Independent Willa Simmons and
Shannon Devereux are not ready to
share their homes with anyone.
But two drop-dead gorgeous
strangers in town are about to
change everything…
Proving the truth that there's…

NO PLACE
LIKE HOME

Two talented and emotional writers
bring to you two wonderfully written
and heart-warming romances.

NO PLACE LIKE HOME

The Ties That Bind
GINNA GRAY

Lovers and Other Strangers
DALLAS SCHULZE

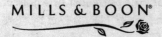

MILLS & BOON®

*MILLS & BOON and MILLS & BOON with the Rose Device
are registered trademarks of the publisher.*

*This collection is first published in Great Britain 2007
Harlequin Mills & Boon Limited,
Eton House, 18-24 Paradise Road, Richmond, Surrey TW9 1SR*

NO PLACE LIKE HOME © Harlequin Books S.A. 2007

The publisher acknowledges the copyright holders of the
individual works, which have already been published in the UK in
single, separate volumes, as follows:

The Ties that Bind © Virginia Gray 2001
Lovers and Other Strangers © Dallas Schulze 2002

ISBN: 978 0 263 85674 3

064-0407

*Printed and bound in Spain
by Litografía Rosés S.A., Barcelona*

The Ties that Bind

GINNA GRAY

GINNA GRAY

A native Houstonian, Ginna Gray admits that, since childhood, she has been a compuslvie reader as well as a head-in-the-clouds dreamer. Long accustomed to expressing her creativity in tangible ways – Ginna also enjoys painting and needlework – she finally decided to try putting her fantasies and wild imaginings down on paper. The result? The mother of two now spends eight hours a day as a full-time writer.

Prologue

*Welcome to Clear Water, Montana—
Population 1,474*

Scanning the sign at the edge of town, Zach Mahoney grimaced. "What the devil are you doing, Mahoney? You should be halfway to Sedona by now, not wasting time on a fool's errand," he muttered to himself.

At the time he'd agreed to this crazy plan he'd been reeling from shock. If he'd been thinking straight he would have told J.T. and Matt to count him out. Hell, he had a good mind to turn his rig around and head for Sedona, and the devil take it.

Zach ground his teeth, knowing he wouldn't. He didn't break his word.

Besides, Kate would give him a tongue-lashing that would blister his eardrums if he didn't see this thing through. His sister, like most women, got emotional when it came to family.

The two-lane highway ran through the center of town, and past the Mountain Shadows Motel on the northern edge. Zach parked his motor home in front of the motel and climbed out.

Inside, he learned from the desk clerk that J.T. and Matt were having lunch across the street at a place called Hodie's. They'd left a message for him to join them there.

Back out on the sidewalk Zach paused to replace his hat and look around. Clear Water nestled in a north/south valley with rolling foothills to the east and the towering peaks of the Rocky Mountains to the west. Other than the spectacular setting, the place was typical of hundreds of other western towns he'd seen while traveling the rodeo circuit—small, sleepy and rugged, a dot of what passed for civilization in a land of incomparable wild beauty.

Though it was April, snow still covered the mountains. They glittered a blinding white in the bright sunshine, and the breeze that swept down their rugged slopes held a bite. Tugging the rolled brim of his Stetson lower over his eyes, Zach huddled deeper into his coat and headed across the street toward Hodie's Bar and Grill.

Like many western ''watering holes,'' Hodie's was a combination restaurant, pool hall and bar. It took a few seconds for Zach's eyes to adjust to the dimness inside, but when they did he homed in on the two men in a corner booth and headed in that direction.

J.T. was the first to spot him.

''Hey, Zach, you made it. Good to see you, bro. Have a seat,'' he offered, sliding over to make room.

The appellation jarred Zach, but his expression remained carefully impassive. He hung his hat and coat on the brass hook attached to the end of the booth and slid onto the bench seat.

Across the table he met Matt's penetrating gaze. More reserved than J.T., he merely nodded and said simply, "Zach."

"You're just in time to join us for lunch."

"No thanks. I've already eaten. I'll just have a cup of coffee." Righting the upside-down crockery mug in front of him, Zach signaled to the waitress.

"You sure you don't want something to eat? This place doesn't look like much, I know, but the food is great. I had dinner here last night after I got in."

"No, I'm good."

"How about—"

"He said he didn't want anything," Matt growled. "Let him be."

"Hey, I was just being friendly. Something you should try once in a while, bro."

Matt gave him a laser look. Unfazed, J.T. grinned back.

Zach took a sip of coffee. The brew scalded his tongue, but drinking it gave him an excuse to remain silent and observe.

No matter how hard he tried, he still had difficulty accepting that he and these two men were brothers. It just didn't seem possible.

Which, he supposed, was normal, given the circumstances. Hell, until six weeks ago, when J.T. and Matt had tracked him down and broken the news to him, he'd had no idea he even *had* brothers. Learning at age thirty-five that he was one of a set of triplets had been a shocker.

At first he'd been certain they were trying to pull some

sort of con, and he'd flatly refused to believe them. To be honest, he hadn't *wanted* to believe them. Kate was his family—all the family he needed.

However, there was proof. Most conclusive of which was the odd irregular-cut wedge of flat silver that each wore on a chain around his neck—a token from a birth mother none of them could remember. Unconsciously, Zach raised his hand and rubbed his through his shirt.

The three jagged, pie-shaped wedges fit together perfectly to form a silver medallion. When whole, etched on one side was an R with a curved line under it, on the other side, in block print were the words, Rocking R Ranch and a post office box in Clear Water, Montana. Beneath the address were the words, ''Your Heritage.''

Whoever she was, for whatever reason, the woman who had given each of them life had left this fragile link to one another and to their past.

Even so…it was still difficult to believe that they were related. They seemed to be as different in every way as any three men could be.

Other than all being six feet two inches tall and having the same general build, they looked nothing alike. Well…maybe, if you looked hard enough, you could see a slight resemblance between J.T. and Matt. They both had vivid blue eyes and dark hair, but Matt's was black, whereas J.T.'s was a mahogany-brown. Zach's own hair was the color of pale wheat, and if he spent too much time in the sunshine without a hat it bleached almost white, and his eyes were green.

The differences between the three of them went deeper than looks, though. Their personalities were nothing at all alike.

A former detective with the Houston police, Matt was tough and taciturn. To Zach's eye, he had the look of a man who had seen too much of life's seamy side to have any illusions left.

On the surface, J.T. appeared to be a lightweight. Movie-star handsome, charming to the ladies and amiable, he seemed to take little seriously. Before quitting his job to try his hand at novel writing, he'd been an investigative reporter for a Houston newspaper—an occupation that had often put him at odds with Matt. It did, however, require intelligence, talent and tenacity, and that made Zach wonder just how much of J.T.'s affability was a clever ploy he used to put people at ease to gain their trust.

He'd read J.T.'s first manuscript, and it was gut-wrenching, insightful and hard-hitting, hardly the work of a shallow playboy.

"By the way, Kate sends her love."

Zach turned his head and fixed J.T. with an unwavering look. "How is she?"

"Terrific. And happy. Did you think she wouldn't be?"

Zach let the question hang between them for several seconds, his eyes narrowing, searching J.T.'s face for the truth.

To his credit, J.T. met the stare without flinching.

At last Zach shrugged, which was as close to an apology as he intended to get. "I just can't get used to you being married to my sister, is all."

"Jeez, man, you make it sound like incest. Kate's your *adoptive* sister. You're not related by blood."

"Yeah, well, we grew up together. She seems a damn sight more like kin than you do."

Matt snorted. "I can sympathize with you there. My last eleven years as a cop, back when J.T. was a reporter, he was a constant thorn in my side. Imagine what a kick in the head it was for me when I found out that he was my brother. The two of us made the connection seven months ago and I still haven't gotten used to the idea.''

"Hey, it was no thrill for me, either," J.T. fired back, his perpetual good humor for once slipping. "But it's a fact, so we're all just going to have to deal with it."

"True. Maybe it'll be easier once we know more. Soon as we eat, we'll get directions to the Rocking R Ranch."

Zach frowned. "Are you two sure you want to do this?"

Matt gave him a sharp look, his coffee mug poised halfway to his mouth. "Why? Don't you?"

"I just don't see the point."

"The point is to get some answers. Maybe meet our mother. Find out why she gave us up."

"Why bother? Look, I've always known I was adopted, and it's never bothered me. Why should it? No kid could've asked for better parents than the Mahoneys. I've sure as hell never felt deprived or been haunted by nightmares, or even felt any curiosity about my biological parents. Maybe you two have some unresolved issues, but I don't. The way I figured it, our mother gave us away, so why should we go searching for her? As far as I'm concerned, the past is past. I say let it go."

Matt looked at J.T. "He has a point."

J.T. snapped, "Look, we're entitled to some answers. At the very least, we should find out our family's medical history in case any of us ever has kids of our own."

"I guess you're right," Matt conceded. "Anyway, Maude Ann and Kate would kill us all if we didn't see this through."

"Okay, fine. As soon as you two finish eating we'll go out to the ranch and get this over with. I wanta be outta here by morning. I got two days to get to my next rodeo.''

The waitress, a plump, fiftyish woman, bustled up to the table. ''Here you go, fellas. Anything else I can ge—''

Her breezy chatter ended abruptly when she glanced at Zach. Her jaw dropped almost to her chest. ''Oh, my stars! You're Colleen Rafferty's boy, aren't you?''

Zach exchanged a quick look with Matt and J.T. ''Maybe.''

''*Maybe?* You mean you don't *know?*''

''No, ma'am. I was adopted when I was two. All three of us were.''

''All three of you?'' Her gaze bounced from one man to the other. ''You mean…you're *triplets?*''

''Yes, ma'am.''

''Oh, my stars.''

''Actually, we came here looking for our birth mother. We have information that she might be from around here,'' J.T. said. ''Maybe you could help us.''

''Well, boys, there's not a doubt in my mind that your mother is Colleen Rafferty. She had a very distinctive face.'' She smiled at Zach. ''You, young man, are the spitting image of her. And I oughta know. Colleen and I were best friends. By the way, my name is Jan Prescott.''

''Nice to meet you, Ms. Prescott. I'm Zach Mahoney, and these are my brothers, Matt Dolan and J.T. Conway.''

''Three different names. Oh, that's just so sad.''

''So her name was Rafferty,'' Matt said. ''Can we assume that has something to do with the Rocking R Ranch? And that she's connected to the owners?''

''I should say so. That ranch has been in Colleen's family for four generations. Her great-great-grandfather,

Ransom Patrick Rafferty, was one of the first settlers around these parts. For the last fifty years or so the ranch has belonged to her daddy, Seamus Rafferty.'' Jan Prescott sniffed. ''A meaner old coot you'll never meet, I'm sorry to tell you.''

''Does Colleen still live at the ranch?''

''Oh, dear, I'm afraid not. Colleen lit out of here close to thirty-six years ago, as I recall. Just boarded a bus one day without a word to anyone, not even me. No one around these parts has seen hide nor hair of her since.

''The rumor going around at the time was that she was pregnant. Back in those days that was a disgrace. I didn't believe it. Gave a few folks a good dressing-down for even suggesting it. But, seeing as how you boys are here, looks like it was true.''

''Could you give us directions to the Rocking R?'' Matt asked.

''Sure. Just follow the highway north about ten miles and you'll see the sign.''

She hesitated, gnawing at her bottom lip, looking from one to the other. ''Look, fellas, I feel it's only fair to warn you, Seamus Rafferty is meaner than a snake. He's not gonna take kindly to you showing up on his doorstep. Fact is, you'll be lucky if he doesn't run you off at gunpoint.''

''We still have to give it a shot,'' J.T. said.

''We're not here to cause trouble,'' Matt added. ''All we want is some information.''

''Yeah, well, good luck getting it. Regardless of how it turns out, though, I want you to know that I'm just pleased as punch that I got to meet Colleen's boys. An' I sure hope you get the answers you want,'' she added, but her expression said she didn't think much of their chances.

* * *

After turning in at the ranch entrance they drove several more miles without seeing anything but rich, rolling grassland on either side of the SUV.

The land rose and dipped in undulating waves, stretching out as far as the eye could see to the east, north and south and to the base of the mountains to the west. Patches of snow still dotted the winter-brown pastures, but in protected spots green shoots poked up to brave the chill. Here and there stands of pine and spruce broke up the rolling landscape. Placid cattle grazed on either side of the narrow dirt road.

Now this was prime ranch land, Zach thought. Exactly the kind of spread he'd always dreamed of owning.

His mouth twisted. Yeah, right. In your dreams, Mahoney. If he saved his money until he was ninety, he'd never have enough to purchase a place even a fraction the size of this one.

The road went down a long incline into a wide, gently rolling valley. At its center sat the ranch house, a sturdy, sprawling, two story structure made of logs and stone. The logs were stained dark brown, the shutters and trim painted cream. A wide porch spanned the considerable width of the house, front and back. It had the look of permanence, as though it had been sitting there for a hundred years or more.

A couple hundred yards or so behind the house, cowboys worked in and around a maze of corrals and the gargantuan barn. Beyond that a bunkhouse, several open-sided hay barns and other outbuildings, which Zach knew probably housed tractors and cattle trailers and other ranch equipment, were scattered around. It was as fine a setup as he'd ever seen…and he'd darn near sell his soul to own it.

A Border collie lay sleeping in a patch of sunshine on the porch. When Matt drove up to the front of the house the animal sprang to her feet and streaked down the steps, barking furiously.

Zach, Matt and J.T. climbed out of the SUV, and the dog continued to growl. Following Zach's lead, they let her sniff their hands. When she was satisfied, the men went up the walk and climbed the steps, the Collie trotting along beside them, tail wagging.

Their knock was answered by an elderly Hispanic woman.

"*¿Sí, señors?*" Her face went slack with shock and she clasped her face between her palms. "*¡Aiee! ¡Madre de Dios!* It is you! Señorita Colleen's *muchachos!*"

Before any of them could respond the woman surged forward, hugging first one, then the other, weeping and babbling in an incoherent mix of English and Spanish.

"Dammit to hell, Maria! What in tarnation are you caterwauling about!" a male voice inside the house bellowed.

Boot heels hammered across the foyer an instant before a gray-haired man appeared in the doorway. Backing up a step, Maria wrung her hands, her worried gaze bouncing back and forth between the four males.

The old man's weathered skin resembled aged leather. He was shorter than Zach and his brothers by about two inches and lean to the point of boniness, but he looked as tough as a pine knot.

"Whoever you are and whatever you're selling, I'm not interested, so get the hell off my property."

As he spoke the old man's gaze skimmed over them, then did a double take, flashing back to Zach. His faded blue eyes narrowed and sharpened as recognition dawned. He stared for the space of three heartbeats before switching to the other two men.

Zach would not have thought it possible, but the old man's expression grew even harder, and his eyes narrowed with pure hatred when his gaze settled on J.T.

"So...she whelped three of you, did she?"

Maria made a distressed sound, which drew the old man's attention. "Get back to your duties, woman. This is no business of yours."

"Are you Seamus Rafferty?"

"That I am." His flinty stare returned to J.T.

"My name is Zach Mahoney. These are my brother's, Matt Dolan and J.T. Conway. We're here because—"

"I know who you are," the old man snapped. "No matter what you call yourselves, you're still Colleen's bastards." He jabbed a bony forefinger at the end of J.T.'s nose. "This one is a dead ringer for Mike Reardon, the sorry, no-good saddle tramp who seduced my daughter. And you." He turned his head and looked at Zach. "You're the image of her."

"So I've been told."

Seamus turned his attention on Matt. "Now, you—you don't favor either of them. You're just a mutt mixture of both." He looked down at Matt's cane, and his mouth curled with contempt. "Got a gimp leg, I see. Not much use to anyone, are you?"

Matt's jaw tightened and his piercing blue eyes flamed.

Zach made a subtle shift, placing himself between Matt and the old man. "We're looking for some information. We're hoping you can help us."

Seamus Rafferty's hard stare swung to Zach and held for an interminable time. Finally he snapped, "Come in. I don't conduct business on the porch." He stomped back inside, leaving them no choice but to follow.

As they walked through the entry hall a young woman dressed in snug-fitting jeans and a Western-style shirt and boots descended the stairs. She was small and wand slim. At first glance Zach took her for a teenager, but drawing nearer he realized she was in her mid-twenties. Her skin was ivory, her eyes blue, her hair black. The thick mane hung down her back almost to her waist, arrow straight and as shiny as polished ebony. Though she appeared to wear no makeup she had the kind of delicate beauty that took your breath away.

Zach wondered who she was. Another of Seamus's grandchildren, perhaps? Or a late-in-life child? Or perhaps his wife?

The last thought was so distasteful Zach dismissed it immediately.

The woman came to a halt on the bottom stair as they walked by, but even so she was still not eye-level with Zach. He realized that she could be no more than five feet two or three—and that her eyes were not blue at all, but a startling violet.

He thought surely Seamus would stop and introduce them, but the old man stomped past the stairs without so much as a glance in her direction.

"Seamus?" she called after him. "What's going on?"

The husky contralto coming from such a small, delicate woman surprised Zach, but he was given no opportunity to contemplate its sexy quality.

"This has nothing to do with you, Willie. Go on about your own business girl, and keep your nose out of mine."

He led them into a walnut-paneled office, took a seat behind a massive desk, then motioned impatiently to the leather sofa and chairs by the fire.

When they were seated he glared at them. "Well?"

"We came here hoping we'd find our mother, but we

learned in town that she left here years ago," J.T. said. "We're hoping that you can tell us how we can get in touch with her."

Seamus snorted. "You expect me to believe that's all you want? Do you take me for a fool?"

"I don't think you want me to answer that."

Matt's quiet comment gleaned a dagger stare from Seamus, but J.T. hurried on. "I don't know what you think we're after, but I assure you, we did come here to look for our mother."

"*You* can't assure me of anything. I don't trust you any more than I trusted that no-good daddy of yours."

A muscle in J.T.'s cheek began to tic and his smiled slipped a bit. "Nevertheless, it's true. We were adopted by different families, and until late last summer, none of us knew the other existed. Matt and I made the initial connection by accident."

"With these," Matt said, pulling his medallion piece out from beneath his shirt and whipping it off over his head.

Zach and J.T. quickly followed suit. Gathering the three pie-shaped wedges, Zach rose and laid them on the desk in front of Seamus. With one finger, he slid the pieces of silver together into a perfect fit. The old man leaned over, scowling as he read the inscription.

"J.T. located Zach a few months ago," Matt continued. "Now we're trying to find our mother. Or, failing that, to at least learn what we can about her. We were hoping you could help us."

"You're barking up the wrong tree. I got nothing to say. That ungrateful girl has been dead to me since the day she confessed that she'd gotten herself knocked up. I threw her out and told her to never come back."

"For getting pregnant?" J.T. looked dumbfounded.

"Women have babies out of wedlock all the time. Some are even planned."

"Not thirty-six years ago they didn't," the old man snapped. "And I wouldn't stand for it today, either. I'll have no harlots or bastards in my family."

"How about her belongings?" Matt inquired. "She must have left something here. Could we take a look at those?"

"Burned it all years ago."

Seamus put his hands flat on the desktop and levered himself to his feet. "Let's cut the crap. I know damned well you didn't come here looking for your tramp of a mother. You came hoping to get your hands on this ranch. Well, I'm telling you that just ain't gonna happen. The Rocking R isn't going to fall into the hands of Mike Reardon's by-blows." He thumped the desktop with the side of his fist. "By heaven, I'll *give* the place away before I'll let that happen."

"That's it. I'm outta here. I told you two this was a bad idea." Zach headed toward the door.

"He's right. C'mon. We don't have to take this." Using his cane, Matt levered himself to his feet and followed.

Zach snatched open the door and strode out—and barreled into the young woman they had seen a few moments before. She hit his chest with an "Oof!" and bounced off.

"Damn." Zach grabbed her shoulders to keep her from falling, set her aside with a terse, "Excuse me, miss," and continued on toward the entrance.

He had a fleeting impression of startled violet eyes and skin like ivory silk, but beyond that he paid her no mind. He was too intent on getting the hell away from Seamus

Rafferty before he lost his temper and planted his fist right in the old coot's sneering face—grandfather or no.

"Seamus, is something wrong?" the woman asked as Matt and J.T. trooped past in Zach's wake. "Who are those men?"

Neither Zach nor his brothers waited around to hear the old man's answer.

"Of all the foul-tempered, suspicious, spiteful old bastards!" Matt snarled the instant they gained the front porch.

"Yeah, Gramps is a bit of a disappointment."

"If that's supposed to be funny—"

"Knock it off, both of you." Zach fixed his brothers with a hard look. "We gave it our best shot and got nowhere. Now can we just drop this whole thing and forget about the past?"

"Suits me."

"I don't think we ought to give up," J.T. argued.

Matt spat out an expletive and rolled his eyes.

"Look, you do what you want, but I'm out of here," Zach said. "As soon as we get back to town, I'm heading for Sedona."

"*¡Pssst! ¡Señors! ¡Señors!*"

As one, they turned to see the woman Seamus had called Maria peeking nervously from around a forsythia at the corner of the house.

"I must speak with you, *por favor. Es muy impor-tante.*"

The brothers exchanged a brief look and moved down the porch to the woman's hiding place.

"Yes?"

Clutching a flat cardboard box to her breasts, Maria glanced around nervously. "You wish to know about Se-ñorita Colleen, *sí? Sus madre?*"

"Yes," J.T. replied. "Do you know where she is?"

A stricken expression flashed over the woman's face. "I…" She shook her head, then cast a quick look over her shoulder and thrust the shirt-size box into Zach's hands. "You take this, *señor. La señorita* sent it to me over thirty years ago."

"What is it?"

"Her *diario.* How you say…journal. Also a photograph that I hid from Señor Rafferty so he would not burn it. Señorita Colleen, she beg me not to tell her *padre* I have the journal."

Matt snorted. "She probably knew he'd destroy it, like he did the rest of her stuff."

Maria nodded. "*Sí,* it is so. *La señorita,* she want me to keep the *diario* safe and give it to her *muchachos* if you ever come here. I am an old woman. I begin to think you will not come while I still live."

A door slammed at the back of the house and Seamus bellowed, "Dammit, Maria! Where the hell are you?"

She jumped guiltily. "I must go." Grasping Zach's arm, she urged, "*Por favor.* Read the *diario.* All your questions, they will be answered."

"To save time, I think we should read it out loud," Zach suggested when he and his brothers entered Matt's motel room a short while later.

"Good idea." J.T. stretched out on one of the double beds and laced his fingers together behind his head. "Why don't you start?"

Matt sat on the edge of the other bed, and Zach settled into one of the room's two chairs. Almost reverently, he lifted the cover off the box and found himself staring at a photograph of a young girl of about eighteen.

She was more striking than beautiful—a female version of the face he saw in the mirror each day—the same blond hair and green eyes, the same thin, straight nose, sharp cheekbones and strong jaw. Her mouth was a bit fuller and softer than his own, but the shape was identical.

It was eerie, looking at that face. The short hairs on Zach's nape and forearms stood on end. No wonder the waitress at Hodie's had been so shocked. And why Seamus had known instantly who they were.

While his brothers studied the photograph, Zach lifted the diary out of the box. The cheap vinyl cover was cracked and split and the pages felt brittle, the edges brown with age.

He looked at Matt and J.T. and cocked one eyebrow. "You ready?" An edgy awareness that they were about to uncover their past pulsed in the air.

"Yeah, we're ready," J.T. said, and Matt nodded agreement.

Zach cleared his throat and turned to the first entry.

"'September 21st. I'm so scared. I'm on my way to Houston, but I don't know what I'll do if my mother's aunt Clara won't take me in. She's elderly, and I barely know her, but other than Daddy she's my only living relative. She never had children of her own, and when she came to the ranch for a visit a few years ago she was kind to me and urged me to come stay with her for as long as I liked. I just pray the invitation will still be open after I tell her about my condition.

"'September 22nd. Heaven help me, I'm too late. I arrived at Aunt Clara's this afternoon and found her house full of people. They had just come from her funeral.

"'I got hysterical, and I must have fainted. A while ago I woke up and found myself lying on a bed in my aunt's guest room. A lady was here with me. She introduced herself as Dr. Chloe Nesbitt and said she had been my aunt's doctor and friend. Then she asked if I was pregnant.

"'When I finally bawled out my story, Dr. Nesbitt was very kind. She said she would talk to Aunt Clara's pastor about my situation. In the meantime, she was sure that I could stay here, at least until the estate is settled. She told me to get some rest and not to worry.

"'How can I not worry? My darling Mike is dead, Daddy has tossed me out, I'm alone in a strange town where I know no one, I have no job, no money, no training other than ranch work and I'm expecting a child in five months! What am I going to do?

"'September 23rd. I can't believe it! Just when things look hopeless, a miracle has happened. Dr. Nesbitt returned this morning with Reverend Clayton and my aunt's attorney, Mr. Lloyd Thomas. Mr. Thomas said that as my aunt's only kin, I will inherit her entire estate! It isn't a great fortune—a modest savings and this small house, is all—but it's a roof over my head, and if I'm careful, the money will see me through until the baby is born and I can get a job. Bless you, Aunt Clara.'"

For the next hour Zach read from the diary. It told of Colleen's struggle to make the money last, her fear of living alone for the first time in her life, of being in a strange place, her shock and joy when she found out she was expecting triplets, and her worries over how she could support herself and three babies. Underlying it all was a desperate loneliness that colored every word and wrung Zach's heart.

Reverend Clayton and Dr. Nesbitt figured prominently in the entries over the next few months. The doctor saw Colleen through her pregnancy, and the reverend and others in his congregation took a special interest in her, offering spiritual guidance and practical assistance and advice.

"'January 24th. Reverend Clayton is urging me to put my babies up for adoption as soon as they're born. He thinks that would be best—for them, and for me. Perhaps he's right. I don't know. But, God help me, I can't. I just can't. I love them so much already. Every time I feel them move, my heart overflows. I cannot bear to give them up, to have them whisked away from me the second they are born and never get to see their sweet faces, never get to hold them. No. No, I can't give them up. I love them. And they are all I have left of Mike.'''

Zach's throat grew so tight he had difficulty forming the words. He thrust the diary into Matt's hands. "Here. It's your turn," he said in a gruff voice.

Matt swung his legs up onto the bed and leaned back against a mound of pillows and continued.

"'February 7th. I'm the mother of three beautiful, healthy boys! They arrived yesterday, two weeks early, but Dr. Nesbitt says they are all doing fine. I have named them Matthew Ryan, Zachariah Aiden and Jedediah Tiernan.'''

"Jedediah Tiernan!" Matt hooted. "No wonder you go by J.T."

"Stuff it, Dolan."

"Do you two mind? Could we just get on with this?"

"Okay, okay." Picking up where he left off, Matt continued.

"'February 9th. Reverend Clayton came by during visiting hours. He offered me a job working in the church's day care center. The pay isn't much, but Reverend Clayton says I can bring the babies to the center. That means I won't have to be separated from them or have the expense of child care. The reverend is such a good man. I don't know what I would do without his help and support.

"'February 10th. The first day home with the boys. I had no idea babies were so much work. I'll write more later when I'm not so exhausted.'"

The entry was typical of the ones during the following year. A picture began to emerge of a young girl struggling to support and nurture three babies alone. To make ends meet she took in ironing in the evenings and on weekends, often working late into the night.

A few weeks before their first birthday Colleen began to mention that she wasn't feeling well. By the end of February her boss at the day care center insisted that she see a doctor, in case she had something contagious. Then came the entry that stunned Zach and his brothers.

"'March 5th. I have advanced ovarian cancer.'"

"Ah, hell," Zach swore and raked a hand through his hair.

"Yeah," J.T. agreed in a subdued tone. "After all she'd already been through, she sure didn't deserve that."

Swinging his legs over the side, Matt sat on the edge of the bed. "Funny. That possibility never occurred to me. I always assumed she gave me away because she didn't want me."

"Deep down, I think we all did," Zach said quietly. "We were too young to understand anything else."

Matt thought that over, then nodded and resumed reading.

"'Dear Lord, what am I going to do? I can't afford to be sick. My babies need me. On top of that, I have no idea how I'll pay for the treatment, but without it I'll surely die. What will become of the boys if that happens? Daddy won't have them. Even if he would, I don't want my boys to grow up under his iron-fisted rule or to bear the brunt of his hatred for their father. God help me. And them.

"'March 6th. I started treatment today. Feel even worse. Nausea is awful.'"

For the next eight months the entries were about the treatment and the ghastly side effects. And her growing financial worries. Within weeks she could no longer work. It was all she could manage to take care of her three toddlers. Left with no alternative, she was forced to go on welfare.

Despite aggressive treatment, her condition continued to worsen, and in December, after nine months of struggle, Colleen accepted the inevitable and wrote of her decision to ask Reverend Clayton help her find homes for her sons.

"'November 23rd. Reverend Clayton and Mr. Thomas, Aunt Clara's attorney, are handling the adoptions. I would like to interview the prospective couples myself, but the family court judge will not allow it. Even though these are private adoptions he demands complete anonymity on both sides, and afterward the adoption records will be sealed.

"'The reverend and Mr. Thomas have tried but they couldn't find a family willing to take three two-year-olds so it appears the boys will have to go to different couples. Oh, how I hate to think of them being separated. They are not only losing me, but each other, as well. But what choice do I have?

"'January 10th. Reverend Clayton has selected three couples. I trust his judgment and I'm sure they will all be wonderful parents, but I can't quite bring myself to commit to them. It shreds my heart just to think about handing my babies over to strangers and never seeing them again. For the boys' sake, though, I have to stop being selfish. They are typical rambunctious toddlers, and I'm so weak now and in so much pain that I can barely get out of bed some days. I worry that I'm not giving them proper care.

"'January 15th. Well, I've done it. I've agreed to the adoptions and signed all the papers. Reverend Clayton had the medallion made and cut, like I asked him, and all the couples have agreed to give them to the boys when they are older. I just hope that someday it will help them find one another again.'"

Matt turned the page, scanned it, then flipped over several more before turning back. "Looks like there's just one more entry. After that there are just blank pages."

"Go ahead. Let's hear it," J.T. said.

'''February 24th. Today was the worst day of my life. I gave my babies away. Two social workers came and took them. I cuddled and kissed them for the last time, and I think they knew something was wrong. As they were being carried out they screamed and cried and held their arms out to me, calling 'Mommie! Mommie!' It broke my heart. Dear Lord, it hurts. It hurts so much I don't think I can bear it. I want to die. Without my babies I have nothing to live for. Please, God. Please. Let me die now. Please.'''

Matt exhaled a long sigh and slowly closed the journal. A heavy silence hung in the room.

Colleen Rafferty was dead. The rush of disappointment and grief took Zach by surprise. For Pete's sake. He had no memories of her. Until he'd seen that photograph he hadn't even known what she looked like. Why did it bother him so much to learn that she was dead?

"Well, that's it. Now we know," J.T. said finally.

Zach gave a little snort. "Yeah. Now we know. For all the good it did us."

Chapter One

The horse snorted and danced in the narrow chute. His ears lay back flat to his head and his eyes rolled, showing white all around.

"Better watch 'im, Zach. This here's one mean sidewinder," one of the handler's cautioned.

Zach nodded, studying the furious bronc with satisfaction. Hellbent was a good draw. Zach knew if he could hang on for the count he'd finish in the money. Maybe even in first place.

Ignoring the canned music and the announcer's deep baritone blaring from the speakers, the crowd cheering on the contestant in the ring, he kept a wary eye on the fractious animal and eased down from his perch on the side of the chute and into the saddle. Immediately he felt the horse's muscles bunch. Squeezing his knees tighter, he wound the reins around his left hand.

"Up next in the chute, from Gold Fever, Colorado, is Zach Mahoney."

A cheer went up, and Hellbent tried to rear, hammering the gate with his hooves.

"Zach is— Whoa! Watch out there, Zach. You got yourself a mean one today."

Between them, Zach and the handlers subdued the horse, but he felt the animal quiver with rage and knew he was in for a wild ride. He tugged his Stetson down more snugly on his head. Wrapping the reins tighter around his gloved hand, he adjusted his position and paused to gather his focus. When he was ready, he raised his right hand.

The gate flew open and Hellbent leaped out into the arena, eleven hundred pounds of bucking, snorting fury, his massive body arching and twisting and spinning.

Zach's hat went flying on the third buck. In rhythm with the violent movements, he raked his blunted spurs over the horse's shoulders and kept his right hand high in the air while his upper body flopped back and forth in the saddle like a rag doll. Every time Hellbent's front hooves hit the ground Zach felt the jarring impact shoot up his spine all the way to the top of his head.

The crowd in the stands became a blur as the horse spun and pitched and did everything in his power to dislodge him. Never had eight seconds seemed so long. Zach's thigh muscles began to quiver from the strain of gripping the horse's flanks, but he gritted his teeth and hung on.

After what seemed like forever, in his peripheral vision he saw a pickup rider move in, and an instant later the horn blared, signaling the end of the ride. Zach grabbed the pickup rider's arm and shoulder, lunged from the saddle and swung to the ground.

''What a great ride! Let's give Zach a big hand, folks,'' the announcer urged.

While the crowd clapped and cheered and the pickup riders caught Hellbent and led him away, Zach scooped up his hat, gave it three hard knocks against his pant leg to remove the dust, set it back on his head and ambled for the pens, doing his best to not limp. With each step pain shot through his left leg and hip—a nasty little memento from the enraged bull that had given him a toss four days ago. Damn. He was getting too old for this.

Most of the cowboys on the rodeo circuit were in their twenties. Some were even in their teens. Zach's mouth took on a wry twist. Yeah, and there's a reason for that, Mahoney, he thought. By age thirty-six they're either too busted up to compete or they've wised up.

Not until Zach reached the exit gate did he allow himself to look over his shoulder and check his score. Yes! The ride had put him in the lead. Not bad for an old man.

By the time he made his way through the clutch of riders and handlers and accepted their congratulations, the last contestant was picking himself up out of the dirt, and Zach knew he'd won the top purse in the bronc riding event. Maybe even Best All Around, as well, but he wouldn't know that for an hour or so when all the events were over. He'd come back then for the finale, but in the meantime he was going to his RV to apply heat to his aching hip and leg.

After retrieving his saddle and bridle, Zach slung them over his shoulder and headed back to his motor home in the camping area behind the rodeo arena. Halfway there a man in a FedEx uniform intercepted him with an overnight letter.

Zach frowned. Who the devil would be sending him a registered letter? He turned the envelope this way and that, but the return address was too faint to make out in the dim light of the parking lot.

When he stepped into the RV his cell phone was ringing. Zach dumped the saddle and bridle just inside the door, tossed his Stetson on the sofa and snatched it up. "Yeah, Mahoney here."

"Zach, it's J.T."

Surprise darted through him. He hadn't heard directly from either of his brothers since they'd they parted company in Clear Water, Montana, nine months ago.

No matter how much Kate and Matt's wife, Maude Ann, might wish otherwise, the brotherly connection just wasn't there.

"Yeah, what's up?"

"Have you gotten an overnight letter from the Manning and Manning law firm yet?"

Zach checked out the return address on the envelope he still held. "It just came. I haven't had a chance to open it yet. How did you know about it?"

"Because Matt and I each received the same letter a couple of hours ago."

"Oh? What's going on?"

"You're not going to believe this. The letters are from Seamus Rafferty's attorney, Edward Manning, notifying us of the old man's death and that we're beneficiaries in his will."

"You've got to be kidding."

"Nope. The old coot passed away yesterday. I called the law firm and talked to Edward Manning. He's waiting to hear from us before scheduling the funeral so he can allow plenty of time for us to get there."

"The hell you say. I'm not going to that old devil's funeral."

"I understand how you feel. That was Matt's first reaction. Mine, too. But the Rocking R meant a lot to Colleen. She obviously felt it was our heritage. If Seamus leaves us so much as one square foot of the place, we owe it to her to accept it.''

Zach rubbed the back of his neck and looked up at the ceiling, torn between resentment and a nagging sense of obligation and loyalty to the mother he couldn't remember. Damn. He didn't need this.

Although…J.T. did have a point.

He sighed. ''All right. I'll go.''

The January wind swooping down the snowy mountain slopes cut to the bone, causing several people to huddle deeper in their coats and shiver. Gray clouds scudded overhead, heavy with the threat of more snow to come. The dank smell of freshly dug, frozen earth hung in the air. From the nearby stand of pines came the raucous cawing of a raven, and in the valley the cattle lowed mournfully, as though aware of the event taking place in the small family cemetery on the slope above the ranch house.

''Dear Lord, we commit unto your keeping the soul of Seamus Patrick Rafferty.'' The minister picked up a handful of dirt and dropped the frozen clods onto the coffin. ''Ashes to ashes. Dust to dust. May God have mercy on your soul.'' Clutching his Bible to his chest, he lowered his head. ''Let us pray.''

Reverend Turner's dolorous voice droned on, but Willa Simmons barely heard him. She was too angry and upset. Refusing to look at the three men standing shoulder to shoulder on the opposite side of the grave, she kept her gaze focused on the casket. They had no right to be there. No right at all.

The sun glinted off one of the coffin's silver handles,

and Willa's eyes narrowed. Her hands curled into fists. It's your fault that they're here. Damn you, Seamus. How *could* you?

"Amen," the reverend intoned, and everyone in the sparse band of mourners echoed the word—all except Seamus's three grandsons. They stood stony-faced and dry-eyed, as they had throughout the service.

Zach Mahoney, Matt and Maude Ann Dolan, J.T. and Kate Conway, Edward Manning, Maria and the ranch hands and herself were the only ones there. A pitiful turn-out for a man's funeral, Willa thought.

It was sad, but Seamus had only himself to blame. Over the years, with the exception of Harold Manning and his son Edward, Seamus had alienated every friend he'd ever had and all of his neighbors and acquaintances around Clear Water.

For an awkward moment the cowboys stood with their hats in their hands and shifted from one foot to the other, looking from Willa to Seamus's grandsons, trying to decide to whom they should offer condolences first.

Edward solved the dilemma for them by turning to Willa with a murmured word of sympathy before skirting around the grave to speak to the three brothers and the wives of the two who were married. The reverend did the same, and the relieved hands quickly followed their example. After muttering a few words, each man wasted no time heading down the hill to the bunkhouse, eager to escape the unpleasant duty and shed his Sunday-go-to-meeting clothes.

When the last cowboy sidled away, Willa slipped her arm through the housekeeper's. "C'mon, Maria. Let's go."

"But, Willie, you have not spoken with the *señors.*"

"Nor do I intend to." Unable to resist, Willa glared

at the brothers before heading for the gate in the wrought-iron fence that surrounded the cemetery.

"Willie? Hold on." Edward called.

The housekeeper turned to wait for the attorney to catch up, leaving Willa no choice but to do the same.

Impeccably dressed as always in a custom-tailored suit, silk shirt and tie, and a cashmere overcoat, Edward looked painfully out of place on the ranch. He was huffing by the time he reached them. Exertion and the biting cold had chaffed his cheeks to a ruddy hue and his styled brown hair was windblown. However, if he was annoyed that he'd had to chase after her it didn't show. His face held only sympathy and tenderness when he took her hand and patted it.

"Willie, I know this is rushing things, but since everyone involved is here, I was wondering if we could go ahead with the reading of the will? I have an early appointment in Bozeman tomorrow."

Willa's gaze shot past him to Seamus's grandsons and the two women. Resentment flooded her. She had been shocked to learn only the day before that her stepfather had rewritten his will to include Colleen's sons. Willa had no doubt that Seamus had left each of them a sum of money merely to ease his conscience. Still, just thinking about it made her bristle.

"By all means. Let's get this over with. The sooner they get their windfall, the sooner they'll leave."

All the parties named in Seamus's will had gathered in the study when Willa arrived, including Maria, Pete Brewster and Bud Langston, the ranch foreman. Only Edward was missing.

Willa took a seat in one of the fireside chairs. Everyone was seated except Zach Mahoney. He stood to one side, by the built-in bookshelves, a little apart from the others, with his suit coat thrust back on either side and his hands in his trouser pockets. While his brothers and their wives talked quietly among themselves, Zach kept silent and waited and watched.

Willa eyed him askance, her mouth tightening. She resented all of the interlopers, but especially this one. There was something about Zach Mahoney—something she couldn't quite put her finger on—that made her edgy and set her temper to simmering. They had barely exchanged half a dozen words, but whenever she was near him her body seemed to hum as though a low-voltage current of electricity were running through her.

Surreptitiously, Willa studied him for a clue to what triggered the reaction, but his chiseled face revealed nothing. Zach wasn't as handsome as J.T., nor did he have Matt's street-tough appeal, rather he had the weathered ruggedness typical of a Westerner.

Even dressed in a suit and tie as he was now, it was apparent in the way he held himself, that loose-limbed walk, and most of all, that aura of quiet strength and self-reliance that radiated from him.

Squint lines etched fan patterns at the outer edges of his eyes and deeper ones ran from his nose to the corners of his mouth. Thick, wheat-colored hair created a startling contrast to his tanned skin. A strong, square jaw, straight nose, well-defined lips and cheekbones sharp enough to cut combined to create a face that had a certain masculine appeal, Willa supposed—if you liked those sorts of rough-hewn looks in a man.

As though he felt her inspection, Zach turned his head, and their gazes locked. The hum of electricity coursing through her body became a jolt. Determined to not let him fluster her, she ground her teeth to keep from shivering and stared back into those deep-set green eyes. They glittered like gems in his sun-scorched face, giving him the sharp, dangerous look of a hungry wolf.

Willa's heart began to pound and her mouth grew dry, but she could not look away. To her relief, the spell was broken when Edward came striding into the room.

"Sorry I'm late. I had to take an urgent call."

He sat at Seamus's desk, snapped open his briefcase, and withdrew a legal-looking document. "If everyone is ready, I'll begin." Edward slipped on a pair of reading glasses and picked up the document. "I, Seamus Patrick Rafferty, being of sound mind…"

The first few pages consisted of the usual convoluted legalese, the upshot of which was several small bequests to the University of Montana and a few charitable organizations. Maria, Pete and Bud were each to receive a modest lump sum and a guaranteed pension when they decided to retire, plus the right to remain on the ranch for life in one of the cottages scattered about the property, if they so chose.

Turning another page, Edward glanced over his glasses at Willa and the three brothers and cleared his throat. "To my grandsons, Matthew Ryan Dolan, Zachariah Aiden Mahoney and Jedediah Tiernan Conway, and to my step-daughter, Willa Grace Simmons, I bequeath the remainder of my estate, including the Rocking R Ranch and all its assets, to be shared equally among them."

"*What?*" Willa shot out of the chair like a bullet. Shaking with fury, she felt the color drain out of her face. "That can't *be!* Seamus wouldn't leave the ranch to *them.* He *swore* over and over that he wouldn't!"

"I'm sorry, Willa, but it's true," Edward said. "Seamus wasn't happy about it. However, despite his threats, in the end he couldn't bear to let the ranch slip out of the family.''

Willa opened her mouth to continue, but Edward stopped her. ''Before any of you say anything else, you should know there are conditions attached.''

'' 'Conditions'?'' Willa repeated in a voice bordering on hysteria.

''Yes. And I feel I must warn you, you're not going to like them.''

''Uh-oh, here it comes,'' J.T. drawled.

''Yeah,'' Matt agreed. ''I knew there had to be a catch.''

''Exactly what are these conditions?'' Zach spoke quietly, never taking his eyes from the attorney.

''You must all live here in this house and work the ranch together for a period of one year.''

''That's outrageous! I won't do it!'' Willa declared.

''If you don't—if any of you refuses to accept the conditions, or leaves before the year is up, then none of you inherits. The ranch and all its assets will be sold in a sealed-bid auction. The money from the sale will be held in a trust fund, from which each of you will receive the sum of ten thousand dollars a year. The remainder of the profits from the fund will go to a number of western universities that offer agricultural and ranching studies.''

''Who will be the executor of the trust?'' Matt made no effort to hide the suspicion in his voice.

''I will.''

''And the sealed-bid auction? Will you handle that, as well?''

''That's correct.'' Edward met Matt's hard stare. ''I know what you're thinking—that's a lot of power for one man. You're right. Normally a board of trustees would oversee a fund of this size and handle the auction, as well. I tried to get your grandfather to set things up that way, but he wouldn't hear of it. Seamus was a difficult man, as I'm sure you discovered.''

"Say we comply with these conditions. What happens at the end of the year?'' Zach asked.

"At that time, if any of you wants out, you may sell your share of the ranch to one or more of the others, but no one else.''

"I should have expected something like this,'' Willa railed. "Seamus always was manipulative and controlling. I just never thought he'd go this far.'' Seething, she paced to the window with quick, jerky steps, then made a frustrated sound and swung around. "This is intolerable!''

Enraged almost beyond bearing, Willa turned the full force of her fury on the brothers, addressing them directly for the first time. "This is all your fault.''

"Now wait just a darned minute,'' Matt began, but Zach raised his hand and silenced him.

He stared at Willa. His face was impassive but those eyes glittered in his tanned face like green ice. "Let's get something straight right now, Ms. Simmons. Whatever devious reasons Seamus had for making us his heirs, my brothers and I did nothing to influence his decision. We came here last year for one purpose—to find our mother. Failing that, we were hoping to get some information about her. That's all.''

Willa's chin came up at a challenging angle. "Not according to Seamus. He said you were three greedy opportunists, just like your father had been, and that you came here hoping to get your hands on this ranch. When you found out your scheme wasn't going to work, you left in a huff.''

"That's not true.''

"Oh, right. I'm supposed to believe you? I don't think so."

"Believe whatever you want. It makes no difference to me. Nor does it change anything."

"It's just not fair," she raged. "Your entire lives you spent less than an hour with Seamus. I've lived here since I was seven years old." She thumbed her chest. "I'm the one who worked this ranch every day for the past twenty years, not you three. I'm the one who was here for Seamus. When he got too old to ride a horse, I relayed his orders to the foreman and the men and worked right alongside them. I'm the one who put up with his bad temper and maliciousness. If you hadn't shown up here, he would have left the ranch to me like he promised."

"Uh, Willie." Edward's expression was a mixture of pity and chagrin. "I'm afraid you're wrong about that."

"What?" Willa stared at him with a blank look. "What do you mean?"

"Before Seamus changed his will to include his grandsons, all he was going to leave you was a few thousand dollars. The only reason he gave you a share of the ranch in this will was to irritate them."

Willa swayed and gripped the back of a chair for support. She felt as though she'd been hit in the stomach with a battering ram. "But...but he always said I'd inherit the ranch someday. He said I deserved it because I was the only one who cared, the only one who'd stuck around. He *promised!* Why would he say that if he didn't mean it?"

"Probably to keep you here. You were a big help to him and he depended on you. As you said, he was good at manipulation. Once he was gone, though, you would no longer be needed."

Another wave of shock slammed into her, and her hold

tightened on the chair back, whitening her knuckles. "You mean...are you saying that I would have had to leave the ranch?"

"I'm afraid so," Edward said gently. "The Rocking R would have been sold in a closed-bid auction, just as it will be if any of you refuses to abide by the conditions."

And she would have been left out in the cold.

Willa closed her eyes. She knew that later, when the hurt was not so fresh, anger would resurface and come to her rescue, but at that moment all she wanted was to curl up in a tight ball and wail out her misery until she was nothing but a hollow shell.

The pain was so great she forgot for a moment where she was, and with whom. Then she opened her eyes and cringed when her gaze fell on the brothers. The knowledge that she had meant so little to Seamus was devastating enough, but having that revealed in front of these men compounded her humiliation. They had the grace to avoid looking at her, but somehow that oblique act of compassion made her feel worse than if they'd gloated, as she had expected them to do.

Gathering her tattered pride around her like a cloak, Willa lifted her chin, squared her shoulders and pulled herself up to her full five feet three inches. Ignoring the others, she turned to the attorney. "I'll challenge the will. Other people heard Seamus promise me the ranch. Maria, for one."

"That's your right, of course. But you should know it will be expensive and it could take years. In my opinion, in the end you'd lose. I'm telling you this as a friend, Willie, not as your stepfather's attorney. Trust me, the will is air-tight."

"I see." Her full mouth folded into a bitter line.

"Then I guess I have no choice but to accept the conditions."

"Maybe you don't have a choice, but we do," Zach said.

"Oh, please." She shot him a look of patent disbelief. "Surely you don't expect me to believe that you would actually turn *down* the bequest. Yeah, right."

"This may come as a shock to you, Ms. Simmons, but we had lives of our own prior to Seamus's death."

"That's right," Matt snapped. "I say to hell with it. And Seamus. I'll be damned if I'll let that old tyrant dictate to me how and where I live my life."

"I agree," J.T. chimed in.

Zach nodded. "I'll admit, that was my first knee-jerk reaction, as well."

"You fools!" Fear that she might actually lose all claim to the ranch wiped away every other consideration. "Do you city slickers have any idea what such a rash decision would cost all of us? What we'd be giving up? I don't like what Seamus has done any better than you, but only an idiot would toss away a fortune of this size. Tell them, Edward."

The attorney rattled off the appraised value of the ranch and last year's revenues.

Matt let out a low whistle, but J.T. was more vocal.

"Holy cow! This place is worth a freakin' fortune!"

"The Rocking R is one of the largest ranches in this part of the country, and our firm's most important client." Edward paused.

"You have exactly two weeks from today, both to make up your minds and to do whatever you need to do and move in. Once you do that, the year begins."

"Mmm. Two weeks isn't much time. We need to talk it over before we make a decision," Zach said.

"Of course. I understand."

"Well, I don't," Willa snapped. "What is the matter with you people? You can't seriously be thinking of refusing? No one throws away a chance like this."

"Miss Simmons, if we do this, it's going to change all of our lives. Yours included. The least we can do is talk it over calmly and take a vote. So why don't you sit down."

"I don't need to talk it over. I can give you my vote right now. I detest the very idea of sharing the Rocking R with you people, but this is my home, and I'll do whatever I have to to keep it. Even if that means putting up with a bunch of greenhorn freeloaders." She stormed out and slammed the door behind her.

Edward winced. "I'm sorry about that. I do hope you'll excuse Willie." Standing, he slipped his reading glasses into a leather case and put them and the will into his briefcase and snapped it shut. "I know it doesn't seem so now, but she's really a nice person and normally quite good-natured and easy to get along with."

"We understand. She's upset, and apparently with good reason."

Matt rolled his eyes at his wife's comment. "Spoken like a psychiatrist. You ask me, she's a spoiled brat."

"That's not fair," Maude Ann protested. "From the sound of it, Seamus has been stringing that poor girl along for years."

"You don't know the half of it," Edward said. "Now, if you'll excuse me, I really must be going. It's a long way to Bozeman. When you've reached a decision, give me a call. If I'm not at my office you can reach me on my cell phone," he said, handing each of them his business card.

He turned to leave, then hesitated. "Uh…it's true that

the Rocking R Ranch is a sizable inheritance, but I feel I must warn you, if you decide to stay you'll earn every penny you get from it. Running a ranch this size is far from easy, and nothing is guaranteed. A poor calf crop, a string of bad luck, a few slaps from Mother Nature can hurt even a place this size. It won't be a piece of cake.''

Zach didn't need anyone to tell him about the hardships and perils of ranching. He knew them firsthand. In college he'd earned degrees in ranch management and business and before going out on the rodeo circuit he'd been general manager of the Carter Cattle Company, better known as the Triple C, a huge spread near Ridgeway, Colorado. Zach, however, saw no need to mention that to the attorney.

''Well, this is certainly an unexpected turn of events,'' Kate said when Edward had gone. ''From what you told Maude Ann and me about Seamus, I thought we'd attend a funeral, then go home with five dollars or some such slap-in-the-face bequest.''

''Yeah, we all did,'' Matt agreed. ''I wonder what made the old man change his mind?''

''My guess is, during our first visit here he somehow picked up on the strain between us,'' Zach said. ''The old coot probably took sadistic delight in that. Like Manning said, he cooked up this whole thing to stir up trouble and make claiming the inheritance as difficult as possible.''

''Right,'' J.T. agreed. ''Wherever he is, he's probably laughing himself silly right now.''

''He's got us in a bind, that's certain. If just one of us refuses to go along with the conditions, we all lose.'' Matt swept the others with a regretful look. ''Much as I hate to, I'm afraid I'm going to have to be the bad guy.

Maudie and I can't just abandon Henley Haven and pick up and move here. The kids we foster need her care.''

"Yeah, well, if it makes you feel any better, I can't ask Kate to give up the Alpine Rose, either. Her parents spent years restoring that house and she's turned it into a profitable business. Added to that, she grew up in Gold Fever. It makes no difference to me where I live. I can write anywhere, but I won't rob her of her home.''

"Before you two start making any noble sacrifices, don't you think you should ask Kate and me what we think?''

"Maude Ann's right. What kind of wife would I be if I stood in the way of your inheritance? Besides, I wouldn't have to sell the bed-and-breakfast. I'm sure I could hire someone to run it for me. And while it's true that I love the Colorado mountains, have you looked around? It's not too shabby here, either.''

"The same applies to Henley Haven,'' Maude Ann stated emphatically. "I can get another psychiatrist to take over for me, and Jane will stay on. And there's no reason why I can't continue to work with abused children. I'm sure there are some here in Montana who need my help.''

"But what about our own kids? They—''

"Will love it here,'' Maude Ann insisted before Matt could finish. "Can you think of a better place to raise five rambunctious children than on a ranch? Or to shelter others? The wide-open spaces will be good for them. And the drier climate will be good for your leg.''

Matt frowned at the mention of his disability. It had been seventeen months since he taken that bullet that had ended his career as a detective with the Houston Police Department and left him with a permanent limp.

"Still…I don't know.''

According to J.T., Matt had become more flexible since marrying Maude Ann, but it was still his first instinct to resist change of any kind. Watching him, Zach could see the struggle going on inside his taciturn brother.

"We're talking about a complete change in lifestyle and careers," Matt argued. "I don't know anything about ranching. Neither does J.T."

"No, but Zach does," J.T. said in a thoughtful voice, beginning to warm to the idea. "And you and I can learn."

"Maybe. Still, we all have to live together in this house," Matt said.

And that, Zach thought, was the real crux of the problem. He, J.T. and Matt might be brothers, but they didn't really know one another. A year ago they had made contact again, but a lifetime apart had created a chasm between them that they couldn't seem to breech.

Kate said they didn't try, and maybe that was true. At best, their relationship was distant, with currents of disquiet and wariness, even an undefined resentment running just below the surface, making them guarded with one another. For whatever reason, the fact remained that they *were* strangers.

"It will be awkward, I guess," J.T. agreed. "But it's not as though it'll be forever. Let's not forget that we're talking about a fortune here. And regardless of what Willa Simmons thinks, we are the rightful heirs. We'd be fools to turn it down. Surely we can manage to rub along together for a year. At the end of that time if anyone is miserable, they can sell out."

Matt looked at Zach. "You've sure been quiet. What do you think?"

"I think I should stay out of this discussion and let the four of you decide. All of you know that owning a ranch is my dream. I'd put up with anything, even Ms. Simmons, to own a part of this place, but I don't think it would be fair for me to try to influence you.''

''Yeah, but do you think we could live and work together for a whole year?''

''Maybe. Maybe not. I'm sure Seamus figured if he threw us together we'd be at one another's throats inside of a week. But one way or another, we won't know unless we try. One thing is certain, though. It's what Colleen would have wanted us to do.''

Chapter Two

Sadie's furious barking and the sound of vehicles approaching caught Willa's attention. Tossing aside the curry brush, she gave her horse an absent pat and walked over to the barn door, arriving just in time to see a caravan of vehicles—a pickup loaded with boxes, three SUVs towing rented moving trailers and a minivan—pull into the ranch yard at the back of the house. Instantly her whole body tightened.

Pete Brewster left the tack he'd been repairing and came to stand beside her. "Looks like they's here."

Gritting her teeth, Willa folded her arms and narrowed her eyes. She watched Zach hop out of the pickup cab and go over to one of the SUVs and say something to Kate as she climbed from behind the wheel.

"Made it just in time," the old man continued, undaunted by Willa's hostile silence. He paused to squirt a stream of tobacco juice into the ground to one side of the

door, then added, "Be two weeks t'morra since the funeral."

"Oh, there was never any doubt they'd make the dead-
line," Willa muttered. "I'm sure they couldn't wait to
get here and claim the lion's share of the ranch."

"'Pears to me you oughta be glad 'bout that, 'stead of
standin' there looking like you just swallered a lemon.
The way I heard it, if they hadn't'a accepted the inheritance, you'd be out on your ear."

Willa glared at the old man, but he paid no attention.
With a huff she returned her gaze to the line of vehicles.

Pete had worked on the Rocking R for almost sixty
years, even before Seamus had inherited the ranch. He'd
taught her to ride and rope and brand, how to string
barbed wire, build a campfire, inoculate and castrate cattle and the other myriad skills that ranch life entailed,
skills Seamus either had not had the time, patience or
inclination to teach her. When Willa had been a child
Pete had been the one who bandaged her cuts and scrapes
and dried her tears if her mother or Maria wasn't around.
He'd also given her backside a wallop a few times when
he'd thought she deserved it. Willa's temper didn't faze
Pete.

"Yes, well…that's what makes it so galling. That and
the fact that they have no to right to this place."

"Well, now, I don't rightly know as how I'd agree
with you there, Willie, seeing as how they's old Seamus's
grandsons, wrong side of the blanket or no. You'd best
accept it, girl. Blood counts fer a lot, 'specially to a feller
like Seamus."

"So I've discovered." She tapped one booted foot
against the hard-packed ground, simmering inside.
"Maybe they have the legal right, but they don't deserve
it. They've never put in so much as a day's work on this

ranch. While I was pouring my blood, sweat and tears into the place all those years, where were they? When Seamus needed them, where were they? They never bothered to call him or write to him or come for a visit their whole lives. Then, when he was so old it was obvious he couldn't last much longer, they showed up with their greedy hands out.''

''You know that fer sure an' certain, do ya?'' Pete rolled his cud of tobacco to his other cheek and slanted her a glinty look out of the corner of his eye.

''Seamus said— Good grief! I don't believe it! Look at all those children! One, two, three—why there's *five* of them.''

''Looks like it,'' Pete agreed.

''Just what we need,'' Willa mumbled. ''A bunch of chattering kids underfoot. They'll be nothing but a nuisance.''

''Oh, I dunno 'bout that. When you was no bigger than a button you tagged after me or Seamus all the time, soakin' up ever'thing like a sponge. Tell you the truth, I plum enjoyed it. Ya ask me, havin' younguns around sorta brings a place to life.''

Willa made a noncommittal sound. It wasn't so much the children who worried her, it was the adults, the five strangers with whom she would have to share her home. Her gaze zeroed in on Zach again. That one in particular bothered her. Just watching him, even from that distance, made her edgy and irritable. What was it about the man?

Willa watched as Maria bustled out the kitchen door onto the back porch, wiping her hands on her apron. The elderly housekeeper hurried down the gravel walkway and greeted the adults effusively then made a big fuss over the children.

She could see that Matt was having a difficult time

persuading the oldest boy to leave the horses in the corral, but after a brief exchange the sulky child climbed down off the corral fence and stomped after the others.

Everyone disappeared inside, and Willa turned to go back into the barn but she stopped when she spotted a red pickup cresting the rise at the top of the road.

Visitors to the Rocking R were rare enough that Willa experienced a dart of surprise. Thanks to Seamus's rotten disposition, with the exception of his grandsons, about the only outsiders who ever set foot on the property were George Pierce, the local veterinarian, and Edward Manning.

Shading her eyes with her hand, she squinted against the glare of the sun and watched the truck descend the road into the valley. It wasn't one of theirs. All the Rocking R pickups were silver-gray. Willa couldn't see who was behind the wheel, but the truck looked vaguely familiar. Who in the world...?

Recognition came with a jolt. Before the shock wore off, her legs were moving. By the time the truck came to a stop in the ranch yard behind the line of parked vehicles she was there to meet it.

"What are you doing here, Lennie?" she demanded, making no effort to hide the irritation in her voice. Not that it mattered. Lennard Dawson was much too self-involved to notice. The man had the sensitivity of a stump.

He flashed what he fancied to be a killer grin. "Why, I came to see you, gorgeous. I figured since Seamus wasn't around to object anymore, I'd drop by and see if you'd like to go out tomorrow night."

Willa barely stifled a groan. She might have known. Eight months ago she'd made the mistake of going out with Lennie. It had been only one date, and she never would have accepted that if Seamus hadn't butted in and forbidden her to go.

Lennie was handsome and as the only child and heir of another local rancher he was probably the most eligible bachelor in that part of Montana. The trouble was, he knew it. Willa hadn't liked him when they were kids, and in her opinion he had not improved with age.

In addition, there had been bad blood between Seamus and Lennie's father, Henry Dawson, for years. Over what, Willa had no idea, as Seamus had refused to discuss the matter, but for that reason alone, had he given her the chance, she would have refused the invitation without a qualm.

Her entire life she'd gone out on only a few dates, and never twice with the same man. Somehow Seamus had managed to run off every male who had ever shown an interest in her. That night his high-handedness had been the last straw, and for once she'd defied him and agreed to meet Lennie in town for dinner.

She'd been ruing that rare act of rebellion ever since.

It had taken no more than five minutes in Lennie's company for her to realize that she still could not abide the man, but he was too conceited to notice. Ever since that night, he'd been acting proprietorial toward her whenever they bumped into each other in town. She'd even heard that he'd been telling people they were a couple. Willa had taken him to task at the first opportunity, but Lennie had just laughed and brushed aside her ire, saying if it weren't for Seamus, they would be. So far, nothing she said made the slightest difference.

Lennie reached for the door handle, but Willa stopped him. "Don't bother getting out. My answer is no."

"Look, we could drive over to Bozeman and take in

a movie. Or just go out to dinner and see what happens after,'' he said with a suggestive wiggle of his eyebrows.

''Nothing is going to happen, because I'm not going out with you. Will you get it through that thick head of yours that I'm not interested?''

Lennie hooked his left elbow over the window frame and gave her a coaxing look. ''Aw, c'mon, Willie. Seamus kept you on a short lead from the time you turned fourteen and developed knockers. It's past time you kicked up your heels, babe.''

''Don't call me babe,'' Willa snapped. ''And trust me, if I ever decide to kick up my heels, it won't be with you.''

Willa heard the back door open and close, and when Lennie glanced in that direction his cocky smile collapsed.

''Who's that?'' he demanded, scowling.

She looked over her shoulder in time to see Zach lope down the porch steps and head for his pickup. He glanced in her direction and nodded, but otherwise ignored them and began untying the ropes securing the boxes in the truck bed.

''That's Zach Mahoney, one of the new owners of the Rocking R,'' she said, unable to hide her resentment. ''He and his brothers and their families arrived just a few minutes ago.''

''One of Colleen's bastards, huh. Everybody in town in talking about them. Is he married?''

''No, just Matt and J.T.''

Lennie's scowl deepened. ''I don't like it.''

''Don't like what?''

''Him living in the house with you.''

''*What?* You don't have the right to like or dislike anything that goes on here, Lennie Dawson.''

She could have saved her breath.

"Damn that Seamus. Don't you see what that scheming old devil was up to? He figured he'd throw you and his bastard grandson together and let nature take its course."

"Seamus may have been autocratic about a lot of things, but he wouldn't go so far as to pick out a husband for me."

"Why not? He tried to force Colleen to marry my old man. He and Seamus even shook hands on a deal. Dad would marry Colleen and take over the ranch when Seamus kicked the bucket."

"That's a lie! I don't believe you."

"Believe it or not, it's true. Hell, Willie, the old coot was a control freak. It bugged the hell outta him that Colleen escaped, so he dangled the ranch in front of her bastards to rein them in. And you're the honey that sweetens the trap. That's the only reason he bothered to include you in his last will."

The statement hit her like a slap in the face. Willa trembled with anger and hurt…and uncertainty. "Get out of here!" she stormed. "Get off this ranch this minute."

"Willa?"

Her head snapped around, and she realized that her raised voice had drawn Zach's attention. He tossed the rope he had just wound into a neat coil onto the tailgate of his truck and took a couple of steps in their direction. "Is there a problem?"

She didn't know which stung the most—Lennie's disgusting insinuations, or having Zach come to her aid.

"No. There's no problem. Mr. Dawson was just leaving."

Lennie's mouth tightened and his face flamed an angry red. Clearly he did not take kindly to being dismissed.

He stared at Willa for a long time, his gaze flickering now and then to the other man. Though Zach's stance was deceptively casual and loose there was no doubt that he was braced for trouble.

"Dammit, Willa—"

"*Goodbye,* Lennie."

A muscle twitched in his cheek. He swore and reached for the door handle again but hesitated when Zach moved closer.

"All right, all right. I'm going." He twisted the key in the ignition and the truck roared to life. "You're obviously too emotional to discuss this rationally. When you've calmed down, think about what I said. You'll see that I'm right."

"Don't hold your breath."

Lennie stomped on the accelerator and the pickup fishtailed as he spun it into a U-turn. Gunning the engine, he tore out of the ranch yard, his tires rudely kicking up dirt and gravel.

Watching the truck shoot up the road at breakneck speed, Willa experienced an odd mixture of fury and disquiet. Lennie was a hothead. She and everyone else around Clear Water had witnessed his temper many times, but she had paid no more attention to his tantrums than she would a small child's. This time, though, she had seen something wild and dangerous simmering in his eyes, and that glimpse had sent an icy trickle down her spine. It galled her to admit it, but she was certain if Zach hadn't been there Lennie would not have let her order him off the ranch.

"Was that guy giving you a hard time, or was that just a lovers' quarrel?"

The question made her jump, and she was even more startled to realize that Zach now stood just behind her left shoulder. Willa was shorter than most men, but he seemed to tower over her, topping her five foot three inches by almost a foot. She was suddenly, uncomfortably aware of his broad shoulders and lean, muscular build, that raw masculinity that surrounded him like an aura, and her nerves began to jitter.

She stepped away and gave him a cool look. "Neither. Lennie Dawson is a neighbor. His father owns the Bar-D, the ranch that borders us to the east. I've known him since I was six."

"Mmm," Zach replied, watching the red pickup disappear over the crest of the hill. "Has he always had a bad temper?"

Willa stiffened, and immediately her anger with Lennie transferred to Zach. "Look, I can handle Lennie. In the future just mind your own business."

Zach shrugged. "Fine by me. I was just trying to help."

"I don't *need* your help. I don't need anything from you." She spun away and stomped back to the barn.

Watching her, Zach shook his head. That's where you're wrong, lady, he thought. You need me, all right. Like it or not, you need me and J.T. and Matt to hold on to this place.

Everything about the woman radiated anger, from those snapping violet eyes to her rigid spine to the defiant set of her jaw. Though on the small side, she was beautifully proportioned, and her leggy stride ate up the ground. Today all that ebony hair was confined in one long braid as thick as his wrist, which bounced and swayed against her backside with each furious step.

He could understand her anger—up to a point. She felt cheated and ill-used, and who could blame her? In her place, he'd feel the same. Seamus had strung her along with false promises, and after putting up with his foul temper and rigid control for most of her life, losing three-quarters of the Rocking R to strangers, never mind that they were the rightful heirs, had to have been a low blow. Discovering that without them she would have lost it all must have been even more galling.

Hell, he couldn't blame her for resenting them. Seamus was the real villain in all this, but the old bastard was gone, and her fury needed a live target.

Okay, he could live with that for a while. It wouldn't be easy, but he'd cut her some slack. At least until the raw hurt eased enough for her to gain a little perspective and look at the situation fairly.

Willa entered the barn muttering a litany of colorful epithets aimed at Zach, Lennie, Seamus and men in general. Sitting on a nail keg in the sunshine spilling in through the open double doors, Pete cast her a cautious glance, then wisely went back to stitching the saddlebag he was repairing.

"How dare Lennie accuse Seamus of using me to further his own agenda," she snarled as she paced to the far end of the barn. "How *dare* he! Idiot. Jerk. Hopeless Neanderthal!"

True, Seamus may not have loved her as his own flesh and blood, as she'd so desperately wanted, but he had accepted her as his stepdaughter and assumed responsibility for her, honoring that obligation even after her mother's death.

Willa had been only fifteen at the time. Seamus could have shipped her off to live with distant relatives, but he had not been a man to shirk his duty.

Still, the sad truth was, Seamus had been perfectly capable of scheming to make a match between her and

Zach. Was that why he had made her a beneficiary in his last will? So propinquity could do its work? He'd clearly had no intention of leaving her any portion of the ranch until after his grandsons showed up.

Seamus may have resented Zach and his brothers, but they had the Rafferty blood that had been so important to him and she had the experience and dedication and love for the Rocking R. If her stepfather had gotten it into his head that a marriage between her and Zach would benefit the ranch, he would have schemed and manipulated to make it happen.

In all things, Seamus had always been so absolutely certain that his way was the right way that he would not have considered such a maneuver wrong. Or insulting to her. Willa snorted. He probably would've thought he was doing her a favor.

"Well, if that was Seamus's plan, it's doomed to failure," she swore. "By heaven, I won't be anyone's brood mare.

"Men!" she spat, earning another wary look from Pete.

Though she'd paced the barn's cavernous length three times, fury still bubbled inside her. Finally she picked up a pitchfork and attacked the stalls, even though they had been mucked out only that morning.

She worked steadily for a couple of hours, until her shoulders ached and the muscles in her arms quivered from the strain. After the stalls were clean and spread with fresh hay she filled the feed and water troughs in the corrals as well as those inside the barn. Occasionally, through the open doors, she glimpsed Zach and his brothers and the children retrieving things from their vehicles and toting them into the house.

When Willa could find nothing else to do she fetched

a can of neatsfoot oil and a soft chamois from the tack room and started applying the lubricant to her saddle.

"I just oiled that saddle two days ago," Pete growled, never taking his gaze from his work. "It don't need it again." Pete had gotten too old to ride and he refused to retire, so Seamus had put him in charge of the tack room, and he guarded his domain with the fierceness of a stock dog with his herd.

"It looked a little dry," Willa said defiantly, and continued to rub the leather.

Pete stood and hung the bridle on a nail. He crossed the barn to Willa's side, took oil and cloth from her and set them aside, then cupped her elbow with his gnarled hand. "C'mon, Willie," he said gently, steering her toward the door. "You can't avoid them folks forever, so you might as well go on inside. Maria's bound to have dinner ready by now. An' from the smells coming from the cookhouse, Cookie's got the men's grub ready, too."

Willa sighed, knowing that Pete was right. "All right, I'm going. I'm going," she mumbled.

Outside twilight had fallen. She murmured good-night to Pete and headed toward the house on leaden feet. She'd rather take a whipping than sit down to a meal with those people.

The heavenly smell of fried chicken greeted her as she climbed the steps to the back porch, and despite the dread she felt, her stomach growled in anticipation. Opening the door, she stepped inside the kitchen and came to an abrupt halt.

For the last eleven years she, Maria and Seamus had rattled around in the huge ranch house. Seamus had not been a talkative man, nor had he been tolerant of what he'd called "women's chatter" at the table. As a result, meals had been eaten mostly in silence, the three of them often exchanging not so much as a word. Now the chatter and bustle of six adults and five children filled the huge old kitchen.

The children were setting the table and indulging in a bit of bickering and shoving as they darted and dodged around each other. J.T. and Matt sat on opposite sides of the long trestle table, drinking coffee and arguing quietly about something. The women carried on a conversation of their own while they helped Maria— Kate at the stove assisting with the cooking and Maude Ann washing the pots and pans and mixing bowls as quickly as the other women finished with them.

Standing a little apart in the doorway that lead into the hall, one shoulder braced against the frame, Zach sipped a mug of coffee and took in the scene in silence, those sharp green eyes missing nothing, including her.

The cacophony of laughter, voices and activity assaulted Willa's senses, making her nerves jump.

"Hello, Willa. We wondered where you were," Maude Ann greeted when she spotted her.

Kate's gaze flickered in her direction. She offered a cautious hello, and J.T. and Matt interrupted their discussion long enough to do the same. Sensing the adults's wariness and the sudden strain in the air, the children stopped what they were doing and stared at Willa with distrust. As though *she* was the one who didn't belong, Willa thought.

Wiping her hands on a towel, Maude Ann turned from the sink with a tentative smile. "I was beginning to worry that you'd miss dinner, but you're just in time."

"Watch out, Willa," Matt drawled. "Maudie's a mother hen. She'll tuck you under her wing with the rest of her chicks if you let her."

"Don't be silly. I just didn't want her to go hungry,

that's all,'' his wife said with a huff, but her eyes danced with affection and humor as she yanked a lock of his hair.

"Ah, the biscuits, they are ready," Maria announced.

"So is everything else," Kate said, carrying a steaming gravy boat and a bowl of salad to the table. "Everybody sit down while I dish up the rest."

The children whooped and made a dash for the table, elbowing one another and jostling for position, but a firm order from Matt put an instant end to the unmannerly behavior.

Kate noticed that Willa still stood rooted to the spot just inside the back door and motioned to the table. "Have a seat. You must be starved after working all day."

Willa wanted to refuse, but she was so hungry she was shaky, and the aromas filling the kitchen were driving her crazy. She shifted from one foot to the other. "I, uh…I have to wash up first. Excuse me."

She expected Zach to move out of the doorway, but he merely shifted a bit to one side to allow her to squeeze by, those cool eyes tracking her all the while.

As Willa scooted past him, her shoulder brushed his chest and a tingle trickled down her spine. He had recently showered, and the smells of soap and shampoo and clean male enveloped her. The heady combination made her light-headed and self-consciously aware that after working in the barn all afternoon she smelled of horses, straw, neatsfoot oil and old leather. Gritting her teeth, she marched down the hall to the powder room.

When she returned everyone was seated, and she took the only chair left, next to the angelic-looking little blond girl.

Matt offered the blessing, and as the bowls and platters

were being passed around the table, Willa felt a tug on her left sleeve. Startled, she looked down into a pair of wide, innocent blue eyes, fixed on her with unwavering directness.

"You ith pretty," the child lisped.

Disarmed, Willa blinked. "Uh…thank you."

"My name ith Debbie, and I'm five. Whath yourth?"

"Willa."

"Wiwa. Thath a pretty name."

"Uh…thanks."

"Not Wiwa, you dumb girl," the African-American boy jeered, rolling his eyes. "She said Willa."

"Tyrone, no name-calling," Maude Ann warned. "You know the rules."

"But she talks like that dumb ole duck in the cartoons."

Tears welled in Debbie eyes and her protruding lower lip trembled. "I ith not dumb. Am I, Daddy?" she appealed, turning her pathetic little face to Matt.

"No, of course not, sweetheart." He gave the boy a stern look. "Apologize to your sister, Tyrone."

"Aw, do I gotta?"

"Yes. Now."

The boy stared down at his plate, his jaw set in a mulish pout. "Sorry."

Maude Ann sent Willa an apologetic look. "Sorry about that. But you know how children are."

"No, actually I don't. I've never been around children."

"Oh. I see." Willa's cool tone was not lost on Maude Ann, and for the first time her own voice had a guarded quality. "Well, we all have adjustments to make. And so you'll know who you're dealing with, let me introduce you to the rest of the children. This is Yolanda."

Starting with the Hispanic girl, Maude Ann worked her way around the table. With the exception of twelve-year-old Yolanda, the Dolans's adopted brood were stair-step in age. In addition to Debbie and eight-year-old Tyrone, there was seven-year-old Jennifer, a quiet, plain child who seemed to be trying to make herself invisible, and a frail-looking six-year-old named Tim.

Willa responded to each child with a cool hello that didn't encourage conversation and returned her attention to her meal as soon as the introductions were finished. They were well behaved, and she supposed they were appealing, but they didn't belong there, and she wasn't interested in getting to know them.

"I know there are a lot of us, and this probably seems like a huge imposition to you, after living here so quietly with your stepfather all those years, but I assure you, the children won't be a problem," Maude Ann added when the introductions were over.

Willa gave a little snort of disbelief and slanted her a look. "Actually, I'm surprised that you brought them here."

Around the table everyone stopped talking and the clank and ping of silverware ceased. Willa could feel ten pairs of eyes fix on her, and in her peripheral vision she saw Maria shaking her head sadly.

As though an iron rod had been rammed down her spine, Maude Ann sat up straighter. Her chin rose and the almost perpetual impish twinkle in her eyes turned to frost. "Really? And just what did you expect me to do with my children during the year we all must be here?"

"Technically, you and the children and Kate don't have to be here at all. The conditions only apply to your husbands and Zach and me."

"Now wait just a minute—" Matt began, but his wife held up her hand to stop him.

"No. I'll handle this." She turned to Willa with an implacable expression. "Where my husband goes, I go, and so do our children. We're a family. If you don't like that, too bad."

"The same goes for J.T. and me," Kate agreed. "You have a lot of nerve even suggesting that we shouldn't be here."

"Look, all I'm saying is, this is a busy ranch. A lot of the work we do is dangerous and cattle and horses are unpredictable. It isn't the safest place to bring a bunch of children."

"Oh, please," Maude Ann scoffed. "Children have grown up on ranches for hundreds of years."

"That's right. You were raised here, weren't you?" Matt demanded.

"Yes, but I was born on a nearby ranch. I wasn't a city kid when my mother and I came to the Rocking R." Willa shrugged. "Actually, you're all going to have a difficult time. There aren't any fancy stores or coffee-houses or restaurants or even a movie theater in Clear Water."

"Don't worry about us. We'll manage," Maude Ann said. "What we don't know, we'll learn."

Zach sat quietly, taking in the clash, but the other adults murmured agreement while the children stared at Willa as though she were a monster with two heads. All except Tyrone, who glared at her and bragged, "Yeah. I'm gonna learn to ride a horse and rope cows an' ever'thing."

Willa shrugged. "Suit yourselves. Just don't say I didn't warn you."

She picked up her fork, took a bite of mashed potatoes.

For the remainder of the meal the others talked among themselves. The only one who spoke to Willa was Maria, and then only to give her a scolding in rapid-fire Spanish, which Willa knew she richly deserved.

It had been a stupid thing to say. The instant the words had left her mouth she'd known that she had gone too far. But, darn it! She was feeling so prickly and on edge. Out-of-sorts and outnumbered.

Zach said little, but the others, including the children, carried on a lively conversation.

Willa's appetite had fled, and she spent most of the meal moving the food around on her plate. When the children were sent upstairs to brush their teeth and shower and get ready for bed, she scraped back her chair. "I'm going to turn in, too."

She made it only as far as the front hall when Zach caught up with her.

"Willa. I want to talk to you."

"Not now. I'm tired. I'm going to bed." She put her hand on the newel post to start up the stairs, but Zach clamped his hand around her upper arm and spun her around to face him.

"What do you think you're doing? Let go of me! I have nothing to say to you."

"Good. Just keep your mouth shut and listen." He bent forward until his face was mere inches from hers. Willa's heart skipped a beat. Fury blazed in his normally cool green eyes. His face was a taut mask, his jaws so tight he spoke through his clenched teeth. "Listen to me, Willa Simmons. You can unleash your anger on me and Matt and J.T. all you want, but if you ever, *ever* again strike out at those kids or my sister or Maude Ann, or upset them in any way, you'll answer to me. Is that clear?"

"I didn't mean to upset anyone. I was only trying to point out the downside of living here."

"Bull. You're between a rock and a hard place, and that frustrates the hell out of you. You can't run me or my brothers off without losing the ranch, so you thought you'd see if you could get rid of the wives and kids. That way you wouldn't feel quite so outnumbered. Nice try, but it won't work. We're here to stay. All of us. Is that clear?"

Humiliation, shame and temper tangled together inside Willa, but it was pride that saw her through. She tilted her chin at a regal angle. "Yes. Perfectly."

"Good."

Chapter Three

Willa rose earlier than usual the next morning. In the kitchen, over Maria's objections, she grabbed a couple of hot biscuits and made her escape, and moments later she drove her pickup out of the yard.

At the ranch entrance she turned north onto the highway and headed for Helena.

It wasn't Willa's nature to run away, and her conscience pricked her as she punched the accelerator, but she kept going. She simply wasn't up to facing Zach and his family just yet, not after the night she'd just had. She had behaved badly and she'd paid the consequences. Long after she'd heard the others come upstairs she'd lain awake, staring at the ceiling, wrestling with her guilt and anger. Even when she'd finally fallen asleep she had tossed and turned fitfully.

Willa justified the trip by telling herself she had to pick up the new boots she'd had made. Never mind that there was no hurry, and that anyone from the ranch who was going to Helena within the next few weeks could have picked them up for her. She wanted to do it herself. Anyway, she deserved a day off now and then, didn't she?

Willa was so unaccustomed to having leisure time she hardly knew what to do with herself, but she forced herself to delay her return as long as possible.

At ten after eleven that evening she pulled into the ranch yard. The house was dark except for the light in the kitchen, but Willa wasn't surprised that Maria had left it on for her. Intent on getting upstairs without waking anyone, she eased open the back door as quietly as possible.

"Oh. What are you doing still up?"

Seamus's grandsons sat at the kitchen table, watching her.

"Waiting for you." Zach gestured toward the chair opposite his. "Have a seat. We need to talk."

Willa didn't budge. "What now? It's late and I'm tired."

"And whose fault is that? If you hadn't run off, we would have had this discussion at breakfast."

"I did not 'run off.' I had some errands to run."

He simply looked at her. She tried to weather that steady gaze, though she felt a guilty blush spread over her face. "Oh, all right. We'll talk." She jerked out a chair and plopped down with a huff. "What is so important that it couldn't wait until morning?"

"Before we go any further, we need to decide who's going to be in charge of the ranch operation."

Shock slammed through Willa, jerking her head back. "What do you mean, who's going to be in charge? *I'm* in charge."

An uncomfortable silence filled the room as the three

men exchanged a look. Finally, J.T. cleared his throat. "Well, the thing is, since we all own equal shares of the Rocking R, my brothers and I feel that we should take a vote on that."

"That's right," Matt agreed. "Let's face it, you can't run a place like this by committee. There can only be one person giving orders."

"I agree with that. I just don't understand why we're having this conversation. None of you city slickers knows beans about ranching. I'm the only one with experience."

"Uh…that's not exactly true," J.T. corrected. "Zach has ranching experience."

"A rodeo cowboy?" She gave a scornful laugh. "You want to put a rodeo cowboy in charge of this ranch? Are you crazy? This may surprise you, but on the Rocking R we don't spend a lot of time riding our bulls."

"Actually, Willa, Zach has worked on a ranch before."

"Oh, please. Hiring on as a wrangler at some hardscrabble little spread between rodeos hardly qualifies him to ramrod a spread the size of this one."

"You don't understand. Zach is highly qualified for the job. He has—"

"Never mind, J.T." Zach watched Willa, his expression inscrutable. "I don't think she wants to hear any of that."

"But—"

"No, it's okay. She's entitled to her opinion. Just as we are to ours. Which is why we're going to vote."

"Then I vote that Zach should be in charge," Matt said.

"So do I," J.T. concurred.

"Since I agree with them, that settles it." Zach's cool

gaze drilled into Willa. "From now on, I'll be giving the orders. Are we clear on that?"

Willa's hands curled into fists. The fierce emotions roiling through her set off a trembling deep inside her body. She gritted her teeth and glared at him, too furious to speak.

Zach cocked one blond eyebrow. "Well?"

"Fine!" she snapped. "Go ahead and play cowboy. Just don't come whining to me six months from now when we go belly up." She exploded out of the chair so fast it toppled and crashed to the brick floor, but she paid it no mind and stomped toward the back door. She had to get out of there—*now*—before she blew apart.

"Willa, wait. We have some other decisions to make."

"Make them yourself. No matter what I want, the three of you will outvote me, anyway."

The back door slammed with a force hard enough to rattle the windows and make the brothers wince.

J.T. gave a long, low whistle. "Man, that is some temper."

"Yeah." Zach stared at the door, a furrow creasing between his eyebrows. "But she has reason to be angry. I hated to deal her another blow, but I don't think we had a choice."

"Maybe we could have been a little more subtle about it."

Matt snorted at J.T.'s suggestion. "And just how were we supposed to do that, Einstein? There is no gentle way to strip someone of their authority."

"Oh, I don't know. Zach could have taken over bit by bit over a period of time."

"And you don't think she would've notice? Yeah, right. That lady is as possessive of this ranch and her position as a dog with a meaty bone."

"I agree," Zach said. "You don't maneuver around a strong-willed woman like Willa. Anyway, clean and quick is usually less painful in the long run.

"As for the other things we need to hash out, I think we'd better give her time to cool down. We'll continue this discussion in the morning."

"Fine by me. I'm ready to turn in. I'm beat." Matt stood and stretched, then unhooked his cane from the back of his chair. He limped away a couple of steps, then stopped and looked back at his brothers with a wry half smile. "The funny thing is, Willa assumes because we're triplets we're going to agree on everything. Man, is she in for a shock."

Willa always rose early, and the following morning was no exception, even though once again she had gotten little sleep.

After storming out of the house the night before, she'd made a beeline for the barn, as had been her habit in the past whenever she'd been upset or smarting from Seamus's criticism. There she had paced and ranted and cursed at the rafters. At one point she'd hauled off and kicked a galvanized pail almost the length of the structure. Of course, that had made a terrible racket and frightened the stock, and she'd had to take time out to quiet them, but, oh, it had felt good to vent her fury.

Finally, with the worst of her rage spent, Willa had wrapped her arms around her horse Bertha's neck and poured out her woes into the animal's sympathetic ear. Of all the unpleasant changes and low blows she'd endured in the past few weeks, this one was by far the worst. The usurpers were taking over, and there wasn't a blessed thing she could do to stop them.

It wasn't until hours later that Willa had returned to

the house and tiptoed upstairs to her room. Still upset, she had slept poorly until just before dawn when she had to get up.

Confident the others were still asleep, Willa dressed and braided her hair and went downstairs. She intended to once again grab a biscuit then saddle up and ride out before anyone stirred, but to her surprise, when she approached the kitchen she heard raised voices.

"No, dammit! I won't do it."

"Why not? You're the logical one."

Stunned and fascinated by the unexpected friction between the brothers, Willa paused outside the swinging door.

"Why? Because I've got a busted leg? Just because I walk with a limp doesn't mean I can't ride a horse or drive a truck."

"Have you ever ridden a horse?"

"No, but I can learn. I'd helluva lot rather be out in the fresh air than cooped up inside all day."

"Actually, Zach, it would be better for Matt to be involved in some sort of physical work," Maude Ann offered cautiously. "He needs to exercise his leg as much as possible."

Willa slipped inside the kitchen in time to see Zach rake his hand through his wheat-colored hair. The others were so intent on their discussion they didn't notice her standing just inside the doorway.

The three brothers and Maude Ann and Kate sat at the table, drinking coffee, while Maria prepared breakfast.

"All right, then J.T. will keep the books."

"The hell I will!"

"Dammit, J.T., what's *your* problem? You're a writer. You're going to be inside working at a desk a lot of the time, anyway."

Well, well, isn't this interesting, Willa thought. She looked from one man to the other, enjoying herself immensely.

"All the more reason to get away from a desk for part of each day. You're nuts if you think I'm going to be stuck inside while you and Matt are out enjoying the wide-open spaces and the fresh air. Besides, I'm lousy at figures."

Zach heaved a long-suffering sigh and massaged the back of his neck. "Look. First of all, ranching isn't fun and games or some kind of lark. It's long hours of hard, back-breaking, muscle-straining, dirty, sweaty physical labor. Sometimes it can be damned dangerous, as well."

"Don't worry about me. I can handle it," Matt vowed.

"Me, too," J.T. echoed.

"How? Neither one of you has ever even been on a horse before, for Pete's sake."

"Then teach us to ride."

"I won't have time."

"Fine, then I'll find someone who will. Because there's no way you're going to turn me into a pencil pusher. I quit the police force rather than take a desk job, and I'm sure as hell not going to be stuck with one here. You got that, Mahoney?"

"For once, I have to agree with Matt," J.T. said.

"Oh, great. Just what this place needs—*three* greenhorns on horseback."

The drawled statement brought six heads swiveling in Willa's direction in time to see her hook her thumbs into the front pockets of her jeans and saunter toward the table. Matt and J.T. shot her an annoyed look, but the women regarded her with a mixture of wariness and concern.

Willa tilted her chin. No doubt they knew about that

discussion last night and that Zach had usurped her place as boss. Well, if they were looking for signs of tears, they were going to be disappointed. She was mad as hell, not hurt.

"Good morning." Kate gestured toward the chair beside her own. "Come join us. We're trying to decide who does what."

"So I gathered."

Zach focused on his most pressing problem. "Can you keep books?"

"No." It was a bald-faced lie. In Seamus's later years, when his eyesight had begun to fade, she'd helped him with the accounts, but of all the jobs on the ranch, bookkeeping was her least favorite, and she wasn't about to take it on to help Zach.

"Great. That's just great."

"I'll do the books, Zach," Kate offered quietly. "Giving Maria a hand with meals and doing the books should keep me busy."

"The children and I will help out around the house, too," Maude Ann volunteered. "And we can put in a garden. I noticed there isn't one now, and I do love fresh veggies. Maybe we can build a coop and raise some chickens, too. It would be nice to have fresh poultry and eggs."

The changes were coming too fast. For Willa it was like being chased by a swarm of bees, and she instinctively resisted.

"And what about me? What am I supposed to do?" Everything about Willa—her expression, the thrust of her chin, her tone—was a belligerent challenge. If Zach thought he could stick her in the house with the women, he had another think coming.

"What were your duties before Seamus became ill and you started relaying his orders?"

"I did whatever needed doing. Usually I worked alongside the men."

"Then that's what you'll continue to do," he said matter-of-factly, taking the wind out of her sails.

At the very least she had expected he would assign her menial chores that were reserved for the newest, most inexperienced hands. At worst, that he would relegate her to the house and domestic chores. She'd been prepared to fight him tooth-and-nail over either.

Zach turned to his brothers. "I want to make one thing clear. If you two insist on working outdoors alongside me, then you're going to darn well pull your own weight and put in an honest day's work. Is that clear?"

Both men bristled.

"Hey! I may have a bum leg, Mahoney, but I'm no slacker. I can work you into the ground any day of the week."

"That goes for me, too," J.T. declared.

"Fine. Just so we understand one another." Zach looked at Willa. "Can you give them riding lessons?"

"No." She sipped her coffee and eyed him defiantly.

"Okay, who do we have on the payroll who can teach these two yahoos to ride and rope and the rest of the basics?"

Willa gritted her teeth. She was spoiling for a fight and wouldn't you know he'd refuse to cooperate. "Your best bet would be Pete. He's almost eighty and arthritic but he was practically born in the saddle. He's been working here since he was sixteen, and he taught me to ride."

"Okay, I'll talk to him after breakfast. Now, the next—"

A high-pitched scream from the front of the house cut

him off in midsentence. The shrill sound made the hairs on Willa's forearms and the back of her neck stand on end.

"What the hell!"

"Holy—!"

"That's Jennifer!" Maude Ann bolted out of her chair. She shoved open the swinging door at a dead run and raced for the front hall. Everyone else followed right on her heels.

The screams continued, running together in one long, ear-piercing sound. By the time they burst into the foyer Willa was at the back of the group.

Jennifer stood by the open front door, rigid, trembling with fright and shrieking. Her face was chalk white, her stricken gaze fixed on the outside of the door.

Both Zach and Matt cursed and Kate and Maude Ann gave a shocked cry.

"*¡Dios mio!*" Maria closed her eyes and crossed herself and began to recite a fervent prayer under her breath.

"Aw, hell," J.T. muttered. "What a thing for a kid to see."

"What? What is it?" Skidding to a halt behind them, Willa wriggled her way to the front of the group, and gasped. "Oh, my, Lord."

Nailed to the outside of the front door was a dead gopher. Between the animal and the door hung a bloodied piece of paper.

Maude Ann dropped to her knees and snatched the child into her arms. Turning away from the gruesome sight, she pressed the girl's face against her shoulder.

"It's all right, baby. It's okay. Momma's here, love," she crooned over and over, stroking the child's back.

The girl locked her arms around Maude Ann's neck in a death grip. "I—I'm s-sorry, Momma. I w-wasn't going anywh-where. I—I just w-wanted to…pet the d-d-doggie," she sobbed against her mother's shoulder.

"That's okay, baby. You didn't do anything wrong. It's okay, baby. It's okay."

Striding forward, Zach snatched the paper free and slammed the door shut, removing the animal from view.

"There's writing on it," J.T. pointed out. "What does it say?"

Zach scanned the sheet of paper. It was lined and ragged along the left side, obviously torn from a spiral notebook. "It says, 'Get out, Bastards. You're not wanted here.'"

His head snapped around toward Willa. "Is this your doing?"

"*Me?* Of course not!" she denied, but all around the others were staring at her, their expressions accusing. Even Maria looked sad. "How can you even ask that?"

"Easy. You've made it plain that you don't want us here."

"That's true, but I'm not a fool. Why would I try to run you off? If any of you leave, I lose everything I've ever wanted. Do you honestly think I'd do something that stupid?"

"What I think is that temper of yours sometimes overrules your common sense."

"That's not true!"

A stony silence stretched out as everyone eyed her with suspicion and hostility. Zach stared at her so long she had to fight the urge to squirm.

The tense silence was broken when the other four children came clamoring down the stairs, barefoot and in their pajamas and still rumpled and rosy from sleep. "What's goin' on? What's Jennifer screaming about?" Tyrone demanded, knuckling both eyes.

"Yeah, she woked me up," Debbie grumbled.

"Nothing to worry about. She just had a little scare, is all," Matt said. "But since you're up, you kids go get dressed. Maria will have breakfast ready in two shakes, so move it."

Taking charge, Kate hurried up to where the children stood. "C'mon, gang, you heard your dad. Time to rise and shine." That produced a chorus of grumbling, but she herded them back up the stairs.

"C'mon, let's get Jennifer out of here." Matt glared at Willa one last time and put his arm around his wife and daughter and led them into the parlor. "It'll be okay, sweetheart. I won't let anything hurt you," he murmured, stroking the shivering child's arm.

"I'll get a crowbar and take care of that mess on the door," J.T. offered quietly. "Maria, would you get me a scrub brush and a pail of soapy water and some rags."

"Ah, *sí*. Come, with me, *señor*."

As the pair headed for the back of the house, Willa risked another glance at Zach. Those cool green eyes still bore into her.

"I didn't *do* it," she insisted through clenched teeth.

He continued to stare at her, so long she began to think he wasn't going to speak to her at all. Finally he nodded. "Okay. If you say so. But if you didn't, who did?"

Chapter Four

Over the next few days the question seemed to hang in the air. Unanswered. Silently accusing.

Zach and the others said they believed her, but Willa knew that they were merely withholding judgment. She could see it in their eyes, hear it in their carefully neutral tones.

Matt was barely civil, and even gregarious J.T. had become reserved toward her. The women were polite, but they'd dropped all previous attempts at friendliness.

"Well, fine. Let them believe whatever they want. What do I care, anyway?" Willa muttered to the blazing sunset. Her horse snorted and bobbed her head, as though in complete agreement.

Willa sat slumped in the saddle, her lower body moving to the rhythm of Bertha's plodding walk. They had been riding fence line all day, and both she and the horse were bone-tired.

Those people were nothing to her, she told herself adamantly. Just a bunch of greedy city slickers and a pack of rowdy kids. Fact was, she didn't like them any more than they liked her. Not any of them.

No matter how many times she said it, however, the truth was, like them or not, it hurt that anyone could think she was capable of such a vile act. Willa felt maligned, and even after five days her pride still smarted from the insult, which kept her temper simmering.

Most of the blame she put squarely on Zach. He was supposed to be the boss, wasn't he? The leader? If he truly believed her, he could have convinced the others.

She avoided them all whenever possible, especially Zach. If he gave her a choice, each morning she opted to tackle jobs that took her as far from where he was going to be as she could get. Those times when she was forced to endure his company she tried to ignore him, but so far she had not succeeded even once.

Despite her best intentions she always ended up taking verbal potshots at Zach. She criticized every decision he made, everything he did, the way he did it and when he did it, even when she knew he was right. She constantly compared his methods to Seamus's and sneered at any changes Zach implemented.

It was foolish of her and nonproductive, and she knew it, but she could not seem to restrain herself. Merely being around the man made her hackles rise and her skin tingle as though it were covered in a prickly rash.

For his part, Zach never flared back at her, no matter how much she picked at him or how cutting her comments, and that was the most irritating thing of all. He would simply give her one of those long, unreadable looks and go about his business, as though she were no more than a pesky mosquito buzzing around.

"Insufferable jerk," she swore. "The man either has a thick hide or the patience of Job. Or he's dumber than dirt."

Willa sighed. Much as she'd like to believe the latter, she knew it wasn't true. After being around him only a few days, it was obvious that Zach was an intelligent, logical man.

Everything was changing, Willa thought morosely. And she was powerless to do anything about it.

She looked around at the glorious sunset backlighting the mountains and streaking the sky with reds and purples and golds, and she sighed again. The only thing that remained the same was the land.

Her previously quiet home was now a beehive of activity and noise, and she resented it. Never mind that she'd always hated the tomblike quiet and emptiness of the huge house in the past, or that she'd often longed for some female companionship, women her own age with whom she could talk. She hadn't chosen to share her home or the ranch or her life with these people. They had been thrust upon her.

Worst of all, she was turning into a shrew, and she hated that.

What in heaven's name was the matter with her? It was true, she'd never been a pushover. From an early age she'd learned to stand her ground, even if it meant locking horns with Seamus. If she hadn't he would have run roughshod over her. Even so, contrariness and bad temper had never been part of her basic makeup.

Inevitably after every attack on Zach, Willa felt small and ashamed—but she simply couldn't stop herself from lashing out at him. Or bring herself to apologize.

Deep down, though she didn't like to think about it, Willa knew that, at least in part, her reaction to Zach sprang from fear that Lennie was right about Seamus scheming to get her and Zach together. No way was she going to let that happen.

There was more behind her prickliness than just self-protection, though. It was also a reaction to Zach usurping her position at the ranch.

She had expected at least some initial resistance from the hands, but none had materialized. It was painful and demoralizing to stand back and watch how easily Zach stepped into Seamus's boots. All the men, including the old-timers she had known all of her life, not only accepted him as their boss, they looked up to him and obeyed his orders over hers. Even Pete.

Maria had accepted the newcomers totally, as well. She adored the children and was devoted to Kate and Maude Ann and thought the three men were *"Muy macho."*

Willa felt betrayed on all sides, unfairly accused and more alone than ever. Her response was to lash out—and to attack whatever job that needed doing with a vengeance. Driven by hurt feelings, simmering temper and offended honor, she worked herself into a state of near exhaustion every day.

The sun went down in a blaze of glory as Willa dismounted and led Bertha into the barn. Zach's horse was in his stall, contentedly munching grain, and the rest of the horses were in the corrals. As usual, she was the last one to come straggling in. She was probably late for dinner again and in for a lecture from Maria.

Willa unsaddled the mare, gave her fresh food and water and a cursory rubdown. "I'll be back later, girl, and give you a good currying. I promise," she said, and hurried toward the house.

To her surprise and delight, Edward Manning sat at the kitchen table drinking coffee with Zach. Maude Ann and Kate were helping Maria prepare dinner, and from the den came the sounds of the television and children squabbling.

Like the gentleman he was, Edward rose as soon as he spotted her. "Ah, Willie. There you are."

"Edward, it's so good to see you." She flashed him a beaming smile and rushed forward with her arms outstretched.

He was taken aback by her enthusiastic greeting, which didn't surprise her. They were casual friends and had never been particularly close. However, since the funeral she'd been feeling woefully outnumbered, and she was so happy to see a friendly face she couldn't restrain herself.

With his usual aplomb, Edward recovered quickly and accepted her hug, though he couldn't quite suppress a little grimace of distaste when he got a whiff of the "horsey" smell that clung to her.

As Willa stepped back from Edward's embrace they heard groaning and the sound of footsteps. Walking with a painfully slow, slightly bow-legged gait, J.T. and Matt entered the kitchen from the main hall. Every step produced a groan and a grimace of pain from both men.

When he spotted their guest, J.T. gritted his teeth and stretched his lips in a strained smile. "Hey, Edward, good to see you."

Matt just nodded.

Grinning, Willa watched them hobble to the table. Matt carefully lowered himself into a chair, groaning louder as his sore backside came into contact with the seat.

"Aren't you going to have a seat, J.T.?" she asked, making no effort to hide her amusement.

"I'll stand, thanks." He cautiously leaned a shoulder

against the wall, making certain his rear end did not come into contact. "In fact, I may never sit again."

"Matt and J.T. have been learning to ride," she explained to Edward with a grin.

"Ah, I see. That explains a lot."

Willa turned her attention back to Edward. "I haven't seen or heard from you since Seamus's funeral, and that was almost a month ago. I was beginning to think you'd forgotten me."

"Hardly. I could never forget you, Willie, you know that. The Rocking R is still my number-one client. But I do apologize for neglecting you. For the past two weeks I've been tied up in political business in Helena. Although I did asked my secretary to convey that message. Don't tell me she didn't call."

"No, I haven't heard from her."

"She called," Zach said.

Willa shot him an accusing glare. "Why wasn't I told?"

"The message didn't seem to be directed to you personally, and I wasn't aware that you were expecting Mr. Manning."

Ever the diplomat, Edward jumped in before Willa could utter a blistering retort. "Oh, well. No harm done. You all seem to be settling in nicely, and I assume, since you haven't contacted my office, that no legal problems or questions have arisen so far."

"Now that you mention it, we have had one disturbing incident," Zach said.

Willa stiffened, but he ignored her and explained about the dead gopher and the note. By the time he was done, the attorney was frowning.

"Do you have any idea who would do such a thing?"

"No. We've drawn a blank." Zach and his brothers

carefully avoided so much as a glance Willa's way. On the other side of the kitchen the women were suddenly busy.

"It doesn't make any sense." J.T. grimaced and adjusted his position against the wall. "What motive would anyone around here have to run us out? We haven't had time to make enemies."

"Ah, but Seamus didn't exactly endear himself to the folks around Clear Water," Edward replied.

"What's that got to do with us?"

Edward shrugged and spread his hands wide. "Who knows? Sins of the father, maybe?"

"Or in this case, the grandfather," J.T. muttered.

"The motive could be simple jealousy," Matt said. "Or greed."

"Greed?" Edward shook his head. "How can that be? The only ones who would stand to gain if you were to give up the ranch are a few universities. I can't believe anyone from those institutions would stoop to scare tactics to drive you out."

"Neither can I. However, there is one individual who would profit." Matt stared at Edward. "You."

"Me?"

"I don't believe it," Willa exclaimed. "First you accuse me. Now Edward?"

"You accused Willie?" Edward looked stunned. "But…that doesn't make any sense."

"I agree," J.T. said. "And neither does accusing you. What's the matter with you, Matt? That's just plain crazy."

"He's right, you know. All I would get is the normal executor's fee."

"I've done some checking. That fee is a percentage of

the trust, which in this case would amount to a hefty sum.''

''So is my annual retainer as your attorney.''

''True, but it's not nearly as much as you'd get as executor of the trust.''

Exasperated, Willa threw up her hands. ''For Pete's sake, Matt! The Mannings have been our attorneys for years. Seamus had absolute trust in Edward's father and Edward. They were his friends!''

''Do you seriously believe I would risk my professional reputation and my political future, not to mention possible criminal prosecution, to sneak out here and kill some hapless creature and nail it to your door?'' Edward shuddered fastidiously. ''Please. Anyway, I've been in Helena for weeks. You can check that if you'd like.''

''I intend to.''

Edward tipped his head to one side and studied Matt's tough-as-nails face. ''You don't like me much, do you, Matt?''

''I don't know you.''

J.T. groaned. ''Don't pay any attention to him. Matt was a cop. He has a suspicious mind and an innate distrust of lawyers.''

''I can't say that I care much for reporters, either,'' Matt added, fixing J.T. with a pointed look.

''Hey, bro, lighten up, will you? I repented my ways, remember. I'm a novelist/cowboy now.''

Matt snorted. ''Some cowboy. You can barely stay in the saddle.''

''Hey! You're one to talk.''

''All right, that's enough, boys,'' Maude Ann drawled, dumping a stack of place mats on the table. ''It's time for dinner. Darling, would you go tell the kids to wash up and come set the table?''

Matt groaned as he started to rise, but J.T. waved at him to stay put. "I'll go. I'm already on my feet."

"Edward, you will join us, won't you?" Kate asked as she and Maria began to placed platters and bowls of food on the table.

"Thanks, but—"

"Please, Edward, do stay," Willa urged, laying her hand over his. "We can do some catching up over dinner. You can tell me how your political plans are going. Are your friends in Helena still urging you to run for mayor?"

"Ah, no fair," he teased. "You know how much I love talking politics."

"Then you'll stay?"

The other women added their pleas, and he gave in.

Willa made certain that Edward was seated next to her, and throughout the meal she devoted all her attention and conversation to him and ignored everyone else. She listened attentively to his every word and laughed at his attempts at humor.

When dinner was over she tried to persuade him to spend the night, but he insisted he had to return to Bozeman.

Willa walked with him to his car, which was out front where he always parked. It would never occur to Edward to enter the house through the back door.

"How is it going?" he asked kindly when they reached his car and were alone for the first time. "Everything working out all right?"

Crossing her arms over her midriff, Willa shrugged and looked away at the night sky. "Okay, I guess. I still hate this arrangement, but there's nothing I can do about it. At least none of us has committed murder yet."

Edward chuckled, then patted her shoulder. "Buck up.

You can take it, kiddo. I promise to stop by more often in the future, and you know you can always call me at my office or at home if you have a problem, don't you?"

"I know. Thanks, Edward."

He dropped a brotherly kiss on her forehead and climbed into his car. Willa stood where she was, watching him drive away. When his car's taillights disappeared over the crest of the hill, she headed for the barn.

She was halfway down the wide middle aisle before she realized she was not alone. "Oh." She stopped abruptly. "I didn't know you were in here."

Zach squatted on his haunches, examining the gate of the stall two down from Bertha's. An open toolbox sat on the ground at his side.

He glanced over his shoulder at her. Those cool green eyes did a quick sweep of her face and body. "What? Has your lover gone already? I thought you'd still be making out in his car."

Willa narrowed her eyes. "First of all, I do *not* 'make out in cars' as you so elegantly put it, and second, Edward is *not* my lover."

"Yeah, well, you'd never know it by the way you hung all over him during dinner."

Willa sucked in a sharp breath, so incensed all she could do for a moment was gape at him. "I *did not* hang on Edward," she denied hotly when she found her tongue. "I was merely enjoying a conversation with an old friend. Trust you to read something dirty into a perfectly innocent act."

"All I know is you sure seem to have a lot of 'good friends.' First Lennie Dawson, now Edward." He fished a screwdriver out of the toolbox and went to work tightening the screws on the stall gate. "Do they know about each other, by the way?"

"There is nothing to know," she snapped. "Not that it's any of your business."

Willa turned to leave, then changed her mind and spun around again. Jaws clenched, she stomped to Bertha's stall, jerked the gate open and stepped inside. She had as much right to be there as he did. She'd be darned if she'd let him run her off.

Bertha whinnied a greeting and nudged Willa's shoulder. Despite her anger, she smiled and reached into her shirt pocket for the sugar cube she'd stashed there during dinner. Bertha lipped the treat from her palm, and Willa leaned her forehead against the horse's neck and stroked her. "You big baby," she murmured.

She loved Bertha more than anything or anyone on earth. Seamus had surprised her with the ten month old filly for her twenty-first birthday. The animal was the only thing of any great value that he'd ever given her. For that matter, it had been the first time since her mother's death that he had bothered to acknowledge her birthday at all.

Ever since then Bertha had been her most prized possession. Not just because she had been a gift from Seamus, but because the animal loved her in return—totally and unconditionally. That was something Willa had never been sure of from any of the people in her life—not her mother, not Seamus, not even Maria or Pete.

For those few moments as she petted Bertha, Willa forgot about everything else, including Zach, but when a quick glance revealed that he was watching her she stiffened and snatched up the curry brush.

Sweeping the brush over Bertha's hide in long, vigorous strokes, she studiously ignored him. She was braced for more of his sarcastic remarks but after several moments when none came she risked another sidelong glance and saw that he'd returned to working on the gate.

They worked in silence for several more uncomfortable moments, but then some imp of mischief prodded Willa. Casting another look his way, she smiled slyly and began to softly sing "Rhinestone Cowboy."

From the corner of her eye she had the pleasure of seeing Zach stiffen. The screwdriver stilled and his jaw clenched. Willa fought back a grin. Until now, her gibes and insults had had no effect whatsoever on Zach, which had exacerbated her anger all the more. No matter what she'd said or done, it had all slid off him like water off a duck's back. It was insulting. He might as well have come right out and said her opinion of him was of no importance.

Enjoying herself, Willa sang a little louder and put an extra twang into the lyrics.

She expected him object at any second, but instead he flexed his shoulders and went back to tightening screws. She sang the entire song twice, but for all the reaction she got you would think that Zach was deaf. By the time she'd finished she was seething. Was the man made of stone?

Unable to bear his silence an instant longer, she finally snapped, "What are you doing over there, anyway?"

"Isn't it obvious? I'm repairing this gate."

"What for? We keep only the most valuable horses in here. The rest of the riding stock is kept in the corrals or the pasture next to the yard. Bertha, here, is out of a long line of prize cutting horses, and I assumed you stabled that stallion you ride for the same reason, but the rest of our stock are just work horses."

"Not that black stallion in corral four. He's a beauty."

"True, but he's also meaner than a snake and unridable. That's why he's being sold."

"Not anymore, he's not."

"What do you mean? I've already found a buyer in Dallas willing to take him." Bertha nickered and shifted uneasily at her harsh tone. "Mr. Henderson is driving up next week to pick him up."

"I called Henderson and canceled the deal."

"You *what!*" Willa slammed down the brush. "You can't do that!"

"It's done." He tossed the screwdriver back into the toolbox and closed the lid, then stood up and swung the gate back and forth to test it.

Willa let herself out of the stall and marched over to him. "You had no right—"

"I had every right. I'm in charge now. Remember?"

She ground her teeth and glared. Paying no attention to her impotent rage, Zach calmly picked up the toolbox and headed for the back of the barn to place it on a shelf. Willa followed right behind.

"It makes no sense to keep that animal. If you'd bothered to ask, anyone could have told you that Satan can't be ridden. All he's good for is breeding. This is a cattle ranch, not a horse farm. If a horse can't be ridden he's no good to us."

"I'll ride him."

"Ha! Better men than you have tried. At one time or another every hand on the place has. Satan has been the cause of more broken bones than I care to count. Sooner or later he's going to seriously injure someone, maybe even kill them. And you think you're going to break him. Fat chance."

"I said, I'll ride him."

Zach placed the toolbox on the shelf and strode back

down the aisle toward the front of the barn. Willa dogged his steps.

"Oh, of course. How silly of me. I forgot, you're the big rodeo star." Dropping the simpering voice, she made a disgusted sound. "Believe me, it'll take more than a broken down bronc buster to ride that horse. Who do you think you are, John Wayne? You're going to have to stick on his back a heck of a lot longer than a measly nine seconds to break him, and that can't be done."

"I don't intend to break him. I'm going to gentle him first, then ride him."

She let out a derisive hoot. "That'll be the day. Do let me know when you plan to perform this miracle, won't you? I'd like to sell tickets."

"That's it!" He stopped and whirled around so quickly that she slammed into his chest and would have bounced off if he hadn't grasped her upper arms.

Surprise formed Willa's mouth into an O, but the fury in those silvery eyes silenced her. "Dammit, woman! You've been snapping at my heels like a vicious little terrier for weeks now," he snarled. "I know you got a raw deal from Seamus, and for that reason I've tried my damnedest to be patient with you, but enough is enough."

His explosive reaction had taken her by surprise, but Willa wasn't one to remain intimidated for long. She tipped her chin up at a pugnacious angle. "Oh? And what are you going to do about it? Beat me?"

"Don't think I'm not tempted to turn you over my knee and blister your butt. But I won't. I've never struck a woman in my life and I don't intend to start now."

"Then there's not much you can do about it, is there?" she said smugly.

Zach's eyes narrowed. "Don't count on it, little girl. There's more than one way to shut you up."

His mouth slammed down on hers, cutting off the sassy retort that was forming on her tongue before she could make a sound. Willa was so stunned she froze.

Then the heat seared through the icy shock. It slid through her veins like molten lava, flushing her skin, melting her bones. The smell of him was all around her— a potent male scent, musky and erotic. It made her light-headed and weak and sent a tingle down her spine.

Zach was in complete control. His mouth rocked over hers, hard, insistent, devouring. Unbearably exciting.

Silently, he commanded her to open to him, and she obeyed mindlessly. When his tongue plunged into her mouth and stroked against hers, passion flared like a gasoline-fed bonfire. The greedy flames shot skyward, consuming her.

Willa moaned as her knees buckled, but when she began to slump, Zach simply tightened his hold on her arms. She hung there between his big, calloused hands like a rag doll as the kiss went on and on. Her heart thrummed and her head spun and her body throbbed and yearned as it never had before.

As suddenly as it had begun, the kiss ended. Zach set her away from him at arm's length, holding her steady while she settled. She blinked at him, bewildered and disoriented, still lost in the daze of passion. "Wha...? Why....?"

Slowly, his stern face came into focus, and as the reality of what had just passed between them came crashing down on her she felt the cold slap of rejection, followed instantly by the most pride-rending mortification she had ever known.

Then, from outside the barn she heard the noisy approach of a group of riders, and she knew why he had ended the kiss so abruptly. That knowledge, however, did not alleviate the terrible humiliation.

"We don't have much time before someone barges in here, so listen up," Zach growled, giving her a little shake. "Let that be a warning. Those who play with fire can expect to get burned, so unless you want more of the same, in the future you had better keep that sharp tongue of yours sheathed. Got it?"

Too embarrassed to fight back, Willa bobbed her head once and prayed the ground would open up and swallow her. When Zach released her she staggered back a couple of steps. The instant she regained her balance she bolted for the door.

"Hey, Willa, how's it goin'?" one of the cowboys called when she emerged from the barn. The others offered similar greetings.

Normally she would have stopped and shot the breeze for a while, but this time, muttering a barely audible, "Evening," Willa ducked her head and stomped past them, her knees threatening to buckle with every wobbly step.

The men stared after her, slack-jawed. "Well, if that don't beat all. Whaddaya s'pose put a burr under her saddle?"

"More likely who. She's prob'ly been buttin' heads with the boss again."

The comments brought a blush to Willa's cheeks, making her profoundly grateful for the darkness.

To her great relief, no one was in the kitchen when she entered the house. Maria always retired to her quarters and put her feet up after dinner, and from the sounds coming from the den, everyone else was in there.

When she reached the safety of her room she leaned

back against the closed door and squeezed her eyes shut, nearly sick with shame and self-loathing.

What on earth was the matter with her? Why hadn't she fought him? She could have kicked or bitten. Or used her fists, for that matter. Instead she had just stood there like a stump and let him kiss her senseless.

Groaning, Willa folded her arms over her middle and rocked back and forth as though she had a bellyache. Dear Lord, she had just meekly let him do as he pleased, docile as a sacrificial lamb. Worse, she'd actually enjoyed the searing rush of sensations and emotion, wallowed in them, mindless to everything but Zach and the way he made her feel. The way he made her burn for him. Like some love-sick teenager.

Most humiliating of all, the kiss had not affected Zach in the least. He hadn't been trembling or flushed or weak in the knees. He had just stood there, pinning her with those icy eyes, steady as a rock. She wanted to kick him. Hard. Then she wanted to shrivel up and die.

The instant Willa disappeared through the barn door Zach relinquished his steely self-control, and as his knees buckled he plopped down onto a bale of hay, shaken to the core. The kiss was supposed to have been a warning to Willa, but it had backfired on him. He felt like he'd been run over by a loaded cattle truck. He propped his elbows on his knees and held his head in his hands. ''Aw hell!''

Chapter Five

Willa had never dreaded anything in her life as much as she did facing Zach the next morning, but when she entered the kitchen he barely glanced her way. Throughout breakfast he behaved the same as he always did, saying little beyond discussing the work schedule for the day or any possible change predicted for the weather. After a while she realized that he had put that sizzling kiss in the barn out of his mind, just as though it had never happened. At first Willa didn't know whether to be relieved or insulted, but his disinterest grated on her and set her temper to simmering.

So did the memory of his warning. Playing with fire, indeed. If he thought the encounter would scare her into meekly accepting his dictates, he was sorely mistaken.

He had caught her off guard, that was all. That's why she had behaved like a docile idiot. It wouldn't happen again.

Neither her anger nor Zach's maddening indifference lessened her need to escape, however, and when he mentioned that he wanted someone to drive to Bozeman and pick up the tractor engine they'd had rebuilt, she volunteered.

The trip took most of the day. When Willa drove into the ranch yard that afternoon she spotted the Dolan kids sitting on the top rail of the corral, cheering and clapping. She parked the truck by the tractor barn and walked over to see what all the fuss was about.

She arrived just in time to see the chestnut gelding J.T. was riding rear up when he jerked the reins too hard. He let out a shout and slid backward over the cantle and right off the horse's rump, and hit the ground flat on his own behind, raising a cloud of dust and a chorus of groans from the kids.

Then all hell broke loose.

Matt doubled over the front of his saddle and guffawed. The sudden loud sound so close to his mount's ear startled the horse. The Appaloosa whinnied and rolled his eyes and went into a side-stepping dance.

Matt's laughter cut off instantly. Dropping the reins, he flung his arms around the animal's neck and held on for dear life, scaring the horse all the more and sending the animal into a series of bucks. Inspired, J.T.'s loose mount ran around the perimeter of corral, tossing his head and kicking out with his hind legs every few steps.

"Dang blast it!" Pete roared.

J.T. scrambled to his feet, hobbled over to the side and hopped up on the first board of the corral fence to avoid being kicked or trampled. Grinning, he called, "Hey, Matt! Having a little trouble with your horse?" He let out a whoop. "Ride 'um, cowboy!"

Pete chased after horse and rider with his funny, bow-legged gait, shaking his fist. "Dang blast you dang-blasted ornery good-fer-nothin' critters!" After several tries the old man finally snagged the Appaloosa's trailing reins, but the horse merely pulled him along. Digging in his heels, Pete grabbed the bridle with both hands and hauled back on it. "Whoa, horse. Whoa. Settle down you good-fer-nothin' hay-burner." The horse kept going, and heels of Pete's worn boots dug twin tracks in the dirt. "Leggo o' his neck, dang it! You're gonna choke the beast!" he barked at Matt.

When the Appaloosa finally steadied and came to a stop, Pete swung on J.T. "Dag nab it, man, don't just stand there laughin' like a fool! Catch your horse!"

Willa crossed her arms on the top rail of the corral fence and grinned. This was the most fun she'd had in months.

Both men were ready to call it a day, but Pete wouldn't allow that. He believed in getting right back on a horse after a fall. "Now get back up on them horses and let's see if you can get it right this time."

Reluctant and grumbling, Matt and J.T. remounted and cantered around the perimeter of the corral, their backsides slapping leather with each stride.

"Move with your horse, dammit! Catch his rhythm! I don't wanta see no daylight 'tween your arses an' them saddles. An' keep them heels down!"

Willa shook her head. Pitiful. Just pitiful.

Disgusted, she turned away. After stopping by the barn for a bridle, she headed toward the fenced pasture that butted up to the ranch yard. That morning when she'd realized that she wouldn't be riding out with the men, before leaving for Bozeman she had turned Bertha out to graze.

Tyrone raced up from behind and fell into step beside her.

"Whacha doin'?"

Willa gave the boy a sideways glance and kept moving. So far she'd managed to avoid the children except at mealtime. She had no idea how to deal with kids and was uncomfortable around them. "I'm going to saddle my horse and go join the men."

Tyrone scrambled onto the board fence and looked around at the thirty or so head of horses scattered over the pasture. "Which one's yours?"

"The black mare with the white star on her forehead." Willa unlatched the gate and stepped inside.

"What's a mare?"

"A female horse."

"Man, you ain't ever gonna catch 'er," he said with cocky certainty. "Uncle J.T.'s still chasing his horse around, an' that's a little bitty ole pen."

"Yeah, well, I'm not your uncle J.T." She stuck two fingers into her mouth and produced a piercing whistle. The black's head came up and she trotted over to Willa.

"Hey, cool! How'd you get 'er to do that?"

"She's my horse. I trained her." Willa patted Bertha's neck and let the mare nuzzle her hand, then slipped the bridle over her head.

The boy fell into step beside her again as she headed back to the barn. She kept her eyes straight ahead and pretended he wasn't there, but Tyrone was not a child who would be ignored.

"Will you show me how to train a horse?"

"You don't have a horse."

"My momma says I can have one soon as I learn to ride. We're all gonna learn. 'Cept for Debbie. She's just a baby."

Willa led Bertha into the barn. Tyrone dogged her heels, peppering her with questions about everything he saw. She kept her answers short, almost curt, but that didn't discourage him.

"Whacha putting that on 'er for?" he ask when Willa positioned the saddle pad on Bertha's back.

"It protects her hide from chaffing." She slung the saddle over the animal's back, hooked the near stirrup over the horn and began to fasten the cinch. Tyrone crowded in so close to watch the operation he got right under the mare's belly, and she had to yank him back and give him a sharp reprimand. That didn't deter the boy one iota.

"Will you teach me to ride?"

"I don't have time. Ask Pete."

"He's busy teaching Dad and Uncle J.T. They're at it every day. An' he says after that it'll be time for roundup and he'll be busier than a one-armed paperhanger."

Willa bit back a grin. How many times had she heard Pete use that expression?

It was true, though. They would all be putting in long hours in the saddle, which meant a constant stream of tack repairs. "Well, I guess you'll just have to wait until summer when spring roundup is over."

"I can't wait that long. I gotta learn now."

"What's the rush?"

"I just gotta, that's all."

"In that case, you'll have to find someone else."

Tyrone cocked his head to one side and studied her with disconcerting directness. "Miss Maudie said you'd say no."

Willa slanted him a look of mild surprise. "You call your mom by her first name?"

"Sometimes." He skipped ahead of her as she led Bertha back out into the sunshine. "She's not my real mom, you know. My real mom didn't want me. Miss Maudie says that's just 'cause she's a drug addict."

Willa stopped in her tracks. "What?"

"Yolanda's folks didn't want her none, either. They dumped her on the side of the highway. An' Jennifer's old man blew away her real mom, an' Debbie was abused. Tim, too." The boy narrowed his eyes. "His old man was one *meeean* dude. He's the one who shot Matt in the leg."

"Good Lord."

"That's why we was all sent to live with Miss Maudie. She's a sigh-ki-trist," he added proudly. "She coulda made big bucks if she'd'a wanted to, but she loved kids so she took in fosters like us."

"Maude Ann's a psychiatrist?" Willa's gaze darted to the woman who was hammering together a chicken coop on the other side of the ranch yard. That gorgeous earth mother was a shrink? She couldn't believe it.

"Yeah. An' when she married Matt they 'dopted all five of us. Now we're a family and cain't nobody take us away from 'um. An' we got two new uncles and Aunt Kate, too."

Willa had no idea what to say. How *did* one respond to such stunning revelations? All she managed was a wan smile.

Feeling a need to escape those big brown eyes and that disturbing innocent candor, she climbed into the saddle. She'd hoped the boy would take a hint, but Tyrone wasn't finished.

He shaded his eyes with one hand and squinted up at her. "An' you know what else? Momma says now that we're livin' here, you're part of our family, too."

"What?" Stunned anew, Willa glanced at Maude Ann

again, then back at the boy. "You must have misunderstood her."

"Nuh-uh. That's what she said." The boy looked down at the ground and scuffed the toe of his athletic shoe in the dirt, then slanted her a sly look out of the corner of his eye. "So, you gonna teach me to ride or not? Momma says family is s'posed to help each other out."

Willa's mouth twitched. Why you crafty little devil, she thought with reluctant admiration. You almost had me there for a second. "Sorry, kid. Like I said, I'm too busy."

"Aw, shoot." He kicked a clod of dirt across the yard, then hooked his thumbs into the side pockets of his jeans and trudged away, the picture of dejection.

Willa watched him for a moment. Pete was right—that one was a pistol.

Zach slung a hundred pound sack of seed into the back of his pickup, then paused to arch his back and glance around. It was only the first of March and snow still covered the ground, but from the number of people in Clear Water it looked as if he wasn't the only one gearing up for spring.

As he turned to retrieve another sack from the stack piled up next to the door of the ranchers's co-op a red pickup screeched to a stop beside his truck and Lennie Dawson and two other men climbed out. Sparing them no more than a glance, Zach walked by the trio, hefted another sack onto his shoulder and carried it back to the pickup.

"Hey, you! You're Zach Mahoney, aren't you?" Lennie barked. "One of Seamus's bastard grandsons."

Zach's jaw clenched, but he kept working. "That's right."

"I want to talk to you."

"Oh? About what?" Zach slung a sack into the pickup bed and turned back for another one without breaking stride.

Lennie followed on his heels. "I'm Lennie Dawson."

"I know who you are."

"Yeah, well, here's something maybe you didn't know." He stuck out his jaw. "Willie Simmons belongs to me."

Zach experienced a rush of distaste. Willa was a high-tempered, annoying thorn in his side, but the thought of her being romantically involved with this guy was unsettling.

Outwardly he didn't react in any way. He simply continued transferring sacks, working in a steady, slow rhythm.

"Hey, Mahoney! Did you hear what I just said?"

"I heard you."

"Yeah, well I'm warning you—stay away from her."

"That's going to be difficult, since we live in the same house." Zach dumped a sack and turned to go back for another but this time Lennie blocked his path.

The first time he'd encountered this man Zach had pegged him for a swaggering bully, and nothing he'd seen so far had changed his mind. Though several inches shorter than Zach, and probably twenty pounds lighter, he stood braced for a fight, his hands fisted and his chin outthrust. Flanking him on either side, his buddies had assumed the same challenging position. Zach doubted that he would have been quite so eager for a confrontation if he'd been alone.

"You know what I mean, smart guy." Lennie reached

out and poked Zach's chest with his forefinger. Zach narrowed his eyes. "You keep your hands off of her, you hear? Willie is mine. An' I don't share what's mine." He poked him again. "You got that?"

Zach stared at him. He itched to ram his fist into the arrogant little weasel's face just on general principles, but he resisted the urge. The locals were already wary of him and his brothers simply because they were Seamus's grandsons. They hoped to eventually overcome the old man's reputation, but getting into a brawl after being in the area only a month wasn't exactly the best way to start off.

For all he knew, Dawson could be telling the truth. Willa had denied any involvement with the guy, but who knew. Maybe that scene he'd witnessed had been a lovers' spat, after all.

Finally he nodded. "Yeah. I understand. Now, if you excuse me, I have more seed to load."

Lennie appeared taken aback by Zach's attitude. He clearly had expected an argument, had probably hoped for one. After a moment his surprised expression turned into a smirk. "Sure. Just don't forget what I told you, Mahoney. C'mon, fellas." Motioning for his friends to follow, Lennie swaggered back to his pickup.

Zach watched them drive away, his eyes narrowed beneath the broad brim of his Stetson. Had Willa told him about that kiss they'd shared in the barn? Was that what had prompted that attempt at intimidation?

If so, Lennie had wasted his breath. He'd already decided that nothing like that would happen again. He didn't even want to think about it.

He had meant the kiss to be punishment. Yeah, right. That plan had backfired on him the instant their lips had touched. He had never experienced passion that strong before. It had sizzled and arced between them like light-ening, and rocked him right down to the ground. He knew that Willa had been just as stunned.

And just as displeased.

Zach was grateful that the men had returned when they had and interrupted them. Otherwise, he was very much afraid that within minutes he and Willa would have been rolling in the hay in one of the empty stalls, tearing off each other's clothes.

That would have been disaster, of course. An affair between them was out of the question. Not to mention just plain stupid. The woman couldn't stand him, for Pete's sake. To her, he was the enemy. They were reluctant business partners, and that's all they would ever be. Period.

Still, merely thinking about how she had felt in his arms sent heat straight to his loins. Annoyed, Zach cursed and went back to loading seed. When done, he slammed the tailgate shut, climbed into the cab, gunned the engine and made a screeching U-turn out onto the highway, headed for the ranch.

Beyond being a royal pain in the rear, Willa meant nothing to him, he told himself. But he sure as hell couldn't say much for her taste in men.

Willa spent two days helping a crew of men repair a stock tank in a part of the ranch that was inaccessible by truck. Unable to get a front-end loader to the site, they had to do the job by hand. It was backbreaking work, but since Zach was busy elsewhere, it seemed to her the best place to be.

Willa put her back into the work, shoveling dirt, hauling rocks and stacking them against the earthen bank for reinforcement, right along with the men. They finally finished close to sundown the second day, and the men headed for the ranch headquarters and the hearty supper Cookie was sure to have simmering on the stove. Willa, however, declined to go with them, saying she wanted to check the fence line in the next pasture before calling it a day.

The truth was she was not in any hurry to return home. Most evenings she delayed doing so until the last possible minute, even though that usually earned her a scolding from Maria. In addition, tonight she simply wanted some time to herself. In the past, she'd done some of her best thinking riding fence.

By the time Willa finally returned to the ranch house and saw to Bertha's needs it was full dark. Expecting to find the others seated around the table, she braced herself, but when she entered through the back door Maria was alone in the kitchen and pots still simmered on the stove. The housekeeper looked up and smiled.

"Ah, there you are. The others, they were getting worried about you, *niña*."

"Where is everyone?" Willa asked.

"Upstairs, getting dressed. Today is Tyrone's birthday, remember? Dinner tonight, it will be special. A birthday party."

Willa groaned. "And I suppose everyone else has gotten him a gift."

"*Sí.*"

"Oh, great. That's just terrific. Somebody might have told me."

"But, *niña*…everyone, they have been talking about it for days." Maria's confusion turned into a scowl. "You were not listening, again, eh, *muchacha?*"

"No, I was listening, I, uh…I guess I just forgot." Maria had been right, though. Most often she simply tuned out the conversation around the table. Partly out of exhaustion, but also to maintain a distance from the others. It was easier that way.

"Humph!" The look in Maria's eyes said she didn't believe her, but she shooed Willa toward the door. "At least go shower and make yourself pretty for the boy. You smell of horse. Now go, go. It is getting late."

Willa started for the door, then paused and gave Maria a considering look.

No matter how hard she worked or how far she rode, she had not been able to dismiss from her mind the shocking things Tyrone had told her. Over and over she'd told herself that it couldn't be true. What kind of people—parents, no less—would do such things to children? He must have made it up. Or at the very least he'd exaggerated.

"Uh, Maria...has Maude Ann or Matt said anything to you about the children? Why they were in foster care?"

"Ah, *sí.*" She crossed her hands over her heart and shook her head sadly. In an emotional voice, and pausing now and then to dab at her eyes with the hem of her apron, she related each child's story, confirming in ghastly detail what Tyrone had said earlier. By the time the housekeeper had finished, Willa was appalled and outraged. And sick at heart.

She had always considered her own childhood a miserable one. Most of her life she had striven in vain to win Seamus's love and approval. Almost from the day that she and her mother had arrived at the ranch she had figured out that the only thing that mattered to her stepfather was the Rocking R. So she had thrown herself into ranch work and learned everything she could about the business and tried to make herself indispensable to him.

It had been a foolish quest that had been doomed from the start, she realized now. Seamus had wanted a son, and nothing any girl child could have done would have ever been enough.

Still, those years of verbal abuse and emotional coldness she'd endured from him were nothing compared to what these children had survived.

"Life has been cruel to these little ones. But that is all over. They belong to Señor and Señora Dolan now. *Gracias a Dios.*"

"Yes. Yes, thank, God." Willa left the kitchen and climbed the stairs in an appalled daze. She felt as though an aching, fist-size knot had lodged beneath her breast bone. Suddenly she was fiercely glad that Maude Ann and Matt had adopted Tyrone and the other children, and that they'd brought them there, to the Rocking R, where they would be safe and loved.

In honor of the occasion, dinner was in the dining room that night. Willa couldn't remember the last time they had used the impressive formal room. Probably when her mother was still alive.

She dressed in her new burgundy-and-gray-print, ankle-length skirt, burgundy sweater and gray suede dress boots, her freshly washed hair loose. She felt a bit self-conscious, but when she entered the dining room and saw that everyone else had dressed up, her misgivings faded. It helped that Kate and Maude Ann's eyes lit up when they spotted her.

"Willa! How pretty you look," Maude Ann exclaimed.

"You certainly do." Kate circled around her. "Oh, my, I love your outfit. You should wear a dress more often."

"There's, uh…there's not too many occasions that call

for dressing up around here. Jeans are more practical.'' She didn't bother to mention that Seamus discouraged the practice. The few times she had bothered to put on a skirt or dress he'd snarled that she looked like a gussied-up tart.

''If this is the kind of merchandise they have in Helena I can see that one of these days the three of us are going to have to drive over there together and hit the shops,'' Kate said, fingering the soft drapy skirt.

Together? The three of them on a shopping spree? Like…like girlfriends? Willa blinked at the two women. Was this Kate's way of saying she wanted them to be friends?

The idea was alien to Willa, and it filled her with both dread and longing. She had never, not once in her life, had a close female friend. Or gone shopping with another woman, other than her mother or Maria.

Willa had no experience with girlfriends. Even though she'd yearned for female companionship for most of her life, the very idea made her feel awkward and uncomfortable. She wasn't sure she knew how to relate to women as friends.

The door between the kitchen and dining room swung open, and Maria entered carrying an enormous dish of enchiladas, which Tyrone had requested for his birthday dinner.

While Kate and Maude Ann helped Maria bring in the steaming platters, Willa pulled an envelope from her pocket and slipped it in among the gaily wrapped gifts stacked on the sideboard.

She turned from doing so, and her heart skipped a beat when she discovered that Zach was staring at her. He stood by himself by the bay window on the opposite side of the room drinking a beer, those green eyes glittering at her over the rim of his glass.

Resisting the urge to turn away, she set her chin at a mulish angle and stared right back. Instead of having the good manners to look away, as she expected, he held her gaze for an interminable time, while her heart thudded against her ribs and a hot blush rushed to her cheeks. Then his gaze slid slowly down her body, from her loose swinging hair all the way to her fancy new boots, lingering along the way at her breasts, her waist, and the flare of her hips beneath the swirly skirt.

The intense scrutiny unnerved her, but as panic began to beat its wings against the walls of her stomach, Maude Ann announced that dinner was served. Relieved, Willa hurried over to the table.

Tyrone was seated in the place of honor at the opposite end of the table from Zach. Beaming from ear to ear, the boy made the most of his privileged status and soaked up all the attention coming his way. After dinner he blew out his candles with one gusty exhale and ripped into his gifts like a tornado while all the other kids crowded around his chair.

He received a video game player and several games from his parents, a robot action figure from J.T. and Kate, a baseball glove from Maria and various toys from his siblings. When all the boxes were opened he picked up Willa's envelope and tore it open without much interest. Willa could see by his bored expression he was expecting it to be a card.

"It's just a dumb ole note," he said, making no effort to hide his disgust when he pulled out the single sheet of paper.

"Tyrone, mind your manners," Maude Ann warned.

"Yeah, before you get too bummed you'd better read it, sport. It might be a treasure map, for all you know."

Tyrone shot his father a "yeah, right" look and unfolded the paper. "This en...tit..."

Kate leaned over and scanned the first line. "Entitles."

"This entitles the bear...er to one pair of cowboy bo...oots and—" He looked up, his eyes growing huge. "One pair of cowboy boots! Wow!" His gaze darted back to the paper, his face growing more animated as he read. "And free...ri...riding les...sons. Hot dog! Riding lessons! I'm gonna have riding lessons!"

"Hey, great, tiger. Whose gift is that?" J.T. asked.

Tyrone's gaze shot down to the bottom of the page. He looked up again, his eyes wide. "It's from Willa!"

A stunned silence followed, and Willa found herself the focus of ten pairs of eyes.

"What? Why are you all looking at me like that?"

"Oh. Nothing," Maude Ann replied. "It's, uh...it's just that...well...this is very kind of you, Willa."

"I thought you said you didn't have time to teach me how to ride."

"I don't. But I decided to take the time. I'll knock off early on Tuesdays and Thursdays and you meet me in corral one at five sharp. Okay?"

"O-*kay!*"

"Good. Tomorrow I'll take you to town for those boots."

"You mean...just you and me?"

"Sure."

To Willa's astonishment, Tyrone's eyes grew suspiciously moist. Suddenly he scrambled down from his chair, raced around the table and flung his arms around her neck. "Thanks, Willa."

She patted the child's back awkwardly, at a loss.

Like most children, Tyrone rebounded quickly and the emotional moment passed. He and the other kids inhaled bowls of chocolate cake and ice cream before the adults had eaten half of theirs and took off for the den to play with his loot.

Still shaken by the boy's reaction, Willa excused herself as soon as they'd gone.

"Don't rush off. Stay and have some coffee, why don't you," Kate urged.

"No. Thank you. I, uh, I'm tired. It's been a long day. Good night."

She barely made it to the bottom of the stairs when Zach caught up with her.

"Willa, wait up."

She stopped with one foot on the first step and shot him a wary look. "What do you want?"

His lips twitched. "Nothing bad. Relax, will you? Not everything between us has to be a battle, you know." She jumped when he put his hand over hers on the newel post, and her heart took off at a gallop. The touch of that calloused palm against her skin sent heat zinging up her arm. "I just wanted to say thanks. That was a nice thing you did. Tyrone is in heaven."

She could see that he hadn't expected that kind of gesture from her. Actually, she was having second thoughts herself. It had seemed like a good idea when she'd written the note, but now she wasn't sure. What did she know about kids? Especially a rambunctious one like Tyrone? What if she couldn't handle him? What if he got hurt?

"I'm glad he's happy," she replied stiffly.

"Yeah, well…Tyrone can be a handful. I thought maybe I'd give you a hand with those lessons. If that's all right with you?"

Willa narrowed her eyes as a painful suspicion began

to take hold. "Why don't you be honest? You didn't follow me out here to thank me. You and the others still think I'm responsible for scaring Jennifer. Now you're worried that I mean to harm that boy." She snatched her hand from beneath his. "Regardless of what any of you think, I'm not a monster."

"I wasn't implying that you were. I simply thought you could use some help. Dammit, Willa, will you wait a second."

Ignoring him, she climbed the stairs with her back ram-rod-straight.

Zach watched her go, exasperated and at the same time filled with reluctant admiration. Willa wore her pride like an iron cloak.

But damn if she didn't look fantastic in that swirly skirt and sweater. He couldn't recall ever seeing her in anything but jeans and a shirt before.

She had obviously just washed her hair, and the scent of jasmine drifting from it had nearly driven him wild. Usually she wore her hair in a braid or pulled back with a clip. Tonight that glorious ebony mane hung loose and arrow-straight almost to her waist. Beneath the entryway chandelier the shiny strands shone with the blue-black sheen of a raven's wing, swaying and sliding like a silk curtain with every furious step she took.

Zach's fingers itched to dive into that thick mass, feel it warm against his skin, slithering through his fingers.

Damn, Mahoney. What the hell are you doing fantasizing about Willa Simmons? The woman despises you. Even if she didn't, there was no way he was getting involved with that little spitfire.

All right, so there was some sort of weird chemistry going on between them. After that mind-blowing kiss in the barn a couple of weeks ago, he could hardly deny that. But so what? Hell, she wasn't even his type. He preferred women who were sweet and gentle and domestic. Not temperamental tomboys.

Willa disappeared into the upstairs hallway, and Zach heaved a sigh. "Damn prickly woman. One of these days you're going to collapse under the weight of that chip on your shoulder. If I don't knock it off first, that is.''

Chapter Six

Willa was convinced that cattle were the most ornery critters God ever made. After a winter of drifting the range, they had grown wild and balked at being driven anywhere, especially cows that had recently dropped spring calves. The stubborn beasts hid out in the most inaccessible places, invariably bolted in the wrong direction when flushed out, and did their best to make a cowboy's life miserable.

Willa spent hours in the saddle riding hell-for-leather through brush and rocky gullies and up and down steep slopes, flushing out strays and recalcitrant new mothers and their young. It was dirty, strenuous work that she could have left to the men, but she used her simmering anger to push on, even when she was close to dropping.

After working without letup for more than an hour, Willa paused on a bench of land above the meadow where they were gathering cattle that day and dismounted to give the mare a rest. She ground-hitched the horse and left her cropping grass, and walked over to the edge of the drop-off to watch the busy scene below.

Even from that height she could hear the incessant racket made by the two hundred or so head they had rounded up so far. Kept bunched in a circle by four men and Sadie, the cattle milled about restlessly, bawling and clacking horns and kicking up a cloud of dust, even though patches of snow still covered much of the ground. Periodically other hands rode up, driving in one or more animals to add to the herd.

Willa's gaze locked on the big man wearing a sheepskin-lined denim jacket and a gray Stetson. Her mouth tightened. Arrogant, overbearing oaf.

By the morning following Tyrone's birthday and that insulting encounter with Zach, her hurt had turned to full-blown anger. Even now, three weeks later, the memory of the doubt and worry in his eyes—and the others', as well—still rankled. That they could think she would deliberately hurt a child was the most scurrilous, contemptuous insult she had ever endured.

So far she had given Tyrone four lessons without any serious mishaps. The boy had missed a lesson when he'd been kept after school one day, and another time she had gotten so busy she'd forgotten to knock off early, causing him to miss another. Wisely, Zach had kept his distance.

Tyrone was awkward and—despite his bravado—a bit afraid of the horse, which had made progress slow, but he was hanging in there. The little cuss was determined, she'd give him that. With that kind of gutsy focus Willa was certain that he would eventually overcome his fear and get the hang of it.

Below, Zach rode over to the herd and said something to J.T. and Matt. Watching him, it annoyed Willa that even from that distance he stood out from the rest of the cowboys. Like it or not, she had to admit there was something about him, something that drew your eye, that set him apart from the other men.

Zach was a commanding figure, a big, broad-shouldered, imposing man in his prime who sat a horse with a loose, easy grace. Still…it was more than just his height and impressive build. He seemed to have an aura of quiet authority about him.

Zach worked right along side his men, charging in and out of ravines and thick brush at breakneck speed and doing any other dangerous or dirty job that needed doing, but no one would ever doubt that he was the man in charge.

On foot, Zach's brothers had the same commanding air about them, even Matt, despite his limp.

As Zach rode out of camp again, Willa's gaze wandered over to Seamus's other grandsons. A reluctant half smile played around her mouth as she watched Matt cut off a cow that tried to bolt. She had to hand it to them. He and J.T. had stuck to the riding lessons with a gritty determination that she hadn't expected of two city boys.

Over the past weeks their riding ability had improved enough that Zach now allowed them to work with the men. However, they did not yet display the same confidence and prowess in the saddle as Zach, nor had they quite mastered the skills of roping or bulldogging, which was why he had assigned them the relatively simple task of riding herd on the stock that had been brought in.

Willa's gaze drifted irresistibly back to Zach as he came riding up out of a draw, driving a bawling cow and her two calves into camp. A tingle danced over her skin, as it always did whenever she saw him, even from afar.

She gritted her teeth and told herself the sensation was the result of intense dislike.

In the distance south of camp a cowboy crested a rise, riding flat-out. When he spotted Zach he waved his hat above his head and began to shout. Willa tensed.

Zach had been about to ride out after more strays, but he whirled his horse around and waited. When the rider pulled his lathered horse up alongside Zach he started gesturing wildly, and even from that distance Willa could sense his agitation.

Something was terribly wrong.

Willa raced back to her horse, vaulted into the saddle and headed down to camp as fast as Bertha could safely pick her way down the slope.

When she arrived in camp Zach was shouting orders. Already she could see some of the men riding south, slapping leather all the way.

"What is it?" Willa demanded, riding up beside him. "What's happened?"

"Stretch! Dooley! Come with me! We got trouble!" Zach shouted to the two men who came riding into camp driving three cows and two calves. He whirled his horse and raced over to where his brothers were circling the herd. Willa followed.

"What's up?" J.T. asked.

"We've got a half mile of fence down on the southern border. All the cows we've rounded up so far are out on the highway. Several have already been hit by motorists and killed."

"A half a mile of downed fence? That's impossible. Unless…"

"Unless it was cut," Zach finished for Willa, his mouth grim.

He turned back to his brothers. "You two and Jake

stay here with the herd. I'll send someone out later to relieve you and spend the night with this bunch. Send the next man who rides into camp to the barn to load a pickup with reels of barbed wire and staples and get it out there, pronto. As soon as they come into camp, tell the rest of the men to hightail it to the south border along the highway. C'mon, Sadie,'' he commanded, and when he kicked his horse into a gallop, the dog raced alongside him.

Willa dug her heels into Bertha's flanks and took off after them.

"Go back. Stay with Matt and J.T.'' he shouted when she rode up beside him. "The men and I will handle this.''

"Forget it. I'm going. Those are my cattle, too, remember?'' Besides, she wanted to get a look at that fence.

Zach didn't waste time arguing.

They found pandemonium when they reached the southernmost boundary of the ranch. At least three hundred head of cattle had wandered out onto the highway. An eighteen-wheeler had slammed into a small bunch and jackknifed. Willa could see at least five dead cows scattered over the asphalt and along the verge. The big rig sat askew across the highway and partly in the bar ditch, blocking traffic.

This part of Montana was sparsely populated, making traffic light, but even so lines of pickups and semi-rigs were backed up in both directions.

It took the better part of four hours to clear the carcasses and wrecked truck off the highway and to round up the meandering cattle. Some had wandered more than two miles. Willa, Zach and several of the men drove them back onto Rocking R land while another crew frantically worked to repair the fence. The last thirty yards or so of wire was strung by lantern light.

It was close to nine when Willa, Zach and the men came dragging in. She was so exhausted she could barely put one foot in front of the other. Worse, she was very much afraid that she had sprained her right wrist, possibly even cracked a bone. She held her arm close to her body, hoping to hide the injury. Later, she'd catch Maria alone and get her to bind it for her.

Zach didn't look as though he felt much better than she did. His face was smudged with dirt and sweat and gray with fatigue.

They were met at the back door by three worried women.

"Ah, *muchacha. ¡Pobrecito!*" Maria exclaimed, wringing her hands. "Sit. Sit, before you fall on your face, and I will get your dinner."

"Don't bother. I'm too tired to eat. All I want is a hot shower and a chance to sleep for about twelve hours straight," Willa mumbled.

"What foolishness is this? You must eat to get your strength back. Now sit."

She gave Willa's shoulder a downward push, and her knees buckled. With a groan, she collapsed into the nearest chair like a dishrag. She crossed her arms on the table, carefully cradling the injured one, and lay her head down.

"First let's see about that wrist."

Willa was so tired she barely heard Zach, and the next thing she knew his calloused hand clasped her forearm. Despite exhaustion and pain, his touch set her nerve endings to tingling.

Her head popped up and she tried to pull away, but it was hopeless. Though gentle, his grip remained firm.

"Let me go. What do you think you're doing?"

"Be still. This arm needs tending. It's already swelling."

"No, it's fine. Just a little strain is al— Ow!"

Zach probed the puffy flesh, then clasped her hand and gently rotated it. Willa groaned and put her head down again, fighting nausea.

"It doesn't appear to be broken, but to be safe you should have it X-rayed tomorrow. In the meantime it should be tightly wrapped."

"Out of my way. I will take care of my *niña*. Ah, *pobrecito*. Such a foolish girl."

Willa heard a thunk, and the next instant she felt her hand being immersed in warm soapy water. Maria fussed and tutted while she washed her hand and arm up to her elbow, then dried it tenderly and wound an Ace bandage around the injured wrist.

"There. All done. Now you will eat."

Willa didn't have the strength to argue, or to even go wash up the rest of the way. Besides, she knew she wouldn't win. Vaguely she was aware of Kate and Maude Ann fussing over Zach. She heard plates clunk down on the table, one just inches from her face. The tantalizing aroma of roast beef drifted to her nose. Her stomach growled, but she was too tired to stir herself.

"Have J.T. and Matt gotten back?" Zach asked.

"Yes. About an hour ago," Kate replied. "They ate and went upstairs to shower. They should be down any minute."

As though on cue, the two men came through the door from the hall. "Hey, Zach. How'd it go?" J.T. said.

"We had a helluva time doing it, but I think we rounded up all of the cattle that weren't killed. It took a while to get that semi-tractor out of the bar ditch and clear the highway. And to get the fence mended, but we finally managed it.''

"How many did we lose?" Matt ask.

"Seven cows, nine calves.''

Maria poked Willa's shoulder. "Wake up, *muchacha*, and eat.''

Groaning, Willa forced herself upright and picked up her fork. Her stomach growled when she took a bite of roast beef, but she could barely summon the energy to chew...or to hold her eyes open.

"Was it deliberate sabotage, like you suspected?''

"Oh, yeah. Dobie and Chuck were repairing fence in the far south pastures today. They said when they rode by that section this morning the fence was fine. When they came back by this afternoon on their way to the barn it was down. Every strand of wire had been cut off at the posts.

"My guess is, it was done as soon as our men were out of sight. Some of the stock had wandered so far by the time we got there they had to have gotten out hours before.'' Zach reached into the pocket of his shirt, withdrew a folded piece of paper and tossed it to Matt. "I found this nailed to one of the posts.''

Willa sat up straighter, her attention caught. "You didn't say anything to me about finding a note.''

Zach shrugged. "You were busy.''

"What does it say?" J.T. demanded.

Matt unfolded the paper and frowned. The lined sheet had been torn from a spiral notebook and was ragged along one edge—just like the one that had been nailed to the front door a few weeks ago. "It says, 'You were warned. Get out now while you still can, or you'll regret it. This is just the beginning.'''

J.T. gave a low whistle. "Damn. Somebody wants us out of here bad."

"Yeah, but who?" Zach looked at Willa. "Do you have any ideas?"

She stiffened. "What's that supposed to mean?"

"I was hoping you might think of someone who'd do something like this. Like maybe your boyfriend."

"Which one," she asked with nasty sweetness. "You seem to think I have so many."

"Oh, c'mon, Willa. You can hardly blame Zach if he does," Maude Ann gently scolded. "A pretty girl like you? Why, you ought to have men lined up from here to the highway."

That caught Willa by surprise. She blinked at Maude Ann, delighted by the compliment and not wanting to be.

"I'm talking about Lennie Dawson. I ran into him in town a few weeks back. He went out of his way to let me know that you belonged to him."

Willa's gaze snapped back to Zach. "He did *what?*"

"He also warned me to keep my hands off of you." Those steady green eyes bore into her, and she knew he was remembering that night in the barn. He'd certainly put his hands on her then. And kissed her senseless, to boot.

She felt her cheeks heat, but she refused to let him make her squirm. "Damn that Lennie," she snarled. "I'll kill him."

"So...does that mean he isn't your boyfriend?"

"Of course he isn't! I told you that."

"You've never gone out with him?"

Willa winced. "Once. *Once!* And then only because Seamus forbade me to."

"Now there's a good reason," Matt muttered. His wife elbowed him in the ribs and shushed him.

J.T.'s forehead wrinkled. "I don't get it. If you're not involved with this Lennie character, then why is he telling everybody that you are?"

"For one thing, he's full of himself. Lennie always wants what he can't have. Telling him no is like waving a red flag in front of a bull. Plus, he wants—"

Willa could have kicked herself. She hadn't meant to mention Lennie's ridiculous claim to anyone. It had been a blatant lie. She stared down at her plate and hoped Zach would let the matter drop. She should have known better.

"He wants what?"

She shot him an annoyed look. "If you must know, I think he and his father want to get their hands on the Rocking R. Before you three showed up they, and everyone else around here, thought I would inherit the entire ranch, which is why Lennie started pursuing me. I figured out that much long ago."

"What about now?" Zach probed. "You think he's willing to marry you for a quarter of what he'd originally hoped to gain?"

Willa's cheeks heated. Put so bluntly, the question was insulting, but since she had brought the matter up, she couldn't very well object, although she suspected Zach was enjoying her discomfort.

Tipping up her chin, she looked him in the eye. "Yes, I do. Even a quarter share of the Rocking R, added to the Bar-D, would more than double the Dawsons' holdings.

"Besides, I think Lennie and his father are determined to at least get my part of the Rocking R. They've got this crazy notion that the whole shebang should have gone to Henry when Seamus died."

"What? Why would they think that?"

"It doesn't matter. I'm sure Lennie made the whole thing up to annoy me."

"Tell us, anyway."

"It's ridiculous. Lennie claims his father and Seamus had a deal. Henry would marry Colleen and take over the Rocking R after Seamus died. But I don't believe him. Seamus wouldn't do that. Lennie will say anything to get what he wants."

"No, *muchacha*. It is true."

Six pairs of eyes turned to Maria. The housekeeper stood by the kitchen sink, wringing her hands, her expression pained.

"Maria, what are you saying?" Willa demanded.

"When *la señorita* is seventeen, the *señor* he betroth her to Señor Dawson, a man twenty years older than *la señorita*." Maria huffed and made a face. "The Bar-D, it is not so *grande* as the Rocking R. Señor Dawson, he is a greedy man and he has much envy for this place. To get his hands on it, he is willing to sacrifice his pride and change his name to Rafferty so the babies from the marriage will carry on the name. Señor Rafferty, he say Señorita Colleen, she owe him this much."

"And our mother agreed to that?" Zach demanded.

"Oh, no, no. Señorita Colleen, she had much spirit, and she refuse to marry Señor Dawson. She love Señor Mike. He is one of the *vaqueros* who works for Señor Rafferty. When she tell him, the *señor* is *furioso*. He dismiss Señor Mike and order him to leave Montana.

"But Señor Mike, he love Señorita Colleen. He get a job at another ranch near Clear Water, and he and *la señorita*, they meet secretly and make plans to…to…"

"Elope?" J.T. suggested.

"*Sí*, elope." Maria sighed. "Before they can marry, Señor Mike, he is killed. Something frighten his horse.

The animal, he rear and fall on top of him. Not long after that, the *señorita* knows she is with child.''

"And when Seamus found out, he tossed her out on her ear,'' Zach finished for her with disgust.

"*Sí.* She ruin his plans, and he go a little *loco.* By the time he cool off, his pride will not let him go after her.''

"That's assuming he wanted to,'' Matt mumbled.

"*Sí.* With the *señor,* it is not easy to know what is in his heart. In the beginning he believe the *la señorita* will not survive alone, that she will give up her baby and come crawling back, begging his forgiveness, and marry Señor Dawson, as he wishes. But the years they go by, and the *señorita,* she does not come.

"Then a minister in Houston, he telephone Señor Rafferty and tell him Señorita Colleen *es muerto.*''

"So he knew when we first came here that she was dead?'' Matt snapped. "Why the hell didn't he just tell us straight-out?''

"I do not know, *señor.* Señor Rafferty was an unhappy man. Sometimes he strike out in strange ways.''

"I didn't notice our mother's grave when we buried Seamus,'' Zach said quietly. "I'd like for you to go up there with us tomorrow, Maria, and point it out.''

Her eyes filled with tears and her chin began to quiver. "I cannot do that, *señor.* The minister who called, he say it is *la señorita*'s last wish to be buried beside her *madre* in the family cemetery here on the ranch.'' She made the sign of the cross and dabbed at her eyes with her apron. "But the *señor,* he say no. He told the man of God to bury her in…in…*la sepultura de los pobres.*''

J.T. and Matt exchanged a puzzled look. "Where?''

"A pauper's grave,'' Zach supplied in a voice tight with fury.

"Why that sorry—'' Matt bit off the tirade and

clamped his jaw tight. Anger radiated from him like a red aura.

Shocked, Willa stared at the housekeeper. Seamus had always been foul-tempered and unforgiving, but even so, she couldn't believe he would do such a thing to his own child. Apparently, however, he had.

Zach looked at his brothers. "I think we should find Colleen's grave and have her body brought here for reburial. Agreed?"

Without hesitation, J.T. and Matt nodded and murmured their approval.

Zach turned his attention back to Willa. "Do you think Lennie's father has been nursing a grudge all this time?"

"Probably." She yawned and fought to stay awake. "There's been bad blood between him and Seamus ever since my mother and I came here. I never knew why, but this explains it."

"Do you think Henry Dawson is bitter enough to be behind these incidents?"

"It's possible, I suppose."

"I see where you're going with this, Zach," Matt said. "But it doesn't hold up. Why would Dawson try to run us out? Unless he can afford to purchase the ranch in the event we default, he'll be better off if his son marries Willa."

Zach looked to Willa again. "Can he afford to purchase the Rocking R if it went up for sale?"

"I doubt it. Even if he used the Bar-D for collateral, he couldn't borrow enough for the purchase price."

"So Matt's right. The only way Dawson and his son would gain is if Lennie married you."

"Please. There is no *way* I'd ever marry Lennie Dawson."

"Yes, but does he believe that?"

"He should. I've told him often enough." Willa sighed and her shoulders slumped. "But knowing Lennie, probably not. His ego is so big he can't imagine there's a woman alive who wouldn't jump at the chance to be Mrs. Leonard Dawson.

"Look, I'm too tired for this. Could we continue this discussion in the morning?"

Without waiting for an answer, Willa scraped back her chair and stood up.

"It seems to me that pretty much eliminates the Dawsons as the ones behind the attacks," J.T. said as she trudged across the kitchen. "Which means we still don't have a clue who's behind this."

"You're right." Matt tossed the note down onto the table. "We don't have any more to go on than we did before."

As exhausted as she was, the remark still set fire to Willa's temper. At the door she paused and looked back at them over her shoulder, her expression tight with resentment.

"Wrong. This note may not tell us who is behind the vandalism, but it certainly proves that it wasn't me. In case you've forgotten, I was working up at Henchman's Meadow with the three of you all day."

"My alarm clock didn't go off."

Willa burst through the kitchen door, hopping on one foot while pulling a boot on the other one, no easy task using one hand. "Usually I wake up before it makes a sound. Wouldn't you know, the first time I oversleep the blasted thing doesn't go off."

"It is no big thing, *nina*. You needed to rest." Maria plunked an iron skillet down on the stove. "Sit down and relax and I will cook you breakfast. Last night you took only a bite of food.''

"Don't bother. Just wrap up a couple of biscuits. I'll eat them on the way to Henchman's Meadow. There are still plenty of cattle up there that need to be rounded up.'' She held on to the back of a chair and stomped her foot down into the boot.

Kate stood at the sink washing dishes while Maude Ann dried them. The two younger women and Maria exchanged a wary look. Maude Ann cleared her throat. "Uh…actually, Willa, you aren't working today.''

She looked up and blinked. "Excuse me?''

"Zach asked Kate to take you to the hospital in Bozeman to have your wrist X-rayed.''

"He what?''

Doing her best to ignore Willa's dangerously quiet tone, Maude Ann rushed on. "I would take you, myself, of course, but I always try to be here when the kids get home from school.''

"I've already called and made an appointment,'' Kate added. "We should leave in about an hour.''

"Forget it. No one is taking me anywhere.''

"Now, *nina,* Señor Zach, he is only trying to do what is best for you. He say you need to rest. And you know you must have a doctor look at your arm.''

Willa's gaze flashed to Maria, who was wringing her hands and looking incredibly guilty. "You turned off my alarm clock, didn't you? He told you to turn it off. Why that —''

"Ah, no, *nina.* The *señor,* he is worried—''

"Yeah, right.''

"Willa, wait! Where are you going?'' Kate cried.

"Where I go every day. To work. Zach Mahoney may

have taken over the Rocking R but he is *not* taking over
my life.''

''But what about your appointment?''

In reply, she slammed the door behind her.

Willa fumed every step of the way to the barn. By the
time she reached it she had worked up a good head of
steam.

''Here now. What're you doin' here?'' Pete demanded
when she stormed inside. ''I 'spected you'd be halfway
to Bozeman by now to see the doc.''

''My wrist is fine. It's just a slight sprain.''

''Izzat so? Then why're you holdin' it against your
belly that'a way?''

''I'm fine. Don't fuss.'' She lifted her bridle off the
nail with her good hand and stepped into Bertha's stall.
''Would you please come help me saddle her? It's a bit
awkward with one hand.''

''Uh-uh. Not me. Zach left strict orders that you was
to see the doc and rest today, an' that's all. I ain't about
to cross the man just 'cause you got a burr under your
saddle.''

''He left *orders?* Why that arrogant, overbearing…
Fine, then. I'll do it myself.''

''Suit yerself. Just don't 'spect any help from me.''

Putting a bridle and saddle on a horse one-handed
proved to be incredibly difficult. Willa grunted and
strained and cursed and struggled. Pete watched the
whole thing with a disgruntled expression, shaking his
head occasionally. The operation took her the better part
of an hour, and by the time she had finished she was
panting and exhausted and her injured wrist was throbbing like a son of a gun. Nevertheless, she grabbed the
pommel with her left hand and swung herself up into the

saddle. As she walked Bertha out of the barn, Pete followed behind her.

"Now that you're saddled up, just where is it you plan
on goin'?" he asked dryly.

"Up to Henchman's Meadow to help with the
roundup."

Pete snorted. "Well, then, little gal, you jist wasted all
that time and effort fer nothin'. Zach's just gonna send
you right back here."

"He wouldn't dare."

"Oh, he'd dare, all right. Why, he's jist liable to toss
you over his shoulder and haul you back hisself. Face it,
Willie, when it come to strong wills, you've met your
match in that man. He's a patient one, but if I was you,
I wouldn't push him too far."

Grinding her teeth, Willa held her throbbing arm
against her side and glared down at the old man, but she
knew he was right. Her act of defiance could well turn
into humiliation if she showed up at the roundup camp.
But dammit! There had to be something she could do to
show him he couldn't run her life.

She glanced around. Two men were repairing a corral
gate nearby and another was filling the water troughs. A
second later her gaze lit on the group of cattle in the pen
next to the barn. She stared at the small herd as an idea
began to take shape in her mind.

Standing up in the stirrups, Willa called out to the men.
"Skinny! Leroy! Taggert! Stop what you're doing and
come over here."

"What're you up to now, little gal?" Pete demanded,
glaring at her suspiciously.

"I'm going to take those men and drive this bunch up
to the high country."

"What! Are you crazy?"

"There's no reason they can't be driven to summer pastures. None of the heifers is going to drop a calf and the bulls we didn't want to use for breeding have already been castrated."

"There's plenty a reasons 'sides them. The main one bein' Zach ain't ready to move them animals yet. He plans to take them up with the rest of the herd when roundup is over."

"In the meantime, they're just standing around consuming feed."

"Zach thinks it's too early to move 'em. We could have us a blizzard up in the high country yet. It's happened a'fore."

"It won't this year. Spring has settled in nicely."

The three men walked over. "You wanted us for something, Willie?"

"Yes. Saddle up and get those cattle out of the pen. We're taking them up the mountain."

The men exchanged an uncomfortable look. "Uh, the boss said we was to get these repairs done."

"Now I'm telling you to stop and help me drive these cattle."

The tall, lanky man called Skinny scratched the back of his neck. "I don't know. The boss didn't say nothing about moving cattle."

"I don't care what Mr. Mahoney said. I'm ordering you to saddle up and move these cattle. Now."

"Yes, ma'am."

"I'm tellin' you, Willie, you're making a mistake," Pete argued when the men disappeared into the tack room to get their gear. "Zach's gonna have a conniption."

"Let him. I'm moving those cattle."

Chapter Seven

The first thing Zach noticed when he rode into the ranch yard a few hours later was the empty pen.

He dismounted in front of the main barn and stalked inside. He found Pete in the tack room.

"Where the devil are the cattle that were in the holding pen?" he demanded.

The old man glanced up at Zach's thunderous expression and winced. "Willie's drivin' 'em up to the summer pasture on Devil's Cup Mountain."

"She's *what?* Why didn't you stop her? I made it clear that I didn't want to start the drive to the summer ranges for another two or three weeks. The weather this time of year is too unreliable."

"I tried to tell 'er, but she weren't in no mood to listen. Come tearin' in here madder'n a wet hen 'bout three hours ago, bound and determined to defy you." Pete shot a stream of tobacco juice into his copper spittoon and darted Zach a sly look. ''Willie always was an independent little cuss. She don't take kindly to being ordered 'round, even when it's fer her own good.''

Zach bit out an expletive. ''That little idiot. I knew sooner or later that temper of hers would land her in trouble. Dammit! This morning the weather channel predicted a severe snowstorm would hit the high country by late afternoon.''

The old man's head jerked up, alarm clouding his faded blue eyes. ''By now they're over halfway there. We gotta do somethin'.''

Zach spun on his heel and stalked toward the door. ''Saddle a fresh horse for me. And add a bedroll and saddlebags. And a bag of grain. I'll go round up emergency supplies.''

Zach rode hard, following the swath of churned earth the herd had left across the rangeland and up into the foothills. Once through the cut in the mountains the trail began a steep climb, leaving him no choice but to slow the gelding's pace.

Frustrated, Zach urged the horse upward at a speed just shy of reckless, giving silent thanks for Pete's years of experience. The old man had chosen well. The barrel-chested gray wasn't the fastest or the biggest, or even the handsomest horse on the ranch, but he had stamina and he was sure-footed as a cat.

There were several places on Devil's Cup Mountain that the Rocking R used for summer pasture, but from the direction Willa was taking she was heading for a high meadow called Cowboy Basin. She and the men had better than three hours' head start on him, but Zach knew the herd would slow them down. Cattle balked at climbing and had to be prodded every step of the way up a mountain. He figured he'd catch up with them a mile or two before they reached the summer range.

He clucked his tongue and nudged the gray's flanks almost constantly, urging him upward, all the while keeping a wary eye on the sky. Ominous, low-hanging clouds were moving in fast from the northwest. The higher he climbed, the darker the sky became and the colder it got.

Just past the halfway point he felt the first sting of sleet hit the back of his neck. He pulled a long fleece scarf out of his coat pocket, looped it over his Stetson to hold it on and wound the ends around his neck and the lower half of his face. Turning up the collar of his coat, he kicked up the gray's pace. A quarter mile farther up the trail the sleet turned to snow.

Zach's heart began to pound. Surely by now Willa would have realized what a precarious position she had gotten herself and the men into and turned the herd around, he told himself. Any minute now he should meet up with them coming down the mountain. When he did and he got his hands on Willa...

Clenching his teeth, he pushed the thought aside and forged on doggedly.

Five minutes passed. Ten. Twenty. The wind kicked up and the temperature began to plummet. The farther up the mountain Zach went, the harder it snowed and the worse visibility became. Snow quickly covered the ground, obliterating all sign of tracks and it swirled so thick that Zach had to lean forward in the saddle and strain to make out landmarks.

Luckily, he'd spent most of the previous two weeks riding the high country with a couple of the old hands. Taking advantage of the spell of mild weather, they had led pack trains to each of the line camps and stocked the cabins with supplies for the cowboys who would be riding herd on the cattle throughout the summer. In the process he had learned the territory.

It was bitter cold and getting colder. The snow was blowing almost sideways now. Worry gnawed at Zach's gut like a sharp-toothed animal. He had grown up in a small mining town high in the Colorado Rockies. He knew how easy it was to get disoriented in a snowstorm.

His heart gave a leap. Up ahead through the curtain of white he thought he saw something move. Nudging his horse forward, he cupped one gloved hand to his mouth and called out. "Hell-looo!"

The wind whipped the greeting back in his face, but as he drew nearer he could make out a large, dark, shifting mass and beside it the hunched shape of a rider on horseback. He rode within five yards of the herd before the man spotted him.

"Zach? Is that you? Man, am I glad to see you."

"Dammit, Skinny! What the hell are you doing up here?"

"Well, uh…you see, boss, Willie, she ordered us to help her move these cattle, an'—"

"You take your orders from me, not from Willa. You're supposed to be repairing corrals. When I assign a man a job, unless I tell him otherwise, I expect him to complete it. You got that?"

"Yessir, boss."

Zach cast a furious look around. Bunched together in a tight circle, their backs dusted with white, the cattle appeared as a shifting grayish-brown blob through the blowing snow. On the far side of the herd, he could barely make out the shadowy shapes of two other riders, but both were too large to be Willa.

"Where is she?"

"Looking for strays. Willie'd decided to turn around

and head back when five or six head took off into the brush. She told us to hold the herd here and wait for her. But me'n Leroy and Taggert, we're gettin' worried. She's been gone 'bout twenty minutes. Maybe a little longer.''

Zach's head snapped around. The look he gave the cowboy was hard enough to cut steel. ''That's too long. Why the devil haven't you already been out looking for her?''

Skinny's Adam's apple bobbed. He looked like a man going to his own execution. ''Willie ordered us to stay with the herd.''

''If you yahoos had followed my orders as well as you seem to follow Willa's, none of us would be in this mess.'' Fighting to control the fury and fear swelling inside him, he clenched his jaw and looked around. ''Which direction did she take?''

''North, right through them bushes.''

''All right. While I go look for her I want you three to take this herd down the mountain as fast as you can.''

Even through the swirling white, Zach thought he saw the man pale. ''In this? We'll be lost in ten minutes. If we don't fall off a cliff first.''

''Here, take this.'' Zach dug into one of the saddlebags and pulled out a compass and handed it to him. ''Tell the point man to keep a close watch on the ground and keep a steady southeast course. In an hour or so you should be out of the worst of the storm, and if you don't dawdle you'll make the foothills by dark. From there the going is fairly easy. Now get these cattle moving. You're burning daylight.''

Zach didn't wait around to listen to any excuses. He nudged the gray and rode into the brush.

Conditions were growing worse. The snow fell faster and thicker and the wind began to howl, whipping the icy flakes into a frenzy. Within minutes Zach found himself in a whiteout.

He didn't bother searching the ground for her horse's tracks. The snow had wiped out all traces of those. In any case he knew how easy it would be to miss seeing her in the swirling maelstrom. While he stared at the ground he could pass within a few feet of her and never know it. So he rode slowly, his eyes constantly moving, straining to peer through the shifting white veil. Every few seconds he pulled down the scarf, cupped his mouth with both hands and yelled Willa's name.

He had no idea how long he searched. It seemed like hours. He was cold to the bone. Icy crystals clung to his eyebrows and lashes above the scarf. He was beginning to lose feeling in his toes and the tips of his fingers. Zach knew he had to seek shelter soon or perish, but he couldn't bring himself to stop searching. Willa was out there somewhere.

It was pure accident that he found her. He stopped to get his bearings, and in a brief instant of partial clearing he spotted the ghostly form of a horse and rider slowly crossing his path a few feet ahead.

"Willa!"

Giving no sign that she'd heard him, she rode on at the same plodding pace, hunched over, her coat collar turned up all around. Then the wind shifted, and the curtain of white swallowed her up again, and terror grabbed Zach by the throat.

"Willa, stop!" He kicked his horse's flanks, and the startled gelding leaped forward. In three long lopes he had her in sight again, but her lack of response and slumped posture only increased his fear. Lord, had she frozen to death in the saddle?

"Wil-laaa! Wil-laaa!"

Her head came up like a deer testing the wind for a sound.

"Here! I'm here." Shouting over the howl of the wind, he rode up beside her, grabbed Bertha's reins and brought her to a stop.

"Z-Zach?" She stared at him, her frost-rimmed lashes blinking owlishly.

"Yeah, it's me. Are you all right?"

First shock then abject relief flashed across her face. "You found me. You found me." She grabbed his arm as though making sure he was real, then squeezed her eyes shut and pressed her quivering lips together. "I thought…I thought I was going to die."

"Yeah, well, we both may yet if we don't get out of this storm. C'mon." He expected her to argue when he pulled the reins from her stiff fingers, but she was either too scared, too exhausted or too frozen to complain. He wrapped Bertha's reins around his gloved palm, turned in the opposite direction and led her through the blinding whiteness.

It would be dark soon. Zach knew that to attempt to descend the mountain at night in a blizzard would be suicide. In any case, the trip would take too long. Willa was half frozen and needed shelter—now. Their only hope was to find the line camp.

Seconds before spotting Willa he'd caught a glimpse of a giant tree that had been struck by lightning and split into a huge vee. He knew that the cabin was approximately ten feet due east of the dead pine. Willa had ridden right past it.

Luckily, Zach possessed an unerring sense of direction. He'd also taken the precaution of bringing another compass.

In good weather, from where they were he could have

tossed a stone and hit the log structure, yet it seemed to take forever to reach it. The exhausted horses plodded through the drifts with their heads down.

The puffs of vapor from the animal's nostrils froze instantly into tiny ice crystals. The wind shrieked around them like a banshee, tearing at their clothes and stinging their exposed skin.

Zach had expected Willa to question and argue, but she remained silent, which kicked his anxiety up another notch. He glanced over his shoulder and saw that she sat hunched deep in her coat. She had her head down and the wide collar turned up to meet the brim of her Stetson, shielding her face. She didn't utter a sound until he brought the horses to a stop.

Looking up, she saw the cabin, and surprise then utter relief passed over her face. Zach couldn't hear her over the wind, but he saw her lips form the words, "Thank God."

Focused on keeping them alive, he wasted no time on conversation. He dismounted and tied the horses to the hitching rail. Willa was so cold and stiff he had to lift her out of the saddle and carry her inside. For once she didn't fight him.

He shouldered the door shut behind them, muting the howling fury of the storm. The weak, grayish glow seeping in through the lone window provided barely enough light to see, but Zach strode directly to the small table in the center of the room. Hooking the toe of his boot around a spindly leg, he pulled out a wooden chair and sat her down.

The temperature in the room was only slightly warmer than that outside. Willa hugged her arms tight and shivered.

"I'll get a fire going," Zach said tersely.

He pulled a box of kitchen matches from a shelf and lit the kerosene lamp that hung from a bracket attached to the wall. Then he hunkered down in front of the pot-bellied stove, opened the small door and began pulling split logs and kindling from the wood box on the floor. He worked with quick efficiency, his jaw clenched tight against the seething emotions bubbling inside him.

The one-room cabin was a crude log structure, meant to house a cowboy through the summer months. An ancient hand pump mounted on the counter that served as a kitchen brought water into the cabin from a well, but that was the extent of the plumbing—or any other modern convenience. There was no electricity. The old pot-bellied stove did double duty as a heat source and a cook range. A white enamel chamber pot was tucked beneath the bunk built into the corner, but unless the weather was inclement most cowboys simply grabbed a roll of tissue and headed for the bushes when nature called. For those who were too fastidious—or too chicken—to bathe in the icy waters of a mountain stream, a galvanized tub hung on a nail by the stove.

When Zach had a good blaze going, he stood and dusted off his hands. "There, you should start feeling some heat soon."

"Th-thanks."

Maybe it was the brevity of her answer, or the pathetic quaver in her voice. Or maybe it was simply the sight of her sitting there huddled in that big coat, shivering, her creamy skin reddened by the cold and ice melting on those long ebony lashes. Whatever the reason, that one shaky word snapped the last thread of Zach's patience.

For the past several hours emotions had roiled inside him like a churning cauldron, but he had kept a tight lid on those feelings and turned all his energy and focus on finding Willa. Now that lid blew off like an exploding pressure cooker.

"Thanks? *Thanks!*" His fist came down hard on the table, making both it and Willa jump. "That's all you have to say?"

"I…"

"What the *hell* did you think you were doing, driving that herd up here?"

"D-don't you dare r-raise your v-voice to m-me," she flared back, but her chattering teeth robbed the protest of its heat and spoiled the effect.

"I'd like to raise more than my voice. What I ought to do is turn you over my knee and blister your butt."

"Y-you wouldn't d-dare!"

"No, I wouldn't. But only because you're female. Believe me, if you were a man I'd flatten you."

As it was, Zach itched to grab her by her shoulders and shake her until her teeth fell out. Knowing he had to put space between them, he swung away and stomped to the window, but he was too upset to remain still and began to stride back and forth across the small cabin. His boot heels struck the puncheon floor like hammer blows.

"Dammit, woman!" he raged, flinging his arms wide. "You countermanded my orders, put your life and the lives of those men in danger, worried Pete sick and nearly cost this ranch several hundred head of cattle. And for what? Because I had the gall to ask you to take one day off and go see a doctor? Damn. What a monster I am."

"Y-you didn't a-ask—"

"Quiet!" he roared. "I don't want to hear it!"

Willa was so startled, she shrank back in the chair and goggled at him.

Zach stalked from one side of the cabin to the other like a caged lion. Every cell in his body quivered with tension. He felt as though he was suddenly too big for his skin and might burst apart at any second.

"Up until now I have been patient with you, dammit. For four months you've criticized and argued and opposed me at every turn. You resent me and my brothers—especially me, it seems. You don't want us here. You don't think we have a right to this ranch. Okay, I got that. Hell, I even understand it. But let me remind you—*I* didn't write that damned will," he bellowed, thumbing his chest. "*I'm* not the one who gave you a raw deal. That was Seamus. Not me."

"If you hadn't—"

"I said *quiet!*" He jerked to a halt and jabbed his finger at the end of her nose. "Not another word until I've had my say."

Her mouth went slack and her eyes widened. Whether he'd startled her into silence or she was afraid to speak, he didn't know. At that moment he didn't care.

When he was certain she would remain silent he resumed his restless pacing. "Like it or not, this is the hand we've all been dealt. You either accept that or we all lose."

"I kn-know tha—"

This time he silenced her with a look. "I'm through being patient. From now on I'm not going to tolerate any more of your guff. Or any more stunts like the one you pulled today."

Willa opened her mouth to speak, thought better of it, and snapped it shut again.

Zach stopped in the middle of the floor and pressed the heels of his hands to his temples. "Dammit, woman, you drove those cattle up here just to defy me. Of all the reckless, stupid, irresponsible..." He shook his head, at a loss.

"I—I didn't expect it to snow."

The mumbled replied enraged him even more. "Give me a break! You've lived here all your life. You know spring in the mountains can be treacherous. Why the devil did you think I wanted to wait a few more weeks?

"No. Never mind, don't bother to answer that. You weren't *thinking* at all. You saw a chance to strike out at me and took it. Consequences be damned."

Guilt flickered across her face, and he knew he'd hit the mark. Cursing roundly, he started pacing again, but when he reached the opposite wall he swung back and pinned her with an accusing glare.

"Do you have any idea how close you came to losing your life out there?" he shouted, flinging an arm out toward the window. "If I hadn't found you when I did you wouldn't have lasted another ten minutes. And believe me, it was dumb luck that I found you at all. Hell, we both could have died out there. I'd been searching for you for hours."

Willa blanched at that, and pressed her trembling lips together. "I—I know," she murmured in a subdued voice. "I was s-so scared. Oh, Lord, I haven't even thanked you yet. I'm so sorry, Zach. I'm—"

"Forget it. I don't need your thanks." Zach stopped pacing and looked into those stricken violet eyes, his chest so tight he could barely breathe.

"Hell, I can't deal with this right now," he growled, and stomped for the door. "I've gotta go see to the horses." He paused to cram his hat down tighter on his head and arrange the scarf again, then he stepped out into the teeth of the storm.

After the brief respite it seemed even colder, and Zach caught his breath at the first slap of icy wind. Visibility was no more than a couple of feet. Keeping one hand on the outside of the cabin wall at all times, he untied the horses and led them around back and into the small lean-to. It wasn't the warm barn that Bertha usually enjoyed, but both horses would be sheltered from the wind and snow, and their shared body heat in the small space would keep them warm enough to survive.

Zach worked quickly, methodically, using the chores to keep his churning emotions at bay. By the light of a battery-powered lantern, he unsaddled the animals and rubbed each one down with a wad of hay, then covered them with horse blankets he found on a shelf. After breaking the ice on top of the rain barrel located just outside the door, he dipped up a bucket of water and gave each animal a drink. He then poured grain from the sack he'd brought with him into a galvanized trough.

Finally, though, he ran out of things to do, and his emotions caught up with him. Overwhelmed him.

When he thought about what could have happened— what had almost happened—a hard shudder shook his big frame.

The adrenaline that had kept him going for the past few hours drained away in a whoosh, leaving him suddenly shaky and weak in the knees.

With an agonized groan, he leaned against the gray gelding and rested his head against the animal's back.

While the two horses munched contentedly, Zach rolled his forehead against the coarse horse blanket, shaken to the depth of his being. It hadn't been anger that had made him tear into Willa, as she no doubt believed. It had been fear at how close he had come to losing her.

Zach groaned again, but he couldn't deny the truth any longer. He would have been concerned about anyone lost in a storm and done his best to find them. However it had been more than mere concern he'd experienced while searching for Willa. It had been gut-wrenching terror that he would not find her in time, and heaven help him, the thought of that had been unbearable.

The depth of his feeling stunned and appalled him. "Damn, Mahoney, have you lost your mind?" he raged at himself. "Willa Simmons is a pain-in-the-butt, smart-mouthed little spitfire. Any man who takes her on will have his hands full. She's not even your type, for Pete's sake."

The lecture didn't do one whit of good. Somehow she had gotten under his guard and stolen his heart, something he would have sworn no woman could ever do.

Zach shook his head. That he'd allowed himself to fall for Willa Simmons, a feisty little hellion who couldn't stand the sight of him, made him feel foolish.

Of all the women in the world, why this one? Though he'd always been a bit of a loner, he'd never had any trouble attracting women. The barrel racers who followed the rodeo circuit and the groupies who hung around the shows had gone to great lengths to gain his attention. For the most part he had ignored their overtures, although that had seemed to only make them more determined.

Not that he'd lived like a monk. While traveling the circuit he'd had a few long-term relationships, mainly out of need and loneliness, and because he preferred serial monogamy to one-night stands.

He'd liked all of the women well enough. A couple he'd been genuinely fond of, but his feelings had never gone deeper than that. In his thirty-six years he'd never let a woman get that close. Until now.

Not that he was in love. Okay, so maybe his feelings for Willa went deeper and were more intense than anything he'd ever experienced before. To even imagine his life without her in it brought pain, but that didn't mean he was in love with her.

Dammit, he didn't want to be in love with any woman. That was not an emotion he trusted. From what he'd observed, it blinded you to a person's true character, often hiding their less than admirable traits until it was too late.

That had certainly been the case with his adoptive mother. After being widowed, in a love-struck haze, she had married a charismatic charmer who'd claimed to be a man of God, but who was in reality a charlatan and a criminal. And a wife abuser.

Zach had learned from her mistake.

Although…now that he thought about it, no one could say that Willa had ever bothered to hide her flaws and put her best foot forward around him.

There was no pretense or guile in the woman. With Willa, you always knew where you stood. She didn't conceal her feelings or opinions behind a polite facade or pretend to be anything but what she was—feisty, willful and defiant, often rash. A real handful. She was also loyal, hardworking, honest, kind to old folks and children, although she was learning her way with the latter and still a bit awkward. She was also friendly and loving with those she cared about. Many times, when she hadn't known he was around, he'd seen her laughing and chatting with the men or giving Pete or Maria a hug and an affectionate kiss on the cheek.

Zach's mouth twisted. Hell, it was probably her unaffected, straightforward manner that had gotten past his guard. He knew all her faults, all her weaknesses and shortcomings, and despite them—maybe even because of them—he was crazy about her.

He'd felt the attraction from the first moment he'd seen her. Desire had slammed through him like a freight train going ninety when he spotted her standing on the stairs that day he and his brothers had come to the ranch to confront Seamus, but he'd chalked that up to nothing more than lust. A basic, animal attraction. Then he'd found out who she was, and realized that she hated him and his brothers. He'd thought her animosity would cancel out the attraction, but he was wrong.

Over the past months that pull had not faded, had in fact grown stronger, though he had refused to admit it until now.

Zach supposed that adage about opposites attracting was true. He tended to be reserved and played his cards close to his chest. Willa was an open book, candid and unrestrained, and out-going around those with whom she was comfortable. He tended to think things through and plan a course of action. Willa reacted impulsively, letting her emotions guide her. Not always wisely, perhaps, and sometimes with disastrous results, but always with genuine conviction.

One thing was certain, life with Willa might be a wild ride and give a man one headache after another, but it would sure as hell never be dull.

He made a disgusted sound. Yeah, right. Dream on, Mahoney. No way in hell that's ever going to happen. The woman would as soon give you a good, swift kick in the shins as look at you. Dammit to hell! Wouldn't you know he'd fall for the one woman who hated his guts?

She'd probably laugh her head off if she knew he was out here in the freezing cold, mooning over her like some infatuated teenager. Grinding his teeth, Zach straightened and squared his shoulders. The only thing he could do was to keep his distance and hope she never guessed that he cared for her.

Chapter Eight

Willa felt wretched.

She had behaved badly. Again. Zach had every right to be furious with her. To hate her, even, after what she'd done. He was right; she could have cost three men their lives. As it was, she'd come darn close to losing her own.

Tears of self-loathing welled in her eyes. She put her head down on the table and groaned. What was the matter with her? When would she ever learn to use her head and stop letting her emotions control her?

If she weren't so contrary, none of this would have happened, she thought glumly.

Willa sniffed, thoroughly disgusted with herself.

The truth was, from the beginning she had cast Zach in the role of villain and blamed him for everything. Partly because he was an available target and partly because that was easier than accepting Seamus's perfidy. Most of all, however, because he aroused feelings in her that she had never experienced before—hot, jittery, uncomfortable feelings that she didn't have a clue how to handle, except to strike out in anger.

She desperately needed to believe the worst of him, but she had to admit, doing so was getting harder all the time. Day by day, as she'd gotten to know him, it had became more and more obvious that Zach was not the grasping, greedy opportunist she had first assumed him to be, but a decent, intelligent, hardworking man who had a deep love for the land and ranching and the knowledge to manage both.

Yet, even knowing that, she still responded to him with prickly antagonism. It seemed to be an instinctive reflex over which she had no control.

Some of her behavior toward Zach could be traced to Lennie's door, as well. Darn him. If he hadn't planted the seed in her mind that Seamus had written his will as he had to manipulate her and Zach, maybe she wouldn't be so leery. It would be just like the domineering old devil to try to control them from the grave.

Well, it wasn't going to work. She would not—absolutely would not—allow him to do that. Which meant she didn't dare get too friendly with Zach. She couldn't risk falling for him, and Willa had a terrible suspicion if she ever let her guard down she might. Lord knew, he already stirred her emotions more than any other man ever had.

Nevertheless, her relentless antagonism toward him had to stop. The man had saved her life, for Pete's sake. And he'd risked his own to do it. They didn't have to be friends, but it wouldn't kill her to be polite. He deserved that much.

She sat up and wiped her teary eyes with her fingertips. When he came back she would apologize. She would also thank him for saving her life. And in the future, she would be polite to him, she swore. Even if it killed her.

She would start by making herself useful.

Willa jumped up and went to the counter and rummaged through the crude cabinets underneath and located a can of coffee and a blue-speckled enamel coffeepot, the kind they used on a campfire.

A short while later she was hunkered down in front of the potbellied stove, stuffing more wood into the firebox when the door banged open and Zach stepped inside carrying a load of firewood in his arms and saddlebags and a bedroll over his shoulder. A blast of frigid wind and snow blew in around him until he shouldered the door shut again.

Standing, Willa held out her hands to the heat rising from the stove's surface and peeked at him out of the corner of her eye. Without so much as looking at her, Zach stomped across the room and dumped the wood into the woodbox.

"I made some coffee. Would you like some?"

He glanced at her, his expression remote. "Later. Right now I need to bring in more firewood. We're going to need it tonight. While I do that, why don't you start dinner?"

"Dinner?"

He cocked one brow. "Don't tell me you can't cook."

"Oh, and I suppose you can?" she snapped before remembering her vow to be cordial.

"Nothing fancy, but I manage. I figure if you eat, you ought be able to feed yourself. You can't always expect others to put a meal on the table for you."

Put that way, Willa couldn't very well argue, but knowing he was right didn't take away the sting. Though she knew she worked as hard or harder than anyone else on the ranch, the matter-of-fact statement made her feel inadequate and lazy, as though she were some spoiled little rich girl who never lifted a finger.

Hurt and defensive, she ground her teeth and hitched one shoulder. "I guess not. But since Maria has always done all the cooking, I never had to learn. Anyway, I prefer ranch work."

"So do I." Willa was certain she saw disdain in his eyes, but he turned and headed for the door. "All right, I'll do the cooking," he said over his shoulder. "But you can at least make yourself useful and man this door for me."

Zach hauled in five more loads of firewood. When the woodbox overflowed he dumped the extra on the floor beside it.

"Do we need so much?"

"If you want the fire to last until morning, we do. I'm sure as hell not going out in that storm in the middle of the night to get more."

His tone instantly put Willa's back up. She opened her mouth to make a pithy comment, then closed it again and ground her teeth harder. "Yes, of course. I should have realized."

Zach raised an eyebrow. Clearly he had expected a more heated reply.

He stomped the snow off of his boots and knocked more off of his long duster before shucking out of the garment and hanging it, along with his scarf and hat, on wall pegs by the door, but he did not remove the heavy coat he wore underneath. The woodstove had raised the temperature in the cabin, but it still hovered around freezing.

In the kitchen area, Zach located another kerosene lamp, lit it and placed it in the middle of the rickety table.

He returned to the counter and primed the old pump with a jar of water kept under the sink for that purpose, then worked the handle up and down until water gushed out into a chipped enamel dishpan. After washing his hands, Zach pulled a kettle from beneath the counter, filled it with water and set it on one of the stove's two burners to heat while he went to work. The coffeepot simmered on the other.

"Can I help?"

Zach arched one blond eyebrow. His green eyes fixed her with a look that made her cheeks heat.

Determined to do something useful, she poured a cup of the strong "cowboy" coffee and set it on the counter beside him. Zach barely acknowledged the gesture with a curt "Thanks."

"You're welcome. I'll, uh…I'll set the table."

The meal of canned stew and biscuits that Zach prepared was surprisingly delicious. Either that, or Willa was so ravenous anything would have tasted like ambrosia. If you didn't count the bite of roast beef she'd had for dinner the previous night, she hadn't eaten since lunch the day before.

She had psyched herself up to apologize and wanted to get it over with. Throughout the meal she waited for an opening to broach the subject, but Zach's expression did not encourage conversation. Every time she tried to initiate a discussion he was cool and distant and responded with a curt reply meant to cut her off, so for the most part they ate in silence.

Finally she couldn't stand the hostile silence a minute longer.

"All right, that's it. I've had enough of your cold shoulder," she announced. "I'm sorry, okay? I'm really, truly sorry. You're right, I shouldn't have driven those cattle up here. It was a reckless, irresponsible, stupid thing to do.''

He stopped eating and fixed her with a hard look. ''So why did you?''

Willa exhaled a gusty sigh and grimaced. ''Just what you said. My temper got the best of me.''

He opened his mouth to speak, but she raised her hands and silenced him. ''I know, I know. I had no reason to get so angry. You were just trying to look out for my welfare. But the thing is, I've had a lifetime of Seamus ordering me around and directing my life. When he died I swore I'd never let anyone do that again. I guess when I found out you'd already made an appointment for me with the doctor and arranged for Kate to drive me, you hit a nerve.''

''So you decided to strike back by defying me. But why the cattle? There were plenty of other things you could have done that would've angered me without risking lives and property. Hell, you came up here totally unprepared. You didn't bring any food with you or emergency gear or even a winter coat.''

''I know, I know. It was an impulsive decision. I was just so angry I wasn't thinking. I felt as though I had to do something or I was going to explode.'' She spread her hands. ''Driving the cattle to summer range just happened to be the first thing that occurred to me.''

''Great. So every time you get ticked off at me over some imagined insult you're going to pull another stunt like this?''

''No! At least…I hope not. From now on I'm going to do my darnedest to think things through before I act. I promise.''

Doubt glittered in his green eyes. ''I don't know.

That's one helluva temper you've got, lady. It's not going to be that easy to control.''

"But that's just it. I've never had what you'd call a volatile temper until—" She stopped abruptly and caught her lower lip between her teeth. "Uh, that is…"

"Until my brothers and I moved in? Is that what you were about to say?" When Willa reluctantly nodded, he just looked at her, his expression remote, unreadable. "In other words, I rub you the wrong way." He shook his head and snorted. "Well, that's not likely to change, is it? And I'm sure as hell not going anywhere. So there goes your good intentions."

"Okay, fine, don't believe me. Don't accept my apology," she said in an offended voice.

"I didn't say that. I know you're sorry and that you didn't mean any real harm."

"You do?"

"Sure. You don't have a malicious bone in your body. Trust me, if I didn't believe that, you and I would have had a showdown long before now. You're just frustrated because you feel you've been cheated. Hey, I agree. You have. But I can't do anything to change that. You need a target for all that anger, and since you hate my guts, I seem to be elected."

"I don't *hate* you!" she exclaimed, appalled that he would think such a thing.

"Really. You could've fooled me."

Willa held his gaze for a long time, unsure what to say. She couldn't very well explain that he made her feel things she'd never experienced before, that he made her aware of her own body, her own femininity in ways that made her feel vulnerable and edgy. Or that she was afraid of where those feelings would lead.

She certainly couldn't tell him that she suspected Seamus had set them up, hoping to manipulate them into marriage. That would be too humiliating to bear, especially since she did not seem to have the same effect on Zach that he had on her.

No. It was better if she let him believe she disliked him.

"All right. So we won't ever be friends. But since it looks like we're going to be stuck here together for a while, do you think we could possibly call a truce, at least for the duration? I don't relish the thought of spending the next day or two locked in battle. It's too exhausting."

Zach regarded her over the top of his tin coffee mug. "Fine by me."

"Good."

They both returned their attention to the meal, and for several minutes a peaceful, if tentative, silence stretched out, the only sounds the scrap of spoons against tin. They were almost finished when, out of the blue, Zach said, "So, since we're being so cordial, mind if I ask you a friendly question?"

Willa shot him a wary look. "I suppose not."

"How *is* your wrist?"

"It's fi—"

His eyebrows shot skyward, and she stopped abruptly, chagrined when she realized the reply and her strident tone had been an automatic response. "Sorry. Habit. Actually, it hurts like the very devil."

"I thought it might. I noticed you've been favoring it. Let's have a look."

Before she realized his intent, Zach's took her hand and pushed her coat sleeve up as far as he could. "Mmm. No wonder it hurts. Your bandage has come loose. It needs to be rewrapped. Let's slip your arm out of this sleeve, okay?''

''I...okay.''

With Zach's help, she worked her arm free, but by then her wrist was throbbing. She gritted her teeth as he unwound the loose bandage. A livid purple discolored her skin halfway up to her elbow and over her hand, even in between her fingers.

''Can you flex your fingers?''

''I think so.''

''Good. Now slowly rotate your hand. How does that feel?''

''It hurts, but it's not too bad. Just a throbbing ache. It's only excruciating when it's under stress, like when I grip something or have to pull with that hand.''

''Mmm.'' He slid the kerosene lamp closer to her hand and leaned in for a better look.

Willa's breath caught. When her lungs began to function again her breathing was shallow and rapid. She stared down at the top of Zach's head, at that shock of wheat-colored hair, and her heart did a funny little flip-flop in her chest. Each individual strand glittered like burnished gold in the lamplight. This close, she could smell it—some sort of citrusy shampoo mixed with his tantalizing male scent.

''That's one heck of a bruise. It also looks a bit more swollen than last night, but that's probably because you used it too much riding up here.'' He gently pressed on the puffy flesh with his forefinger. ''Does that hurt?''

Willa was so distracted the question didn't register at first. ''Uh, n-no. It's just sore.'' In truth, all she could feel was the warm touch of that calloused finger against her skin.

"I think it's just sprained, but I'd feel better if you had a doctor look at it when we get off this mountain."

"I, uh, I will."

He glanced up at her. His face wore the same fathomless expression, but for once surprise and a touch of humor glittered in his eyes. "What, no argument?"

"It hurts."

"Ah." He carefully wound the Ace bandage and clipped it in place. "There. That will keep it immobile, which will help ease the pain."

He looked up again, and their gazes met. Held.

Their faces were so close she could feel his breath feathering over her skin like a caress. Neither moved. The air seemed to have grown suddenly thick. Willa's heart began to pound so hard she felt a vein in her neck pulsing, heard the heavy beat reverberating in her ears. Fluttering wings of panic beat in her stomach. Still, she could not move, could not look away from those hypnotizing green eyes.

A howling gust of wind rattled the door, and Zach's head whipped around toward the sound, breaking the spell.

"I brought a first-aid kit with me," he announced abruptly, and shot to his feet. "I'll see if I can find some painkillers for you."

He strode away and rummaged through the saddlebags he'd dumped on the floor beside the door. Willa closed her eyes and slumped in the chair, and the breath she hadn't realized she'd been holding came whooshing out.

"Here you go. Hold out your hand." Willa complied, and he shook two tablets out into her palm. "That should dull the pain somewhat."

"Thanks."

"No problem." He picked up their bowls and started

to move away, but she grasped his coat sleeve and stopped him.

"Zach, wait." She gazed up at him, feeling horribly awkward but determined to speak her piece. "I never thanked you for saving my life. I just want you to know that I appreciate what you did."

"You don't have to thank me. I would have done the same for anyone."

She didn't doubt that, but it hadn't escaped her that she would have died if he hadn't come after her...and then the Rocking R would have belonged entirely to him and his brothers. "That may be, but it was me you risked your life to save, and I am grateful. I just wanted you to know that."

He stared at her for a moment, his expression, as usual, unreadable. Finally he dipped his chin in a quick nod and carried the bowls to the counter.

Willa cleared the table of the remaining items, and while Zach washed up, she dried. They worked in silence for a while, but that soon began to grate on her nerves, and she searched for a safe topic of conversation.

"So...how long were you a rodeo rider?"

"Ten years."

"Really? Then you didn't start until you were in your mid-twenties. Isn't that a little old to take up such a dangerous occupation?"

He slanted her a look out of the corner of his eye and kept scouring the stew pot. "I was twenty-six. And, yeah, I guess you could say that."

She waited for him to elaborate. When he didn't she probed a little deeper. "So what did you do before that?"

"In college I majored in business and ranch management. After graduation I worked as assistant manager of the Triple C Ranch in Colorado."

Willa gaped at him. "You managed the Triple C?"

"Yeah. You've heard of it?"

"Of course I've heard of it. Everyone in ranching has heard of the Triple C. It's one of the few spreads in the country that rivals this one." Recalling the assumptions she'd made about his ranching experience, Willa felt absolutely foolish. "You might have told me."

"Would it have made any difference?"

She thought that over, and sighed. "Probably not."

"That's what I figured."

"With a job like that, why on earth did you leave it to take up rodeoing?"

Zach swished the tin bowl he'd just washed through the pan of rinse water and handed it to her. "Working on the Triple C was great, but I wanted a place of my own. After four years I realized that I needed to do something with the potential to earn large chunks of money fast. There are some rich purses in rodeos. Particularly the big ones like those in Houston or Dallas. If you consistently finish in the top five or so and avoid getting busted up, you can sock away a good chunk of change."

"And did you?"

"I did all right. I won my share of events, and I lived frugally. I figure, barring any major injuries, I was about two years away from having enough saved to buy a spread in Texas that I've had my eye on. Nothing on the scale of this place, mind you, but a sweet little setup all the same."

"Was your adoptive father a rancher? Is that how you got interested in the business?"

"No, he was a mining engineer. He was superintendent of one of the last gold mines in the Colorado Rockies. I think he was a little disappointed when I didn't follow in his footsteps, but mining just wasn't for me. As far back as I can remember all I've ever wanted to do was ranch. It's just something that's in my blood.''

Yes, it would be, Willa thought. She studied his profile, that strong face with its sharply chiseled features, and for the first time a feeling of acceptance settled over her.

The absolute rightness of Zach and his brothers inheriting the Rocking R suddenly struck her with such blinding clarity that she wondered how she could ever have denied it. This place had been carved out of the wilderness by generations of Raffertys before them. Had it not been for Seamus's controlling nature and rigidity, Zach, J.T. and Matt would have been born here, grown up here, and eventually have inherited the whole kit and caboodle. The Rock R was their heritage, not hers.

Oh, she had worked the land and given the ranch her all for twenty years, but it had never quite been hers. Not the way it was Zach's. Or Matt's or J.T.'s. If anyone was the interloper here, it was her, she realized with a pang.

"How about you?" Zach asked, handing her a rinsed cup. "I know you said you were born on a small ranch near here, but it's unusual for a woman to get so involved in the day-to-day operation of a place like you have. What sparked your interest in ranching?"

"Oh, that's easy. I was trying to impress Seamus."

"Why, for Pete's sake? The man was a tyrant."

"True, but he was also the only father figure I had, and I realized soon after my mother and I moved here that the only thing that mattered to Seamus was the Rocking R. So I set about learning everything I could about ranching." A wry half smile tipped up one corner of her mouth. "At first I thought that would please him. Later, when I was a bit older, I figured if I made myself indispensable to him, he would have to love me.

"It didn't work, of course. At best, he tolerated me. I don't think Seamus was capable of loving anyone. It's just too bad I didn't realize that until I was grown."

"How old were you when you came here?"

"Six. My own father died when I was barely five years old. I don't have any memory of him at all—just a few old photos. My mother tried, but she couldn't work the ranch by herself, and a year after my dad's death the bank foreclosed. We were about to be turned out on the street when Seamus came to our rescue. I guess he figured since she'd already had one child, she would be a good breeder. He offered her marriage and lifetime security. All she had to do was give him a son.

"Mother didn't love him, nor did he love her, but our situation was desperate."

"I guess it's safe to assume your mother didn't produce the way Seamus planned."

"Oh, there was one pregnancy after another just like clockwork for five years, but the babies were all stillborn. And none of them was the son Seamus wanted. I understand that the same thing happened with his first wife, your grandmother, after Colleen was born."

"Sounds to me like the problem lay with Seamus."

"Yes, the doctor suspected he carried a defective gene, but Seamus refused to accept that. His determination to father a son cost two good women their lives. My mother died giving birth to her fifth stillborn daughter. Your own grandmother died with her sixth."

"You said he ran your life. How so?"

"He decided what I could do, where I could go and when. He even told me what I could and couldn't wear, with whom I could associate—which was no one outside this ranch."

"Why did you let him get by with it? You sure don't have any trouble defying me."

"I wasn't a meek little mouse, if that's what you mean, but I knew not to push him too far." Willa dried the Dutch oven and put it away. "At first I didn't rebel because I was trying so desperately to gain his approval. Later, after my mother died, I was afraid if I crossed him too much he wouldn't let me stay here. He hadn't adopted me, so he wasn't under any obligation. He could have sent me to an orphanage, and that thought terrified me. Also, by then, it seemed the only thing in my life that I could count on to always be there was this ranch."

Zach gave her a long searching look, but he didn't comment.

When they finished the dishes he added more wood to the fire. Then he dragged the rolled-up mattress off the bed and tossed it onto the floor in front of the stove. "We'll sleep here where we'll get maximum heat," he announced.

Willa's mouth fell open. "We? We! What do you mean, *we?* If you think I'm going to sleep with you, you can just forget it!"

Chapter Nine

"Relax. Your virtue is safe." Zach hunkered down on one knee and spread a silver space blanket out on the floor in front of the stove then untied the cords holding the thin bunk mattress and unrolled it on top. He didn't bother to look up.

"Darn right it is, because I'm not getting into bed with you."

"You don't have any choice. Neither of us has." He shook out the bedroll blanket and spread it on top of the mattress.

"That's what you think. Lay a hand on me, Mahoney, and you'll be walking funny for a week."

Zach stood up and dusted off his palms, his movements fluid and unhurried. Willa backed up a step.

"Oh, for the love of— Will you cut that out? I'm not going to force myself on you."

She didn't look convinced, and he rolled his eyes.

"Look, the temperature outside is about fifteen and dropping, and all we have is one wool blanket and the two space blankets I tossed into my saddlebags. This little stove can't heat the whole cabin. It was only intended for cooking, and maybe to knock off the chill on a summer night. Hell, you could freeze meat over there in the corners right now. The only way we're going to keep from turning into a couple of popsicles is to sleep right here," he insisted, pointing to the makeshift bed at his feet.

Willa crossed her arms and hugged them tightly to her middle. "We could sleep in shifts," she suggested hopefully.

"Trust me, before this night is over we're going to need to share our body heat."

Just the thought of that made Willa's stomach muscles quiver.

Zach went to the door and took his duster from the peg and slipped it on. "I'm going to step outside for a few minutes and give us both some privacy. I suggest you make use of the facilities while I'm gone," he said with a pointed glance at the chamber pot under the bunk frame. "And I'd hurry if I were you. I'm not standing around out there for very long."

He was out the door before she could reply. When it banged shut behind him Willa practically leaped across the room and dragged out the white enamel pot.

She had barely zipped up her jeans when he returned amid a blast of freezing air and snowflakes. He shed his duster and shook off the snow, but instead of hanging it back on the peg he carried it across to the mattress and dropped it onto the floor, then shucked out of his heavy inner coat and dropped it on top of the wool blanket. "Give me your coat."

"What for?"

"We'll be warmer, not to mention more comfortable, if we use our coats as cover. Now hand it over."

Willa complied reluctantly. Shivering, she rubbed her arms and watched him arrange her coat and his over the wool blanket then lay the open slicker over both. "Don't just stand there freezing. Take your boots off. By the time you're done the bed will be ready and you can jump in."

While she hooked the heels of first one boot then the other into the bootjack by the door, Zach shook out another silver space blanket and covered the slicker and coats.

By the time her boots were off Willa was so cold any qualms she had about sharing a bed with Zach had vanished. She scampered across the cold floor and dove into the bed.

Scooting over as close to the stove as she could get, she pulled the covers up to her ears. Mercifully, the coats still held their body heat, and as the blessed warmth soaked in she almost groaned.

Lying huddled in the cocoon of coats and blankets, Willa watched Zach squat down in the small space between the bed and the stove and build up the fire. He worked steadily, seemingly impervious to the cold. With each movement the muscles in his back flexed and rippled beneath his flannel shirt. From that angle his shoulders looked impossibly broad. Helpless to resist, her gaze traveled downward, tracing the beautiful taper of his back to his lean waist and narrow hips. He really was a fantastic male specimen, she thought, as a swarm of butterflies seemed to take over her stomach.

"There, that should hold us for a while." He rose, and Willa heard him cross the room and pull off his boots. A second later she heard his belt hit the floor with a clunk. She pressed her lips together as her heart rate kicked up another notch.

One by one, the kerosene lamps went out. Moments later a draft blew in and raced up her backside when the edge of the cover lifted and Zach slipped in beside her. Willa squeezed her eyes shut and lay as still as a stone.

When he was settled, Zach turned onto his side, toward her, and hooked his arm over her middle. At the first touch Willa nearly jumped right out of her skin.

"What do you think you're doing? Stop that!" she cried when she felt herself being hauled backward. She tried to scoot away but she was no match for his strength.

"Will you settle down?"

The deep rumble of his voice right above her left ear sent another shockwave rippling through her. With every word, his warm breath dewed the side of her face and stirred the loose strands of hair at her temple.

"This is a single bed. For both of us to fit on it, we're going to have to snuggle close. Anyway, we'll stay warmer this way." With his hand splayed over her belly, he tucked her into the curve of his body until they fit together like two spoons.

Willa's breath caught. The feel of that hard, utterly masculine body pressing against her back set every pulse point in her to throbbing.

She couldn't argue with his reasoning, though. Already his heat was seeping through the layers of their clothing. She felt it from the back of her neck all the way to the soles of her feet. Willa welcomed the warmth, but the intimacy of their position shocked her to her core. Never in her life had she been this close to a man.

Nor had she ever been so aware of her body, or its needs. She had to stifle a groan. It was foolish and crazy, stupid even, and if he knew, no doubt he would laugh, but heaven help her, it felt wonderful to be held in his arms.

She tried to fight it, but Zach's nearness filled her with a longing so intense it was almost pain. To her horror her nipples had hardened and were suddenly so tender they ached, and that private place between her legs throbbed and yearned.

Trying to ease the ache, she shifted, and immediately froze. She stared, wide-eyed, into the semidarkness, her heart pounding. Apparently, Zach was just as affected by her nearness as she was his. She felt the hard evidence of that pressing against her backside.

Awareness overwhelmed her. With acute sensitivity, she could feel every square inch of contact between their bodies, feel his chest rise and fall with each breath he took, hear its sibilant hiss in her ear. She could even feel the steady thump-thump of his heart tapping against her back.

His smell surrounded her, masculine and earthy, and so erotic it made her head spin.

Every nerve ending in Willa's body had come alive as though electrically charged. She closed her eyes and breathed deeply and tried to banish the scorching desire, but it was hopeless. She was so tense her entire body was stretched as taut as a piano wire.

"Dammit, woman, will you stop worrying," Zach growled in her ear. "I already told you, I'm not going to attack you."

"I...I know that."

"Oh, yeah? Then why are you trembling?"

"I..." Willa bit her lower lip and again willed herself to relax, but it was no use. The hot, shivering longing that suffused her would not be denied.

Though he didn't move, she sensed Zach's sudden tension.

"Willa?"

Her throat grew so tight it hurt. She could not have made a sound to save her life.

Rising up on one elbow, Zach eased back enough to pull her onto her back, but she stubbornly kept her face turned away. "Willa?" he repeated softly. He gripped her chin with his fingers and turned her face toward his. "Open your eyes, Willa, and look at me," he commanded in a voice like warm velvet.

Awash with embarrassment, she pressed her lips tightly together, but after a few moments she gave in to the inevitable. As though weighted with lead, her long lashes lifted and her feverish gaze met his. In the soft glow coming from the stove's firebox she saw his pupils widen, saw something flicker in those depths, something hot and a little wild. And unbearably exciting.

Not quite steady, his big hand cupped the side of her face. "Willa." This time he said her name in a husky whisper. His gaze roamed her face, delved deep into her eyes. His calloused thumb swept over her cheek, touched the corner of her mouth, and when her lips quivered she heard his sharp intake of breath.

Then his eyes grew heavy-lidded and his head angled to one side and began a slow decent.

Every cell in Willa's body trembled with excitement and anticipation. Her breathing grew rapid and shallow. Her heart pounded so hard the heavy tom-tom beat reverberated in her ears.

With his lips mere inches from hers, Zach stopped and waited, giving her one last chance to stop him.

In some tiny part of her brain that still functioned with a grain of sanity, Willa knew that stopping was the wise thing to do. The right thing to do. Zach had no idea that he might be playing right into Seamus's hands. At the very least she should warn him of what she suspected. He had a right to know that it was possible they had been set up. No doubt, he would be as appalled as she was.

She could not let them fall into the old man's trap. All it would take was a word from her, a shake of her head, and Zach would back off, of that she was positive.

He stared down at her, his eyes sizzling with desire, waiting. Willa opened her mouth to say the words that would end this now, before it was too late, but she couldn't do it. She simply could not. Lord help her, she wanted this. Needed this.

Instead she whispered his name, soft as a caress.

Something flickered in his eyes, something hot and hungry and so erotic it sent a shiver down her spine.

Then his lips were on hers.

There was nothing tentative or restrained about the kiss. It was firm and sure and spoke of easy confidence, his lips rocking greedily over hers as though he could not get enough of her. It was the kiss of a man who knew exactly what he wanted and intended to have it.

Though inexperienced, and on some level, aware that she was out of her league, Willa let her instincts guide her. Winding her arms around Zach's neck, she kissed him back with all the passion, all the pent-up longing that pounded through her, and when he silently urged her to open her mouth she complied without hesitation.

The first intimate touch of his tongue against hers sent a shock of intense desire jolting through Willa. She clutched him tighter and welcomed the sensual invasion, eagerly following his lead, twining her tongue with his in an ageless mating dance.

Then his hand closed over her breast, and when his

thumb rubbed back and forth over her nipple Willa's breath shuddered to a stop.

The pleasure was so exquisite she moaned deep in her throat.

Zach tensed at the sound and tore his mouth from hers. "Dammit to hell!" He jackknifed to a sitting position, braced his elbows on his updrawn knees and clutched his head between his hands.

Willa felt instantly bereft, and for a second she was so disoriented she couldn't think. She stared at his broad back and hunched posture and blinked several times. "Z-Zach?"

"I'm sorry. Damn, I'm so sorry."

"S-sorry? You're…sorry?" Around the edges of her consciousness, she felt the chill of humiliation creeping in.

"You have every right to be furious. Hell, I ought to be horse-whipped. I just finished assuring you that I wouldn't force myself on you. Then two minutes later, what do I do? I'm all over you, that's what. What kind of man does that make me? And to think, I pride myself on keeping my word."

He clutched his head tighter and cursed vividly.

Willa's eyes widened as understanding dawned. She reached out her hand to touch him, then thought better of it. "Zach, no, it wasn't like that. You mustn't blame yourself. I—I knew what I was doing."

He glanced at her over his shoulder and shook his head. "No. You had a bad scare tonight. And now here we are, trapped alone together in an isolated cabin in a howling storm. You're upset and not thinking clearly."

"That's not true. I—I wanted you to kiss me."

"Dammit, Willa, I wanted more than just a few kisses.

And believe me, if I hadn't stopped when I did, we would've done a whole lot more.''

''I know that,'' she insisted, trying to ignore the blush that heated her cheeks. ''And I wanted that, too. So you see, you have no reason to blame yourself.''

He shot her a sharp look, and for an instant she thought she saw desire rekindle in his eyes. Then he shook his head and it was gone. ''No. You're too vulnerable right now to make that kind of decision.''

His refusal to believe her was beginning to get under her skin. ''That's just not true. I'm not a child. I knew exactly what I was doing.''

''Oh, yeah, right. For Pete's sake, Willa, just this morning you would've like nothing better than to see me strung up by my thumbs. If you had been yourself you would've fought me like a wildcat, and you know it. So let's just drop it, okay. I promise it won't happen again.''

''Well,'' Willa huffed, and flounced over onto her side. ''So much for Seamus's big plan.''

''What?'' Zach twisted around and shot her a hard look. ''What plan? What are you talking about?''

''Nothing.''

''Nothing, hell.'' He grasped her shoulder pulled her onto her back again. ''What did you mean, 'So much for Seamus's plan'?''

Willa grimaced. Once again, she'd let her temper overrule her good sense. Would she ever learn? ''It's just a silly theory that Lennie has about Seamus's will. There's absolutely no proof that he's right. I shouldn't have mentioned it.''

''Tell me, anyway.''

Willa gave him an annoyed look. ''Oh, all right. He thinks Seamus's will was nothing more than a scheme to trick you and me into...well...''

"Into...? C'mon, spit it out."

"Okay, if you must know, into marriage," she snapped.

"*What!*" His head jerked back as though he'd been slapped.

"Lennie believes that Seamus thought if he threw us together on a daily basis nature would take its course and you and I would eventually get married. If that happened, then the ranch would remain in the family, and I would be compensated for all my years of hard work and dedication." She shrugged. "Of course, he hadn't counted on your rigid sense of ethics," she added in a resentful voice.

"Why that sorry son of a—"

"There's no point in getting upset. We don't know if it's true. It could merely be Lennie's suspicious mind at work."

Zach shot her a look. "You knew the old man better than anyone else. What do you think?"

Willa was sorely tempted to lie so he would drop the matter, but she couldn't. She sighed. "Seamus was certainly capable of doing something like that."

"That's what I thought."

"But that doesn't mean he did. It's still just a theory."

"Yeah, one that makes perfect sense. It would explain why he had a change of heart about making me and my brothers his heirs." Zach mulled the idea over a few moments, his mouth grim. Then he exploded. "Damn that old coot! *Damn* him! I *won't* be manipulated."

"What does that mean?" she asked uneasily. "You wouldn't throw away the ranch because of a suspicion, surely."

"No. I'm angry, not stupid. I wouldn't do that even if I had proof that the old buzzard had tried to direct our lives to suit his own purposes. What I can do, though, is make damned sure his little scheme doesn't work.''

Willa took immediate offense. ''Trust me, you have nothing to worry about,'' she declared huffily. ''It does take two, you know.''

''Hell, I know that. Naturally I assumed that you wouldn't like being a pawn in Seamus's little game any better than I do. I am right, aren't I?'' he asked, watching her.

''Yes. Of course.''

''That's what I thought. Look, we might as well admit it. As unlikely as it seems, there is an attraction between us. After what just happened, I don't think either of us can deny that. But we sure don't have to act on it. Right?''

Willa nodded. ''Right.''

''Fine. Then we have no problem.'' Lying back down on the mattress, Zach turned onto his side and ordered bruskly, ''Now let's get some sleep. It's been a long day.'' As Willa turned over to face the stove again he draped his arm across her waist, but this time he didn't pull her close.

Lying motionless, she stared at the fire through the glass in the stove door. Zach couldn't have made his feelings clearer if he had spelled them out on a marquee: he wasn't interested.

Oh, he wasn't adverse to a roll in the hay when the opportunity presented itself. After all, he was a man. That didn't mean his emotions were involved. Men didn't necessarily equate sex and love. She might be a novice when it came to romance and male/female relations, but she'd spent her life almost exclusively among men. She'd overheard them talking enough to know that much.

Zach certainly wasn't interested in any sort of serious or permanent relationship. Not with her.

It shouldn't matter. In fact, she ought to be delighted, but the truth was, she wasn't. His rejection hurt.

Willa's eyes filled with tears. It was time to admit the truth, she thought dejectedly. At least to herself. Like it or not, welcomed or not, her feelings toward Zach had changed dramatically.

For two months, ever since that cold February night in the barn when he had kissed her, she had been restless and edgy, filled with a vague hunger that seemed to grow more insistent with every passing day. At first she had adamantly refused to admit that the encounter with Zach had been the cause, or that it had affected her at all. She simply had a bad case of spring fever, she'd told herself. It would pass.

However, instead of fading, the raw nerves and undefined yearnings had intensified. They tugged at her constantly, haunted her dreams, distracted her at the most inopportune times, made her feel vulnerable and desperate.

She'd tried to deny the feelings, tried to banish them by constantly whipping up her anger against Zach, but that ploy had failed miserably.

Now she realized that his kiss had stirred slumbering passions in her that, once awakened, would not be pushed aside.

Ever since that night, she'd wanted to feel his lips on hers again, wanted to experience that exquisite, heart-stopping pleasure. She'd buried those yearnings deep and had refused to acknowledge them. Until now...when it was too late.

A tear spilled from the corner of her eye and soaked

into the mattress. A sad, wry smile twitched the corner of her mouth. What a fool she'd been all these months.

Like an idiot, she'd told Zach about Lennie's stupid suspicions, and now any chance of him developing feelings for her was lost.

Long after Willa had drifted off to sleep Zach lay awake, staring into the semidarkness, his mind and heart in turmoil. The more he thought about what she'd told him the more convinced he was that it was true. That cantankerous old devil had set them up.

Oh, he'd been clever about it. He'd made J.T. and Matt beneficiaries, as well, so his scheme wouldn't be obvious.

Zach thought about the private detective's report he'd found in Seamus's file cabinet. It had contained a thorough dossier on each of them, including the most private details of his and his brothers' lives. The report had been dated three months after their first visit to the ranch. Had the discovery that one of his grandsons was single prompted the old man to hatch the scheme? Zach's mouth twisted. How convenient for him.

In her sleep, Willa made a small sound and shifted closer. The move put her enticing little bottom into firm contact with the fly on Zach's jeans. He nearly groaned when she wiggled into a more comfortable position, rubbing innocently against him.

In the faint light from the fire he studied the curve of her cheek, the delicacy of her eyelids and the way her lashes lay like lush ebony fans against her white skin. Gently, so as not to wake her, he tucked a loose tendril of hair behind her ear.

The hell of it was, he cared for Willa. She had become important to him in ways he could never have imagined. Each morning when he got up, the knowledge that she would be there made his day seem brighter. He looked forward to seeing her across the table from him at mealtime. Having her with him while they worked around the ranch, no matter how prickly she was, gave him an odd feeling of contentment. He like the way she looked, the sound of her voice, her laugh, the way she walked. He liked everything about her, even that fiery temper.

Just when he'd found a woman who meant the world to him, he finds out the old man had handpicked her for him. Just the thought of it made Zach see red. Damn you, Seamus, he raged silently.

The sly old coot had set a trap, and like an idiot he'd walked into it. But he wasn't about to take the bait.

Willa awoke alone the next morning. The fire had been stoked and was blazing brightly and a pot of coffee boiled on the stove. Zach's coat and slicker were gone, and she assumed he was seeing to the horses. Jumping out of bed, she made a dash for the chamber pot and sent up a prayer he would not return for a few minutes longer.

Twenty minutes later the door opened and he came in carrying another load of wood. He gave her a quick look and a muttered, "Morning," and went to the woodbox and dumped the split logs.

She polished off the leftover biscuit she was eating and washed it down with a swig of coffee before returning the terse greeting.

"That storm must have been just a freak weather system moving through," he announced as he straightened and dusted off his palms. "It stopped snowing around midnight, and now it's sunny and mild out there. The snow is melting fast. While you finish eating and tidy up, I'll go saddle the horses."

"We're leaving?" She had thought that they would

probably be stuck there for at least another day or two. Not that she was complaining. The prospect of another day and night alone with Zach was painful to contemplate.

"Yeah. It'll be rough going in spots, but it should get easier the lower we go. The heaviest snowfall was above seven thousand feet. Besides, there's probably a search party out looking for us already. So get a move on."

Normally Willa would have bristled at his tone, but she was distracted by a stab of guilt. Until that moment she hadn't given a thought to how distressed the folks back at the ranch must be. Kate, in particular, would be worried sick about Zach.

They rode single file with Zach leading the way. The temperature had climbed into the high sixties, and the snow was mushy and wet and melting into little rivulets everywhere. Though the horses plowed easily through the rotten snow, Zach kept a slow pace, keeping a sharp eye out, knowing the slightest misstep could be disastrous.

An hour out, and barely a quarter of the way down the mountain they came around a bend and met the search party coming up the trail from the opposite direction. The group consisted of three of their oldest hands, and Zach's brothers.

"Zach!" J.T. called the instant he spotted them, and spurred his horse forward. "Man, are we ever glad to see you, bro." His gaze darted behind Zach to Willa, and his grin widened. "And you found Willa. Thank God for that."

"Are you two okay? Either of you hurt?" Matt demanded as he and the others reached them. They crowded around, adding their own words of relief.

"We're fine. We found the line camp before dark and spent the night there."

Matt's face remained stern but the relief in his eyes was obvious. "Girl, you scared us all witless," he barked, only to relent a second later, his hard mouth stretching into one of his rare smiles. "But it sure is good to have you back safe and sound. Just don't pull another stunt like this again. Okay?"

"I won't. I promise." She was stunned and amazed by the brothers' concern. She had expected them to be worried about Zach, but not her.

When they arrived at the ranch she was even more surprised by the greeting she received from Kate and Maude Ann. Amid tears and murmurs of heartfelt relief, the two woman and Maria crowded around her the instant she dismounted and hugged her fiercely.

"Oh, Willa, we've been so worried. Thank heaven, you're all right," Maude Ann declared.

"I don't think any of us slept a wink last night," Kate added. "But I knew if anyone could find you in that storm it would be Zach."

The children attacked her en masse, wrapping their arms around her waist and legs and clinging so tight she couldn't move. When they finally released her, Pete stepped up.

He scowled and squirted a stream of tobacco juice into the dirt. "I oughta turn you over my knee, that's what I oughta do. Scarin' an old man thata way." Then he snatched her against his chest and hugged her tight, his gnarled hands clutching her as though he'd never let go. "Willa. Oh, thank God."

She turned, and her eyes widened. "Edward. I didn't expect to see you here. Don't tell me they called you."

"No, no one called me. Although, I wish they had. I arrived this morning shortly after the search party left. When I learned what had happened my heart nearly stopped.'' He grasped her upper arms and inspected her. ''Are you okay?''

Willa knew she must look as though she'd been jerked through a knothole backward after the past forty-eight hours, especially to someone as fastidious as Edward, but she smiled and shook her head. ''Yes, I'm fine. But thanks for asking.''

''Good. I've been pacing the floor for the past four hours. We all have.'' He looked at Matt and J.T. ''Your wives filled me in on what else has been going on. Have you told them yet?''

Zach was instantly alert. ''Told us what?''

''No, not yet,'' J.T. replied, looking uncomfortable.

Matt scowled. ''We were going to give them a chance to relax and recover before we unloaded that on them. Thanks a lot.''

''Oh. Sorry...I didn't realize—''

''All right, somebody tell me what's happened. Now.''

''We got trouble, Zach.'' Matt said in a somber voice. ''While you were gone yesterday someone shot our best bull and gutted him like a fish.''

Chapter Ten

The senseless attacks continued with no letup. A week after the storm, someone dynamited the stock tank that Willa and the men had repaired earlier in the spring. Ten days after that, Zach, Matt, J.T. and the rest of the men returned one evening to find every tire on every vehicle in the ranch yard slashed. Three weeks later, someone spray-painted a satanic symbol on the side of the barn.

As spring gave way to summer the vandalism began occurring more frequently. More troublesome, the acts, and the notes that were often found nearby, had begun to take on sinister overtones.

Cattle were slaughtered and left in the pastures to rot. Others were mutilated pitifully and in so much pain they had to be put down.

One morning, about to leave on a shopping trip to Bozeman, Maude Ann and the kids discovered one of the barn cats had been killed and left out on the windshield of her van. On the front seat was a note warning that one of them could be next.

After that incident, Zach, with the wholehearted support of Matt and J.T., issued orders that the women and children were not to go anywhere alone, not even into Clear Water for groceries. Wherever Willa worked on the ranch she was to be in the company of at least two men at all times.

The instant the edicts were issued Zach glanced at Willa. "Any objections?"

That he had expected her to balk at the restriction was obvious, and she admitted to herself that as little as two months earlier she would have done so automatically, simply to oppose him. Abashed, she shook her head. "No. It makes sense. Whoever is doing this is obviously unbalanced. I'm not anxious to be his next victim."

That earned her a long, considering look from Zach and almost comical, stupefied stares from everyone else sitting around the table.

All of the attacks near the house had taken place while the men and Sadie, the dog, were working miles away. Pete spent his days in and around the barn, but the old man was hard of hearing and too frail to be of much protection for the women, so Zach assigned two men, armed with rifles, to remain at the ranch headquarters every day and to patrol the grounds.

After the first animal was discovered butchered they all feared for Sadie, who had recently whelped a litter of six, so Zach moved the dog and her pups into the house, much to the delight of the children.

After each incident the sheriff was called. He spent hours at the ranch, going over the sites and conferring with the men, particularly Matt, but they had no leads, other than the notes torn from a spiral notebook, which Matt had saved as evidence.

A feeling of uneasiness permeated the ranch and everyone on it. You could see it on the somber faces of the men, the way everyone constantly looked over their shoulder and scanned the area around them everywhere they went.

It was standard procedure for every man to carry a rifle in his scabbard while out on the range. In the high country you never knew when you'd run across a cougar or rattlesnake or some other unfriendly critter. Also, if an injury occurred you could fire the gun to signal for help. Now, however, the men had started strapping on handguns, too. The cowboys looked like an armed posse out of a Western movie, Willa thought wryly.

The precautions made no difference. The attacks continued with more frequency than ever. A watering hole was poisoned and the vet had to be called out when over thirty head of cattle sickened. An unusual number of horses turned up lame, the result of blows to the legs. A prime pasture was set on fire, and Zach and the men battled the blaze for over thirty hours. They were staggering with exhaustion by the time they finally put it out.

Zach was furious, and though he did not say so, he was worried, as well. So were his brothers. They discussed sending the women and children away until whoever was responsible was caught, but Maude Ann and Kate flatly refused to budge.

"Forget it. There is no way I am leaving you, J.T.," Kate declared. "Anyway, Willa can't leave. If she does you all lose the ranch."

"That's right. And if she stays, Kate and I stay, too. We won't leave her alone here with no women for moral support. Besides, the ranch is our home now, and that creep isn't going to run us off of it,'' Maude Ann added.

The men argued and pleaded. Matt and J.T. even tried issuing ultimatums, but Kate and Maude Ann stood firm, and in the end their husbands had to accept defeat.

Since the night of the storm, Willa's feelings had changed, not only toward Zach, but toward his family, as well. The concern his brothers and sisters-in-law had shown for her safety when she and Zach returned after the storm had disarmed her, and once she lowered her guard and her prickly hostility began to fade she started to see all of them differently.

Gradually, Willa discovered that she truly liked both women.

Maude Ann, a born earth mother, was warm and open and utterly natural. Kate, though a bit more reserved, was friendly and pleasant and just as congenial.

Willa was still cautious and reserved around the brothers, but after months of listening to their conversations she began to understand how the events of their lives had shaped them into the men they were.

There was Matt, the former police detective, with his penchant for rules and order and doing what was right. On the outside Matt appeared stern and unapproachable, but Willa had witnessed his gruff tenderness with the children numerous times, and she had come to realize that behind the stern facade was an old softie.

J.T. was a charmer. His quick grin and easy banter made him appear a lightweight, but that breezy manner hid a keen intellect and a kind heart. Willa suspected the devil-may-care attitude, like Matt's penchant for order and constancy, was J.T.'s way of dealing with the pain of loss.

Then there was Zach—the strong, silent type, a stoic

loner who carefully guarded his feelings. He was a difficult man to get to know, but Willa had learned enough about him to realize that Zach was a man of bedrock-solid ethics and morals, a man whom a woman could trust with her life—and her heart—if she could ever break through that protective wall he'd built around himself.

Of course, in her case, she admitted with a dejected sigh, even if she could manage to do that, he would probably still reject her, thanks to Seamus and his scheming.

Intellectually, Willa knew it was for the best. Neither she nor Zach would allow themselves to become Seamus's puppet. However, that message had not yet gotten through to her heart, or her body.

Whenever she and Zach were in the same room the air still hummed with a sizzling awareness that seemed to grow stronger with each passing day. Sparks of electricity arched between them if they accidentally touched, and when their gazes happened to meet, the dark emotions swirling in his eyes made her weak in the knees.

Beyond those brief, isolated moments, though, Zach was so preoccupied with the troubles that Willa doubted he gave her more than a passing thought when he wasn't around her.

Unfortunately, she couldn't *stop* thinking about him. He occupied her mind nearly every moment of the day and she dreamed of him almost nightly. In her mind she relived that kiss in front of the fire over and over. She thought often about how wonderful it had felt to sleep in his arms, to cuddle next to that big, warm body.

During mealtimes or whenever Willa worked in Zach's vicinity, her gaze was drawn to him like a moth to a flame. And each time her heart did a crazy little dance in her chest.

The reaction made her feel foolish and lovesick, but she couldn't stop herself. He was so utterly masculine, at times just watching him walk across the ranch yard with that rangy, loose-limbed stride caused her to catch her breath.

One evening after dinner, when she spotted him in the main corral working with Satan, she couldn't resist strolling over to watch. The Dolans and the Conways and all the children were already there, and some of the hands had gathered to watch, as well.

Zach did not attempt to saddle the stallion or ride him. He didn't even put a bridle on the animal. He merely stood in the middle of the circular corral while Satan trotted nervously around the perimeter, ears back and eyes wild with hate and distrust. Zach merely turned slowly in place, keeping the enraged stallion in sight at all times, talking to him in a soft, calming voice while he gently tossed a soft rope made of loosely braided cotton rags over the horse's back and pulled it back. He repeated the action again and again, letting the animal grow accustomed to the touch and the sound of his voice.

''What's he doin' that for?'' Tyrone demanded from his perch on the fence rail.

''I'm not sure,'' J.T. replied absently. ''Trying to calm him down, I guess.''

''Is the horsie scared?'' Debbie asked, her blue eyes wide.

''He doesn't want to be ridden, that's for sure,'' Matt replied.

Willa moved over to the group and climbed up on the fence with the kids. ''Satan is scared, all right. He's scared he's going to be eaten.''

All five children looked at her with horrified expressions, their eyes big as saucers.

''We don't eat horsies,'' Jennifer stated with childlike outrage. ''We ride them.''

''Yes, but Satan doesn't know that. He's mostly wild, and his instincts tell him to flee from all other animals, and that includes man. Or, if he's cornered, to fight with all his might because they may eat him. So what your uncle Zach is trying to do is teach him not to fear him or his touch.''

Willa was amazed at Zach's patience. And his gentleness. He kept tossing the rope and murmuring to the stallion tirelessly. She could see that the horse was confused and trying to figure out just what this human was up to.

Finally, after perhaps twenty minutes, Satan grew tired and came to a stop, bobbing his head and snorting, but still keeping a wary eye on Zach. He continued to toss the rope, but now each time he moved a step or two closer. Watching him out of the corner of his eye, Satan continued to bob his head and blow softly through his nose.

Finally, when Zach was close enough, he slowly reached out and ran his hand down the horse's neck. A quiver ran over Satan's hide, but he didn't shy away.

Emboldened, Zach wrapped both arms around the animal's neck, stroking him constantly as he murmured encouragement in his ear. Willa was amazed that Satan tolerated the touch, but he just stood there, his ears moving back and forth.

''Why's he huggin' 'em?'' Timothy asked.

''Shh. Just watch,'' Matt replied.

After perhaps ten minutes of stroking and soothing, Zach released the horse and turned his back and walked away five steps and stopped. Satan followed him and nudged his shoulder. Keeping his back to the horse, Zach changed direction and took a few more steps. Again Satan followed and nudged his shoulder.

Over and over, Zach repeated the maneuver, and every time Satan stuck with him. When he took a bridle off the fence post and slipped it on, the horse accepted it with merely a twitch of his ears. Constantly murmuring reassurance and stroking, Zach put the saddle pad and saddle on the horse. Satan shifted uneasily but he calmed under Zach's hand and allowed him to tighten the cinch.

He soothed the horse for a few minutes more, then grasped the saddle horn and put his foot in the stirrup. Everyone held their breaths.

Zach carefully lifted himself up and swung into the saddle. Satan sidestepped and bobbed his head, and his front hooves lifted a few inches off the ground, but he settled when Zach patted his neck and murmured to him.

For a moment they remained motionless while Zach stroked and murmured. Then he gave the horse a gentle nudge and the black stallion started walking. Another gentle nudge sent him trotting easily around the enclosure.

All around the others exclaimed in subdued tones of amazement. Willa watched horse and rider, her throat tight, her eyes misty. She had never seen anything so beautiful or so touching in her life.

In that moment of startling clarity, she realized that she wasn't merely attracted to Zach. She was in love with him.

He was everything she had ever dreamed of finding in a man, she realized—strong yet gentle, patient, intelligent, kind, hardworking, passionate and sexy. Everything about him appealed to her—his raw masculinity, his rugged good looks and lean, muscular build, that air of quiet authority that he wore with such ease.

Willa bit her lower lip and fought back tears. Dear Lord, she was in love with Zach—completely, irrevocably, head-over-heels in love with him. And it was hopeless.

Willa did her best to squash her feelings for Zach, or at least ignore them. To avoid him she reverted to her former behavior of retreating to her room immediately after dinner, and she volunteered for work assignments that took her out of his immediate vicinity. At mealtime, when avoiding him was impossible, she never spoke to him directly and tried never to make eye contact with him.

None of her efforts worked. Day by day she fell more in love. Too inexperienced with men and love to know what else to do, Willa nursed her feelings in silence. She thought about confiding in Maude Ann, but she was still too unsure of the tentative friendship between herself and the other women. Confiding in Kate was out of the question since she was Zach's adoptive sister. As for Maria, much as Willa loved her, she knew the old woman couldn't keep a secret for spit. So she said nothing and dealt with the emotional turmoil as best she could.

Except for winter, late summer was the slowest season on the ranch. The majority of the cattle were pastured in various high mountain valleys. The branding, castrating and inoculating had been completed. The hands took turns manning the line camps, working in one week shifts, and those who were not in the mountains spent the late spring plowing, planting, fertilizing and irrigating the pastures. In summer they completed any needed repairs, and made hay and stored it in the pole barns scattered around the winter range.

During spring and fall roundups, everyone worked from sunup to sundown. In mid-summer, however, many of the men found time on Saturday night to go in to town and raise a little hell at the local dance hall, Hody's.

After a day of dusty, hot work driving the haybaler, Willa had just showered, changed and joined the others in the kitchen when Zach walked in. Wearing clean jeans and a clean shirt, he had that shower-fresh scrubbed look and smelled of soap and shampoo.

Willa's heart gave its usual little flutter at the sight of him. Turning away, she went to the stove and poured herself a cup of coffee. She carried it to the back window and gazed out. Several of the men, scrubbed and spit-polished for their Saturday night outing, were climbing into pickups.

"My, don't you look nice, big brother," Kate commented. "Is that a new shirt?"

"Sorta. And thanks. Don't bother setting a place for me tonight. I'm going to go into town with the men, maybe shoot some pool and have a few beers."

J.T. grinned. "And maybe latch on to some pretty little thing to two-step with too, I'll bet. Huh, bro?"

Willa's head snapped around. He was going into town?

Unfazed by his brother's teasing, Zach shrugged. "There's always that possibility, I guess." His gaze met Willa's in a long, searing look. Then he blinked, and the contact was broken.

"I'd better get going. I'll see you all tomorrow."

As he went out the door Willa turned back to the window and watched him stride down the walk and climb into his truck. Her heart felt like a lead weight in her chest.

Willa worked like a demon through the remainder of the summer and through the fall roundup, wearing herself

out each day so that she barely had the energy to eat
before falling into bed and almost none to mope over
Zach.

She volunteered for the dirtiest, most strenuous jobs—
anything to keep her mind off of him. He had gone into
town four more evenings since that first time, and each
time he hadn't returned until after midnight. Willa knew
because she'd still been awake and heard him come in.
She wondered if he'd met someone—and who she was.

Eventually the roundup was over, the herd had been
culled and all but the breeding stock and this year's crop
of calves was on its way to market, leaving Willa to
wonder how she would ever get through the winter,
cooped up in the house with Zach.

She was nibbling at her dinner, mulling over that problem when Maude Ann interrupted her.

"So what are you going to wear, Willa?"

Willa didn't hear her at first. Then she noticed that
everyone was staring at her expectantly, and she blinked.
"What?"

"I said, what are you going to wear?"

"Wear?"

"To the After Roundup Dance at the Grange Hall? It's
this Saturday night."

"Oh. I'm not going."

"What do you mean, you're not going. Of course you
are. We're all going."

"No, you don't understand. I never go to these things.
I haven't since I was fifteen." She didn't bother telling
them that Seamus had disapproved and forbidden her to
attend.

"Then it's high time you did," Kate insisted.

"No, I—"

"Willa," Zach said her name softly, and her gaze snapped to meet his. He was watching her, his green eyes steady and glittering with some deep emotion. "We're trying to build some goodwill and rapport with our neighbors and overcome Seamus's reputation around here. For that reason it's important that we all attend the Grange dance and socialize."

"But...but I don't have anything to wear." Though the classic female complaint, in Willa's case it was true. Other than the wool skirt and sweater she'd bought on impulse months ago, and the black dress she kept for funerals, the only thing in her closet were jeans and shirts.

"Is that all?" Maude Ann laughed. "Trust me, sweetie, that's a problem we can fix in no time with a quick shopping trip to Bozeman or Helena."

"No, really, I couldn't."

"C'mon, Willa, it'll be fun," Kate urged. "We'll go tomorrow, just the three of us."

"And an escort," all three men stated in unison.

"There. All done." Maude Ann stepped back and studied her handiwork with a satisfied smile.

Kate came rushing into Willa's bedroom from the hall. "Here, I finally found the necklace I was looking for. See, it'll will be perfect with your dr—" She stopped short, staring. "Oh, my. Willa, you look gorgeous."

"The's boo-ti-ful," Debbie declared dreamily. "Ithin't the, Jennifer?"

"Uh-huh. Just like a princess."

Leaning against either end of Willa's dressing table, elbows propped on the top and chins resting in their hands, the two little girls gazed at her in wide-eyed admiration. Lying stretched out on her belly across the bed, Yolanda did the same.

Willa stared at her reflection in the mirror. She barely recognized herself.

The "quick" shopping trip to Helena had turned into a whirlwind, all-day spree that had resulted in her being outfitted with a whole new wardrobe. Trying to resist Maude Ann and Kate in a shopping mode was pointless, Willa discovered. It was like trying to tame twin tornadoes with your bare hands.

They had simply overwhelmed her, dragging her from store to store, department to department, bullying her into trying on mountains of clothes. Willa had never seen anyone sort through racks with that kind of concentration and speed.

The two women worked as a team. While one helped her in and out of one outfit after another, the other kept bringing more and more things for her to try on, and each one was given a critical once-over by both women.

They hadn't stopped at clothes, either. They had dragged her around stores buying shoes, purses, jewelry, makeup, perfume, scarves, even a hat with a little veil hanging from the broad brim, though where in the world she would ever wear such a thing, Willa didn't know.

Then today she had been in the middle of giving Yolanda a riding lesson when Kate and Maude Ann had descended on her and dragged her inside, declaring it was time to get ready for the dance. Willa had protested that she didn't need four hours to shower and change her clothes, but she hadn't reckoned on Kate and Maude Ann.

The two women had hustled her straight into the shower, and when she'd stepped out she'd discovered that the serviceable, plain cotton undies she had laid out to wear had been replaced by a pair of bikini panties and a strapless bra made of scraps of black silk and lace. Kate and Maude Ann had then bullied her into donning a pair of outrageously sexy, strappy, red high-heeled sandals and her new silk robe.

Then the beauty regime had begun.

Willa had endured a facial, a manicure and a pedicure. She was lotioned and perfumed and her eyebrows plucked. Kate piled her hair on top of her head in an elegant arrangement with several tendrils hanging loose around her face and neck. When she was done, Maude Ann went to work with the array of new cosmetics that she had been cajoled into buying the day before.

The result was the stunning creature staring back at her from the mirror.

"Okay, time to get dressed. Stand up."

Still fascinated by her new look, Willa obeyed Maude Ann's command, docile as a lamb, and the next thing she knew the women stripped off her robe and slipped a little wisp of a red dress over her head and zipped it up.

Held up by two tiny straps, the dress hugged her upper body like a second skin before flaring out from her waist to fall in billowy folds around the middle of her calves.

Willa stared at her reflection, stunned. She had never dreamed she could look so elegant and attractive, or so...so...sexy.

Kate slipped the necklace around her neck and fastened the matching gold earrings in her lobes, then stepped back with a self-satisfied grin. "There. Perfect."

"Yes, and I have a gold-and-black evening shawl that will be the perfect wrap with that dress. Willa, honey, you're going to knock 'em dead tonight."

"Okay, we'd better get a move on. The men are downstairs, straining at the bit to leave. Maudie and I took care of our makeup and hair earlier, so just give us a minute to slip into our dresses and we'll all go down together.''

The reaction Willa received was worth every second of the torture Kate and Maude Ann had put her through.

The men were standing at the foot of the stairs when they descended. J.T. and Matt complimented their wives lavishly, but when they caught sight of her they both did double takes and their jaws dropped.

Willa barely noticed. She was aware of only Zach. He stared at her with an almost predatory intensity, his green eyes sizzling as they ran slowly over her, from the top of her fabulous up-do all the way down to her red-tipped toes peeking out of the strappy high-heeled sandals, then back again.

''Wow, Willa, I'm so used to seeing you in jeans I hardly recognized you,'' J.T. said. ''You look great.''

''Yeah,'' Matt agreed. ''You clean up real good, kiddo.''

Kate giggled and Maude Ann rolled her eyes. ''Matt, honestly.''

''What? What did I say?''

''Ignore these two bozos.'' Zach stepped forward and took her hand. ''You're beautiful,'' he said softly.

While her heart started beating in a snare-drum roll, Willa smiled shyly and murmured a quiet, ''Thank you.''

''Well, if we're all ready, shall we go? We can all ride together in the van.''

''Thanks, Maudie, but I'll take my truck, just in case any of us wants to leave early. Willa and I will follow you.''

Chapter Eleven

Zach didn't give her a chance to object. Taking the evening shawl from her, he draped it around her shoulders, placed his hand against the small of her back and ushered her out the door.

Which was just as well, Willa thought, sitting in the passenger seat of Zach's truck, watching him skirt around the front. She didn't know what she would have said, or even if she would have had the strength to object. The truth was, she wanted to be with him.

Zach climbed in behind and wheel and started the engine. While they waited for the others to get into the van he turned those steady green eyes on her. "You comfortable?"

Lord, no, she thought. How in heaven's name could she be comfortable, when she was tense as a drawn bow? "Yes. I'm fine, thanks," she lied.

The Grange Hall was only about five miles south of

the ranch entrance, halfway between the Rocking R and town, for which Willa was profoundly grateful. What in heaven's name had possessed Zach? He had been adamant about keeping his distance from her, and all summer, except for a few sultry looks, he had kept that vow. Now he had practically kidnapped her.

They made the short drive in silence. Zach was in one of his intense moods, and Willa was so confused and excited she was tongue-tied and in no shape to carry on a conversation. In any case, she had no idea what to say to him.

At the Grange Hall he parked beside the van and cut the engine. When he made no move to get out, Willa glanced his way and found that he was staring at her through the fading light. Instantly her nerves began to jump.

"You really are beautiful."

The husky murmur and the heat in his eyes rendered her mute. All she could do was stare back at him, mesmerized.

Next to them, the others climbed out of the van and slammed the doors, and the spell was broken. Without a word, Zach baled out of the truck and came around to her side.

Inside the hall the women were left standing alone while the men took their wraps to the coatroom. Maude Ann immediately took advantage of the opportunity and nudged Willa in the ribs.

"Zach is certainly being masterful tonight," she said with a teasing grin. "I think he's smitten."

"Oh, no, you've got it all wro—"

"Willa?"

She turned and saw a group of young men around her age approaching.

"It is you. See, guys, I told you it was Willa." He flashed her a grin. "Remember me. I'm John Finley. We went to school together."

"Actually, we all did," one of his buddies inserted. "I'm Bobby Lehmann, and this is Travis Howard and Neil James."

"Of course I remember you. Good grief, it's not as though I've been gone these past eight years. I see all of you in town from time to time."

"Yeah, but not looking the way you do now," Travis blurted.

Their dumbfounded expressions brought a wry smile to Willa's lips. When they had attended school together she had not been one of their crowd and none of them had given her so much as a second glance. Granted, that had probably been because she was Seamus's stepdaughter and he had kept her so confined. Still, their lack of interest had hurt.

Before she could introduce Kate and Maude Ann, John Finley, who had always been the most aggressive of the four, stepped closer and smiled. "How about it if you and I get reacquainted while we dance?"

Taking her acceptance for granted, he reached for her hand, but before he could make contact Zach's fingers clamped around his wrist. "Forget it, fella. The lady's with me."

John looked as though he was about to challenge the claim—until he met Zach's stare. "Hey, sorry, man. I didn't know. I just wanted to chat with an old friend, that's all."

"No harm done." Zach released him, and the four men turned away and disappeared into the crowd.

"You know, Zach, if you want to build a rapport with

our neighbors, that's not exactly the way to go about it,''
Maude Ann drawled.

"He'll get over it."

"What's up? Did we miss something?" J.T. asked as
he and Matt joined them.

"Not really." Zach took Willa's elbow. "Let's
dance."

"I'm sorry, I can't." She gave him an apologetic look.
"I don't know how to dance. I never had an opportunity
to learn."

"Then it's time you did. C'mon, I'll show you. It's
easy."

"No, Zach, really, I can't." Panic fluttered in her
chest, but he ignored her protest and tugged her toward
the dance floor.

"Zach—"

"Just relax and follow my lead," he said, turning her
into his arms. "You'll do fine, I promise."

Instead of assuming the normal stance, he wrapped
both arms around her waist and pulled her close, and at
the first contact with his body Willa was lost.

With a sigh, she closed her eyes and rested her cheek
against his chest.

His hands roamed up and down her back, molding her
to him from shoulder to thigh. Willa shivered and gave
herself over to him as he began to sway in rhythm with
the slow music.

He was right, she discovered. It was easy. Their bodies
moved together as though they were one person. The
country and western song had a heavy, sensual beat, and
as the singer crooned out the crying lyrics of love lost, a
tingle shuddered through Willa.

The feel of Zach's body pressed against hers, moving
to the provocative rhythm, was so erotic she felt as

though she were melting. His body was warm and wonderfully firm, and the clean scent of him surrounded her, making her senses swim.

Zach lowered his head and rested his chin against her temple, and Willa sighed again and snuggled her cheek against his chest. Dear Lord, this felt so good, so right.

The song ended and another began, this one faster. Instead of releasing her, as she expected, he swung her into the dance, twirling her around the floor in step with the energetic beat, leaving her no choice but to follow.

Willa had no idea how long they stayed on the floor or for how many dances. She didn't care. Dreamily, she was aware of the other couples gliding by, of the looks she and Zach were receiving, but they didn't matter. Often one of the couples would be Kate and J.T., and now and then, during the slow dances, Maude Ann and Matt, but even they registered on her consciousness only remotely. Willa's whole world had been reduced to just her and Zach. She floated through the evening on a cloud of happiness and pleasure, her body vibrating with a delicious excitement.

Suddenly the music stopped and the band leader whooped, "Okay, guys and gals take your places. It's time for a *line dance!*"

Easing Willa back a half step, Zach raised an eyebrow, but she laughed and shook her head. "I don't think I'm ready for that yet."

"Okay, I guess you've earned a break." He wrapped his arm around her waist and led her off the floor.

When they reached the sidelines Willa's nerves began to jump again. Now what? she wondered. How did one behave with a man after they had practically made love on a dance floor? Or perhaps she was making too much of it. Maybe Zach danced that way with all women. The thought didn't set well, but she had to face that possibility.

Suddenly she felt tongue-tied and awkward. She had no idea what to say or what to do with her hands, but Zach solved the problem for her.

"Would you like something to drink? I think they have punch and beer."

"Yes, please. Punch would be lovely."

He touched her cheek and looked into her eyes, and the proprietary gleam she saw there sent a thrill rocketing through her. "I'll be right back," he murmured. "Don't go away."

"I won't."

Floating on air, Willa watched him walk away. Winding his way through the crowd toward the drinks table on the other side of the hall, Zach stood head and shoulders above most of the other men, and to her eyes he was by far the handsomest.

"Haven't you made a big enough spectacle of yourself without drooling over that bastard?"

Willa jumped and swung around. "Lennie. I didn't see you there."

Flanked by two of his friends, Lennie Dawson leaned against the wall a few feet away, glaring at her.

He straightened and stalked over to her. Up close she saw the wild look in his eyes and uneasiness trickled down her spine. He was simmering with rage.

"Did you think I wouldn't be here? That I wouldn't see you hanging all over that Mahoney character? Flaunting yourself in front of him?"

"I wasn't—"

"Don't lie to me. I heard all about that night you spent with him up in the mountains," he snarled. "The way you kept turning me down, I figured you were just playing hard to get, so I backed off to give you a little time to come to your senses. And while my back is turned you start cheating on me with one of Seamus's bastards. Just like the old man wanted.''

Willa sucked in a sharp breath, but before she could deliver the blistering set-down that was on the tip of her tongue, Lennie raged on.

''Just look at you,'' he sneered. ''You got yourself all floozied up for him, didn't you? You look like a painted slut.''

''Why you rude, egotistic, overbearing twit. I don't have to stand here and listen to your insults.'' She tried to walk away but he stepped in front of her.

''I'm not through talking to you.''

''Too bad, because I'm through listening. Get this through that thick head of yours, Lennie. What I do and with whom I do it is none of your business. I am *not* interested in you. Never have been, never will be. Not if you were the last man on earth.''

Rage contorted his face. ''You bitch.''

Pain exploded in Willa's cheek as Lennie struck her across the face. Willa felt hands grabbing her to keep her from falling and heard the shocked gasps and murmurs from the people nearby, but before she could recover her balance Zach stepped between her and Lennie and smashed his fist into the other man's face.

''Hey!'' Lennie's buddies yelped.

The blow sent Lennie flying backward. He landed hard on his backside at the feet of his friends, blood gushing from his nose.

Kate and Maude Ann pushed their way through the crowd and hovered protectively over Willa. ''Are you all right?'' both women asked.

Lennie struggled to his feet with the help of his cohorts. Wiping his bloodied nose on his shirtsleeve, he looked over the top of his arm at Zach with pure hatred. "C'mon, guys, let's get him," he snarled.

"Need any help?" Matt and J.T. stepped forward, flanking Zach on either side an instant before Lennie cut loose with a growl and he and his friends charged.

After that, everything happened so quickly it was almost a blur.

Zach blocked Lennie's blow with one arm and with his other fist delivered a punch to his stomach that doubled him over. J.T. elegantly ducked his man's first swing, sidestepped the second and felled him with a karate chop to the back of the neck as he stumbled past. At the same time Lennie's other friend came at Matt swinging an empty beer bottle, but a cane whack across his forearm sent the bottle tumbling to the floor and dropped the man to his knees, holding his arm and howling in pain.

Before any of the downed trio could move, Zach, J.T. and Matt jerked them up by the backs of their shirt collars, bundled them out through the open double doors of the hall and tossed them down the steps. Lennie and his pals landed in a tangled heap in the gravel-and-dirt parking lot.

Zach stared down at Lennie, his eyes glacial. At his sides his hands curled and uncurled, again and again. "I'm going to count to ten, Dawson." His voice grated from between clenched teeth. "If you're not out of here by the time I'm done I'm going to whip your sorry butt from here to Clear Water and back."

"That's…that's assault!" Lennie blustered. "I'll have you arrested!"

"One. Two."

"You all heard him," Lennie cried, addressing the

crowd that had gathered behind Zach and his brothers. "He threatened me."

"Three."

"Threat? What threat? I didn't hear anybody threaten Lennie, did you, Harvey?"

"Uh-uh, not me."

"Me, either," several others chimed in.

"Four. Five."

"You dirty little coward," another man jeered. "You're the one who started it all."

"Six."

"That's right. If anyone files assault charges it oughta be Willa."

"Seven."

"All right! All right! We're going."

"Eight. Nine."

The three men scrambled to their feet and nearly fell over one another hobbling across the parking lot for Lennie's pickup.

Within seconds the red truck careered out of the parking lot, sending up a shower of gravel, then burning rubber as it took off down the highway toward town.

Zach turned and began pushing his way through the crowd amid a flurry of compliments and back-thumping. Following him, Matt and J.T. received the same treatment.

"I'd like to shake you fellas' hands. He had it coming."

"Good job. Lennie Dawson ain't nothin' but a bully."

"That's right, he's been running roughshod over folks hereabouts for years."

"About time he got his comeuppance. Those friends of his, too."

Zach accepted the praise with gritted teeth and kept

moving. ''Thanks, but if you'll excuse me, I need to see about Willa,'' he said over and over with an edge of impatience.

He found her sitting on the sidelines between Kate and Maude Ann, holding a wet cloth to her cheek and looking shaken. A cluster of curious women fluttered nearby.

Zach hunkered down in front of her and took her free hand. ''How bad is it?''

''I'm okay. Really,'' she insisted automatically. Willa did not quite meet his eyes, and he realized that she was more humiliated than hurt.

''Her cheek is bruised, but I don't think the bone is broken,'' Maude Ann supplied.

Zach bit off a shocking curse, then shot to his feet, pulling Willa up with him. ''I'm taking her home.''

''Good idea,'' J.T. agreed.

''Yeah, we'll all go,'' Matt stated, but when he cupped Maude Ann's elbow to lead her out she held back.

''Whoa. There's no reason for us all to leave. I'm sure that Zach can look after Willa just fine.''

''I agree with Maudie,'' Kate said.

Their husbands gaped at them. ''You want to stay? After what just happened?'' Matt demanded.

''Of course. Darling, it's all over now and the evening is young.'' Now that the excitement was over the band had started playing again and Maude Ann nodded toward the couples who were beginning to take to the floor. ''Besides, Kate and I want to dance some more. Don't we, Kate?''

''Oh, yes. Definitely.''

''Good, that's settled then. Have a good time.'' Hooking his arm around Willa's waist, Zach wasted no time leading her away.

Matt and J.T. gaped at their wives with identical bewildered expressions.

"I swear, Maudie, I've never known you to be insensitive. That poor girl has been traumatized and hurt. I would think that you of all people would want to comfort her."

"Yeah, you, too, Kate," J.T. added. "It's not like either one of you to think of yourself first."

The women exchanged a look and rolled their eyes.

"Poor darlings. They really are clueless, aren't they?"

"Totally," Kate agreed.

"What does that mean? Clueless about what?"

Maude Ann patted Matt's cheek. "Kate and I aren't being selfish, darling. Or insensitive. Actually, we're doing Willa and Zach a favor. For heaven's sake, hasn't either of you noticed what's going on between those two? There's enough heat between them to melt a glacier."

The two men looked thunderstruck.

"Are you telling us…"

"I don't believe it!"

The brothers looked at each other and shook their heads. *"Willa and Zach?"*

On the drive home Zach gritted his teeth and silently cursed Lennie Dawson. He still itched to throttle the little weasel. Unconsciously, his fingers squeezed the steering wheel as though it were Lennie's neck.

He had been returning with a cup of punch for Willa and a cold brew for himself when he saw the little creep pull back his hand and slap Willa. Zach knew the image was burned into his brain forever. He couldn't remember ever being so angry.

He only wished he had done more to the bastard than punch him, he thought, tightening his fingers around the steering wheel once again. Dammit, no one hit a woman in his presence. Especially not this woman.

He glanced at Willa, and his rage spiked anew. She sat huddled on the far side of the bench seat in a defensive posture with her arms folded over her middle, her face turned away, gazing out the passenger window at the dark night. The blow she took had knocked her elegant hairdo loose, and now it listed to one side and sagged over her right ear.

"You okay?"

She spared him only the briefest glance before turning back to the window. "Yes. I'm fine."

"Does your cheek hurt?"

"No. Not anymore."

Zach sighed and turned the truck in at the ranch entrance. Ever since leaving the Grange Hall he'd gotten the same type of uncommunicative response whenever he spoke to her. For the rest of the drive along the twisting, turning ranch road he remained silent, as well.

Zach parked the pickup out back and they entered the house through the kitchen. The instant they stepped inside, Willa murmured a quiet, "Good night," and headed for the front hall and the stairs, but he put a hand on her arm and stopped her.

"Willa, wait. Let me take a look at your cheek."

"That's not necessary. It's okay."

"Humor me."

Only the dim glow of the light above the stove that Maria had left burning for them illuminated the room. Zach flipped on the overhead light and cupped her face with both hands and tilted it up. Frowning, he inspected the red mark on her left cheek. "It's red but the skin isn't broken." He lightly touched the puffy area with his forefinger. "Does that hurt?"

Willa shook her head.

Merely looking at the angry red splotch brought Zach's anger rushing back. "Dammit, why did he hit you?"

"Lennie has a bad temper."

"Yeah, so you said before. But what set him off to-night?"

"Does it matter?"

"It sure as hell does to me. So tell me."

For a moment he thought she wasn't going to answer. Then she hitched one shoulder. "He was jealous. Of you."

"I see." Zach's thumbs stroked along her jaw, the tender underside. "And does he have reason to be?"

The deep timbre of his voice sent a shiver of longing through her. Willa stared at the plaid pattern of Zach shirt. His nearness was having its usual effect on her system, making her head swim and her pulses pound and filling her with trembling awareness. She wanted so much to lay her head on his chest and feel his arms enfold her again, but she didn't dare.

All evening she had been floating in a foolish, rosy-colored dream, but Lennie's sudden appearance had brought her back to earth with a thud, reminding her that a future with Zach was not in the cards.

"Willa?"

She tried to turn her head away, but he wouldn't let her.

"Look at me," he commanded in a husky whisper.

There was no place to go, no place to hide. She couldn't even summon up a spark of defensive anger. Defeated, she slowly raised her head and looked at him helplessly, knowing that all she was feeling was there in her eyes for him to see.

Something flickered in the green depths of his eyes,

something hot and intense. She felt his sudden stillness, the faint tremor in the hands cupping her face.

"Willa." This time he whispered her name like a caress. He examined her face, feature by feature, then his gaze dropped to her mouth, and his eyes grew heavy-lidded as his head tilted to one side and began a slow descent.

Watching him through the screen of her lashes, she waited, her heart pounding, wanting his kiss so much she could barely breathe, and at the same time aching with sadness at the futility of it all.

As his lips closed over hers, Willa moaned and stepped into the kiss, wrapping her arms tight around his lean middle.

Releasing her face, Zach slid his arms around her and pulled her tightly against him. All the quivering awareness, all the pent-up longing that had been building between them throughout the evening, throughout the long, busy spring and summer, exploded. He kissed her deeply, passionately, as though he would devour her.

Willa responded in kind, holding nothing back, greedily giving and taking all the pleasure she could in these few glorious moments, knowing that all too soon it would be taken from her.

Her hands clutched his back, roamed frantically over the broad expanse. Innocently, driven almost mad by the need to touch him, she snatched the tail of his shirt loose from his jeans and slipped her hands underneath. With a sigh of satisfaction she ran her palms over his bare flesh, glorying in its warmth, its firmness, her fingers alternately clutching and kneading.

A low groan vibrated from Zach's throat and he tore his mouth from hers. "I want you," he rasped. "Dear heaven, how I want you."

"I—I want you, too."

"Then come upstairs with me. Now. Let me make love to you."

The husky words vibrated with so much passion a shiver rippled through her. "I want to, Zach, but…how can we, when this is probably what Seamus planned?"

"The devil with Seamus. I've been giving this a lot of thought. Hell, I've hardly thought about anything else since that night in the line camp. I finally realized that if we deny this thing between us just because we suspect the old man plotted to get us together, then he's still controlling our actions, and we end up hurting only ourselves. It would be like cutting off your nose to spite your face.

"This has nothing to do with Seamus, or this ranch, or with the two of us being in close proximity day to day. It's not as though you're the only female in the area. I've met a few others since I've been here. I even took a couple of them out.

"I tried to tell myself that I just needed to be with a woman. Any woman. That if I started seeing someone else I would stop thinking about you constantly."

Hurt coursed through Willa. Merely suspecting that he was seeing someone else, she had suffered searing jealousy every night that he'd gone into town, but knowing for certain, hearing him admit it, was so much worse.

"I see," she said, her voice frosty with hurt. "In that case, maybe you should be asking one of those women to sleep with you." She tried to pull away but he grasped her shoulders and refused to let her go. Willa turned her head away, refusing to look at him.

"Willa, listen to me. It didn't work. Nothing happened. I didn't want either of those women. They both let me know that they wanted to go to bed with me, but I wasn't interested. And do you know why?''

She gazed at him warily out of the corner of her eye, her expression still mulish and distrustful. ''Why?''

''Because they weren't you.'' Crooking his finger under her chin, he turned her face toward his again. He looked into her eyes, and his voice deepened. ''It's you I want. Only you.''

Hope fluttered in her chest. She searched his face, his eyes, and all she saw there was unflinching honesty.

''To hell with Seamus and his plotting. This is just me wanting you and you wanting me,'' he continued in the same low tone.

Happiness began to percolate, effervescing from somewhere deep inside Willa like tiny champagne bubbles. Slowly her mouth curved into a smile and she slid her hands up over his chest and clasped them behind his neck. ''Take me upstairs, Zach.''

Before all the words were out of her mouth he swooped her up into his arms. Willa gazed at his determined profile, her heart thudding, excitement and dread nearly suffocating her. She had to tell him. He had a right to know. She had to.

Zach shouldered open the swinging door and strode into the hall, and when he'd gained the foyer he took the steps two at a time.

He did not slow his pace until they were inside his room. Coming to a halt beside the bed, he looked deep into her eyes. ''Are you sure this is what you want? If not, say so now. I'm not sure I'll be able to stop if we go on.''

Tell him. You have to tell him, now before it's too late. ''Zach, I...there's something you should know. I...''

''Yes?''

"I…" She gazed at his rough-hewn face, flushed with passion, the desire blazing in his eyes—for her—and instead of the words she intended to say she answered his question, truthfully from her heart. "I want you to make love to me. I've never been more sure of anything in my life."

He pressed a quick, hard kiss on her mouth, and placed her on her feet. Willa was so nervous her knees were weak, and when he slid his hands over her shoulders and up the sides of her neck she shivered. "You looked beautiful tonight," he whispered. "But I've been wanting to do this all evening."

She felt his fingers in her hair, and a second later the pins scattered across the floor and what was left of her elegant hairdo came tumbling down. He picked up handfuls of the slippery strands, lifted them, let them slide through his spread fingers and cascade around her shoulders and back like an ebony silk curtain, all the while watching as though mesmerized. "Lovely," he murmured.

Then his gaze drifted to her face, and he bent his head and kissed her again, as though unable to resist. Willa sighed and leaned in closer, then smiled against his lips as she felt his hands winnow through her hair again. Not until the kiss ended and she felt a tickle of cooler air against her lower back did she realize that he'd unzipped her dress. Instinctively, she crossed her arm over her chest to hold up the sagging bodice.

Zach smiled. "Shy? Don't be. Not with me. I want to see you. I've dreamed about this for months."

"You…you have?"

"Mmm. Watching you in those tight jeans every day has been driving me slowly out of my mind."

His words thrilled her. All this time, she thought with

amazement, while she had been almost sick with love for him, Zach had been fantasizing about her.

Gathering her courage, she swallowed hard and slid first one strap, then the other off her shoulder, all the while holding his gaze. As the dress slithered to the floor she saw the fire leap into his eyes. Trembling with nerves, she stood in front of him wearing only the sexy little black lace panties and bra and red, strappy high heels.

"Ah, sweetheart." Zach reached out and ran his forefinger along the top edge of the bra, leaving a line of fire on the pearly mounds of flesh that swelled above it. "You take my breath away."

His trailing finger reached the clasp at the center front of the bra and flipped it open, and the strapless scrap of lace fell to the floor. Willa shivered and resisted the urge to cover herself.

Then Zach's hands were there, cupping her breasts, lifting, stroking. He bent his head and kissed the soft flesh, ran his tongue around one rosy aureole, then pulled it into his mouth. Willa's head lolled back and she squeezed her eyes shut, moaning at the delicious sensation that tugged all the way to her feminine core. Had she not been clutching his shoulders for support she would have surely collapsed in a heap.

With a sudden urgency, Zach released her, and as the cool air struck her wet nipple she moaned and reached for him, but he ignored her plea and swept her up into his arms and moved closer to the bed. With one knee sunk into the mattress, he paused and looked into her eyes. His face was dark and rigid with passion, his eyes glittering like diamonds. "I meant to go slow, but I can't. Not this time. I've wanted you too long."

"Oh, Zach."

He laid her down on the mattress, and in one smooth

motion stripped away the lacy panties and sandals. Then
he went to work on his own clothes. Willa watched him,
fascinated, her heart pounding wildly in her chest.

He yanked off his boots and socks and straightened.
Gripping the lapels of his Western shirt, he gave them a
yank, and the gripper snaps came loose with a rapid rat-
tat-tat-tat-tat, like a tiny machine gun firing. He snatched
off the shirt and tossed it over his shoulder. Next he
hooked his thumbs under the waistband of his jeans and
underwear and shoved them to his ankles and kicked
them off. All the while, he watched Willa watching him.

The mattress dipped, and he came down beside her.
He took her mouth in a ravenous kiss and ran his hand
over her body, cupping her breast, sweeping his thumb
across the nipple until it stood up like a pebble, then
abandoning the soft mound to skim over the long curve
of midriff and waist and hip.

He trailed kisses over her cheek, her jaw, down her
neck. "You taste heavenly," he murmured, nuzzling the
silky valley between her breasts. He explored her navel,
her hipbone, the silky juncture where her thigh met her
body. Then his fingers found that nest of tight, black
curls.

"Zach. Oh, Zach."

Willa shifted restlessly, almost delirious. She was
swamped with so many new and wondrous sensations she
couldn't think. She could only respond, and at his silent
urging, she parted her thighs for him. Then his fingers
stroked that warm, wet part of her that yearned for him,
and she moaned and arched against his hand.

A low, desperate growl rumbled from Zach, and he
quickly moved into position between her thighs. Willa
was on fire, her body hot and feverish, but gossamer
wings of panic fluttered around the edges of her mind

when she felt his sex nudge her. She struggled to think, to remember.

"Zach...I..."

Then it was too late.

He thrust into her, and she felt a searing pain. It lasted only a moment, but she could not hold back the cry that tore from her throat.

"What the—"

Braced on his arms above her, Zach stilled and stared down at her in horror. "Willa? What—?"

He started to withdraw, but she clutched his shoulders and pleaded, "No! Don't stop. Please, don't stop."

"Dammit, Willa—"

"Please." She gazed up at him, her eyes entreating, and arched her hips, taking him deeper. "Please."

Zach gritted his teeth, but when she lifted again he was lost. With a groan he started to move, slowly, watching her face for signs of distress, but all he saw there was relief and building pleasure. He watched her eyes glaze with it, her lips part. She began to move with him, arching her hips to meet every thrust.

"Put your legs around me," he rasped.

She obeyed, and her eyes widened as he thrust deeper, faster. Her breathing became labored and rapid, and she began to turn her head from side to side on the pillow and to make small, frantic sounds.

Zach stared down at her in awe, amazed and unbearably excited by her innocent ardor. He could see the passion building in her, hear it in her desperate little moans.

"Oh. Oh. Oh, Zach. *Zach!*"

"Go with it, baby. Let go," he growled.

Willa cried out, and he felt her sweet, pulsing contractions tighten around him, and his control began to slip. Arching his back, he threw his head back and pressed deep, and a low, guttural sound of ecstacy rumbled from his throat as his own climax overtook him.

Zach collapsed on top of her and struggled to catch his breath. Willa sighed and wrapped her arms around him and ran her palms up over his back.

That feather-light touch instantly jarred him back to his senses, and he withdrew from her and rolled out of bed.

"Zach?"

Jaw set, he stalked across the room and snatched up his jeans and stepped into them. He heard a rustling sound, and from the corner of his eye he saw Willa sit up in the bed and pull the sheet up to her armpits.

"Zach?"

The anger and guilt bubbling inside him boiled to the surface and he swung on her. "A *virgin!* Why the hell didn't you tell me?" he shouted.

"I...I..."

"Dammit, you're twenty-six! How can you still be a virgin?"

"I—I told you I haven't dated much. Seamus...Seamus didn't approve. After I turned twenty-one and could defy him I had a few dates, but I never went out with any of them more than once. I think he scared them off somehow. So..." She broke off and pressed her lips together and watched him nervously.

"And you let him get by with that?"

"I—I'm sorry you're disappointed."

"Don't be ridiculous. I'm not disappointed. I'm angry. Dammit, you should have told me. I never would have touched you if I'd known you were a virgin."

"I see." Willa ducked her head and stared at her fingers, which were nervously plucking at the sheet.

"Damn." Zach paced to the window, then swung back

and plowed both hands into his hair, holding his head as though to keep it from exploding. "Well, the damage is done now. There's only one thing to do. We'll get married as soon as possible. Tomorrow, if I can arrange it."

Willa's head jerked up. "What?"

"I'll call Edward in the morning. Maybe he can pull some strings for us."

"Forget it." Tossing back the sheet, Willa jumped out of bed and snatched up her dress from the floor.

"Okay, if you don't want Edward to help, we'll go through normal channels."

Willa stepped into the dress and yanked up the zipper. "No, I mean forget the whole thing. I'm not marrying you. Period. This is the twenty-first century, for heaven's sake! I will not marry a man simply because he feels obligated to make an 'honest woman' out of me." She grabbed up her bra and panties and stomped for the door. "So you can take your proposal and stuff it, Mahoney!"

"Willa, come back here. That's not what I meant."

Ignoring him, she kept going. Zach cursed and stomped after her down the hallway. "Will you stop and listen to me. Dammit, I didn't even use any protection. You could be pregnant."

She stormed into her bedroom, and turned back, blocking the door. "If I am, then I'll deal with it. Alone."

Zach opened his mouth to argue, but she slammed the door in his face and turned the lock. He spewed a string of curses and banged on the door with the side of his fist. "Dammit, woman, open this door!"

"Stop that! You'll wake up the children. Just go away. I have nothing more to say to you."

He stopped pounding and looked down the hall toward the children's bedrooms and cursed again, this time under his breath. "All right, all right. I'm going," he said, pitching his voice just loud enough for her to hear him through the door. "But this isn't the end of it. We're going to talk about this in the morning."

He stalked back into his room and slammed the door. Too agitated to sit, his hands clenched at his sides. "Stubborn woman," he snarled at the ceiling. What the devil was the matter with her? After what they had just shared, he knew she cared for him. So why was she being so obstinate?

He reached the window and turned to pace back to the other side of the room, but after only two steps he spotted one of her shoes. Zach bent, picked up the red sandal and sat on the edge of his bed. He stared at the tiny shoe, turning it around and around in his hand. How did women walk in these things? It had a three-inch heel and was nothing more than a couple of straps and a thin sole.

The corners of his mouth twitched. It sure was sexy, though. The silvery innersole bore the impression of her toes, and he smiled wider this time, remembering the sassy red nail polish on them. When she had come sashaying down those stairs in that swirly red dress and these little-bit-of-nothing shoes it had been all he could do not to ravish her on the spot.

He'd never felt this way about a woman before. He was crazy about her, and she was tying him in knots.

Zach sighed and rubbed his thumb back and forth over one of the red straps. "Dammit, Willa, why won't you marry me?"

Chapter Twelve

Leaning back with his chair tilted on its rear legs, Zach sipped his coffee and watched the hall door over the rim of the mug.

Tying on her apron, Maria came into the kitchen through the side door that led to her quarters. When she spotted Zach, she jumped and let out a squeak and slapped her hand over her heart.

"Señor Zach! You startled me. You are early this morning."

"Yeah." He nodded toward the stove. "I already made the coffee." Immediately, his gaze returned to the swinging door. He had a hunch Willa would try to sneak out early. He'd come downstairs almost an hour ago to make sure that didn't happen.

Maria followed the direction of his gaze, and wisely went about her business, saying nothing.

Just as Zach suspected, a moment later Willa pushed

through the door. Two steps into the room she stopped short. He cocked one eyebrow. "Going somewhere?"

"What are you doing here?"

"Waiting for you." He gave her a searching look and his tone gentled. "Are you okay?"

"My cheek is fine."

"That's not what I meant. After last night, I thought you might be a little…uncomfortable."

Willa gave him a go-to-hell look and headed for the back door.

The front legs of Zach's chair hit the floor as he sprang to his feet and blocked her path. "You aren't going anywhere until we have that talk we should have had last night."

"Forget it, Mahoney. I'm leaving." She sidestepped first one way, then the other, but each time he mimicked the action. "Will you stop that!"

Maria stopped working and watched them with avid curiosity, her gaze bouncing from one to the other.

"We have to talk, Willa."

"We most certainly do not! I have nothing to say to you. Now get out of my way."

"Or you'll what? Face it, sweetheart, I'm bigger and stronger than you are, and just as stubborn."

"You wouldn't dare use brute force on me."

"Wanna bet?"

"Why you sorry, low-down, good-for-nothing—"

"Hey! Hey! What's all the racket about?" Matt demanded, limping into the kitchen. J.T., Kate and Maude Ann followed behind him. "We could hear you two yelling at each other all the way upstairs. You wake those kids before it's time for them to get up and I'll personally knock your heads together." He limped over to the stove to get some coffee. "So what's the problem here?"

"Your brother won't take no for an answer. *That's* the problem."

"What?" Both Matt and J.T. stiffened and drilled Zach with identical icy stares. The women looked stunned. "What did you do to her?"

A guilty flush crept up Zach's neck and face. "This is between Willa and me, so just stay out of it."

"I have nothing more to say to you. Get out of my way."

"Oh, no, you don't," he warned, matching her side-step again. "You're not going anywhere until we settle this."

"It is settled!" she yelled.

"Dammit, will you calm down and listen to reason?"

"Reason? *Reason!* Don't you dare talk to me about reason, you…you…throwback! Now get out of my way!"

She feinted to one side, then darted around him on the other. Zach made a grab for her arm, missed, and snagged the back of her shirt instead, jerking her to a halt. Willa shrieked and twisted around, swinging.

"Hey, that's enough! Break it up, you two." Matt stepped between the pair.

J.T. grabbed Zach's arm. "Let her go, Zach."

"Dammit—"

Matt jutted his head forward until he and Zach were nose to nose, eyeball to eyeball. "You heard him," he growled. "The lady wants to leave. Let her go. And remember, there are two of us."

Jaw clenched, Zach stared back, weighing his chances. "Damn," he finally snapped, and released the shirt. Willa shot out the door like a bullet.

"*Muchacha!* Your breakfast!"

Ignoring Maria, she kept going and ran to her pickup.

An instant later the engine roared to life, and the tires kicked up gravel when she stomped on the gas and sped out of the yard.

"Great. Just great." Zach turned cold, furious eyes on his brothers. "Don't either of you ever do anything like that again."

"Hey, bro, you can't expect Matt and me to stand by and do nothing while you manhandle a woman."

"I wasn't going to hurt her, for Pete's sake. I just wanted to talk to her."

"That's not how it looked from where we stood," Matt replied. "What the devil happened between you two last night, anyway?"

"Obviously not what we thought was going to happen," J.T. drawled.

Kate put her hand on her brother's arm. "Zach, what's wrong? You and Willa were getting along so well at the dance before that thug Lennie hit her. Why is she so upset with you now?"

"Damned if I know." Zach raked his hand through his hair and began to pace. "All I did was ask her to marry me, and she hit the roof."

"You asked her to *marry* you?" Kate stared at him with her mouth hanging open.

"Jeez, bro, isn't that kind of sudden?"

"I know. I know. I didn't intend to ask her this soon, but then after we got home last night we—" He broke off and scowled at them. "Look, just forget it, okay. This is a personal matter between Willa and me. I'll work it out."

"Oh, no, you don't. You can't just leave us hanging," Maude Ann insisted. "Besides, how can we help you if you don't tell us what the problem is? So spit it out. What happened when you and Willa got home?"

Zach glared at them, but all five just waited with expectant expressions. Finally he sighed and raked both hands through his hair again. "After we got home, I took a look at her cheek and tried to comfort her and... well...one thing led to another and—"

"Aha! So what we thought was going to happen *did* happen. Jeez, bro, you must not have done it right if she's that mad."

"Knock if off, J.T., and let him finish," Matt barked.

Zach shot J.T. a quelling look, and started pacing again. "Anyway, the thing is...it was Willa's first time. But she didn't tell me, and by the time I realized it, it was too late."

Matt gave a long, low whistle.

"Oh, man, that's a heavy responsibility," J.T. murmured, sobering.

"Yeah, well, I chewed her out for not telling me. I told her if she had I wouldn't have touched her, but the damage was done, so we would get married. That's when she hit the roof and started acting completely irrational."

Maude Ann rolled her eyes. "Big surprise. No wonder she's got her nose out of joint."

"Oh, Zach, how could you?" his sister groaned.

"What? I was trying to do the right thing."

"Jeez, bro, I sure hope you didn't say *that* to Willa."

"Man, you really bungled things." Matt shook his head and gave him a pitying look. "Hell, Zach, even I know you don't ask a woman to marry you without first telling her that you love her."

"He's right," Kate said. "No woman wants a man to marry her because he feels it's his duty. She needs to know that she's loved and wanted so much that her man can't bear the thought of a life without her."

"I can't! Dammit, I've never felt this way about any

woman before. Surely she knows that I wouldn't have ask her to marry me if I didn't love her.''

''Oh? And just how would she know that?''

Zach glared at Maude Ann, unable to come up with a reasonable answer. After a moment he heaved a sigh, grimacing. ''Ah, hell. I guess I really shot myself in the foot, didn't I? I swear to you, I was already thinking marriage, but I was going to court Willa for a couple of months first, then propose. What happened between us last night just made it seem more urgent, that's all.''

''Then I suggest you tell her that,'' Kate advised. ''But I warn you, don't be surprised if she doesn't believe you.''

''Damn. So, it's hopeless?''

''Not necessarily,'' Kate replied. ''All I'm saying is, be prepared. It's going to take a lot of effort to convince her. You may be in for a long, hard struggle.''

''I'll damn well lay siege to her if I have to,'' he declared.

Zach began to pace again, muttering under his breath about Willa's stubbornness and his own stupidity. Halfway across the room he stopped and glared at his brothers. ''Wipe those grins off your faces. You two are really enjoying this, aren't you?''

J.T.'s grin widened. ''Hey, after the grief you gave me when I wanted to marry Kate, can you blame me? Anyway, I gotta tell you, man, seeing my calm, always-in-control brother so frazzled is a pure delight.''

Except for a light in the kitchen, the house was in darkness when Willa drove into the ranch yard that night.

She parked beside the barn and went inside and flipped on the dim overhead light. Immediately Bertha whinnied and her head appeared over the front of her stall. ''Hi, girl,'' Willa murmured, stroking the mare's forehead. ''Did you miss me today?''

''It's about time you showed up.''

Willa jumped and spun around, her hand over her racing heart. ''Zach! What are you doing here?''

''Waiting for you. I knew you'd look in on your horse before you sneaked up to your room.''

''So you lay in wait in the dark to ambush me,'' she snapped.

Zach shrugged. ''Whatever it takes. So, where were you all day?''

''I went to a movie in Helena. Not that it's any of your business.'' She'd also spent hours moping in a park and more just aimlessly driving around, but she wasn't going to admit that to him. She didn't dare let him know how much he'd hurt her.

She stomped around him to the feed bin, half expecting him to reach out and grab her, but he kept his distance and merely watched her.

''By the way, I've already fed your mare.''

''Oh.'' She dropped the scoop back into the bin and closed the lid. ''In that case there's no reason for me to stay.'' She swung around and headed for the door with a determined stride.

''Willa, I love you.''

The quiet declaration stopped her in her tracks and sent a shaft of pain through her heart. She turned slowly and looked at him, her eyes accusing. ''Don't you dare say that to me. Not now.''

''I know, I know. I should have told you last night. My only excuse is, I was rattled. But it's true all the same.''

''I don't believe you.'' Her voice was low and quivering with hurt and anger. It was all she could do to not burst into tears.

"Nevertheless, I do love you. I swear it."

"Stop it! Stop saying that!"

She headed for the door again, but before she'd taken two steps Zach was blocking her path. She hadn't known a man his size could move that fast.

"Willa, listen to me—"

"No! You'll say anything to get your way, all because of some outdated code of honor. Well, I'm sorry if you have a guilty conscience about what happened, but I refuse to have a martyr for a husband. Now get out of my way."

"Okay, I will, if you'll answer just one question?"

She eyed him warily. "Oh, all right. Go ahead."

Zach looked deep into her eyes. "Do you love me?"

Willa sucked in a sharp breath. "That's not fair. You can't—"

"Do you?"

She tried to turn her head away, but he grasped her chin and refused to let her. "Look at me, Willa," he commanded in a voice like velvet. "Look at me."

When at last she raised sullen eyes to meet his gaze he went on in the same softly insistent tone. "If you can look me straight in the eye and honestly say, 'I don't love you, Zach' then I'll never bother you again. Can you say that, Willa?"

Her chin began to quiver and her eyes grew moist. "I...I..."

"Say it, Willa."

Her eyes accused him. "Why are you doing this to me?"

"Say it," he whispered.

She tried, but she couldn't force the words out. Finally she closed her eyes and shook her head. ''I...I can't.''

''Thank God for that,'' Zach exclaimed, and snatched her into his arms. He cradled her close and rubbed his cheek against the top of her head. ''If you'd said that to me it would have killed me.''

He loosened his hold just enough to lean back and look at her. Willa's heart jumped when she saw the gleam in his eyes.

''Zach, no—''

''I have to. I've nearly gone insane these past twenty-four hours. If I don't kiss you soon I'm going to blow apart.''

''You don't understand. This changes noth—''

Zach's mouth settled over hers, swallowing up the words. She tried to resist, pushing at his shoulders, but it was a weak effort at best and pointless. This was Zach, and she loved him so much it hurt.

The lushness of the kiss, its power, its seductiveness were impossible to resist. At the first touch of his lips against hers, the tingling heat coursed through her veins and set her pulse to beating like a tom-tom.

After a night of crying, followed by a day of licking her wounds, her emotions were running just below the surface, making it impossible to hold back her response.

With a groan, Willa succumbed and wrapped her arms around his neck, kissing him back greedily, hungrily, her passions soaring. Vaguely, she felt herself being lifted, carried, then they were lying together in one of the empty stalls on a pile of fresh hay. It crackled beneath them as they kissed endlessly and clung to each other, its pungent grassy scent rising all around them, filling the air with its sharp sweetness.

There was no time for foreplay, and no need. Driven

by the anxiety and raw emotions of the past twenty-four hours, their desire reached fever pitch within seconds. They worked frantically to get free of their clothes. Soon buttons and zippers and clasps were dealt with, but needs were desperate, demanding, and neither could wait long enough to strip completely. Shirts were yanked open, jeans and underwear shoved down and kicked off partway. Then, in a move as natural as breathing, Willa opened to him, and Zach sank into her silky warmth.

For several moments the only sounds in the dimly lit barn were the stomp of hooves and an occasional soft whicker from the horses stalls, the crackle of hay, and lovers' soft sighs and gasps and whispered words of passion.

The end, when it came, was explosive, eliciting a long, moaning cry from both of them. Then only the hiss of their labored breathing broke the ponderous silence.

After a moment Willa became aware of a piece of straw poking into her back and shifted. Zach raised up on his forearms and smiled down at her, one blond eyebrow cocked. "Am I too heavy?"

Their intimate position, combined with the wild disarray of their clothes and the dawning awareness that they had just made love in the barn, a literal "roll in the hay," brought a blush to her face. Barely able to meet his gaze, she shook her head.

Zach's chiseled lips turned up at the corners. All the hard edges in his face seemed softer. He had that relaxed, slumberous look of a satisfied male. Lowering his head, he placed his forehead against hers and looked into her eyes. "Tell me again that you love me."

"Zach, don't." She pushed at his shoulders. "Let me up."

He rolled off of her, and she sat up and fastened her

bra and started buttoning her shirt. Zach sat up, as well. She knew he was watching her, but she kept her gaze focused on her task.

"Willa? What's wrong?"

She glanced at his puzzled expression and sighed. "Zach, nothing has changed."

"What do you mean? You do believe that I love you, don't you?"

"What I believe is, you're a moral and honorable man who always tries to do what's right. Right now you think that means marrying me." Her jeans and panties were bunched below her right knee. She stood and stuffed her left foot into the empty pant leg and pulled them up.

"How can you say that. After what just happened?"

Willa looked up from buttoning the waistband on her jeans, her face sad. "Oh, Zach, all that proves is you desire me. That's not a difficult response to get from a man. And it's certainly not enough to convince me that we could build a life together."

Over the next few days Zach was even more quiet and distant than usual, but Willa knew he hadn't given up. He watched her with brooding intensity whenever they were in the same room or working within sight of each other.

Everyone else had picked up on his black mood and they all watched what they said and tiptoed around him as though they were walking on eggs, making the atmosphere in the house extremely uncomfortable.

The only solution Willa could think of was to avoid Zach as much as possible, and each morning she grabbed a biscuit and headed for the barn before the others gathered for breakfast.

Four days after making love with Zach the second

time, she entered the barn at daybreak and was surprised when she didn't see Pete. "Pete? Are you here?" she called as she headed for Bertha's stall.

She was halfway there when someone grabbed her from behind, clamping one hand around her waist and the other around her mouth, cutting off her instinctive scream.

Her first thought was it was Zach, but then she realized that the man was smaller.

"I've been waiting for you, bitch," Lennie growled in her ear. "You've been leaving early these past few days, so I figured this would be the best time to catch you alone."

Willa struggled to twist free, but Lennie laughed and tightened his hold painfully. "Go ahead, fight me. It won't do you any good. You're coming with me."

Revulsion shivered through her. He'd been watching her.

"The trouble was that stupid old man was always here before you left the house and you never ride out without three or four cowboys with you. But I took care of the old geezer."

Pete! Dear Lord, what had he done to Pete?

"Now we're going up into the mountains, just you and me. And when I'm done with you, Mahoney or no other man will ever touch you again. C'mon. Let's go. My truck is hidden over behind the pine grove."

At first, all she'd felt was revulsion and disgust, but now real fear coursed through her and she began to twist and buck and kick.

"Stop that! It won't do you any good. Dammit! I've got a gun. If you don't stop I'll shoot you right here—*Ow!*"

He hopped on one foot and grabbed his leg where

Willa's boot heel had made hard contact with his shin. The instant his hand left her mouth she threw back her head and screamed.

Zach was halfway to the barn when the bloodcurdling sound stopped him in his tracks, raising the hairs on the back of his neck. Willa! His hesitation lasted only a fraction of a second, then he pounded for the barn.

The screams were cut off as suddenly as they erupted, just as Zach charged inside. The sight that greeted him brought him skidding to a stop. Lennie Dawson had Willa in a choke hold, with a gun to her temple.

"Stop right there, Mahoney, or she's dead!"

"Let her go, Dawson."

"Not on your life. She's coming with me."

Zach shook his head, his eyes fixed on Lennie. "I don't think so."

"I'll shoot you if you don't get out of the way," he screamed. "Damn you! If I can't have Willa, no man will. Especially not you."

The wild look in Lennie's eyes unnerved Zach, though he was careful to not let his uneasiness show. Eaten up with jealousy, the younger man hovered on the brink of insanity.

"Zach, please go. Please," Willa pleaded. "He means it."

"No. I'm not going to let him take you. He'll have to kill me first."

"That's a better idea, anyway," Lennie raged. "This ranch should have been mine. Willa should have been mine, and you stole both of them. You deserve to die, damn you!"

"Put the gun away, Dawson," Matt ordered. He and

J.T. entered the barn and took up a position on each side of Zach.

"Get out of here!" Lennie shrieked. "My quarrel is with him, not you two."

"Anyone who tangles with our brother has to deal with Matt and me, too," J.T. informed him.

"And with us, as well," Maude Ann stated calmly. She and Kate stepped inside the barn and stood shoulder to shoulder with their husbands and Zach, flanking the men on each side.

Appalled, the three men paled. "Maudie, you and Kate get out of here. Now," Matt bellowed.

"Jeez, Kate, have you lost your mind?"

"Sis, J.T.'s right. Get out of here. If you want to help, go call the sheriff," Zach said.

"He's on his way. I called as soon as we heard Willa scream and Matt and J.T. took off for the barn. And Maudie and I aren't leaving, so forget it."

"That's right." Maude Ann looked Lennie right in the eye and tilted her chin at a challenging angle. "Mr. Dawson, you really should have given this more thought before you decided to harm any of us, because we're a family, and that includes Willa. And families protect their own."

In the distance the wail of a siren could be heard, growing steadily louder. Zach took a step forward, and the others moved with him. "Drop the gun, Lennie. It's over."

"No! No, stay back! Or I'll shoot you all!"

Zach shook his head and edged forward another step. So did everyone else. "You may get one of us, maybe even two, but you can't stop us all."

"At least I'll get you."

"Please, Zach, go back. Go back," Willa sobbed.

"Shut up!" Lennie tightened his hold on Willa's neck, nearly choking her. "I'm gonna enjoy this." Lennie turned the gun directly at Zach and took aim at his heart.

Clawing at the arm encircling her neck, Willa struggled to get air and at the same time raised her knee and kicked back as hard she could. She landed a vicious blow squarely on Lennie's kneecap. He howled and the gun's booming report echoed through the barn. Zach let out an "Oof," spun around and went down.

"Zaaach!" Willa fought like a wildcat, clawing and scratching and kicking to get free, but Lennie stubbornly hung on. Cursing her and hobbling, he raised the gun again, but before he could fire, Matt and J.T. jumped him and wrestled him to the ground, taking Willa down with them.

Calling Zach's name over and over, she wriggled and squirmed and frantically worked herself free of the pile of men and scrambled on her hands and knees to his side. "Zach. Oh, Zach," she sobbed. With Kate and Maude Ann's help, they rolled him over onto his back, and Willa cried out when she saw the bloodstain spreading on his shirt.

"Easy," Maude Ann cautioned in her calm, physician's voice.

"What in the cat hair is goin' on?" Groaning, Pete staggered out from behind a stack of hay bales, holding his head.

"Pete! Thank God. Are you all right?"

"Far as I can tell, Willie."

"What happened?"

"Well now…one minute I was dippin' up grain outta the feed bin, an' the next thing I know, I'm waking up behind the hay bales to a godawful noise what sounded like an explosion. If that ain't bad enough, now some fool's comin' with a siren wailing like a banshee. Dang, I got me a knot on my noggin you could wear a hat on. I think somebody conked me.''

"That was Lennie. And he shot Zach."

Pete frowned, focusing on Zach's prone body. "How bad is he?"

"It probably looks a lot worse than it is," Maude Ann answered. "Kate, would you go get my medical bag? It's in the armoire in our room. And call an ambulance while you're there."

The sheriff's car screeched to a halt outside the barn as Kate ran out the door. She paused just long enough to say something to him and gesture toward the barn, then ran for the house, where Maria was standing on the back porch, wringing her hands.

"What's going on here?" Sheriff Denby demanded, taking in Zach's prone and bloodied form and Lennie struggling to break free from Matt and J.T.

When they explained what happened, the sheriff smiled contemptuously at Lennie. "Always knew you'd get in real trouble someday, Dawson."

"You can kiss my—"

The sheriff slapped Lennie upside the head. "Watch your mouth in front of the ladies, boy." He pulled the younger man's arms behind his back and snapped a pair of handcuffs on him. "Lennie Dawson, you're under arrest for attempted murder, attempted kidnapping, felony menacing—"

"And assault," Pete added. "He whopped me over the head."

"And felony assault. You have a right to remain silent. If you relinquish that right…"

When the sheriff finished reciting Lennie's Miranda rights he shoved him down onto the floor and asked Matt and J.T. to keep an eye on the prisoner while he checked out his truck.

Kate raced in with the medical bag. "The kids heard all the ruckus and they're pretty upset. I told Maria to keep them at the house, and that you would be there soon."

"Thanks." With Willa kneeling beside Zach, clutching his hand, Maude Ann went to work. She unbuttoned his shirt and peeled it back, but when she began swabbing the entry wound with a sterile pad his eyes fluttered open. "Willa?"

"I'm here, darling." She squeezed his hand and smiled tearfully. "I'm right here."

"Are you...all right?"

"Yes, I'm fine. Don't try to talk. The ambulance will be here soon to take you to the hospital."

"I...love you."

Willa's lips quivered and a tear spilled over onto their joined hands. "I know. I love you, too."

Maude Ann cleaned out the wound, applied antiseptic and packed it with sterile gauze. Zach groaned when she and Kate rolled him onto his side. "The good news is we won't have to dig out the bullet. It went straight through. And it doesn't appear to have hit any artery or major muscle."

The sheriff came back into the barn carrying several plastic evidence bags. "Looks like Lennie here is your vandal. I found this in his truck—yellow spray paint, butchering knives, dynamite, and a hide with your brand on it."

"I don't get it, Dawson. Why try to run us off? What did you have to gain?"

Lennie gave Matt a surly look. "You mean beside the satisfaction of hurting your brother? That's easy. Money.

Edward Manning paid me five thousand up front, and I was to get another ten when the bunch of you turned tail and ran.''

''I *knew* something was fishy about that guy,'' Matt declared. ''I *knew* it. I had my suspicions about him from the moment we met him.''

''Well, I for one think he's lying,'' Sheriff Denby said. ''I mean, c'mon. Edward Manning is a well-known and respected man in this state. Seamus trusted him implicitly. Hell, he was the only one the old man did trust. Manning is also a wealthy man. He inherited a fortune plus a successful law firm from his old man.

''Not only that, for years he's been positioning himself to make a run for the governor's office. Some say he's going to throw his hat into the ring the next election. Why would he risk all that when he's got nothing to gain by running you off the ranch? No, I think our boy Lennie here is just blowing smoke.''

''I'm telling you, I was acting under orders from Edward Manning. He said get rid of at least one of Seamus's heirs, and to use any means necessary to do it.''

''Now why would Mr. Manning do that?'' the sheriff demanded.

''I don't know. You think he'd tell me? I just do his dirty work.''

''Then it's your word against his.''

''I'm telling you, I'm not taken the fall for this alone. I was acting under orders from Edward Manning!''

''Yeah, yeah.'' The sheriff hauled Lennie to his feet and gave him a shove. ''C'mon, get moving. I got a nice cell in town with your name on it.''

''Sheriff, hold on,'' Matt said. ''Look, I'm not trying to horn in on your territory or step on anyone's toes, but would you mind if I do some checking on Manning on my own? Just to satisfy my own curiosity?''

''I'm telling you, it's a waste of time. But, hey, if you want to give it a shot, be my guest.''

Two days later Willa sat beside Zach's hospital bed watching him doze, when the Dolans and the Conways walked into the room.

''How's he doing?'' J.T. whispered.

Zach's eyes fluttered open. ''I'm okay.''

''Are you sure?'' Kate studied him worriedly. ''You still look pale to me.''

''Don't fuss, sis. I'm fine. Or at least I will be when they let me out of here.''

''He's cranky because they've been keeping him sedated,'' Willa supplied, chuckling.

''I wanted to talk to you,'' he growled. ''But they've kept me so groggy I haven't been able to string two coherent sentences together.''

''Well, cheer up,'' Maude Ann said. ''I spoke to Dr. Bailey, and he told me if there is no sign of infection in your wound, you can go home tomorrow.''

''In the meantime, here's something that should cheer you up.'' Matt tossed a file folder onto Zach's bedside tray.

''What's this?''

''The scoop on Manning. At face value, he appears to be exactly what everyone assumes—a wealthy, successful attorney with a bright future ahead of him. I did some digging, though, and found out the man is broke.''

''How can that be? What about his father's fortune and the law firm? And the retainer he gets from the Rocking R is nothing to sneeze at.''

''It seems our friend Manning has expensive tastes. He

likes to run with the big boys. The movers and shakers. Thanks to a series of bad investments and his extravagant spending, Edward has lost the fortune his old man left him. To maintain his lifestyle and keep up appearances, he's borrowed heavily.

"With his political ambitions within reach and his back to the wall financially, he's desperate for money.

"If we were to forfeit the ranch it would be sold in a sealed-bid auction, and Edward would be solely in charge of the whole thing. It would be a simple matter for him to rig the bidding in favor of his buyer. I suspect he stood to receive a hefty kickback from the sale of ranch, but even without that, his fee as executor of the trust could run into the millions annually."

"That son of a—" Zach bit off the rest of the expletive and demanded, "So do we have enough to have him arrested?"

"Yeah, but on minor charges. All he's done so far is solicit someone to harass us, and Lennie's testimony is uncorroborated. It would be his word against Edwards— a bullying vandal and would-be murderer looking to make a deal versus a well-respected pillar of the community. Who do you think a jury will believe? Even if we did manage to get a conviction, all Edward would get is a fine and a slap on the wrist.

"As to the conspiracy to commit fraud, all we've got is motive and opportunity. Without hard evidence, we wouldn't stand a chance in court. A good defense attorney will rip our case to shreds."

"So there's nothing we can do," Zach demanded angrily.

"I didn't say that. We can't send him to prison, but we can have the satisfaction of making him squirm and derail his political ambitions. In fact, J.T. and I have already taken care of that little matter."

"Yeah, you should of been there, bro," J.T. chimed in, grinning. "We paid Mr. Manning a visit this morning and laid it all out for him. We dismissed him as our attorney, of course, but we also warned him that if he even thinks of running for public office we'll file charges against him and make the public aware of his underhanded dealing. You should have seen his face," J.T. crowed. "I think that hurt him worse than a prison term would."

"Yeah, you're probably right." Zach looked at each of his brothers, gratitude and a new respect, even a hint of affection in his eyes. "Good job. And I want to thank you both for your help. You, too, Maudie and Kate. If you hadn't been there—"

"Hey, bro, you don't owe us any thanks."

"J.T.'s right." Matt gave Zach's uninjured shoulder a squeeze. "That's what brothers do. They stick together."

After Zach's family left he took Willa's hand and looked deep into her eyes, his face serious and just a touch anxious. "I think I'm awake enough now to talk."

She smiled and smoothed back a lock of hair from his forehead. "Okay."

"I seem to have a vague memory of telling you again while Maudie was patching me up, that I love you."

"Mmm, you did."

"And of you saying that you knew. Or was I hallucinating that last part?"

"No, you weren't hallucinating."

"Then you do believe that I love you?"

Willa's eyes grew moist as she gazed down at him. "Oh, my darling, of course I believe you. How could I not, when you risked your life to save me."

"Okay, now that we've got that settled, maybe I can do this right this time." He brought her hand to his mouth and pressed a warm kiss against her palm, looking into her eyes all the while. Then he pressed her hand against his heart. "I love you, Willa, and I will until the day I die."

"Oh, Zach." Her voice quavered with so much emotion she could barely speak.

"Will you marry me, sweetheart?"

Tears slipped over each of her lower eyelids and trickled down her cheeks. "Yes. Oh, yes, my love. I'll marry you."

Zach cupped his hand around her nape and brought her face down for a lingering kiss that made her heart thunder. When their lips parted, he looked into her eyes. "Soon?"

Willa laughed. "Anytime you say."

Three weeks later, on a bright October afternoon, Willa stood at her bedroom window and stared out, marveling at the people wandering through the ranch yard. In all her years at the Rocking R, there had never been this many guests on the ranch at one time, not even for her mother's funeral.

And more were arriving all the time, people with whom they did business and neighbors from miles around, new friends all, thanks to the determined efforts of Zach and his brothers to mend the fences that Seamus had destroyed years ago. There were so many guests the cowboys had taken down a section of fence and turned the home pasture into a temporary parking lot.

Willa's gaze wandered over to the meadow by the pine grove, where a flower-bedecked arch had been set up in front of two groups of folding chairs on either side of a long red carpet, and her throat grew tight with unbearably sweet emotions.

Someone tapped on her door, and a second later Kate and Maude Ann rushed in. "It's time. Tyrone and Timothy are seating the last of the guests now."

Willa smiled and picked up her bouquet and followed Maude Ann downstairs, while Kate held up her train. Pete was waiting for her in the foyer, looking scrubbed and uncomfortable in his tux, but when he saw her his faded old eyes grew misty. "Willie, girl, if you ain't the prettiest thing God ever made, I don't know what is."

She kissed his cheek, making him blush, and whispered, "I love you, too," and looped her arm through his.

Moments later Willa stood serenely beside Pete and watched her attendants, all dressed in long emerald-velvet gowns, walk down the red carpet aisle. First came little Debbie, solemnly strewing rose petals, then her bridesmaids, Jennifer and Yolanda, followed by her two matrons of honor, Kate and Maude Ann.

The stirring opening notes of "The Wedding March" sounded and, proud as punch, Pete led her down the aisle.

Every head turned in her direction, and gasps and sighs sounded all around, but Willa barely heard. Through the layers of tulle and lace, all she saw was Zach. He stood in front of the arch with Matt and J.T. and the minister, looking so handsome in his tux he took her breath away, his intense green eyes fixed on her as though willing her to come to him.

Through the misty veil, Willa glanced around—at the five children she had once resented, at Maude Ann and Kate and Matt and J.T., whom she had considered grasping usurpers, all watching her with pride and affection, waiting to welcome her with open arms into their family, and her heart overflowed.

How much had changed in the past ten months, she thought dreamily. Not just in her life, but for all of them. Zach and Matt and J.T. had forged a strong brotherly bond, the children finally had the safe and loving home they deserved, her own years of isolation and loneliness had ended and she and Kate and Maude Ann had become the dearest of friends.

And most miraculous and wonderful of all, she and Zach had found each other.

Willa and Pete came to the end of the aisle, and when Zach reached for her hand she smiled serenely at him through the veil. They had all started out at odds with one another, but now they had become exactly what Maude Ann had said they were, she thought happily. They were a family, bound together by ties of love.

* * * * *

Lovers and Other Strangers

DALLAS SCHULZE

DALLAS SCHULZE

loves books, old movies, her husband and her cat, not necessarily in that order. A sucker for a happy ending, her writing has given her an outlet for her imagination. Dallas hopes that readers have half as much fun with her books as she does! She has more hobbies than there is space to list them, but is currently working on a doll collection. Dallas loves to hear from her readers, and you can write to her at her website at www.dallasschulze.com.

For Mary Anne, Kathleen and Denise
for all the laughter, the quilting fun
and the friendship

Chapter 1

For the first one hundred years or so of its existence, the town of Serenity Falls had managed to live up to its name. It had been founded in the 1870s by a gentleman of uncertain background but considerable charisma. He liked to say he'd been called to California by a force from the stars, though there were those who suggested that the only stars involved had most likely been worn by members of a posse chasing him out of town. Whatever the reason, there was no question but that he'd ended up exactly where he was meant to be. Where else but California could a man adopt the name of Jonathan Everlasting Reconciliation and not find himself incarcerated in the nearest asylum?

Whatever his background, Brother Rec knew what he was doing when it came to laying out a new town, though there were complaints at the time about the amount of open space he insisted be incorporated into the town's design. What was the point of leaving empty fields sitting cheek by jowl with the houses? Didn't do anything but encourage mice and coyotes. Brother Rec spoke grandly of the need to retain a connection with nature, a close-up view of the good Lord's work here on earth. Folks shook their heads over this foolishness, bought mousetraps and took potshots at any coyotes foolish enough to come within rifle range. As time passed, the mice and the coyotes moved on to less hostile environs and the fields became parks, giving the town a rural quality that was considered one of its biggest charms.

In the early 1890s, Brother Rec left Serenity Falls, taking with him five thousand dollars in town funds and the mayor's sixteen-year-old daughter. The scandal rocked the community, not least of all because the mayor was more upset by the loss of the team of racing mules taken by the eloping couple than he was by the loss of his daughter. Then again, they *were* the finest mules in the county, if not in the state, and Millie Ann had been a pretty girl but not exceptionally bright so perhaps his reaction was understandable.

The town survived Brother Rec's betrayal and, over the next ninety years or so, it also survived two world wars, a depression, earthquakes both major and minor and the advent of cars, television and rap music. Through it all, it remained pretty much what it had started out to be—a smallish town with an unusually strong sense of community.

There had, of course, been crises over the years. There was the flood of '32, when boulders the size of small cars washed down out of the foothills and came to rest in the middle of town. In the midfifties, two lions escaped from a visiting circus, and citizens huddled inside their homes in fear of the ravening beasts.

The lions, possibly confused by the lack of an audience, wandered the streets for a couple of hours before allowing themselves to be recaptured.

The sixties had brought the requisite amount of turmoil—long hair, blue jeans, even a sit-in or two. But all in all, Serenity Falls had weathered the years well.

Of course, there was a time, more than twenty years back, when some citizens had thought the town might be brought to rack and ruin through the efforts of a single individual. Reece Morgan had been a newly orphaned ten-year-old when he came to live with his grandfather. For the next eight years, Serenity Falls had been considerably less serene than usual. If there was trouble, he was bound to be in the midst of it, and if he wasn't actually caught in the act, it was only because he'd just left the scene.

When he left town the day after getting his high school diploma, there was a general sigh of relief. Most folks agreed that he was bound to come to a bad end and they'd just as soon he did it somewhere else. With his departure, Serenity Falls settled back into its usual sleepy contentment.

But, small towns, like elephants, have long memories. When old Joe Morgan died and left his house to his erring grandson, transgressions more than twenty years old were suddenly news again. Those who had known Reece recalled his wild ways and shook their heads over the possibility of his return, but it was generally assumed that he would put the place up for sale as soon as the ink was dry on the title transfer.

Weeks passed. The lawn gradually turned brown under the heat of the summer sun, and the house took on a dusty, unlived-in look, but the expected For Sale sign did not materialize. Neighbors speculated on the possibility that the lawyers hadn't been able to find Reece.

As summer crept toward autumn, the speculation grew more lurid. Reece was dead. He was in prison. He was an underworld drug lord and the Feds were waiting to nab him if he came forward to claim his grandfather's house. Level-headed sorts pointed out that, according to the news and made-for-TV movies, drugs were a highly profitable business. If Reece was head of some sort of drug cartel, it didn't seem likely that he'd risk capture in order to claim a slightly shabby two-bedroom house on a medium-size lot in Serenity Falls. California real estate wasn't what it had been, after all. Besides, if the DEA or the FBI or any other set of initials was staking out the house, their presence would be known. Edith Hacklemeyer lived directly across from the Morgan place and there wasn't a secret agent living who could slip past her sharp eyes.

Eventually the speculation began to die down. There were complaints about the way the house was being let go, comments that its unkempt condition might affect property values. Edith commented acidly that it would be just like Reece to let the place go to rack and ruin out of sheer spite. He never did have any respect for property. Hadn't he once ridden his bicycle right through a bed of her best petunias? No one could tell her *that* had been an accident! No one tried. And no one offered much argument to her assertion that Reece Morgan was trouble—always had been, always would be.

By October, having the old Morgan house sitting empty had begun to seem almost normal, and most of the speculation had died down due to lack of information. But it revived quickly when Sam Larrabee's brother, who worked for the electric company, told Sam that the power was being turned on again.

The word spread quickly. Ex-con, drug lord or walking dead, it seemed that Reece Morgan was finally coming home.

Shannon Devereux frowned at the calendars laid out in front of her. She sighed and then shuffled through the stack of index cards that held information on the classes she was supposed to be scheduling and then looked at the calendars again, seeking inspiration. Finding none, she shuffled the cards a little more before resolutely picking one out.

When she bought the quilt shop four years ago, she hadn't known a thing about running her own business. She'd been looking for a focus in her life, something to fill her days and make the nights seem a little shorter. Patchwork Heaven had proven to be exactly what she needed. She felt a surge of pride as she looked around the shop. Shelves along two walls held bolts of fabric in a rainbow array of colors. Patterns and books were displayed in racks in the center of the shop. The front of the building was almost all glass, letting in sunlight and giving a pleasant view of the tree-lined street outside. At the back of the shop, where Shannon was sitting, were tables for classes, and every spare inch of wall was covered by class samples—a warm, multicolored wallpaper to entice potential students. The arrangement was both efficient and inviting.

She'd done a good job, she thought. Business had increased nicely. For the past two years, the shop had been making a small but steady profit. She wasn't likely to make it into the Fortune 500, but she was solvent and that was more than most small businesses could say. Even better, she loved her work. Most of it, anyway. She looked down at the calendars and the stack of cards and sighed. Where was a scheduling fairy when you needed one?

"You know, there are easier ways to do that." Kelly McKinnon paused next to the table, a stack of bolts in her arms.

"If you tell me that a computer would make this easier, I'm going to fire you." Shannon fingered the edge of an index card, debating whether to slot the hand quilting class on a Saturday morning or Thursday evening. And should it be January or February?

"A computer would make that a lot easier," Kelly said, ignoring the warning.

"You're fired," Shannon said without looking up.

"You can't fire me."

"Why not? You're insubordinate. That's a good reason to fire someone."

"Insubordinate?" Kelly considered the accusation for a moment and then shook her head. "I think insubordination applies only to the military."

"I don't see why they should get to hog all the best words," Shannon said, frowning.

"They're selfish pigs, aren't they?" Kelly said sympathetically.

Shannon sighed and sat back in her chair, looking up at her friend and employee. At five feet one inch tall—if she stretched a bit—with a mop of pale-blond hair and brown eyes that always seemed to hold a smile, Kelly made her think of the illustrations of pixies in old children's books. "You're sure I can't fire you for insubordination?"

"I think you'd have to court martial me instead."

"Too much trouble. You'll have to stay."

"Thanks, boss." Her job security confirmed, Kelly nodded toward the calendars. "You want me to do that for you? It's a lot easier when you can just click and drag the class names from place to place. Saves a lot of wear and tear on erasers. Why did you buy a computer for the office if you're not going to use it?"

"People have been scheduling classes for centuries without using a computer."

"You're afraid of the computer." Kelly's tone made it a statement rather than question.

"I am not," Shannon said defensively. "I just don't see the point in using it to do something that I'm perfectly capable of doing by hand. People are too dependent on computers these days."

"Well, you certainly don't have to worry about that," Kelly said dryly. She set the bolts she'd been carrying on the edge of the table and lifted the top one—a midnight-blue fabric printed with a scattering of tiny gold stars. "You never even turn it on."

"I run it at least once a week," Shannon said. "I figure that will keep its pistons clean."

Kelly slid the bolt of fabric in amongst the other blues, turning her head to grin at Shannon. "Computers don't have pistons. I'll get that," she added as the phone began to ring.

"Maybe I'd like them more if they did," Shannon muttered as she walked away.

She could put away the rest of the fabric, she thought, eyeing the bolts on the edge of the table. It wouldn't really be procrastinating if she was doing something productive, would it? She allowed herself a brief, wistful moment of self-delusion and then resolutely picked up the first index card. If she didn't get this done soon, the winter class schedule was going to be going out next spring.

She heard Kelly say, ''You're kidding!'' in a tone of breathless surprise and then tuned out the rest of the conversation. Kelly McKinnon was one of the kindest, most generous-hearted people you could ever hope to meet. She also happened to be hopelessly addicted to gossip. As near as Shannon could tell, she was the unofficial clearing house for information for the entire town.

It could have been an intolerable character flaw but Kelly's interest came without a trace of malice. She was genuinely interested in everyone—not just what they were doing and with whom but what they were thinking and feeling. Which was probably why people were so willing to tell her things they wouldn't even share with their hairdresser. Besides, Kelly was quite capable of keeping a secret. She might know where all the bodies were buried, but she rarely told anyone where to find them.

With an effort Shannon forced her attention back to the schedules. A strand of strawberry-blond hair fell forward and she tucked it absently back behind her ear. She penciled in the beginning quilt-making class on Tuesday night. Esther McIlroy was teaching that. Esther didn't mind running the cash register to handle any purchases her students made, which meant that Shannon didn't have to be here.

''You'll never believe what Rhonda Whittaker just told me!'' Kelly said as she hung up the phone.

''Don't tell me.'' Without looking up, Shannon sensed the other woman approaching from the front of the shop.

"Don't you want to know?" Kelly asked impatiently.

"Know what?" Shannon went over the penciled line a little more heavily. Tuesday was a good night to learn how to make quilts, she decided. She'd double-check with Esther to make sure it was okay.

"What Rhonda just told me," Kelly said. "Don't you want to know what she said?"

Shannon set the pencil down and looked up, her blue eyes mock solemn. "You've already told me I won't believe it, so why bother to tell me? If I want to hear things I'm not going to believe, I can watch the news."

"This is firsthand information."

"What makes you think Rhonda Whittaker is more trustworthy than Tom Brokaw? Isn't she the one who says she saw Elvis going into a room at that motel on the edge of town?"

"That was Tricia Porter," Kelly corrected her. "And it wasn't Elvis she saw, it was Paul McCartney. And she saw him at the natural foods store, buying organic barley."

"That's sooo much more believable than seeing Elvis," Shannon drawled.

"Well, I think he's a vegetarian."

"Elvis?"

"Paul McCartney," Kelly said impatiently. "I think he's a vegetarian so I guess it's not totally beyond the realm of possibility to see him in a health food store."

"Oh sure." Shannon nodded agreeably. "I bet he flies over from England on a regular basis to buy barley at Finlay's Flourishing Foods for Fitness. The name is probably known all over the world. Or maybe it's that sign out front, the one that says Authentic Foods. I mean, how could Paul resist a chance to get 'authentic' food?''

"I never have known what that means," Kelly admitted, momentarily diverted. "It sort of implies that other stores are selling fake food, doesn't it?"

"I'm surprised they haven't sued for defamation of inventory or something."

"Defamation of inventory?" Kelly's eyebrows rose in question.

"If it's not already on the books, I'm sure there's a lawyer somewhere who could make a case for it," Shannon assured her.

"Probably. But that's not the point."

"What point?"

"Precisely! We've gotten away from the point."

Laughing, Shannon dropped her pencil and leaned back in her chair. "I feel like I've fallen into an Abbott and Costello routine. You're not going to ask me who's on first, are you?"

"I'm trying to tell you what Rhonda Whittaker told me," Kelly said sternly. "And you're not making it easy."

"Sorry." Shannon did her best to look meek, but there was a suspicious tuck in her cheek and her eyes were bright with humor. "What did Rhonda tell you?"

"Reece Morgan is here."

"In the shop?" Shannon's eyes widened in surprise.

"No, you idiot. In Serenity Falls. Rhonda saw him herself. He stopped at the '76 gas station on the north end of town. Rhonda was getting gas there when this mean-looking black pickup truck pulled in."

"How does a truck look mean?" Shannon interrupted. "Did it lift its front bumper in a sneer?"

"Do you want to hear the story or do you want to ask irrelevant questions?" Kelly asked, exasperated.

"I'll be quiet," Shannon promised meekly.

"Thank you." Kelly cleared her throat. "As I was saying, a black pickup pulled in."

"A mean-looking black pickup," Shannon reminded her helpfully.

"And a man got out of it."

"Elvis?"

"Rhonda recognized him right away," Kelly continued, ignoring the interruptions.

"If he was wearing one of those spangled jumpsuits, I wouldn't think that would be very hard."

"It was Reece Morgan."

"In a spangled jumpsuit?"

"He was wearing jeans, a black T-shirt and black boots."

"No sequins?" Shannon asked, disappointed.

"Rhonda said he looked mean."

"She thought his truck looked mean, too." Shannon reminded her.

"Rhonda does sometimes let her imagination run wild," Kelly admitted. "But however he looked, we at least know he's back in town."

"Unless it's really Elvis or Paul McCartney," Shannon murmured wickedly.

Kelly shook her head. "Rhonda wouldn't have been nearly as interested in one of them. She said it was definitely Reece Morgan. They were in the same class. She said she'd have known him anywhere."

Shannon shook her head, her soft mouth twisting in a half smile. Until she moved to Serenity Falls, she'd never lived in the same place for more than two or three years. She couldn't imagine what it felt like to have lived in the same town your whole life, to be able to recognize a classmate from twenty years before.

"I never really thought Reece would come back here," Kelly said.

"His grandfather left the house to him. It seems reasonable that he'd want to go through everything himself."

"From what I've heard of his relationship with the old man, it doesn't seem likely that Reece would come back looking for mementos," Kelly said, shaking her head. "Everyone says they were pretty much oil and water."

"Is this the same 'everyone' who saw Paul McCartney eating oats at the health food store?" Shannon asked dryly.

"It was barley, and even Frank says they didn't get along." Frank was Kelly's husband. "He was a couple of years younger than Reece, but he knew him pretty well since Reece and Frank's older brother were friends. He says Reece's grandfather was a flinty old bastard."

"I can't argue with that description," Shannon said, thinking of the old man who'd lived in the house next to hers. Tall and spare with a military bearing that made no concessions to age, he'd offered her a brief, rather formal welcome when she first moved in. For the next four years, their contact had been limited to an exchange of hellos if their paths happened to cross at the mailboxes. In all that time she couldn't ever remember seeing him smile or even look as if he knew how.

"If Reece has come back to stay, you're going to be living next door to him," Kelly said, giving her a speculative look.

Shannon had no trouble reading the expression in her friend's eyes. She shook her head. "Forget it. I am not going to spy on the man just to satisfy your curiosity."

"No one said anything about spying," Kelly said, all injured innocence. "But living next door to him, you're bound to get to know him."

"I lived next door to his grandfather for four years and the only thing I know about him was that he put out the neatest piles of trash I've ever seen. I think they were color coordinated."

"Reece doesn't sound like the type to color coordinate his trash."

"It's been twenty years since anyone in this town has seen him. He could have changed."

"From hellion to neatnik?" Kelly wrinkled her nose. "Doesn't sound likely."

"Anything's possible." Shannon dropped the index cards on top of the calendars, scooped them all into a haphazard stack and thrust them at Kelly. "Here. Make yourself useful. Feed these into your magic machine and give me back a schedule."

"Aren't you in the least bit curious about Reece?" Kelly asked as she took the papers. "I mean, what if he's an escaped felon or something?"

"Right." Shannon's tone was dry as dust. "If I were an escaped felon, I'd make it a point to hide out in the one place where everyone knew me, in the one place the police would be sure to look for me, in the one place where I couldn't possibly hide my presence. And I'd drive into town, in broad daylight, driving a mean-looking truck, wearing a spangled jumpsuit and buying barley at the natural food store."

"You're getting your celebrities mixed up," Kelly

pointed out, grinning. ''Reece was driving the truck but he wasn't wearing a jumpsuit and no one has seen him eating barley.''

''It's only a matter of time.'' Shannon waved one hand. ''By the end of the day, the rumor mill will probably have him arriving in a spaceship complete with bug-eyed aliens for escort.''

Kelly laughed. ''We haven't had any alien sightings around here since Milt Farmer gave up corn liquor and found religion.''

''With Reece Morgan returning, can aliens be far behind?'' Shannon's smile lingered as she moved toward the front of the shop to wait on the customer who had just entered.

Despite herself, she couldn't help but wonder about her new neighbor. After everything she'd heard about him, she was more than a little curious to actually meet the man in the flesh. The image in her mind was a cross between a young Marlon Brando and the Terminator. What a disappointment it was going to be if he turned out to be a plump, balding accountant.

Chapter 2

Groaning, Reece rolled over and opened his eyes. This must be what it felt like to spend a night on the rack, he thought, as he inventoried an assortment of aches and pains. The last time he could remember sleeping in a bed this uncomfortable, he'd been an unwilling guest in a South American prison.

Blinking the sleep from his eyes, he stared up at the water stain on the ceiling directly over the bed. If he squinted a little, it was a dead ringer for the outline of Australia. He contemplated it with some regret, thinking of wide beaches, cold beer and tall, tanned Aussie girls in very small bikinis. Now *there* was the perfect place for working through a midlife crisis. What on earth had made him decide to come back here—where he'd spent the most miserable years of his childhood?

It was all a matter of timing, he thought as he rolled out of bed and slowly straightened his aching spine. The news of his grandfather's death had come at a time when he was reevaluating his life. A rainy night, a slick road, and he had regained consciousness in time to hear the paramedics weighing his odds of making it to the hospital alive. With the distance provided by shock, he'd pondered the irony of dying in a car wreck. He'd lived with the possibility of his own death for a long time, but he'd always assumed it would come in a more spectacular form—a bullet, a knife sliding between his ribs, a car bomb maybe. It seemed supremely ironic that death should come in the form of something as mundane as having a tire blow out.

He eventually limped out of the hospital minus a spleen and fifteen pounds, neither of which he'd needed to lose but he wasn't complaining. As the doctor had told him several times, he should consider himself damned lucky to be alive at all. It wasn't the first time he'd scraped past death by the skin of his teeth. In his line of work, it was something of an occupational hazard, and he'd lived with the possibility for so long that he didn't even really think about it anymore. But there was something about nearly waking up dead because of a car wreck that had made him stop and take a long, hard look at his life. Maybe it was the mundanity of it—the reminder that his death could be just as meaningless as anyone else's. Or maybe it was spending his fortieth birthday alone in the hospital—the sudden realization that half his life was over that made him question what he was going to do with the rest of it.

It wasn't a real midlife crisis, Reece thought as he pulled clean clothes out of his duffel bag and walked, naked, to the bathroom down the hall. In a real midlife crisis, you did stupid things like quit the job you'd had for the past fifteen years, let go of the apartment where you'd lived for almost as long, and had an affair with a woman half your age. He met the eyes of his reflection in the dingy mirror over the bathroom sink.

Hell. Two out of three and the most boring two, at that. Maybe he should have kept the job and the apartment and just gone for the affair. His mouth twisted in a half smile as he pushed back the shower curtain. Midlife crisis or temporary insanity? Looking at the grudging trickle of tepid water that seemed to be the best the shower had to offer, Reece wasn't sure he wanted to know the answer.

Shannon knelt on the lawn next to the flower bed and tugged halfheartedly at a scraggly patch of dichondra that was matted around the base of a rosebush. Generally, she gardened on the "survival of the fittest" philosophy. Any plant that couldn't survive a little competition was welcome to move to someone else's flower bed. She had neither the time nor the inclination to pamper delicate plants, and she tackled the weeds only when it began to look as if they were going to overwhelm the flowers.

She sat back on her heels and eyed the patch of ground she'd cleared. The weeds weren't really all that bad but it was such a beautiful day that it seemed a shame to spend it indoors. In early November, summer's heat was gone and the winter rains had not yet begun. The air was dry and warm and the nights were cool enough to be refreshing. Closing her eyes, she turned her face up to the sun, savoring the warmth of it against her skin. No matter how long she lived in southern California, she didn't think she'd ever learn to take this kind of weather for granted.

"Good way to end up with skin cancer."

The tart comment made Shannon jump and she stifled a curse when she realized who had interrupted the peaceful morning. Edith Hacklemeyer lived across the street. A short, thin woman on the far side of sixty, she was a retired English teacher who filled her days with gardening, quilting and offering unwanted advice to anyone who crossed her path. She was an unimaginative gardener, a mediocre quilter and a tireless busybody. Since she was both a neighbor and a customer at the shop, Shannon felt obligated to remain on amicable terms with her.

"Beautiful day, isn't it?" She chose to ignore the remark about skin cancer. One of Edith's less appealing characteristics was her ability to find the bad in everything and everyone.

"We need rain," Edith said, frowning at the crystal-clear sky.

"The rain will get here," Shannon said easily. She leaned forward to smooth the soil around a marigold.

"Ought to pull those up and put in some pansies," Edith told her, eyeing the marigold with disfavor.

"It's still blooming, and I like the flowers."

"Never cared much for marigolds. They always seemed a bit tatty looking to me but, even if I liked them, I'd pull them up. Got to get the winter bloomers in early so they can get established with the first rains."

"Mmm." Shannon made a polite, interested noise and tucked a little more soil around the marigold. The bright little blossoms seemed to smile at her and she smiled back.

"I don't envy you." Edith's attention shifted away from the flowers and her pale-blue eyes settled on the dusty black truck parked in the driveway of the house next door.

"Oh, I don't mind waiting a while to plant winter flowers," Shannon said, deliberately misunderstanding.

"I was talking about *him*," Edith said darkly. "I don't envy you having to live right next door to *him*. No telling what sort of trouble *he'll* cause."

"I don't see why he should cause any trouble at all." Shannon let her gaze rest on the truck. She'd taught a class at the shop the night before and the truck had been there when she got home around ten o'clock. Obviously, the grapevine had worked with its usual efficiency and Reece Morgan really was home. After all she'd heard about him, she had to admit that she was more than a little curious to see him in the flesh.

"His kind doesn't need a reason. Trouble comes naturally to that sort."

"You haven't seen him in twenty years. He might have changed."

"A leopard can't change its spots." Edith's tone suggested that this observation was original to her. "Mark my words, things won't be the same now."

"Maybe things could use a little shaking up." Shannon said mildly.

"Not the sort of shaking up *he'll* give them. Can't imagine why he came back here. He wasn't wanted before, and he's certainly not wanted now."

Until that moment Shannon had been reserving her opinion about Reece Morgan. Aside from a mild curiosity, she really hadn't given much thought to the man. But Edith's firm pronouncement that he wasn't welcome set her back up instantly. She had a sudden image of the sort of welcome Edith might have given to a newly orphaned boy twenty years before. And his grandfather—just how welcoming had that stern old man been? She rose to her feet in one smooth movement.

"Actually, I was thinking that it would be neighborly to invite him for breakfast," she said as she dusted her hands off on the seat of her cutoffs.

"Invite him to breakfast?" Edith couldn't have looked more horrified if she'd just announced that she was going to tap dance naked through the center of town. "You can't be serious."

"Why not?" Shannon's smile held an edge that would have warned a more observant woman, but Edith was nothing if not unobservant.

"He's a hoodlum, that's why not. He rode his bicycle through my petunias." She offered the last triumphantly, as if no more profound evidence of wickedness could be given.

"I don't think a man should be judged by a childish prank. If you'll excuse me, I think I just saw someone moving around in the kitchen," she lied.

Shannon walked away without waiting for a response. Behind her, she heard Edith's horrified gasp and then the rapid patter of her sneakers as she scurried back across the street, seeking a protective distance from potential disaster. Shannon knew the other woman would go into her house and immediately go to the front window, which gave her a clear view of the street and everything that went on there. It was that knowledge that kept her walking toward the Morgan house, even as her brief spurt of temper cooled. The last thing she wanted to do was invite a total stranger to breakfast, but she was too stubborn to back down now.

"This is what you get for letting your temper get the best of you," she muttered as she climbed the steps to the porch. "The man is going to think you're a total lunatic."

Shannon jabbed her finger against the doorbell button and heard the faint sound of chimes through the door. She could practically feel Edith's eyes boring into her back. Briefly she considered turning and waving. Such a breach of protocol would probably be enough to get her classified as a hoodlum, right next to Reece Morgan, petunia killer. The thought of Edith's horrified reaction made her smile, and the last of her annoyance evaporated.

This wasn't exactly how she'd planned to spend her morning, but she couldn't deny that she was more than a bit curious about her new neighbor. After everything she'd heard about him, she was prepared for anything from a tattooed refugee from a motorcycle gang to a Milquetoast accountant, complete with pocket protector and taped glasses.

What she was not prepared for was the six feet four inches of damp, half-naked male who pulled open the door. He must have just gotten out of the shower, she thought, staring at an impressive width of muscled chest. A solid mat of dark hair swirled across his upper body and then tapered down to a narrow line that ran across an admirably flat stomach before disappearing into the waist of his jeans. She was astonished by the effort it took to look away from that intriguing line and lift her eyes to his face.

Oh my. It hardly seemed fair that the rest of him matched the body: thick dark hair, worn slightly shaggy and long enough to brush his collar, if he'd been wearing one; sharply defined cheekbones; a strong blade of a nose; and a chin that hinted at stubbornness. Twenty years ago he might have been almost *too* good-looking.

But age and experience had added an edge to his features, refining and sharpening them to something far more potent than mere handsomeness.

None of her imaginings had prepared her for the man standing in front of her. Nor had they prepared her for the way her stomach clenched sharply in sudden awareness—a deeply feminine response to his masculinity. It had been a long, long time since she'd felt anything like it, and the unexpectedness of it had her staring at him blankly.

Reece's first thought was that he'd never seen eyes of such a deep clear blue—pure sapphire fringed with long, dark lashes. His second was that he hoped she wasn't selling anything because he had a feeling that his sales resistance might reach an all-time low under the influence of those eyes.

She didn't *look* like someone who was selling something. She was wearing a faded blue T-shirt that clung in all the right places and a pair of denim cutoffs that revealed legs that went on forever. There was a smudge of dirt on one cheek, and her reddish-gold hair was pulled back in a plain, unadorned ponytail. The stark style emphasized the fine-boned beauty of her features. He caught himself straightening his shoulders and tightening his stomach muscles in an instinctive male response. The reaction both amused and irritated him.

"Can I help you?" he asked when it began to look like she wasn't going to break the silence.

Shannon flushed, suddenly aware that she'd been staring at him like a teenager gawking at a rock star. Completely thrown off balance, she blurted out the first words that came to mind. "Would you like some breakfast?"

"Breakfast?" he said, trying to sound as if he was

accustomed to having beautiful women show up on his doorstep and offer him a meal. What a shame, he thought. She looked perfectly normal, but she was apparently not rowing with both oars in the water.

"I live next door," Shannon said, aware that the invitation hadn't come out as smoothly as she might have liked and trying to salvage the situation. "I didn't mean to sound abrupt. It's just that I wasn't expecting you."

Reece's brows rose. She sounded flustered but sane. He leaned one shoulder against the doorjamb, starting to enjoy the situation. "You knocked on my door," he pointed out gently.

"I know. But I wasn't expecting…you." She waved one hand, the gesture encompassing the six feet four inches of male standing in front of her. His brows went higher and she caught the gleam of laughter in his dark eyes. Sighing, she grabbed for the tattered shreds of her dignity. "I bet you're wondering if you should call for the men with the butterfly nets."

"The thought had crossed my mind," he admitted, and she couldn't help but laugh.

"Can I start over?"

"Go ahead."

She drew a deep breath. "I'm Shannon Devereux. I live next door."

"Reece Morgan." He offered his hand, and she took it automatically, startled by the jolt of awareness that shot up her arm at the light touch.

"I know who you are," she said as she withdrew her hand. She rubbed her fingertips against her palm. "We were expecting you."

"We?" Reece threw a questioning look past her shoulder at the empty street and Shannon cursed the easy way the color rose in her cheeks. This was what she got for letting temper and curiosity get the better of her, she thought. If she'd minded her own business instead of listening to Edith Hacklemeyer, she would still be pulling weeds and enjoying the weather. Instead, she was standing in front of the most attractive man she'd seen in a very long time, confirming his initial impression of her as a blithering idiot.

"I meant that everyone knew you were coming," she said.

"Did they?" Reece frowned uneasily. He'd spent too many years keeping to the shadows to be comfortable with the idea, but he knew there were few secrets in a small town. Besides, it didn't matter anymore, he reminded himself. It was just that old habits were hard to break. "I didn't exactly take an ad out in the local paper."

"You didn't have to. Sam Larrabee's brother spread the word." When Reece gave her a blank look, she clarified. "He works for the electric company. He saw the order to turn on the utilities."

"And *he* took out an ad in the paper?"

"No, he told Sam. And Sam told Alice—that's Sam's wife. And Alice told Constance Lauderman, who probably called—"

"Okay, I get the picture." He shook his head as he interrupted her recitation of the local grapevine. "I'd almost forgotten what this place was like," he said, looking both irritated and reluctantly amused.

"Well, it's a small town, and news does tend to get around."

"I guess it does." Reece slid the fingers of one hand through his still-damp hair.

The movement drew Shannon's eyes back to the

solid width of his bare shoulders and chest, and she felt her stomach clench in helpless awareness. She didn't know what it was about him that brought on this deeply female response. The sight of a bare male chest had never caused this kind of reaction before. It would be nice to believe it was because she'd spent too much time in the sun this morning. With an effort, she dragged her gaze upward and met his eyes.

"Anyway, that's how I knew who you were. I thought you might not have taken the time to do any shopping when you got in yesterday and might like to have breakfast at my house."

Reece rubbed his hand absently across his bare chest. She'd guessed right about the shopping. As far as he knew, the only food in the house was a package of slightly squashed Twinkies he'd bought somewhere in Arizona the day before. On the other hand, he hadn't come back here to develop a social life. He just wanted to put the house in shape to sell and maybe get himself in shape—mentally and physically—while he was at it. No matter how attractive she was, he didn't want to—

"Coffee's already made," she added, as an afterthought.

"Let me get a shirt." The promise of caffeine was too great a temptation. He still wasn't sure his new neighbor was all there, but she was beautiful and she had coffee—the combination was more than he could resist.

He disappeared into the house, and Shannon drew a deep breath and then released it slowly. *Wow.* What on earth had happened to her? It wasn't as if Reece Morgan was the first attractive man she'd met. Kelly had made it her life's work to introduce her to every single, straight, attractive male who came within range—a rapidly shrinking pool, as Kelly reminded her tartly every time Shannon turned down a date. She'd never given any of those men a second thought, had barely noticed them even when they were standing right in front of her. But this man—*this* one made her very aware of the differences between male and female, something she hadn't paid much attention to lately.

By the time Reece returned, she'd regained her equilibrium and was able to give him a casually friendly smile. Whatever she'd felt earlier, it was gone now, and if she felt a slight tingle when his arm brushed against hers, it was probably only because she had a touch of sunburn.

"I thought you could go years without meeting your neighbors in California," he said as he pulled the door shut behind him and checked the knob to be sure the lock had caught.

"In California, maybe, but not in Serenity Falls." She caught his questioning look. "You see, the town is caught in some sort of space-time-continuum warp. You know, like the ones on *Star Trek?* I think we're actually somewhere in the Midwest right now. As near as I can tell, the change occurs just as you pass the town limit sign. If you pay attention, you can actually feel the shift as the very fabric of space folds and deposits you in…oh, Iowa maybe."

"Really? I didn't notice," Reece said politely but she caught the gleam of laughter in his eyes.

She liked the way he could smile with just his eyes, she thought. Of course, so far, there wasn't much about him that she *didn't* like. *Tall, dark and handsome.* The old cliché popped into her head, and she smiled a little at how perfectly it fit him. At five-eight, she was tall for a woman and was accustomed to looking most men in the eye, but walking next to him, she felt small and almost fragile.

As if sensing her gaze, he glanced at her, and Shannon looked away quickly, half-afraid of what her expression might reveal. Distracted, she tapped her fingers against the tailgate of his truck as they walked past.

"It doesn't look particularly mean to me." She immediately wished the words unsaid but it was too late. What was it about him that caused her to blurt out the first thing that popped into her head?

"What?" Reece gave her a look that combined wariness with curiosity, confirming her guess that he had doubts about her mental health. Not that she could blame him, she admitted with an inner sigh. She hadn't exactly been at her best this morning.

"Reports of your arrival spread around town yesterday afternoon. Someone mentioned that you were driving a mean-looking truck."

"Mean-looking?" Reece glanced back at his truck and shrugged. "It's never attacked anyone, that I know of." He frowned thoughtfully. "There was a woman at the gas station yesterday. Skinny, big teeth and a face sort of like a trout. She looked at me like I was an alien with green skin and antennae sticking out of my head."

"Or Elvis in a spangled jumpsuit," Shannon murmured, thinking of her conversation with Kelly.

"No, I think she'd have been less surprised to see him," Reece said thoughtfully.

Shannon's laughter was infectious, and Reece found himself smiling with her. He wouldn't be all that surprised if it turned out that she'd escaped from a mental ward, but he wasn't going to let that stop him from

enjoying her company. Walking beside her, he was
conscious of the long-legged ease of her stride, of the
way the sunlight caught the red in her hair, drawing
fire from it.

"That was Rhonda Whittaker at the gas station," she
told him.

"Whittaker." His eyes narrowed thoughtfully as he
repeated the name. "I think I went to school with her.
She looked like a trout then, too."

Shannon laughed again. His description was wickedly accurate. Rhonda *did* look a great deal like a
trout—a perpetually startled trout.

"Careful. That trout holds a key place on the local
grapevine."

He shook his head. "I'd almost forgotten what this
place was like. Everybody always knew everybody
else's business, and what they didn't know, they made
up."

"According to Edith Hacklemeyer, no one ever had
to make up anything about you."

"Good God, is that old bat still around?" He
stopped at the beginning of Shannon's walkway and
looked at the neat white house across the street. A modest expanse of green lawn stretched from the house to
the street, perfectly flat, perfectly rectangular, cut exactly in two by an arrow-straight length of concrete
sidewalk. The only decorative element was a circular
flower bed that sat to the left of the sidewalk. It contained a single rosebush, planted precisely in the center.
The rest of the bed was planted in neat, concentric rows
of young plants, bright-green leaves standing out
against a dark layer of mulch.

"Of course she's still there," Reece answered his
own question. "The place looked exactly the same

twenty years ago. Every spring she planted red petunias, and in the fall, she planted pansies. It never changed.''

''It still hasn't.'' Shannon wondered if it was just her imagination that made her think she could see a shadowy figure through the lace curtains. She had to bite back a smile at the thought of Edith's reaction to having Reece boldly staring at her house. She touched him lightly on the arm.

''You're not supposed to do that.''

''Do what?'' He looked down at her, one brow cocked in inquiry.

''Look at her house.'' Shannon shook her head, pulling her mouth into a somber line.

''There's some law against looking at her house?'' Reece asked, but he turned obediently and followed her up the walkway.

''You're stepping out of your assigned place in the world order. It's Edith's job to watch you. It's your job to be watched.''

''I'll try to keep that in mind,'' he said, amused by her take on small-town life. ''I can't believe old Cacklemeyer is still around.''

''Cacklemeyer?'' Shannon's gurgle of laughter made him smile. ''Is that what you called her?''

''She wasn't real popular with her students,'' he said by way of answer. ''She's not still teaching, is she?''

''No. She retired a few years ago.''

''There are a lot of kids who should be grateful for that,'' he said with feeling.

''According to Edith, you committed petuniacide on at least one occasion,'' Shannon commented as she stepped around a small shrub that sprawled into the walkway. She glanced at him over her shoulder. ''She seemed to think it was a deliberate act of horticultural violence.''

"It was." His half smile was reminiscent. "She acted like that flower bed was the gardens at Versailles. If she was in the yard when I rode my bike past her place, she'd scuttle out and stand in front of it, glaring at me, like she expected me to whip out a tank of Agent Orange and lay waste to her precious flowers.''

"So you lived up to her expectations?"

"Or down to them." He shrugged. "Sounds stupid now."

"Sounds human. Hang on a minute while I move the hose," she said as she stepped off the path and walked over to where a sprinkler was putting out a fine spray of water.

In an effort to avoid staring at her legs like a randy teenager, Reece focused his gaze on the house instead. It was a style that he thought of as Early Fake Spanish—white stucco walls and a border of red clay tile edging a flat roof, like a middle-aged man with a fringe of hair and a big bald spot. The style was ubiquitous in California, a tribute to the state's Spanish roots and its citizens' happy acceptance of facades. In this case, age had lent something approaching dignity to the neat building. The front yard consisted of a lawn that appeared to be composed mostly of mown weeds and edged by two large flower beds that held a jumble of plants of all shapes and sizes in no particular order. Reece was no horticulturist but he was fairly sure that Shannon was growing an astoundingly healthy crop of dandelions, among other things.

"I don't advise looking at my flower beds if you're a gardener," she said, following his glance as she rejoined him. "I'm told that the state of my gardens is enough to bring on palpitations in anyone who actually knows something about plants.''

''What I know about plants can be written on the head of a pin.''

''Good. I may call on you for backup when the garden police come around.'' For an instant, in her cutoffs and T-shirt, her hair dragged back from her face, her wide mouth curved in a smile, her eyes bright with laughter, she looked like a mischievous child. But she was definitely all grown up, Reece thought, his eyes skimming her body almost compulsively as she stepped onto the narrow porch and pushed open the front door. It took a conscious effort of will to drag his eyes from the way the worn denim of her shorts molded the soft curves of her bottom.

The last thing he wanted was to get involved with anyone, he reminded himself. He was here to clean out his grandfather's house and maybe, while he was at it, figure out what he was going to do with the rest of his life. He didn't need any complications. Breakfast was one thing, especially when it came with caffeine, but anything else was out of the question.

And if his new neighbor would be willing to start wearing baggy clothes and put a paper sack over her head, he just might be able to remember that.

The interior of the house continued the pseudo-Spanish theme of the exterior. The floor of the small entryway was covered with dark-red tiles, and archways led off in various directions. Through one, he could see a living room, which looked almost as uncoordinated as the flower beds out front. A sofa upholstered in fat pink roses sat at right angles to an overstuffed chair covered in blue plaid. Both faced a small fireplace. The end table next to the sofa was completely covered in magazines and books. In one corner of the room, there was a sewing machine in a cabinet. Heaped over and around it and trailing onto the floor, there were piles of brightly colored fabric. The comfortable clutter made it obvious that this was a room where someone actually lived, and he couldn't help but compare it to the painful neatness of his grandfather's house—everything in its place, everything organized with military precision. The whole place had a sterile feeling that made it hard to believe it had been someone's home for more than forty years. Pushing the thought aside, Reece followed Shannon through an archway on the left of the entryway.

The kitchen was in a similar state of comfortable disarray. It was not a large room but light colors and plenty of windows made it seem bigger than it was. White cupboards and a black-and-white, checkerboard-patterned floor created a crisp, modern edge, but the yellow floral curtains and brightly colored ceramic cups and canisters added a cheerfully eclectic touch.

"Have a seat," Shannon said, gesturing to the small maple table that sat under a window looking out onto the backyard.

Reece chose to lean against the counter instead, his eyes following her as she got out a cup and poured coffee into it.

"Cream or sugar?" she asked as she handed him the cup. "I don't actually have cream, but I think I've got milk."

"Black is fine." Reece lifted the cup and took a sip, risking a scalded tongue in his eagerness. But it was worth it, he thought as the smooth, rich taste filled his mouth. "This is terrific coffee," he said, sipping again.

"It's a blend of beans that I buy at a little coffee

shop downtown. They roast it themselves.'' She opened a cupboard, stared into it for a moment and then closed the door.

"You do your own grinding?"

"I haven't figured out yet whether or not it actually makes a difference but the guy who runs the shop sneers if you ask him to grind it for you."

Shannon opened the refrigerator door, and Reece felt his stomach rumble inquiringly. It had been a long time since dinner last night, and if she cooked half as well as she made coffee, breakfast was bound to be special. Relaxing back against the counter, he sipped his coffee and allowed his eyes to linger on her legs with absentminded appreciation while he entertained fantasies of bacon and eggs or maybe waffles slathered in butter and maple syrup or—

"How do you feel about Froot Loops?"

Chapter 3

"I haven't really given them much thought," Reece admitted cautiously.

"I don't suppose you'd be interested in having them for breakfast?" she asked. "I have that and Pepsi."

"Pepsi?" An image of multicolored, sugar-coated bits of cereal floating in a sea of flat cola flashed through his mind, and his stomach lurched. "On the Froot Loops?" he asked faintly.

"Of course not!" Shannon's nose wrinkled in disgust. "*With* it, not poured over it."

It seemed a marginal improvement. Reece took another swallow of coffee and tried to decide just how polite he should be in turning down her offer. It seemed a pity to offend someone who made coffee this good.

Shannon sighed abruptly and pushed the refrigerator door shut with a thud. She turned to face him, her hands on her hips, her chin tilted upward. "The truth is, I don't cook." Her tone mixed apology and defiance. "In fact, I'm a complete disaster in the kitchen. I live on frozen dinners and junk food. Coffee is the only thing I can cook without destroying it, and that's only because it's an automatic pot."

"You invited me to breakfast," he reminded her mildly.

"I know." She sighed and spread her hands in a gesture that might have been apology. "It was Edith's idea."

"Cacklemeyer suggested you should ask me to breakfast?" His brows rose in disbelief.

Shannon shook her head. "She said I shouldn't. She came across the street while I was working in the garden."

Reece took a fortifying swallow of coffee and tried to sort out the conversation. "She walked across the street to tell you *not* to invite me to breakfast?"

"Not exactly." She scowled and shoved her hands in the back pockets of her cutoffs. His eyes dropped to the soft curves of her breasts, pure male appreciation momentarily distracting him from both the conversation and the emptiness of his stomach. "She came across the street to tell me to pull my marigolds and that you were sure to cause trouble. So, I told her I liked marigolds and that I was going to invite you to breakfast. I hadn't planned on it, obviously."

"The marigolds or breakfast?" he asked, fascinated by her circuitous conversational style.

"Breakfast," she said, her eyes starting to gleam with laughter. "I knew I liked marigolds but I *didn't* know I was going to invite you to breakfast until she annoyed me."

"So this was all part of a plot to irritate Cacklemeyer?'' A more sensitive man would probably be offended, Reece thought.

"I don't think you could call it a plot." Shannon's tone was thoughtful. "If it had been a plot, I would have planned a little better and bought some decent food. Oh, wait!" Her eyes lit up suddenly. "There's a box of waffles in the freezer, but I don't think I have any syrup. I have grape jelly, though," she added hopefully.

Reece barely restrained a shudder. Her idea of "decent" and his were not quite the same. Nothing—not the best coffee he'd had in months, not five feet eight inches of long-legged, blue-eyed, dangerously attractive redhead—could make him eat toaster waffles spread with grape jelly.

Shannon must have read something of his thoughts, because her hopeful expression faded into vague suspicion. "Are you a health food nut? One of those people who only eats roots and berries and never lets a preservative touch their lips?"

Reece thought about the Twinkies lying on the seat of the truck. "No, I've got nothing against an occasional preservative." He finished off his coffee—no sense in letting it go to waste—and set the cup down, trying to think of a tactful way to make his escape.

Seeing his vaguely hunted expression, Shannon felt a twinge of amusement. Not everyone shared her casual attitude toward food. "Not a fan of grape jelly?"

Reece caught the gleam in her eye and relaxed. "Actually, I'm allergic."

"To grape jelly?" Shannon arched one brow in skeptical question.

"It's a rare allergy," he admitted.

"I bet." She told herself that she wasn't in the least

charmed by the way one corner of his mouth tilted in a half smile. "Fred and Wilma are on the jelly glass," she tempted.

"The Flintstones?" Reece shook his head, trying to look regretful. "That's tough to turn down, but my throat swells shut and then I turn blue."

"Really?" Her bright, interested look startled a smile from Reece.

"I hope you're not going to make me demonstrate."

"I guess not." Her mouth took on a faintly pouty look that turned Reece's thoughts in directions that had nothing to do with breakfast. He reined them in as he straightened away from the counter.

"Maybe I can take a rain check on breakfast?" he asked politely.

"I'll get an extra box of Cap'n Crunch next time I go shopping," she promised, and he tried not to shudder.

"You did what?" Her eyes wide with surprise, Kelly turned away from the pegboard full of sewing notions, a stack of chalk markers forgotten in her hand.

"I invited him to breakfast," Shannon repeated.

"That's what I thought you said." Kelly came over to the cutting table where Shannon was making up color-coordinated packets of fabric and leaned against its edge, her expression a mixture of disbelief and admiration. "You just sauntered up and offered him bacon and eggs?"

"Froot Loops," Shannon corrected her. She slid a cardboard price tag onto a length of lavender ribbon before tying it around a stack of half a dozen different pink fabrics. "I didn't have any bacon. Or eggs."

"Froot Loops? You invited Reece Morgan over for

Froot Loops? And you waited until now to tell me?''
It was difficult to say what Kelly found most shocking.

"Yesterday was your day off. And there's nothing
wrong with Froot Loops. I eat them all the time.''

"You could have called me at home.'' Kelly grumbled. "And Froot Loops aren't exactly what I'd call
company fare.'' She shook her head, her dark eyes
starting to gleam with laughter. "I'd have given anything to see his face when you put the box on the
table.''

"Actually, the box didn't get that far.'' Shannon began folding the next stack of fabric.

It was Tuesday morning, the sky was gray with the
promise of rain that probably wouldn't show up for
another month and there were no customers. It was a
perfect chance to catch up on a few things around the
shop. And to indulge in a little gossip. Glancing at
Kelly's stunned expression, Shannon couldn't deny that
she was enjoying being the one with astonishing news
to deliver.

"Apparently, Froot Loops and Pepsi are not among
his favorite breakfast combos.''

"Who can blame him?'' Kelly pulled her face into
a comical grimace. "If he really is a mob boss, he's
probably already put a contract out on your life just for
suggesting it.''

"I thought he was supposed to be a vegetarian zombie.''

"That's Paul McCartney.'' Kelly picked up the
chalk pencils and carried them over to the notions wall
to hang them up.

"Paul is a zombie?'' Shannon looked surprised. "He
looks so normal.''

"No, he's a vegetarian.''

"Does that mean he can't be a zombie?"

"Zombies pretty much have to be carnivores, don't you think?" Kelly wandered back to the cutting table and reached for the roll of ribbon and began snipping it into eighteen-inch lengths. "I mean, how frightening would it be if a bunch of squash-eating undead were roaming the streets?"

"I guess it would be pretty frightening for the squash." Shannon tossed another fabric packet into the box.

"I suppose," Kelly agreed absently. "What's he like?"

"Who?"

"Reece Morgan." Kelly's tone was exasperated. "Who were we talking about? And if you mention Paul McCartney, I'm going to brain you with the nearest blunt object."

"I wasn't going to mention him," Shannon lied meekly.

"Good." Kelly set the ribbon aside, lifted a bolt of fabric from the stack leaning against the side of the cutting table, clicked open a rotary cutter and began slicing off half-yard chunks. "You're the first eye witness I've talked to, so tell me what the infamous Reece Morgan is really like. Did he send shivers up your spine?" she asked, grinning.

"Not that I noticed." At least not the kind of shivers Kelly was talking about. If there had been a small—practically infinitesimal—shiver of awareness, she was keeping it to herself. The last thing she needed was for Kelly to turn her matchmaking eye in Reece Morgan's direction.

"Is he mean looking? Does he have a patch over one eye? Antennae growing out the top of his head? A nose ring? Wear three-inch lifts and a girdle? Tell me all.''

"He doesn't need a girdle," Shannon said, remembering the muscled flatness of his stomach. "Or lifts. He's tall. No eye patch, nose ring or antennae that I noticed. And I didn't think he was mean looking, though I imagine he could be. He has dark hair, dark eyes."

"Good-looking?" Kelly asked, folding the end of the fabric and pinning it to the bolt.

"I think most women would say so," Shannon offered, careful to sound neither too interested or suspiciously indifferent.

"Well, who cares what men think? Unless..." The bolt of fabric hit the table with a thud as a possibility occurred to her. "Do you think he's gay?"

"No," Shannon answered without hesitation.

"Are you sure?" Kelly shook her head as she began folding the fabric she'd just cut. "Because it seems like every good-looking, single man in the state of California is these days."

Shannon could have told her that Reece Morgan was more likely to turn out to be the world's first squash-eating zombie, but she settled for a half shrug and mild reassurance. "I'm pretty sure."

Kelly folded in silence for a moment then sighed abruptly. "Well, it's certainly going to disappoint a lot of people."

"People are going to be disappointed that he's not gay?" Shannon asked, startled.

"Not that." Kelly grinned. "They're going to be disappointed if he's normal. I mean, what's the point of having a bad boy come back to town if he's not bad anymore?"

"I see what you mean. I hadn't thought of it that way." Shannon shook her head sadly. "When you think of it, it was pretty inconsiderate of him. The least he could have done was get his nose pierced or maybe file his teeth."

"Exactly." Kelly looked wistful. "I was really hoping for black leather and chains."

Shannon's brows rose. "Does Frank know about this?"

"Not for me, silly. For Reece Morgan. He could at least have worn a black leather jacket and maybe an earring. For heaven's sake, even stockbrokers are wearing earrings these days!" She shook her head at the unfairness of it.

"The man's an inconsiderate lout." Shannon looped a ribbon around the next stack of fabric.

"So, what did you do about breakfast?" Kelly asked.

"Well, I offered him toaster waffles and grape jelly but he said he was allergic to grape jelly and took a rain check." Shannon dropped the fabric packet into the basket and waited for Kelly's reaction. She wasn't disappointed.

"Toaster waffles and jelly?" Kelly stared at her in horror. "You actually eat that?"

"Not voluntarily, but there wasn't anything else in the house."

"What did he do?"

"Actually, I think he turned a little pale."

"Who can blame him?" Kelly muttered and then giggled. "I'd love to have seen his face."

"It was...interesting," Shannon admitted, grinning at the memory of Reece's poorly concealed revulsion. "But he managed to remain polite."

"I'm almost sorry to hear that," Kelly said.

"I suppose you'd rather he'd threatened me with bodily harm?"

"Well, you have to admit that the man is starting to sound depressingly normal. In fact, he sounds downright dull."

The bell over the door jangled, saving Shannon the necessity of a response. *Dull?* she thought as she turned to greet the customer who'd entered. That was just about the last word she could imagine applying to Reece Morgan.

There was nothing like a small town to make you appreciate the joys of living in a city, Reece thought as he rolled his shopping cart into place behind a middle-aged woman wearing a hot-pink jumpsuit and purple sneakers. In the fifteen years he'd lived in D.C., no one had ever gawked at him over a pile of bananas or waylaid him in the dairy aisle to offer condolences on his loss and, in the next breath, ask what he planned to do about the condition of his lawn. He'd been discreetly eyed by a young woman pushing a cart full of baby food and disposable diapers, blatantly stared at by an old man carrying a six-pack of Coors and a bag of pretzels and nearly mowed over by a toddler trying to escape parental supervision.

Obviously, shopping at Jim & Earl's Super Food Mart had been a mistake. It was just a few blocks from his grandfather's house, which meant it was convenient, not only for him but for his neighbors, who apparently found his presence a source of endless fascination. He didn't even have to turn his head to know that the skinny blonde in the next checkout line was studying the contents of his cart as if trying to commit a complete inventory to memory. If only he'd thought of it sooner, he could have thrown in half a dozen boxes of neon-colored, fruit-flavored condoms and a couple cases of tequila so the local grapevine would have something really interesting to talk about. As it was, he doubted they were going to be able to do much with the news that he'd been seen buying boneless chicken breasts and bok choy.

He listened with leashed impatience as the cashier quizzed the woman in the pink jumpsuit about the health of every member of her family, clicking her tongue in sympathy or exclaiming with delight, as necessary. If only her hands moved as fast as her mouth, she could win the grocery-checking Olympics, Reece thought acidly. She paused, a box of bagels in her hand, her mouth forming an *O* of amazement as the customer detailed the results of her niece's breast reduction surgery and he bit back a groan. At the rate she was going, he stood in real danger of growing old and dying before he made it up to the register. He turned his head to see if there was a shorter line—or a longer one with a deaf and dumb cashier—and forgot all about his irritation.

His coffee-making, Froot Loop-eating neighbor was walking toward him, though he might not have recognized her if it hadn't been for the unmistakable reddish-gold gleam of her hair, which was caught up in a soft twist at the back of her head. The T-shirt and shorts had been replaced by a silky-gold blouse and a calf-length skirt in shades of rust and moss green. He couldn't help but feel a pang of regret that those incredible legs were covered, but he had to admit that there was something tantalizing about knowing just what that flowing skirt was hiding. She looked older, more sophisticated and just as delicious, he admitted, letting his gaze skim over the soft curves and angles of her.

He hadn't set eyes on her since their not-quite-breakfast encounter a little more than a week ago, but he'd thought about her more than he liked to admit. More than was smart for a man who wanted no entanglements, because, even on a short acquaintance, he was fairly sure that Shannon Devereux was not the sort of woman to fall into a casual affair with a currently unemployed ex-government agent who just happened to be living next door to her for a few weeks.

Shannon looked up and saw him. Her eyes widened in surprise and then she smiled and Reece found himself thinking that maybe Serenity Falls wasn't such a bad place after all. She walked over to him, a mesh basket hanging over her arm.

"You know, recent studies indicate that people who eat large quantities of fresh vegetables are twice as likely to develop cauliflower ears."

"I didn't know cauliflowers had ears," he said, responding to the unconventional greeting without missing a beat.

She widened her eyes in surprise. "Of course they have ears. How else could they know what's being said on the grapevine?"

His smile widened into a quick grin that made Shannon's breath catch. Over the past week, she'd almost convinced herself that her new neighbor couldn't possibly be as attractive as she'd thought. Her imagination, fueled by months of whispered speculation about the mysterious Reece Morgan, had exaggerated his looks, created an image to suit his two-decade-old reputation. But the way her pulse stuttered when she looked up and saw him forced her to admit that no exaggeration had been necessary. Not when you had six feet four inches of dark-haired, dark-eyed, solidly muscled male standing right in front of you. Even on its best days, her imagination couldn't improve on that reality.

With an effort she pulled her eyes away from his face and glanced at the contents of his shopping cart. Clicking her tongue, she shook her head in disapproval. "You don't plan on buying that stuff, do you?"

Reece's expression shifted to wary amusement. "You're not going to tell me that they've decided that vegetables are carcinogenic, are you?"

"Not yet, though I'm fairly sure that further research will eventually prove Brussels sprouts were never intended to touch human lips," she said darkly. "But that's not the point now." Shannon flicked her fingers at the bags of vegetables and the package of boneless chicken breasts. "You actually have fresh ginger in there."

"And that's a bad thing?" Reece wondered if he should worry that her circuitous conversational style was starting to seem almost normal. The skinny blonde in the next line was craning her neck in what she probably thought was a subtle attempt to eavesdrop on their conversation. Reece ignored her.

"It hardly suits your image." Her soft mouth primmed into a disapproving line. "Think about it. Bad boy returns home and buys vegetables? What kind of a message does that send?"

"Bad boy?" Reece repeated, not entirely pleased. "Is that what I'm supposed to be?"

"Of course." She seemed surprised that he had to ask. "According to local myth, you were the scourge of Serenity Falls."

"Scourge?" He was caught between irritation and

amusement. "I think that's overstating things a little. I may have raised a little hell, but I didn't exactly pillage and burn the town."

"You're forgetting the petunias," she pointed out.

"One flower bed and I'm a scourge?" How did she manage to pull him into these conversations?

Shannon looked regretful. "In a town this size, it doesn't take much." She shifted her shopping basket from her right hand to her left, and her voice took on a self-consciously pedantic tone that, for some reason he couldn't fathom, made Reece wonder if her mouth could possibly be as soft as it looked. And wouldn't *that* set the grapevine humming—news that that Morgan boy had kissed his very attractive neighbor right in the middle of the food mart with God and half the town looking on. With an effort, he dragged his attention back to what Shannon was saying.

"Actually, the Bad Boy is a classic figure in Western mythology. An important character in both film and literature. Think of James Dean."

"James Dean?" Reece's upper lip curled. "Kind of a skinny little twerp, wasn't he?"

Shannon's eyes widened in horror, and she pressed her free hand to her chest as if to protect her heart from the shock. "James Dean? The king of cool? You're calling him a twerp?"

"Couldn't have weighed more than one-fifty soaking wet and with his shoes on. Maybe if he'd eaten his vegetables, he'd have bulked up a little."

Shannon's mouth twitched and was sternly controlled. "Don't you think that would have spoiled his lean and hungry look? It's hard to seem tragically misunderstood when you look like you could eat hay with a fork."

"So only the scrawny get sympathy?" Reece shook his head. "Doesn't seem quite fair to me."

"I'm told that life isn't always fair."

"I've heard that rumor."

"Do you have plans for Thursday?" she asked, changing the subject abruptly.

"Thursday?" he repeated blankly.

"Thanksgiving?" Shannon arched her brows. "You know, turkey, dressing, pumpkin pie. Pilgrims shaking hands with the Indians they're eventually going to wipe out. The fourth Thursday in November when we all get together and eat too much? This coming Thursday? Do you have plans?"

"Not that I know of," Reece admitted cautiously.

"Well, you're welcome to join the crowd at my house," she offered. "It's nothing formal. People just drop by."

"Are you cooking?" he asked involuntarily, visions of freeze-dried turkey flashing before his eyes.

Shannon's quick, throaty laugh made the skinny blonde sidle closer in an attempt to overhear what was being said. "Don't worry, it's potluck. Everyone brings something, and I've been strictly forbidden to set foot in the kitchen."

"No Froot Loops?"

"Only in the stuffing," she promised solemnly. Looking past him, she nodded toward the checkout counter. "Looks like you're up next."

Turning, Reece saw that the woman in the pink jumpsuit was paying for her purchases and the cashier was giving him a distinctly ominous look of bright-eyed interest.

"Watch out for Agatha," Shannon said, confirming his concern. "She can wring information out of granite.

If the Inquisition had had her, they wouldn't have needed the rack.''

"Great, a full-service store," Reece muttered as he pushed his cart forward. "They bag your groceries while they pump you for information."

"Just say no," Shannon advised solemnly but she was grinning as she turned away without waiting for a reply. "See you Thursday, maybe."

Not likely, Reece thought as he began loading his groceries onto the conveyer belt. He didn't want any involvement and, while attending a potluck Thanksgiving dinner along with half the town wasn't exactly a prelude to a passionate love affair, it was too…neighborly. Too friendly. It suggested that he had a place here, which he didn't—not now, not twenty years ago.

He glanced over his shoulder in time to see Shannon disappear down the frozen food aisle. It was nice of her to invite him, but he was perfectly content with his own company, on Thanksgiving or any other day. Still, he had to admit that it would be interesting to see if she really did manage to slip Froot Loops into the stuffing.

Chapter 4

For the past few years, the fourth Thursday in November had been just another number on the calendar to Reece, and he was perfectly content to keep it that way. So what was he doing standing on Shannon Devereux's doorstep holding a spinach salad?

The door opened, saving him the necessity of having to come up with a satisfactory answer to his own question. He'd been expecting Shannon and had to adjust his gaze five inches lower and his thinking fifty years older. Suspiciously black hair topped a thin, wrinkled face. Reece had heard of someone applying makeup with a trowel, but he'd never seen anyone who looked as if they might actually have done just that until now. Foundation, blusher, concealer and possibly a bit of spackle coated every inch of skin from forehead to chin. False eyelashes, black eyeliner and royal-purple eyeshadow were balanced, more or less, by stoplight-red lipstick that had bled into the fine lines around her mouth.

Her clothing was no less colorful. A purple sweat-shirt with a design of teddy bears at a picnic topped a pair of hot-pink pedal pushers. Her calves were bare and colored a streaky orangey brown that suggested either a severe nutritional problem or a badly applied tan-in-a-bottle. Purple sneakers with pink glitter and black laces completed the ensemble.

"What is that?" Her voice, surprisingly deep for a woman, brought Reece's dazzled eyes back to her face. She was staring at the bowl in his hands, dark eyes full of suspicion.

"Spinach salad."

"Does it have meat in it?"

"No."

Her dark eyes flickered suspiciously from the bowl to his face. Reece half expected her to insist on an inspection, but she must have decided he had an honest face or maybe it just occurred to her that spinach salad was an unlikely place for meat to lurk. Whichever it was, she shuffled back into the entryway, letting the door open wide, spilling laughter and voices out into the warm afternoon.

His first impression was of wall-to-wall people. His second and third impressions pretty much confirmed the first. There were people standing in the entryway, clutching plastic cups holding liquid of assorted colors. There were more people in the living room, sitting on the sofa, the chairs, perched on the hearth, leaning against the wall next to the front windows. Yet more people standing in the hallway, which he assumed led back to the bedrooms. Everywhere he looked, there was someone standing or sitting. Fat people, skinny people, old, young, enough variations of skin tone to make a liberal cheer or a conservative weep. Male, female and…well, he wasn't willing to hazard a guess about the one wearing the leather pants and a pink Mohawk.

"You can take that out to the patio."

Reece blinked and focused his attention on the woman who'd let him in. Compared to the Mohawk wearer, she looked downright conservative. "Patio?"

"Go through the kitchen," she said, reading the question he hadn't asked.

Reece nodded his thanks and made his way across the entryway. He exchanged greetings with three total strangers and one woman who looked vaguely familiar before ducking through the doorway into the kitchen. More people. Food smells. Voices raised in argument over the correct way to make gravy. He had enough experience in hand-to-hand combat to lay odds on the skinny woman. Her opponent was male and outweighed her by a good forty pounds, but size wasn't everything, and the way she was gripping the wooden spoon suggested she meant business. He was willing to bet that roux was going to win out over slurry, whatever the hell that meant.

And then he was outside and there were more people but they were scattered across the surprisingly spacious patio and out onto the lawn, still dull and mostly brown from summer drought. The weather was typical of a southern California autumn—clear blue skies and warm enough to qualify as summer in some parts of the country. Not exactly your traditional crisp Thanksgiving weather but nostalgic in its own way. Not so much for the years spent with his grandfather—holidays with the old man had generally been long on tradition, short on feeling—but for the years when his parents were alive. They'd been very short on any recognizable traditions—dinner was as likely to be McDonald's as it was turkey—but there had always been plenty of love and laughter.

"You *did* come."

Reece turned to greet his hostess, feeling that now-familiar little kick of awareness when he saw her. Shannon was wearing a long, soft skirt in some bluey, greeny shade and a simple scoop-necked top that hovered between rust and gold. The color brought out the red in her hair, which was drawn back from her face with a pair of gold clips and left to tumble on her shoulders. Her eyes sparkled, bluer than the sky, sapphire bright and warm. Her mouth was warm coral, and he wondered what she'd do if he kissed her, right here in front of God and half the populace of Serenity Falls.

"How could I resist the possibility of a turkey stuffed with Froot Loops?" he asked, reining in his suddenly raging libido.

Her smile widened into a grin, her eyes laughing at him. "Sorry, I couldn't get near the stuffing. Sally actually held up a cross when I got too close to the oven."

"So, it's safe to eat the stuffing?" he asked, raising one eyebrow.

"Coward. Froot Loops provide an important assortment of vitamins and minerals."

"Not to mention artificial colorings and preservatives," he murmured, following her to the long table, set up on one side of the patio and already groaning under a vast array of bowls and platters.

"I think we can wedge this in here," Shannon said, turning to take the bowl from him. She found a space between a bowl of iceberg lettuce and carrot shreds and an elaborate, layered vegetable aspic. "The turkey came out of the oven a few minutes ago. Sally says it has to rest for half an hour, which seems ridiculous. How much rest can a dead bird need?"

"It's to let the juices settle back into the meat," Reece said absently. She really had the most amazingly kissable mouth.

Shannon gave him a look that mixed surprise and faint disapproval. "You know how to cook."

Reece shrugged. "I'm no Wolfgang Puck, but I've lived alone for a long time. I got tired of going out to eat."

"You can buy a gourmet meal in a box, like any other civilized human being."

"Depends on your definition of gourmet, I suppose," he said mildly. She shook her head in apparent despair.

"Be sure and take some of the aspic," she said, gesturing to it.

"Good?" Reece asked, eyeing it with interest.

"Probably not." Shannon frowned down at the aspic. "Last year, Vangie brought a coffee cake that was so hard someone suggested selling it to NASA to replace the ceramic tile on the shuttle."

"And that's supposed to encourage me to eat the aspic?" Reece asked.

"Oh, I didn't say you had to *eat* it. I just said you should take some." She saw his raised eyebrow and shrugged. "Vangie has sensibilities," she said, as if that explained everything and it probably did.

Reece cleared his throat and tried to look regretful. "Actually, I'm allergic to aspic."

"Aspic *and* grape jelly?" Shannon's eyes widened in surprise.

"Grape—" He caught himself, remembering that first morning when she'd offered him toaster waffles and grape jelly and he'd claimed allergies. He coughed a little. "Not many people know that one of the primary ingredients of aspic is grape jelly."

"Really?" Shannon cast a doubting look at the shimmering aspic. "Wouldn't grape jelly make it purple?"

"The, um, baking soda in the aspic neutralizes the, uh, chemical additives that give grape jelly its characteristic color."

"Wow." Shannon shook her head in amazement. "Have you always been such a good liar?"

"Always. It's a gift." He said it with such simple pride that it startled a quick, choked laugh from her.

His eyes flickered from her eyes to her mouth. She couldn't possibly taste as good as she looked. Could she? He couldn't possibly be thinking about finding out. Could he? Maybe she read something of what he was thinking because her smile faded abruptly and her breath caught a little. Reece dragged his gaze from her mouth, saw the awareness in those clear blue eyes. Did he lean down? Did she sway toward him?

The screen door banged behind him, and Reece straightened, abruptly aware of where he was—standing on a sun-splashed patio with a dozen people in plain sight. Shannon threw him a quick, uncertain smile, a murmured—and unheard—comment and moved past him toward the kitchen door. Reece turned to watch her walk away. The phrase, "Danger, Will Robinson" drifted irresistibly—ridiculously—through his mind.

What the hell had just happened? Nothing. That's what had happened. Absolutely nothing. And nothing *would have* happened, even if they hadn't been interrupted. Right. Nothing would have happened.

Oh, hell. Who was he kidding? If they hadn't been standing right here in front of God and half of Serenity Falls, he'd probably be trying to give her a tonsillectomy with his tongue right about now. And the fact that he was fairly sure she wouldn't have objected did nothing to alleviate the sudden snugness of his jeans. Reece shifted uncomfortably, moving away from the table to lean against one of the redwood support posts, one that happened to be in shadow. Forty freaking years old and he was showing all the self-control of a sixteen-year-old. No, come to think of it, he hadn't made a habit of getting erections in public when he was sixteen.

He wasn't here to start an affair, he reminded himself. The last thing he wanted was any kind of involvement. He had enough to do with cleaning out his grandfather's house and figuring out what to do with the rest of his life. Beautiful neighbors with gorgeous red hair and legs that went on forever did not fit into his plans.

The only way the aspic could have tasted worse was if it had actually been made with grape jelly and baking soda. Reece managed to swallow the single bite he'd taken and then pushed the remainder of it to one side of his plate, concealing it under a slightly wilted piece of iceberg lettuce. The unknown Vangie might have sensibilities but she apparently lacked taste buds.

The food was as eclectic as the guests. Tofu and turkey. Couscous and three-bean salad. Pearls and blue jeans. Retired professors and born-again hippies. It was a guest list right out of a hostess's nightmare or maybe a Marx Brothers movie. Potential disaster lurked around every slice of jellied cranberry sauce and dollop of...what exactly was the brown stuff with the little orange bits in it? Reece poked it cautiously to the side of his plate, hiding it under the lettuce leaf with the aspic.

"Darva Torkelson's family secret rice pilaf," someone said, and Reece looked up guiltily. "The secret is that no one knows what the orange things are, and I haven't found anyone brave enough to actually try tasting it to find out. I'm voting for M&Ms."

A stocky man with stoplight-red hair was standing just to his left, his blue eyes bright with amusement and...expectation? It only took a moment for the memory to snap into place.

"Frank? Frank McKinnon?"

"You know anyone else who looks like Howdy Doody on steroids?" Frank grinned and held out his hand. Reece felt memories flood over him as he shook it.

"How are you, man?"

"Good. I'm good. Is Rich here?" Reece scanned the crowd around the buffet table, looking for more of that bright-red hair. Rich McKinnon had been his best friend during the years he lived in Serenity Falls. The two of them had gone through football, detention, first dates and first cars together. They'd kept in touch for a while after Reece left town—Christmas cards, a few phone calls, but they'd gradually lost touch.

Frank shook his head. "Rich lives in Montana now. He's a gen-u-ine cowboy." He drew out the words with a thick Western drawl. "Got hisself a little ranch with horses and cows and all that good stuff."

"A ranch, huh?" Reece grinned and shook his head. "What happened to becoming a world-famous wildlife photographer?"

"He found out that wildlife photographers spend a lot of time sitting in huts, freezing their privates off, waiting for a ring-necked wallaby to wander into camera range and hoping a hungry grizzly bear doesn't wander by first."

"I can see how that would take some of the fun out of things. How are your parents?"

Ruth and Daryl McKinnon had always treated him as if he were one of their own. They'd had a rambling old house where everything was always covered in a fine layer of plaster dust from the ongoing series of remodeling jobs that were never quite finished. Dogs, cats and kids wandered in and out in an ever-changing parade of fur and faces. It had taken him a while to figure out that only three of the kids actually belonged to the McKinnons, and he never had figured out which of the animals were theirs.

"Dad retired three years ago, and he and Mom bought an RV. They spend most of the year on the road. Kate is married and has a couple of kids. She lives in Boston now, and Rich married a woman with three kids and then they had two more so Mom and Dad divide their time among the grandchildren. They spend a couple of months here in the spring so Mom can catch up on the local gossip and Dad can make sure I'm not running the hardware store into the ground, and then they take off again."

"Did your dad ever finish remodeling the house?" Reece asked.

Frank laughed and shook his head. "Hell, no. When we moved in, three out of four bathrooms were torn apart and the back hall was halfway through a wall-papering job.''

"And three years later, two bathrooms are still without tile and the wallpaper is up but the floor is only half-refinished," a new voice said.

"What can I say? It's genetic," Frank said, his smile softening as he turned to slide one arm around the woman who'd joined them. She was small, not just short but slim, with the kind of delicate build that made Reece think of pixies. Big brown eyes set in a heart-shaped face and a tousled cap of blond hair reinforced the impression. He had the fanciful thought that if she turned he might see wings on her back. But her bright, interested expression was human and familiar. The first few times he'd seen that particular expression, he'd had the urge to check to make sure his fly was zipped or look in a mirror to see if a third eye had appeared in the middle of his forehead, but it hadn't taken long to figure out that it wasn't the possibility of imminent indecent exposure or extra body parts, it was just him. His mere presence was enough to elicit interest.

Reece Morgan, walking, talking scenic wonder.

But unlike the elderly man who'd gaped at him while he was buying cleaning supplies or the trout-faced woman at the gas station that first day, Kelly McKinnon didn't stare at him as if he was a two-headed calf at the county fair. The curiosity was there but banked, about what you'd expect from a woman meeting someone who'd known her husband twenty years ago.

She said the town must have changed a lot since he'd lived here before and Reece agreed that it had. She asked where he lived and he told her he'd been living in D.C. and added that he'd given up his apartment and wasn't sure where he was going to settle when he left Serenity Falls.

"Maybe you'll decide to settle here," she said, taking a bite of dinner roll.

"I don't think so." The statement left room for doubt, and he frowned. "I'm just here to clean out my grandfather's house," he added firmly. "Get it in shape to sell, then I'll move on."

"Got a place in mind?" Frank asked. He used the side of his fork to cut a mushroom-soup-covered green bean in two. "Somewhere to settle?"

"Nowhere in particular," Reece admitted. He poked another bit of the brown stuff under the lettuce leaf with the aspic.

"Just going to travel?" Frank asked. "The romance of the open road, huh?"

Reece mumbled something around a bite of really excellent scalloped oysters and hoped Frank would take it as agreement. In his experience, the open road offered little by way of romance, unless you happened to *like* lumpy mattresses and bad food.

"So, you're running the hardware store now," he said, steering the conversation away from his possible future plans.

Frank was willing to go along with the change of topic and, for the next few minutes the conversation moved easily from hardware stores to the housing development that was going up on the west edge of town, to old acquaintances. Reece was surprised at how many of the names he remembered and even more surprised to feel a twinge of nostalgia at some of the memories Frank evoked. He hadn't exactly been brimming over with warm and fuzzy feelings when he left here but maybe there had been more good times than he'd realized.

"Well, all I can say is that it's a crime to use the word *Thanksgiving* in connection with such a barbaric display." The raspy comment preceded the arrival of the old woman who had answered the door for him earlier. She stomped to a halt next to Kelly, every scrawny, makeup- and glitter-covered inch quivering with indignation.

"Hello, Mavis," Frank said. Reece caught a glint of mischief in his blue eyes before he added, "Happy holiday."

The innocuous greeting had an immediate and startling affect. Mavis drew herself up, her eyes narrowing in a glare that should have withered Frank on the spot. "Happy? *Happy?*" she repeated, her deep voice lending resonance to the word. "What's happy about a day on which millions of innocent creatures are slaughtered in the name of celebration? Death and destruction. *That's* what you're celebrating. Death and destruction."

Kelly gave her husband an exasperated look before putting her hand on Mavis's arm. "No one is celebrating death and destruction. People have to eat, and you know that not everyone feels the way you do about—"

"You." Reece tensed as those dark eyes pinned him to the pillar behind him. "Do you know what you're eating?"

Reece thought of the alleged rice pilaf and the inedible aspic and thought he could answer, with some truth, that he *didn't* know, but he had a feeling that pleading ignorance wasn't going to do him any good.

He was almost relieved when Mavis continued without waiting for a response.

"Turkey." She fired the word at him. "You're eating turkey."

"Umm, yes," Reece admitted cautiously. He shot Frank a questioning look, but the other man just shook his head, eyes bright with laughter.

"Are you aware that that was once a living, breathing animal with hopes and dreams?"

"Dreams?" Reece repeated, looking at the half-eaten slice of turkey on his plate.

"A future," Mavis continued ruthlessly.

"He coulda been a contenda," Frank murmured. His Brando imitation was not the best Reece had ever heard, but it was good enough to startle a snort of laughter from him. Mavis swelled up like a pouter pigeon, narrow chest expanding, dark eyes flashing beneath their awning of false eyelashes. Kelly shot her husband a look of mixed amusement and annoyance and thrust her plate at him before setting her hand on Mavis's sinewy arm.

"Ignore him," she told the other woman. "He just doesn't understand." Head bent in attentive sympathy, she led the other woman away from the turkey-laden table.

"*I* don't understand?" Frank muttered, staring down at the plate she'd handed him. "This from the woman with a turkey haunch the size of a small pony on her plate?"

"I think it was the bit from *On the Waterfront* that showed a certain lack of sensitivity," Reece suggested.

"Hell, I was just trying to show that I understood the sacrifice this turkey had made." Frank managed to balance his wife's plate on a nearby planter and cheerfully transferred the rest of her lunch to his plate. "Mavis is a vegetarian."

"Yeah, I kind of gathered as much. Either that or she's got a thing for turkeys." Reece chewed thoughtfully on piece of turkey. "What do you think a turkey dreams of?"

"Thanksgiving being canceled," Frank said promptly, and the two men snickered.

They ate in companionable silence for a while. Reece's eyes drifted over the guests, thinking again that they were an unlikely mixture. He saw Shannon standing on the summer-browned lawn, talking to a skinny young man with a prominent Adam's apple and thinning hair. As he watched, the guest with the pink Mohawk and indeterminate sex approached, and the three of them stood talking together.

"She certainly does believe in mixing her guest list." Reece was hardly aware of speaking the thought out loud until Frank answered.

"Shannon?" He followed Reece's gaze, grinning at the eclectic little group. "It's not exactly a guest list. It's more a case of Shannon collecting stray puppies. Pretty much anyone who doesn't have somewhere else to go is welcome."

Stray puppies? Stray puppies? Was that how she thought of him? As a stray with nowhere else to go? The idea stung, all the more so because there was an element of truth to it. He hadn't exactly been overwhelmed with invitations for the holiday. But that didn't make him a stray, for god's sake. It wasn't as if he hadn't had anywhere else to go. He had options.

He had a standing invitation to spend the holiday with his ex-wife and her family. Never mind that it had been left standing for the past ten years because he and

Caroline liked each other best when they were a few thousand miles apart. The point wasn't whether or not he'd *wanted* to go. The point was he *could* have gone. He could have gone back to Virginia, admired the fall foliage, thrown a football with his son. He hadn't seen Kyle since the beginning of summer. Almost six months ago. Too long.

And if he didn't want to go back to Virginia, he could have stayed home, could have fixed himself a steak dinner and eaten it while he watched football on his grandfather's ancient television.

Frank had shifted from updating him on old acquaintances to giving him a running commentary on the other guests. The one with the pink Mohawk was female, if you could judge by the name, which you couldn't always these days, but Becky seemed an unlikely name for a boy. Then again, it seemed an unlikely name for someone dressed like that. Spike maybe or Squeaky, but Becky conjured up images of pinafores and ankle socks, not pink Mohawks and skin-tight leather. Maybe she was another one of his neighbor's "strays," Reece thought, feeling a quick little pinch of irritation.

The irritation lingered in the back of his mind, niggling at him as he let Frank pull him into a conversation with a balding man who bore no resemblance to the quarterback who'd made all the girls swoon when they were in high school together. It tugged for his attention as he watched Shannon chat with an elderly woman with blue hair and a sweet smile, and it was still there when he saw her laughing with a group of children who were playing tag in the backyard.

Strays, he thought as he watched her head off a potential brawl between Mavis and a heavyset man who looked prepared to use lethal force in defense of the turkey leg he was clutching.

Stray puppies. The phrase echoed in his mind as he helped clear the tables and then break them down for storage. Well, maybe some of the guests were lost souls but he wasn't. It hadn't been loneliness or an excess of holiday spirit that had brought him here. It had been something a little more basic. His eyes followed Shannon as she and another woman wrapped the leftovers. She'd taken her shoes off at some point and, barefoot, with the soft skirt swishing around her calves and her hair tumbling down her back, she looked both earthy and elegant—a gypsy in silk.

Lust, Reece thought. Not turkey, not the chance to mingle with a guest list right out of central casting for eccentrics, not a desire to give thanks for anything, except maybe the soft curves of the female body and the bright glint of laughter in a pair of blue eyes. Okay, so lust *and* liking. It was a scary combination. Lust was simple. You either acted on it or you didn't and, one way or another, you were done with it. Liking was more complex. Liking suggested friendship, and friendship meant ties, connections, things he wasn't looking to add to his life right now.

Then again, maybe he was making a bigger production out of it than it really should be. His eyes on Shannon, Reece folded one metal leg against the underside of the table. Really, did it have to be a big deal? Like. Lust. Not a bad combination. It didn't have to lead to anything more than say, oh, maybe a blazing hot affair. The thought rolled through his head, creating a sudden, potentially embarrassing pressure against his zipper, making him grateful for the solid screen of the table

as he carried it to the side gate and out to Frank
McKinnon's truck.

By the time he'd loaded the table into the bed of the
pickup and promised Frank that he'd stop by the hardware store and promised Frank's pretty wife that he'd
come to dinner soon, the excess pressure in his jeans
had subsided, but the thought of having an affair with
his Froot Loops-eating neighbor remained.

Why not? The attraction was mutual. He might not
have done much dating in recent years, but he hadn't
forgotten the way a woman looked when she was interested. They were both consenting adults. There was
no reason they couldn't act on that attraction.

He made his way back through the side gate, stepping around a teary five-year-old who'd thrown herself
down in the middle of the walkway and was refusing
to move, despite her father's strained pleas for reason.
The scene in the backyard was one of controlled chaos.
Cleanup, like the meal itself, was apparently a cooperative effort. Well, it was mostly cooperative, he
amended as he watched Mavis and a tall, thin man with
a goatee and painfully plaid trousers square off over
the leftover turkey. He was too far away to hear what
they were saying but it seemed likely that Mavis was
thinking burial with honors and the guy in the loud
pants was thinking sandwiches. They were locked in
an apparent stalemate until Shannon touched Mavis on
the shoulder. A few words, a smile, and the older
woman relinquished the platter to Mr. Plaid Pants, who
wasted no time in carrying his prize into the relative
safety of the kitchen.

Shannon stayed with Mavis, her head bent attentively to listen to what the other woman was saying.
Her hair swung forward in a tumble of red-gold curls.

Reece's fingers curled into his palm in a reflexive urge to touch, to see if her hair was as soft as it looked.

Maybe he'd get a chance to find out.

Shannon waved goodbye to Lillian and Hector Gonzalez, waiting until the elderly couple had tottered their way down the walkway and into their car before she shut the door with a sigh of relief. She leaned back against the door and listened to the quiet. When she was growing up, holidays had meant her and her father eating in a restaurant, listening to perky, piped-in music and trying to think of something to say to each other. Well, *she'd* tried to think of something to say to him. She'd never been sure that the silences bothered him, not then, not at any other time.

There had been a lot of silence when she was growing up, which was probably why she enjoyed the noise and controlled chaos that went along with opening up her home to so many people, but that moment when the last guest left and silence descended again...

"Breathing a sigh of relief?"

Shannon's eyes flew open. Reece Morgan was leaning in the archway that led to the kitchen. Well, not quite the last guest, she amended, looking at him. She'd known he was still here. She known where he was at any given moment all afternoon. A fine thread of awareness had spun between them, a faint line of warmth that had tugged at her senses. She was fairly sure that should bother her, and maybe it would. Later. When she wasn't alone with him. When she couldn't feel this low, electric hum of interest.

It was nearly dark outside and the entryway was dim, lit only by the soft yellow glow that spilled in from the living-room lamp and the sharper white glow of the kitchen light that silhouetted Reece's tall figure.

''No food fights. No medical emergencies and everyone went home smiling,'' she said, answering his question. ''I think a sigh of relief is warranted.''

Reece's brows rose. ''Are food fights and medical emergencies a usual part of the day?''

''Not usual, exactly, but last year Professor Durshwitz thought he was having a heart attack and we had to call the paramedics but it turned out to be indigestion, and the year before that, one of the Brinkman boys threw a dinner roll at his sister. She retaliated and there was a brief flurry of flying rolls. Pretty harmless really until someone hit Edith Hacklemeyer in the forehead with a buttered roll.''

Reece's sharp bark of laughter echoed in the tiled hall, and Shannon's mouth curved in response. ''I don't imagine Cacklemeyer was particularly gracious about it.''

''Well...no, I don't think you could use the term *gracious*. She seemed to think that everyone involved should be drawn and quartered. When no one offered to at least lock Bobby Brinkman in a closet somewhere, she left in a huff.'' Shannon frowned a little, remembering. ''The thing was, it was really hard to take her seriously with this big blotch of butter right between her eyes. She hasn't been back since.''

''I'm not surprised. Cacklemeyer was never big on forgive and forget.'' Reece straightened away from the door and started toward her, and Shannon felt her heart begin to beat a little faster. ''I'm surprised she was here at all since she doesn't seem to be a friend of yours.''

''She doesn't have anywhere else to go, really.'' Shannon watched him approach. The door at her back suddenly seemed like a very good idea, because her knees weren't 100 percent sure they wanted to support her.

"A stray puppy?" Reece murmured, stopping in front of her.

"What?" She tilted her head to look at him. She wished the light was better so she could see his expression, but maybe it was better this way because she wasn't at all sure she wanted him to see what must be in her face, in her eyes. Pressing her palms flat against the door on either side of her hips, she tried to steady her breathing, tried to swallow against the excitement that was swelling in her chest.

"Cacklemeyer." Reece set one hand on the door near her head and leaned toward her. "Is she one of your strays? Frank said you collect strays."

"He did?" She was having a hard time following the conversation.

"Do you think *I'm* one of your strays?" he asked, his voice low, husky, a little dangerous.

His free hand came up, long fingers tracing the line of her jaw. There was nothing particularly sexual about that light touch but she felt it like a thin line of fire running down her body. She stared up at him, searching his expression in the fading light, reading hunger mixed with humor and a trace of distinctly masculine irritation.

"Is that what you think?" he whispered, his head dipping toward hers.

Think? Shannon closed her eyes, her mouth parting in anticipation. She wasn't sure she remembered what thinking was, not with his mouth so close that she could feel his breath on her skin, smell the faint crisp scent of aftershave.

"I'm not a stray puppy," he said against her mouth.

Not a puppy, she thought hazily. A wolf, maybe, all sleek muscle and power but definitely not a puppy, stray or otherwise. Shannon's hands came up, her fingers curling into the solid muscles of his upper arms, holding on to him, holding him. Her breath left her on a sigh as his tongue flickered across the seam of her lips, asking—demanding—entrance. She gave it to him willingly, hunger and need fluttering in the pit of her stomach.

She'd been waiting for this, wanting it since that first moment, when he'd opened the door and stood there bare-chested and damp from the shower. It was everything she could have imagined, everything she hadn't let herself think about. His mouth was warm and firm, shaping and molding hers. He tasted of chocolate cream pie and coffee, of desire and hunger.

There was no slow buildup, no soft, coaxing kisses. Just this…need…that washed over her like the ocean, a warm wet wave that overwhelmed with gentle strength, pulling her under, rolling her, leaving her dizzy and clinging to Reece as if he were the only steady thing in the universe. It was too much, she thought. It shouldn't happen this soon, shouldn't be this much this soon. There should be uncertainty, hesitation, fumbling. Instead, they fit together as if they'd known each other forever. As if they were already lovers.

Reece's hand slid behind her, fingers splayed wide across her lower back, drawing her away from the door and up against his body. Solid, she thought, letting her fingers slide into the thick dark hair at his nape and tilting her head to deepen the kiss. He was so solid and it had been so long, so very long since she'd been held like this. A lifetime since she'd been wrapped in someone's arms, held close and safe. Not that *safe* was exactly the word that came to mind at the moment. Not with her heart hammering in her chest and her knees threatening to give out.

It had never been like this, she thought hazily, tilting her head back into the support of Reece's hand, her breath leaving her on something that was almost a whimper as his mouth slid down her throat in a series of biting kisses. She'd never felt this kind of urgency, this kind of hunger, not even with... Her breath caught again, not with pleasure but with a quick little pinch of fear. It was too much. Too much heat, too much need, too much everything. She didn't want... Reece's tongue stroked across the pulse that beat at the base of her throat and Shannon moaned softly, her fingers digging into his shoulders. Okay, obviously she *did* want. Her body wanted, anyway, but that didn't mean she had to give in to— Oh, my...why hadn't anyone told her that her collarbone was an erogenous zone?

Reece was working his way back up her throat, and Shannon shuddered as he caught her earlobe between his teeth, worrying it gently before releasing it to taste the soft skin behind her ear. It was difficult to remember why this was a bad thing, when long-dormant hormones were stirring, humming a chorus of how good this was, of how much better it could be if she'd just stop thinking, if she'd just give in and let the pleasure take her where it would.

It took a conscious effort to slide her fingers from his hair, to brace her hands on his shoulders—those very wide, very attractive shoulders—and push back from him.

"This is not a good idea," she managed, wishing she sounded more definite.

"Feels pretty good to me." Reece's thumbs rubbed distracting little circles on the points of her shoulders. His smile was crooked, inviting, a little wicked. "Maybe my technique is a little rusty. You could help me polish it up."

"There's nothing wrong with your technique." Shannon turned her head, and the kiss he'd aimed for her mouth landed on her cheek. Making the best of it, Reece slid his mouth a little farther to the right and nibbled on her earlobe. Shannon's knees and her resolve weakened. With an effort, she stiffened both and planted her hands against his chest. "Your technique is just fine," she assured him breathlessly. "I just... It's too fast... This isn't what I want." Honesty and nerves compelled her to add, "Well, I *do* want it but I'm not going to do it."

Reece gave her a speculative look, and she knew he was debating whether or not to try and change her mind. She sternly suppressed the urge to flex her fingers against his chest, to explore—just a little—the solid wall of muscle and tried to look like a woman whose mind was unchangeable. Maybe she overdid it a little, because she saw a glint of humor edge out the speculation. He opened his mouth but whatever he'd intended to say was cut off by the mellow chime of the doorbell. He hesitated a moment and then one corner of his mouth kicked up in a rueful smile.

"Saved by the bell," he murmured.

His hands dropped away from her shoulders as he stepped back, and Shannon told herself that the little pang she felt was relief, not regret. And if she tried hard enough, she might be able to make herself believe it.

Chapter 5

Conscious of the rather obvious bulge in his jeans, Reece retreated through the nearest archway, leaving Shannon to open the door. Standing in the middle of her cluttered living room, he stared blankly at the heap of fabric that nearly covered the sewing machine occupying the corner near the front window.

What the hell had just happened? A kiss. Right. He'd done that before. Not much in the last year or so, maybe, but that didn't mean he'd forgotten what it was like. There was a sort of unwritten protocol to first kisses. Two mouths, four lips, maybe a bit of tongue, a little body heat, some polite groping, a sort of unspoken inquiry about whether or not both parties wanted this to go any further. This had broken all the rules.

Too fast, she'd said. That was an understatement. He'd barely wrapped his mind around the possibility of having an affair with his sexy neighbor before he found himself groping her up against her own front door. Too fast and too much. It was one thing to indulge in a few fantasies about his pretty neighbor with the legs that went on forever and that full lower lip that seemed made for tasting. It was something else to...*want* like this, this much, this fast. If she hadn't called a halt, he'd have taken her to bed or maybe, God help him, have just taken her up against the door.

Which maybe wasn't the best thing to be thinking right before meeting Shannon's older brother.

When the doorbell rang, Shannon assumed it was one of the guests, come back for some forgotten item. Keefe was just about the last person she expected to see standing on her doorstep. Her brother, she reminded herself. Not just Keefe Walker, near total stranger, but her brother. It didn't seem any more real now than it had months ago when she'd suddenly acquired an entire family she hadn't known existed. Four brothers, a mother she'd thought long since dead and an assortment of sisters-in-law and various children whose relationship to her and to each other she'd yet to sort out. It was more than a bit overwhelming to go from being an orphan to having more family than she could comfortably keep track of. She still hadn't quite managed the emotional shift.

"Keefe." It came out more stunned than welcoming, and Shannon felt herself flush when he raised one dark brow in silent comment.

"Shannon."

"I hope you don't mind us dropping by like this." Keefe's wife rushed to fill the silence, giving Shannon a welcome excuse to look away from her brother.

"Of course not." Her smile relaxed, grew warmer

as she looked at the other woman and the sturdy infant straddling her hip. A small, quietly pretty blonde with big blue-gray eyes and a shy smile, Tessa was one member of Shannon's new family who seemed to understand just how overwhelming the Walkers could be en masse.

Shannon made an effort to pull her scattered wits together and stepped back into the hall, opening the door wide in invitation. "Please come in. I'm sorry if I seem a little scattered. The last of the guests just left and I was…" Her voice trailed off as she remembered just what she'd been doing right before they arrived. She shot a glance toward the living room and wondered what the odds were that Reece was still there. Pretty good unless he'd climbed out a window, she admitted with a sigh.

She pushed the front door shut and turned to smile at her unexpected company, suddenly conscious of her bare feet and tousled hair. Not that there was anything about those things that suggested she'd been doing anything…well, anything in particular just before they arrived. Bare feet were just bare feet, and her hair could be tousled for any number of reasons. Feeling a quick spurt of irritation at her own self-consciousness, she quashed the urge to smooth her hair. It wasn't any of Keefe's business what she'd been doing or with whom. Just because he was her brother, it didn't mean he was her…brother. And maybe, in an alternate dimension, that would make sense.

Sighing at her own tangled thoughts, Shannon led the way into the living room. She hoped Reece had strong nerves.

Reece had always considered his nerves to be better than average. It had been pretty much a job requirement since nervous people didn't last long in his line of work. But he had to admit that he could think of a whole list of things he'd rather be doing than trying to exchange light conversation with Shannon's rather large older brother. He fought the urge to smooth his hair where Shannon's fingers had been buried in it and hoped that her mouth didn't look as kiss swollen to everyone else as it did to him. Looking at Keefe Walker, he had an uneasy feeling that not much got past those dark eyes.

Keefe's eyes slid from Reece's hair to Shannon's mouth and then back. Reece met his look calmly, but there was nothing he could do to stop the heat he could feel rising in his face. Blushing like a damned schoolboy, he thought, caught between irritation and amusement. Then again, the last time he'd dealt with a hostile older brother, he'd been sixteen and Lisa Ann Palmerston's brother, home on leave from the air force, had caught the two of them red-handed in the back of Reece's beat-up Corvair. Ritchie Palmerston had threatened him with the loss of several treasured body parts. Something told him Keefe Walker was not much for threats but would probably head straight for dismemberment.

"We were on our way home from Los Olivos," Tessa was saying. "Everyone got together at Rachel's for the…" She looked at Shannon and flushed. "Well, *almost* everyone," she said, flustered. "You, um, weren't there, of course, and Gage is in South America or some such place."

"Africa," Keefe said, the first word he'd spoken since the introductions.

"Africa. South America." Tessa waved one hand to

indicate her indifference to the exact location. The baby—David—chortled and clapped his hands together, pleased with the entertainment. Reece grinned, remembering Kyle at that age. God, how many years ago had that been?

"Either way, he couldn't make it home for Thanksgiving but he'll be back for Christmas." She paused and drew a deep breath, sending Shannon a shy smile. "Anyway, we were on our way home and we thought we'd drop in, since you couldn't make it home for Thanksgiving and this is on the way. More or less."

She looked uncomfortable, and Reece wondered just how far out of the way they'd come for this casual visit. And wasn't it interesting that Shannon had missed out on a family get-together, choosing to stay here and fill her home with a mixed bag of misfits and strays for the holiday? Couldn't be a major breach with her family, or Tessa and Keefe wouldn't be here. On the other hand, the tension in the atmosphere made it pretty plain that there was a problem of some sort.

"I'm glad you stopped by," Shannon said, and Reece gave her points for sincerity. He wondered if anyone else noticed the fine lines of tension bracketing that full mouth. Maybe he should come to her rescue? But short of setting fire to the sofa or faking a seizure, he didn't see a way to cut this visit short. Besides, rescuing her suggested that they were…involved, which they weren't. Never mind that not ten minutes ago he'd had her pressed so close against him that she probably had the imprint of his shirt buttons on her breasts. And this was definitely not the time to be thinking about her breasts, not with her brother standing there looking at him with those dark eyes that saw way too much for comfort.

"Shannon said you're a neighbor?" Keefe asked.

"More or less." Reece leaned against the back of the sofa. Might as well *look* relaxed, even if he didn't *feel* relaxed. "My grandfather owned the house next door. He died a few months ago, and I'm staying there while I clean the place out, get it ready to put on the market."

"So you're not staying on permanently?" There was nothing but polite interest in Keefe's tone, but Reece didn't think it was his imagination that put a hopeful note in the question. There was only one possible response, of course. Never mind that rattling the other man's cage was a testosterone-laden cliché. It was just irresistible.

"Hard to say," he murmured. "The place sort of…grows on you." A glance in Shannon's direction would have overplayed his hand so he kept his eyes on the other man, his expression easy, open, as innocent as he could make it. There was a quick flash of humor in those dark eyes, acknowledgment of the hit, maybe, and Reece let his mouth curve in a half smile. It was practically bonding, guy style.

When he looked at Shannon, she gave him that look of mingled irritation and amusement that was unique to females witnessing obscure male territorial rituals. There was only one possible response to that look. Reece widened his eyes in mock innocence, and her mouth twitched before being sternly controlled.

"Why don't I make a pot of coffee?" she said, apparently deciding to ignore the whole exchange.

"Sounds good," Keefe said. "I'll help you with it."

Reece saw a quick flare of something that might have been panic in Shannon's eyes at the thought of being alone with her older brother, and he had the impulse to offer to help with the coffee, too, but judging from Keefe's expression, it wouldn't be anything more than a temporary stay of execution. Whatever he wanted to say to his sister, he looked determined to get it said. If it wasn't over a coffeemaker now, it might end up being over a midnight snack hours from now. Might as well let him get it out.

He watched them leave and then turned to meet Tessa's shy smile. The baby bounced against her hip, looking at Reece with a bright, interested expression that made him grin.

"So, how old is David?"

Shannon was painfully aware of Keefe's rather large presence in her kitchen as she went through the familiar motions of getting out the coffee grinder and taking the beans out of the freezer. Of her four newly acquired brothers, Keefe was the quietest, the one she found hardest to know. Not that she knew any of them, really. She'd made sure of that, she thought, with a twinge of guilt. She'd been careful to keep her distance from them for reasons she'd been equally careful not to examine too closely.

"You grind your own beans?" he asked.

It was the first thing either of them had said since leaving Reece and Tessa in the living room. Though that had only been a few minutes ago, Shannon's voice felt rusty, as if she hadn't used it in weeks.

"It's supposed to taste better." She shrugged as she twisted the lid on the grinder. "I'm not sure I can tell the difference, really."

The high-pitched whir of the grinder cut off any reply he might have made, and she allowed herself a moment of wistful regret that grinding coffee only took a few seconds. When she shut the machine off, the silence seemed painfully loud. Well, he could just say something, she told herself. She dumped the freshly ground coffee into the filter, inhaling deeply at the rich, brown smell of it. *She* wasn't the one who'd shown up on *his* doorstep with some sort of agenda in mind. If the silence didn't bother him, it certainly didn't bother her. It didn't bother her at all.

She hadn't turned on the overhead light, turning on the milk-glass lamp that sat on the table and one of the fluorescent lamps that were mounted under the upper cabinets instead. She usually found the soft glow of the smaller lights restful, but it would take more than cozy lighting to soothe the tension in the room tonight.

Keefe was leaning back against the counter, hands braced on either side of his hips. The body language was relaxed but his eyes were watchful, still. Shannon fussed with the coffee cups she'd taken from the cupboard, arranging them just so on the Holstein patterned tray.

"So, how was your holiday?" she said, and barely managed to restrain a wince at her own perky tone. Apparently, he had a higher tolerance for uncomfortable silence than she did.

"It was good," he said. "Too much food, too many people for the space. Lots of noise. Gets noisier as the kids get older."

"Sounds nice," Shannon said, trying to remember how many nieces and nephews she had. Three? Four? She felt an unpleasant little pinch of shame that she didn't even know that much.

"We were all sorry you couldn't join us," Keefe said. One corner of his mouth kicked up in a half smile.

"It's been a very long time since we were all together for the holidays."

"I already had other plans," she said, hating the defensive note that crept into her voice. She wanted to sound assured, mature with just a hint of none-of-your-business. Instead, she sounded as if she was making excuses. God, was there some genetic thing about older brothers that made her feel guilty even when she didn't have anything to feel guilty about? Well, not much to feel guilty about.

"It was…I've had this sort of potluck for the last couple of years," she said, even as she told herself that she didn't owe him any explanations. "I, ah, didn't want to disappoint people."

Keefe nodded in apparent acceptance. Shannon looked desperately at the coffeemaker but the carafe was still less than half-full.

"Mom's hoping you'll join us for Christmas."

Mom. Shannon winced away from the word. The small, dark-haired woman with the warm brown eyes was *his* mother but, no matter how much she wished otherwise, she couldn't quite see Rachel Walker as *her* mother. *Her* mother was the ghostly figure in her childhood imaginings, a not-quite-remembered presence. She'd grown up telling herself how things would have been if her mother were alive. *They wouldn't move so often if her mother were alive. They'd have a real home if her mother were alive. Her father would care about her if her mother were alive.* She couldn't help but appreciate the irony when she found out that it wasn't her mother's *death* that had made her life what it was, it was, in an odd way, the fact that she was alive.

"I-I'm not sure what my plans are for Christmas,"

she said finally, unwilling to say yes, not quite able to say no.

A muscle flexed in Keefe's jaw, and Shannon had to look away from the sudden sharpness in his eyes. She stared at the coffeemaker, willing it to drip faster. Out of the corner of her eye, she could see him. He was still leaning against the counter but, where his fingers curled around the edge, the knuckles showed white through his tanned skin. She swallowed and kept her eyes on the coffee, which was still dripping with glacial slowness into the glass carafe.

"You know, for someone who went to a fair amount of trouble to find her long-lost family, you sure don't show much interest in getting to know us." He didn't raise his voice. He didn't need to, not when he could put razor-sharp anger into that easy tone.

"Of course I want to…" He arched one dark brow, and she stumbled to a halt, color flooding her cheeks. No, she couldn't really expect him to believe that, not when she'd turned down most of their invitations and offered none of her own. "I've been really busy," she said, hating the weak sound of the excuse. Shame fueled a jagged little spurt of anger. What right did he have to come into her home and chastise her? She tilted her chin and met his eyes. "I have a business to run. It doesn't allow me much time for a social life."

"Social life?" Keefe repeated the phrase with a deadly lack of emphasis. "Funny, I never thought to put family in the category of a social life."

Shannon flushed and looked away. "You know what I mean."

"No, I don't." He straightened away from the counter. There was nothing threatening about the move but he suddenly seemed to be *looming* over her, and she had to resist the urge to step back, to put more space between them. "I'll tell you what I *do* know. I know *you* came looking for *us*. I know you waltzed into our lives—into our mother's life—waved hello and then waltzed back out again. I know she looked like she'd been kicked in the gut when she said you weren't coming for the holiday." His voice was low and even, but the words hit with the impact of bullets. "And I know I don't ever want to see that look in her eyes again. Maybe you've got a reason for keeping your distance, but just in case it hasn't occurred to you yet, let me point out that you're not the only one involved here."

Shannon wanted to hold on to her anger, wanted to wrap herself in a blanket of righteous indignation, but she couldn't quite manage it because, beneath the anger in his eyes, there was something that told her Rachel Walker wasn't the only one she'd hurt. She opened her mouth to tell him…to tell him— She wasn't sure what she wanted to tell him. That he was wrong, that she did know she wasn't the only one involved, that the last thing she wanted to do was hurt anyone, that she didn't want to be hurt herself.

Before she could sort out her tangled thoughts and come up with actual words, the coffeemaker pinged. Startled, Shannon jumped and jerked toward the counter, staring blankly at the full carafe.

"Coffee's ready," she said stupidly.

Keefe sighed and lifted one hand, running his fingers through his dark hair. "You know, maybe we'd better head home," he said, looking suddenly tired and older. "It's getting late and we've still got a long drive ahead of us. Sorry I put you to the trouble of making coffee."

"No trouble," she murmured.

He started toward the door and, as if it belonged to someone else, she saw her hand come out, her fingers curling into the sleeve of his chambray shirt. "Keefe, I...I didn't..."

He waited, his expression unrevealing as he looked down at her. Shannon bit her lip, fumbling for the right words.

"I-I'll try to be there for Christmas," she said at last. It seemed pathetically inadequate, but maybe it was enough because his eyes were suddenly warm.

"Good." One corner of his mouth curved up in an oddly endearing half smile. "You know, if you give us a chance, you might even end up liking us."

He didn't seem to expect an answer, which was just as well because she could hardly tell him that that was what she was afraid of, that she'd like them, that she'd more than like them.

Feeling as if she'd been through an emotional wringer, Shannon followed him out of the kitchen. She could hear Reece talking, the low rumble of his voice in response to Tessa's lighter, softer tones. When she stepped into the living room, she saw that he was standing in front of the fireplace, the baby was perched on his hip, chewing happily on Reece's knuckle. Tessa was sitting on the sofa, smiling as she watched the two of them. The smile faded when she looked at her husband, her eyes concerned and questioning. Whatever she read in his face must have reassured her because the smile returned, her softly pretty features lighting up with an expression so full of love that Shannon looked away, feeling her heart twist a little with something that wasn't—couldn't be—envy.

Not that looking at Reece was much better. He held the baby with a casual ease that spoke of experience.

It was an unexpected side of her tall, dark and handsome neighbor and made her realize how little she really knew about him. Her skin still tingled with the imprint of his hands, but she didn't know if he had children or if he was—horrible thought—married.

David stopped chewing on Reece's knuckle and pulled back to study his hand with solemn intensity that hinted at deep, philosophical questions.

"Gonna read my palm?" Reece asked, grinning.

"He's probably trying to decide where to chew next," Keefe said, his tone dry. "It's worse than having a puppy in the house."

At the sound of his father's voice, David's head jerked around, his face breaking into a wide, mostly toothless grin. Squealing with delight, he threw himself toward Keefe, heedless of the five-foot gap between him and his goal. Reece caught him easily, fingers splayed across the baby's chest. Grinning, he handed the squirming bundle off to Keefe.

"Looks like he's aiming for a career as an acrobat."

"I think his main goal in life is to see if he can turn all my hair gray before he learns to walk," Keefe said dryly. He shifted his gaze to his wife and raised his eyebrows. "I was thinking maybe we ought to skip coffee and hit the road. It's getting pretty late."

"I was just thinking the same thing," Tessa said, standing up. She gave Shannon an apologetic look. "I hope you don't mind."

Mind? When the alternative was the four of them sitting here, trying to make conversation over coffee that none of them wanted? Shannon just hoped she didn't look as relieved as she felt, because she really did like Tessa.

Goodbyes were mercifully brief, and it was easy to

pretend she didn't see the look that passed between the two men, one of those annoying male exchanges that managed to convey ridiculous testosterone-driven concepts of territorial warnings and responses to same, all with just a glance.

She closed the door behind Keefe and Tessa and, for the second time in less than an hour, breathed a sigh of relief. This had, without question, been the strangest Thanksgiving of her life. An afternoon spent preventing a pitched battle between Mavis and just about every other turkey-eating guest, followed by a kiss that had threatened to leave her toes in a permanent curl and then this visit from Keefe, who'd made her see things about herself that she didn't particularly like. And it was still only seven o'clock.

"You want some help drinking that coffee?" Reece asked, and she turned to look at him, resting her shoulders back against the door. He was standing in the living room doorway, one shoulder braced against the frame.

"Help would be good," she said, surprised to find she meant it. She was generally content with her own company, but for some reason she wasn't particularly anxious to be alone tonight. She pushed away from the door and headed for the kitchen, aware of Reece following her, trying not to think of how good it felt not to be alone with her thoughts right now.

The Holstein-patterned tray was still sitting on the counter, holding four cups and a blue-flowered sugar bowl that didn't match the red spatterware creamer. She'd bought most of her dishes at garage sales and flea markets and, if any two pieces matched, it was purely by coincidence. While she was putting two of the cups away, Reece was lifting the carafe out of the coffeemaker and filling the remaining cups.

"Maybe this will kill the taste of the aspic," he said, lifting his cup—a thick white china mug decorated with a bright-red chicken on one side and a neon-yellow sun on the other.

Shannon grinned as she stirred two spoonfuls of sugar into her own cup. "Poor Vangie."

"*Poor Vangie?*" Reece arched one dark brow and shook his head. "How about some sympathy for the victims? I think that stuff softened the enamel on my teeth."

Laughing, Shannon picked up her cup and tilted her head toward the door. "I've been on my feet most of the day, and I think I hear the sofa calling my name."

If the sofa hadn't been actually sending out signals, it certainly seemed to welcome her. Shannon sighed as she sank into the yielding comfort of the plump cushions. Reece settled in the blue-plaid chair, one ankle propped on the opposite knee. He looked relaxed, at ease in her home, comfortable with the silence between them. She heard the barely audible whoosh as the old gravity-fed heater kicked on. The sound made her realize that the room was on the cool side, not uncomfortably so but enough to provide a reminder that summer was well and truly gone.

Reece took a drink of coffee, the silly chicken mug all but hidden in his big hand. It reminded her of the easy way he'd held Keefe's son.

"Are you married?"

He looked at her, brows raised in a look of mild surprise. "Not anymore. Why?"

"I thought bachelors were supposed to run in terror

at the mere sight of an infant, but you seemed pretty comfortable with David.''

''I have a son,'' he said easily. ''It's been a while since he was that size, but I guess there are some things you don't forget.''

''I guess not.'' She wondered how long he'd been divorced and if he saw much of his son, but couldn't think of a way to ask without sounding nosy.

''We got divorced when Kyle was eight,'' he said, as if reading her thoughts. Or maybe it was just the obvious next question when someone said they were divorced. ''It was an amicable divorce, or as close as you can come when you're talking divorce. Caroline remarried a couple years later, and she and her second husband have two children together. They live in Virginia. Her husband's a lawyer with a big D.C. law firm, and Caroline sells overpriced antiques to people with more money than sense. Charles, her husband, is a decent guy.''

''It's great that you were able to stay on good terms.''

''We worked at it.'' Reece took a sip of his coffee, now tepid and slightly bitter, just like his marriage had ended up, he thought, and then wondered if it was a sign of encroaching middle age when he started finding metaphors in a coffee cup. ''Neither of us wanted Kyle to get caught in the middle of the mess we'd made. Kyle's nineteen now and still speaking to both of us, so I guess we did okay.''

''It's too bad more people don't work at it,'' Shannon murmured. ''Especially when children are involved.''

Reece nodded and wondered what had put the distant look in her eyes. Curled up in the corner of the sofa, those distracting legs curled up under the long folds of her skirt, her hair tumbling around her shoulders in red-gold waves, her expression soft and almost wistful, she looked simultaneously tempting and untouchable. Less than an hour ago he'd been holding her, his fingers buried in her hair, her mouth sweet and warm beneath his. It hardly seemed possible, yet the memory of it was so real he could almost reach out and touch it. It was, in fact, oddly more touchable than the woman herself was at the moment.

"You want to talk about it?" He caught her quick, startled look.

"Talk about what?"

Definitely not cut out for undercover work, Reece thought. Couldn't lie worth a damn. Those big blue eyes slid away from his as if afraid of what he might read there. He debated letting the subject drop. Whatever was bothering her, it was none of his business. He was just passing through, not planning to stay, not planning to get involved. Except he already was involved. Maybe he had been from the moment he'd opened his door to a leggy redhead of dubious sanity. Or maybe it had been the offer of toaster waffles and grape jelly that had done it. Or maybe it was those eyes, looking so…lost. With a sigh for best-laid plans that seemed to be agleying all over the place, he gave up the whole idea of noninvolvement.

"You want to talk about whatever it was that had your big brother all tight-jawed?" he asked. "Feel free to tell me to butt out."

Shannon opened her mouth to tell him—politely— to do just that, but she closed it again without speaking, startled to realize that she *did* want to talk about it. Sort of. Given a choice she would have liked to forget about the whole tangled mess but, since selective amnesia wasn't an option, maybe talking about it would help sort things out in her mind.

"It's a long story," she said, half hoping Reece would grab the excuse to end the conversation. When he arched one brow and looked expectant, she sighed, half relieved, half irritated.

"It sounds like something out of a Dickens novel. Or a soap opera." Shannon paused to take a sip of her coffee. The tepid liquid made her grimace, and she leaned forward to set the cup on the edge of the coffee table. The small delay had given her a chance to sort her thoughts a little and, when she continued, her tone was distant as if she were telling a story about something she'd seen on the news or a movie she'd watched.

"My parents split up before I was born. It was a second marriage for her and she already had four sons. Her first husband was a police officer in Los Angeles, and I guess they were very happy but he was killed in the line of duty. Maybe she was still grieving when she married my father. He was a cop, too, and maybe he reminded her of her first husband." She smoothed her fingers along a fold in her skirt, keeping her eyes on the aimless movement. "Maybe…maybe she really loved him." She released her breath on a long sigh and shrugged irritably. "Whatever. It didn't work out, and they split up before I was born. She got custody but he got visitation rights. I guess things worked out okay for a while, a few years anyway. Then, he showed up to pick me up one day and he just…didn't bring me back."

"Parental abduction," Reece murmured.

"That's what they call it." Shannon leaned her head against the back of the sofa and closed her eyes. "I don't remember much about it. Or about what it was like before he took me. I don't know if it's because I was so young or some sort of traumatic amnesia. I had a few memories of my...family but nothing clear. I grew up thinking my mother was dead. My father moved us around a lot. I suppose he was afraid someone would find out.''

''He must have loved you very much.''

She shrugged. ''I suppose.''

She wanted to believe that, but Shannon couldn't help but think of the lonely years of her childhood, of the silent man who'd seen that she was fed and clothed and educated but had seemed incapable of offering even the simplest gesture of affection. There was a part of her that thought it more likely he'd taken her out of spite and then, once the deed was done, he'd either been too stubborn or too frightened of the consequences to take her back.

Pushing aside the old questions, questions that could never have an answer, Shannon straightened away from the plush cushions and looked at Reece. ''You see before you an authentic milk-carton kid,'' she said, grinning crookedly. ''My face was plastered on dairy products all across America, smiling at people as they ate their breakfast cereal.''

Reece raised his brows and looked impressed. ''That might explain your obsession with Froot Loops.''

Shannon blinked in surprise and then gave a startled little giggle. The few people she'd told about her past had reacted with sympathy and concern. No one had ever *joked* about it.

''I've never met a real celebrity. Should I ask for your autograph?'' Reece asked. His smile widened when she choked on another laugh.

"Talk to my press agent." She'd always found this so difficult to talk about. All the angst and pain. It always seemed so...melodramatic. Never mind that it was all real—all the hurt, all the years lost. She didn't like to talk about it, tried not to think about it but this...this felt good. It felt good to laugh about it.

"Thanks," she said, relaxing back into the cushions, feeling a pleasant lethargy slipping over her. It had been a very long day. Morning seemed a century ago. "I think I needed that laugh."

"Laughter is the best medicine," he said, mock solemn.

"I've heard that rumor," Shannon admitted. She released her breath in a slow sigh. "So, you might as well hear the rest of the story. It's even more like something out of a Dickens plot. My father died when I was eighteen. We'd moved too much for either of us to collect a whole lot by way of household goods, but he had a few boxes that he'd left in storage in Des Moines. I didn't bother to send for the boxes until a couple of years ago, and—here's the part Dickens would have liked—I found these pictures of me with these people who looked vaguely familiar and papers that made it clear my mother hadn't really died when I was born. It was just a little bit of a shock."

Her tone was light but it didn't take much imagination to know what she must have felt, realizing that her father had lied to her, that her whole life had been based on a lie. Reece had had the rug pulled out from under him a time or two, had his entire life turned upside down in the space between one breath and the next. It was never a pleasant experience. The only words that came to mind sounded incredibly banal and meaningless so he said nothing, letting a surprisingly easy silence build between them.

"You know that thing about being careful what you wish for?" Shannon asked suddenly, smiling a little as she looked at him. "I'd spent my whole life wishing I had a big family, brothers and sisters, a mother, roots— every cliché you've ever seen on television. And then I found out I had four older brothers and a mother who wanted nothing more than to welcome me back into the fold."

"But you discovered the family business is white slavery?" he asked, and she grinned and shook her head.

"No. No, they're all really nice." She pleated the hem of her skirt between her fingers, her eyes on the aimless movement. "My...brothers even married nice women and their kids seem nice, too. They're all just..."

"Nice?" Reece finished, when she seemed at a loss for words. She gave a surprised little huff of laughter.

"Exactly. They're just...really nice. Not that I'd want them to be un-nice," she added, frowning a little as she groped for words to explain something she didn't completely understand herself. "I mean, it's great that they were so warm and welcoming. Really great."

"Must be hard, though, hard to wake up one morning and find yourself with a ready-made family, especially when you don't remember them but they remember you. Lot of expectations there."

"Yes." Shannon felt something tight and hard loosen inside her. "Yes, that's it exactly."

That was what she hadn't been able to articulate these past few months. The Walkers had opened their arms and their hearts to her and, when she couldn't do the same, she'd felt guilty and confused and lost. She'd found the warm, loving family of her childhood fantasies, but they were strangers to her. In retrospect, it seemed ridiculous that she could have expected them to be anything else, but there had been a part of her that half expected some mystical emotional connection to spring up the moment she saw them. Blood calling to blood like something out of a Victorian novel, she thought, with a twinge of sad amusement for her own naiveté. Instead what she'd felt was the weight of their expectations and the sharp bite of her own disappointment.

"Family," Reece said. "It's never as simple as it looks in the sitcoms." He lifted his empty cup from the coffee table and stood up. "Definitely a case of false advertising."

Following his lead, Shannon rose, too. "Maybe they should come with warning labels. Professional actors just pretending to be a family—don't try this at home, boys and girls."

He followed her out to the kitchen, setting his cup on the counter next to the sink before turning to look at her. His hand came up, fingers barely touching her lower lip.

"You know, it's been a long time since I've had a big brother interrupt a necking session."

"Necking session?" she arched one brow. "Is that what it was?"

Reece's smile was wicked. "If you have to ask, maybe I need to work on my technique."

"I don't think you need to worry about that," she said primly. She was fairly sure that if his technique got any better, she'd have melted into a puddle in the entryway, but she wasn't going to tell him that.

"I'll take that as a compliment." He brushed his thumb across her mouth and she knew, as surely as if he'd spoken out loud, that he was thinking about kissing her again. She waited, not sure what she'd do if he did. Kiss him back, that was pretty much a given. Based on her one-time experience, she didn't think it was possible to *not* respond when Reece Morgan kissed you.

He let his hand drop, and the moment was gone. Shannon told herself she was relieved. Well, mostly relieved.

"It's been a long day. I should go, let you unwind." He picked up the big glass bowl that had held spinach salad and moved toward the front door.

Shannon followed, suddenly aware of how tired she was. It really had been an incredibly long day. She wrapped her fingers around the edge of the door, leaning against it as he stepped out onto the porch. It was full dark out, and the air was cool and dry. It wasn't the crisp, maybe-it-will-snow weather of picture postcards but there was a feeling of autumn in the air. Maybe it was the collective panic rising from the home of every potential shopper, that humming awareness that there were only four more weeks until Christmas breaking through the post-Thanksgiving-dinner lassitude.

"Thanks for the dinner."

"Even the aspic?" she asked, biting her lip to hold back a smile.

"Don't push it," he said, and she laughed.

Leaning against the door, she watched him walk

down the cracked walkway, admiring the way the faded denim of his jeans hugged his narrow hips. Life was certainly more interesting since Reece Morgan had moved back to town.

Chapter 6

Reece stared glumly at the partially disassembled faucet. He picked up a washer, moved it from one side of an unidentifiable part to the other and looked at it some more.

He could break down an AK-47 in the pitch-dark, working solely by feel, and reassemble it again in a matter of minutes. He could rig a car bomb with not much more than a pocket knife and a wad of chewing gum, turn a tube of toothpaste and a couple of hairpins into a deadly weapon and build a fire in the middle of a blinding rainstorm. He was skilled in several forms of hand-to-hand combat, had fought his way through hostile jungles, the back alley of more than one foreign city and escaped from an enemy prison—twice. His body bore the scars of two bullet wounds, half a dozen close encounters with sharp-edged weapons and the more recent car wreck that had nearly killed him.

For the last twenty years or so, he'd felt justified in

considering himself a man of more than average competence, equipped for survival in even the most hostile of environs. Only now did he realize he had yet to face the ultimate challenge. It was one thing to look death in the eye; it was something else altogether to go head-to-head with a broken faucet.

Still frowning, Reece picked up a bottle of a surprisingly decent locally brewed beer and took a fortifying swallow. A man was supposed to be master of his environment. It was one of the things that separated man from beast, civilization from chaos. Technology—that was the problem. A few thousand years ago he could have just built a hut in the howling wilderness, killed a mastodon or two for dinner and felt pretty good about himself. Now a man needed to understand the intricacies of plumbing before he could be master of his own home.

He'd rather face a mastodon any day.

The sound of the doorbell offered the possibility of retreat with honor. No one could expect him to think about plumbing when there was someone at the door, anxious to either lighten his wallet or save his soul. At this point he didn't care which it was, as long as it didn't involve washers, wrenches or gaskets of any kind.

"Frank." Reece greeted the other man with real pleasure. In the week since Thanksgiving, he'd thought about calling several times and just hadn't gotten around to it. He was glad Frank had taken the initiative. "Come on in."

"Hope you don't mind me just dropping in," Frank said. "You can tell me to go away if you're busy."

"Actually, I had an appointment with destiny but it

was canceled." Reece shut the door and turned to see Frank studying the dimly lit living room.

"Love what you've done with the place," he said, looking at the pile of cardboard boxes that blocked access to the sofa and the mound of bulging black plastic trash bags that blocked half the front window.

"It's called Dumpster decor," Reece told him. "It's the latest thing on the East Coast."

Frank nodded. "I can see why. It's cheap and you can definitely do it yourself."

"Don't be fooled by the apparent simplicity," Reece warned him. "It took me three solid weeks of work to achieve this effect."

"I bet." Frank looked around again. "You got someone coming to get rid of this junk?"

"Tomorrow," Reece said immediately, and Frank chuckled.

"I helped my parents clean out my great-aunt Josephine's house a couple of years ago. I don't think she'd thrown anything out since Truman was in office."

"I think my grandfather has her beat," Reece said, thinking of the stacks of old envelopes saved to use for scratch paper, the balls of string and an entire drawer full of rubber bands that were so old they'd disintegrated at a touch.

"You want a beer?" he asked, leading the way into the kitchen.

"Thanks." Frank nodded approval at the label when Reece handed him an ice-cold bottle. "Good stuff. I know the guy who makes it, Larry Lebowitz. He was in my class in high school. Computer nerd, tape on his glasses, pocket protector, the whole nine yards. Figured he'd vanish into the bowels of some big company and never be heard from again. Went off to San Francisco for a few years then came back with a boyfriend who looks like a refrigerator with a head, bought an old commercial laundry and started a brewery. Everyone thought they were crazy but they've done okay. Won a prize at the State Fair a couple years back.'' He grinned. "And Larry still looks like a computer nerd.'' He took a long pull from the bottle and, when he lowered it, his eyes settled on the pathetic pile of faucet parts on the counter. "Need some help?''

Reece weighed his options. He could give a manly grunt and deny any need for assistance or he could abandon his pride and hope Frank actually knew what all those little parts did.

"You know anything about faucets?'' he asked, choosing a cautious middle ground between denial and shameless begging.

"I run a hardware store,'' Frank reminded him. "There's not much I don't know about faucets. What's the problem?''

"The main problem seems to be that I don't know what the hell I'm doing,'' Reece admitted, tossing pride to the wind in hopes of actually having a working faucet again. "I got it apart okay, but I know there weren't this many parts when I started and I think the repair kit I bought is actually for the carburetor on a '56 Chevy because none of this stuff looks like it goes in a faucet.''

Frank grinned. "Not a do-it-yourselfer, I take it.''

"My idea of doing it myself is picking up the phone to call the manager of my apartment building.'' Reece eyed the other man speculatively. "There's a case of beer in it for you if you can actually put it back together.''

"Bribery." Frank nodded his approval. "I like that, but I'd probably have done it for a six pack." He set the bottle on the counter and began rolling up the sleeves of his blue flannel shirt, eyeing the parts like a man who knew what he was looking at.

"I don't mind paying a fair price for a working faucet," Reece said graciously.

He leaned one hip against the counter and watched as Frank sorted through the parts, setting some aside, shaking his head a time or two as he disassembled some of Reece's tentative attempts to put the thing back together again.

"Man, you're a plumber's wet dream," he said, grinning as he pried apart two items that apparently didn't relate to each other.

"I bought the kit at your store. It was right under a sign that said it was a suitable project for home owners without much do-it-yourself experience," Reece pointed out.

"Yeah, but we didn't say it was suitable for people with severe parts-recognition impairment and a total inability to read a schematic." Frank's grin held cheerful malice.

"Bite me, McKinnon." Reece was too grateful for the help to put much force behind the words.

He finished the last of his beer, debated about getting another one, and then decided it was too early in the day for a second. He dropped the empty bottle in the recycle bin and leaned back against the counter while Frank worked.

Thin sunlight shone through the window over the sink. It had rained the day before and the sky was still overcast, defying the weather reports that had promised clear skies and sunshine. The window faced Shannon's house, and Reece found his thoughts drifting in that direction.

He'd seen her several times in the last week but not to talk to. He was usually halfway through his second cup of coffee about the time she was leaving in the morning. From the front porch he could watch her back out of her driveway. She drove a fire-engine-red Miata that clashed so magnificently with her hair that it was a sort of fashion statement all on its own. She intrigued him, he admitted, and not just because she did interesting things to his libido.

"Have you known Shannon long?"

If Frank was surprised by the abrupt question, he didn't say so. "About as long as anyone, I guess. I was friends with Johnny Devereux before they got married."

"Married!" Reece was too startled to conceal his reaction. "She's married?"

"Widowed," Frank said. "Johnny died three years ago this past August."

Reece stared at him blankly, trying to slot this new information into the image he had of his pretty neighbor with the long, lazy stride and easy smile. "She's awfully young to be widowed," he said at last, the first clear thought to surface out of the tangle.

"Yeah, it was a real tragedy." Frank nodded as he reached for two parts that bore no apparent relation to each other and put them together with a quick twist of his fingers. "She and Johnny had only been married a few months. Johnny was a firefighter and she was working as a receptionist in a dentist's office. A bunch of the local guys got called out to help with a big brush fire in Los Angeles, one of those where they had to call in units from all over the state. It looked like they might be getting it under control then the Santa Ana winds kicked up and they were right back where they started. Johnny and another firefighter were trapped in a wash when the winds shifted. The fire went right over them, not a damned thing anyone could do to get to them.''

Imagining it, Reece felt sick to his stomach. He'd seen what burns could do to the human body. ''Hell of a way to die.''

''Yeah.'' Frank nodded, his round face uncharacteristically somber. ''The other guy made it a couple of days but he was so badly burned that...'' He stopped and shook his head and, after a moment, went back to work on the faucet while Reece stared blankly out the window at the house next door, his mind spinning with the effort of trying to shuffle all this new information into what he knew—or thought he knew—of his neighbor.

''I was a little surprised Shannon stayed on,'' Frank said as he reached for a wrench. ''She'd only lived here a few months and, with Johnny gone, I thought she might sell the house and move away from the memories, but a couple months after he died, she bought the shop.'' He glanced up, saw Reece's blank look and clarified. ''Quilter's Haven over on Sycamore.''

''She owns a store that sells quilts?'' Reece asked, feeling his mental image shift yet again.

''Not the actual quilts. Fabric and stuff to make quilts,'' Frank clarified.

''People make quilts?'' Reece asked blankly. He had a vague image of little old ladies in long dresses hunched over a cloth-covered frame, gossiping while they wielded their needles. ''Enough of them to support a whole shop just for that?''

"Oh, yeah." Frank laughed. "I heard Shannon tell someone once that a quilt shop is a destination business, and she sure was right. Quilters drive all the way from Los Angeles to go to her shop. It's weird because there are plenty of quilt shops in L.A. but they'll drive all the way out here, anyway, like some sort of religious trek.

"I thought she was crazy when she bought the place and I told her so, but she just gave me this little smile and said it would give her something to do, so Kelly and I pitched in and helped her get the place in shape. Kelly went to work for her from day one, and I'll be damned if she hasn't made a success out of it. She's not getting rich but she's turning a profit, which is more than most small businesses manage."

So, his long-legged neighbor was a successful businesswoman. It was difficult to reconcile that with the woman who let a coffee-shop employee intimidate her into grinding her own coffee or the one who would invite a stranger to breakfast to spite her nosy neighbor. On the other hand she certainly had people skills, he thought, remembering the way she'd managed to avert a war over the turkey leftovers last week. That kind of diplomacy came in handy for working with the public.

When he'd seen her going off to work in the mornings, he'd pictured her working in an office somewhere, not running her own business.

Obviously, he had a lot to learn about his temporary neighbor.

"Ohmmm. Ohmmm."

Shannon grinned as Kelly chanted under her breath. "You know, you sound like you're set on fast-forward. I think you're supposed to try for a sort of slow, rhythmic pace. The monks aren't actually racing each other to the finish line.''

"They've never had to deal with Edith Hackle-meyer,'' Kelly muttered darkly. "The woman has the taste of a-an aardvark and all the finesse of a water buffalo.''

"Actually, there are very few aardvark quilters. I think it's the opposable-thumb problem.'' Shannon un-rolled the last yard of fabric from a bolt and set the empty cardboard insert aside. The fabric was a leafy print with brightly colored frogs scattered across it, and they'd sold the whole bolt in two days, so she'd reordered in hopes that the sudden frog frenzy would last until the new bolt arrived.

"Well, I'd rather deal with an aardvark than deal with that woman,'' Kelly said, casting a dark look toward the back of the shop where Edith was looking at fabrics. "Do you know what she said to me?''

"With Edith, almost anything is possible.''

"She said that bleached blond hair tended to make a woman look hard and cheap.'' Kelly smoothed her hand over her streaky blond hair, her eyes bright with annoyance. "I *don't* bleach my hair.''

Shannon choked on a laugh. It was so typically Edith. She hadn't actually said that Kelly's hair was bleached so no one could accuse her of making a personal remark. If Kelly *chose* to take an apparently random remark personally, well, that was hardly Edith's fault.

"I *don't* bleach my hair,'' Kelly whispered fiercely, apparently objecting to Shannon's obvious amusement.

"I believe you.'' Shannon assured her. "I just can't help but admire the way she manages to deliver an insult without ever actually saying anything insulting. You've got to admit, it's a real talent.''

"It's the only one she has," Kelly muttered, moving away from the cutting table as Edith approached with half a dozen bolts of fabric stacked in her skinny arms.

Shannon put on her best, friendly shop-owner smile. "Did you find what you wanted?"

"Eventually." Edith pursed her lips in discontent. "Most of the fabrics are so bright and garish. I don't understand why you don't stock a better selection of quieter, more tasteful prints. *You* wouldn't remember, of course, but those of us who were quilting in the seventies remember the charming little calicos that were available then."

Shannon kept her smile in place, ignoring Kelly's muted growl from behind her. Most of the long-time quilters she knew were grateful for the wide selection of fabrics available to them now and referred to the seventies as the dark ages of quilting.

"There are fashions in quilt fabric, just like everything else. Right now the fashion is for cheerful prints and colors."

"Garish," Edith said, sniffing her contempt.

"Well, I'm glad you found something to your taste," Shannon said, ignoring the comment as she lifted the first bolt off the stack and unrolled the fabric onto the table. "How much of this one would you like?"

"Two yards of each," Edith said. "Whatever I don't need for the top I'll use to piece the back."

Kelly was looking at the stack of fabric and rolling her eyes in disgust, and Shannon bit the inside of her lip to hold back a laugh. She generally tried to appreciate her customers' choices. It was both good manners

and good business, but she had to admit that Edith
made it difficult. She must have looked long and hard
to find six fabrics so dull and washed-out. Paired with
something more vivid, they would have provided the
eye with a resting place and added richness to a quilt.
Mixed together, they looked old and worn-out, even
before they were cut from the bolt. Still, the old rule
about the customer always being right held true, even
when they had no taste.

"Another log cabin quilt?" Shannon asked as she
measured off the fabric. As far as she knew, log cabin
was the only pattern Edith ever made. She turned out
half a dozen log cabin quilts a year, each as uninspired
as the one before it, and donated them all to a woman's
shelter. Shannon tried hard to admire her for the charitable work but it wasn't easy.

"Yes. For those poor, unfortunate women. I feel it's
important to do what I can for those less fortunate than
myself. You do still offer a discount on fabric bought
for charitable purposes, don't you?"

"Of course."

Kelly gave a disgusted snort, or maybe she was just
clearing her throat. Shannon decided to give her the
benefit of the doubt, but to be safe she kept her attention on the fabric. Laughter and rotary cutters were not
a good mix.

"Two yards of the green, too." Edith tapped the bolt
with one finger as if Shannon might need guidance in
telling green from pink. "I understand you've spent
some time with the Morgan boy," Edith said and, between the abrupt change of topic and the word *boy,* it
took Shannon a moment to figure out who she was
talking about.

"He came over for Thanksgiving dinner," she admitted.

"I generally don't interfere in other people's business," Edith said, and Shannon shot an involuntary look at the older woman's nose to see if it had grown. In her experience Edith Hacklemeyer *lived* to interfere. "But I feel it's my duty to offer you some advice."

"Really, it's not necessary." Even as she spoke, Shannon knew it was futile. Nothing could stop Edith when she was on a roll.

"You're too young to remember Reece Morgan from the first time he lived here. Of course, you didn't even live in Serenity Falls, but if you *had* lived here, you would have been too young to remember him."

From somewhere behind a wooden display full of books, Shannon heard Kelly choking back a laugh. Ignoring her, she concentrated on cutting a straight line.

"But I certainly remember him," Edith announced, verbally shrugging off the muddled beginning of her speech. "And let me tell you, he's trouble."

Shannon was surprised to feel a twinge of real annoyance. Usually Edith's pompous pronouncements rolled off her back. The woman loved to complain, especially about things that were none of her business. But this time she found herself remembering the gentle way Reece had handled Keefe's baby son, the way he could smile with just his eyes, and her patience thinned.

"He's been very pleasant," she said mildly. "Very pleasant" seemed like an odd thing to say about a man she'd almost had sex with up against her own front door but it would have to do.

"The devil can charm when he wants to," Edith said, pressing her lips together.

More choking sounds came from behind the books.

Edith cast a frowning look in that direction, but Kelly was either crouched down straightening out the fabric below the book rack or she was rolling on the floor trying to control her laughter. Shannon kept her attention focused strictly on the task in front of her, folding the cut end of fabric neatly over the bolt and pinning it in place.

"As the twig is bent, so grows the tree," Edith continued, dismissing the noise.

Had she memorized an entire book of homilies? Shannon reached for the next bolt and tried to block out the other woman's voice.

"Not that Joe Morgan didn't do his best, but you can't make a silk purse out of a sow's ear."

The bell over the door rang and Shannon looked up eagerly, hoping for an entire busload of quilters to come spilling through the door or even a frazzled mother with sticky-fingered children in tow, anything to provide a distraction.

What she got was Reece Morgan, all six feet four inches of him. He was wearing black jeans that hugged his narrow hips in a way that was probably illegal in more conservative parts of the country and a heavy gray cable-knit sweater that emphasized the width of his shoulders. Droplets of water sparkled against the thick darkness of his hair, courtesy of the light mist falling outside.

His eyes skimmed the shop, one dark brow arching when he saw Edith, and then his gaze settled on Shannon, his mouth curving in a smile that made her knees go weak. She smiled back helplessly. Edith was still droning on, something about troublemakers and spots that couldn't be changed, but it was background noise. Somewhere in the back of her mind she wondered if

she should be worried about that, about the way everything else just faded away except Reece—his eyes, his
smile, the subtle smell of wet sidewalks and damp wool
that came in with him.

The multicolored striped awning sparkling against
the white stucco storefront had caught his eye and, on
an impulse, he'd turned into the small parking lot
across the street. Impulse didn't explain why he'd been
driving down that particular street to start with, but
Reece decided to cut himself some slack and not insist
on an explanation.

Stepping out of the drifting mist into the bright
warmth of Quilter's Haven, Reece was reminded of the
scene in the *Wizard of Oz* where Dorothy opens the
door of the hurricane-tumbled house and steps out of
the black-and-white world of Kansas into the techni-
color sprawl of Oz. The walls were lined with bolts of
fabric in every color of the rainbow. Books with colorful covers were displayed in a low wooden rack. The
space between the shelves of fabric and the ceiling
were covered by a dizzying variety of what he assumed
must be quilts, though they weren't the somber geometric designs of his vague imaginings. Plaid chickens
jostled for space with floral teacups and a penguin carrying a bouquet of daisies. The geometric patterns were
there, too, but there was nothing somber about them.
So much for little old ladies wielding their needles and
discussing the latest doings at the Grange Hall.

He pulled his eyes away from the display and found
himself staring at the back of Edith Hacklemeyer's
head. He'd seen her several times since he moved back.
She spent time in her yard each day, probably using
tweezers to eradicate any weeds foolish enough to lift

their heads in her lawn. But even if he hadn't seen her, he would have recognized that nasal voice. God knew, he'd spent enough hours listening to it as she droned on about dangling participles and the importance of proper punctuation. She was saying something about leopards not being able to change their spots, no matter how much they tried and no one could tell her that *he* had tried all that hard. It wasn't hard to guess who the leopard in question was and Reece felt a quick little spurt of amusement. You had to give the old bat points for consistency. Uproot a few petunias and twenty years later, he was still the spawn of the devil.

He looked past her and met Shannon's eyes and felt his mouth curve in a smile. She was wearing a thin, soft sweater in a warm shade of blue that reflected the color of her eyes. Trim black jeans clung to her hips and those illegally long legs. She'd pulled her hair back from her face with a pair of clips shaped like bright-blue butterflies and let the rest of it tumble onto her shoulders. She looked young and vibrant and ridiculously attractive.

It was getting easier and easier to forget that he was only staying in Serenity Falls long enough to clean out his grandfather's house. Harder to remember that he wasn't looking to get involved with anyone at this point in his life.

With an effort he looked away from Shannon, hearing Cacklemeyer's voice still droning on.

"I always try to take a charitable point of view," she said, a portrait of self-delusion. "But one must face facts, after all, and the fact is that some people are just born to trouble. That's all there is to it. I don't—"

She broke off abruptly as Reece stepped into her field of vision.

"Ms. Hacklemeyer. It's been a long time, hasn't it?"

"Yes, it has, um, been a long time." Her expression made it clear that it hadn't been nearly long enough, and Reece let his smile widen, showing the maximum number of teeth.

"Your flowers look very nice this year."

He heard Shannon choke back a laugh as Edith's eyes widened in a look that mixed indignation with just a touch of fear. Before she could say anything, Kelly McKinnon popped up from behind the book display.

"I'll finish cutting Edith's fabric," she said, moving over to the cutting table and nudging Shannon away from the stack of fabrics there. "I'll take care of business while you talk."

Smiling and prodding, she edged the two of them toward the back of the store and the illusion, at least, of privacy.

"Let me guess," Shannon said. "You've always wanted to make a quilt."

"Actually, I didn't know you *could* make a quilt," he admitted. "Frank dropped by this morning and mentioned that you owned a quilt shop. I was in the neighborhood so…" He let a shrug finish the sentence. No point in mentioning that being "in the neighborhood" had taken him fifteen minutes out of his way. "I wasn't sure what to expect."

"Gray-haired ladies in granny gowns?" she guessed, giving him a shrewd look.

"Pretty much," he admitted sheepishly.

She clicked her tongue and gave him a disapproving look. "Stereotypes. That's not at all politically correct of you. I could give you my standard lecture on the diversity of quilters in America today, but I've got a meeting with a fabric rep in half an hour so I'd only have time to hit the high points.''

Reece tried to look both chastened and disappointed but, from her sudden laugh, guessed that he'd managed to look more relieved than anything else. Her laugh was infectious, low and warm, inviting, and he had a sudden, fierce urge to lean in and see if he could taste that warmth. It took a conscious effort to pull his eyes away.

"Nice place," he said, seeking a distraction.

"Thanks. We do pretty well." Shannon glanced around the shop with obvious pride. "When I first started, it seemed like there weren't enough hours in the day to do everything that needed to be done, but I've got half a dozen women who work part-time now so I don't have to be here every minute of the day. It still takes a lot of time but it's not quite twenty-four hours a day anymore."

"Not many small businesses make it past the first year."

"I wasn't sure I would, either," she said, grimacing at the memory of those first, lean months. "It's taken a while but we're finally showing a profit. I'm not ready for the Fortune 500 but we're in the black and that's more than most small businesses manage." She gestured to the colorful quilts hanging on the walls. "We run a schedule of about forty classes per quarter and most of them fill up. When we bring in a big-name teacher, we sometimes get students from as far away as San Diego, and we've got several block-of-the-month programs that are—"

Shannon stopped abruptly, suddenly aware that she'd been all but lecturing him. She felt herself flush and gave him an apologetic look. "Sorry, I didn't mean to ramble on like that."

"I don't mind. It's interesting."

"Yeah, right." Her eyebrows rose in disbelief. "And I suppose your idea of light entertainment is reading the stock market report."

"Insurance," he said solemnly. "Actuarial tables drive me wild." He waggled his eyebrows up and down, grinning when she gave a strangled little chuckle.

"You must be a laugh riot on a date."

"See for yourself. Have dinner with me tonight."

Shannon's laugh ended on a gasp. "What?" Had he just asked her for a date?

"Have dinner with me," Reece repeated calmly, but there was something in his eyes that made her wonder if he wasn't as surprised by the invitation as she was. "Frank mentioned a new restaurant that opened up where the old library used to be."

"Emilio's," Shannon said. Frank had taken Kelly there for their anniversary a couple of months ago and Kelly had raved about the food.

"That's the one. It's a weeknight so I should be able to get a reservation on short notice."

A date. He'd just asked her out on a date. She hadn't gone on a date in…well, years. She wasn't sure she even knew *how* to date anymore. Food, conversation. She was pretty sure she remembered how to do that part of it. And afterward? A kiss good-night or… It was the "or" that made her hesitate. That wasn't surprising—women had been hesitating over that particular "or" since at least the beginning of the sexual revolution. No, it wasn't the "or" itself that worried her, it was what her answer might be if the question of "or" came up.

Chapter 7

The food at Emilio's was as good as Kelly had said it was. Shannon ordered salmon in a balsamic vinegar glaze and Reece had filet mignon napped with a shallot and red wine sauce. No aspic, he said sadly, giving the menu a disappointed look. It made her laugh and suddenly it seemed silly to be worrying about what the end of the evening might bring. Whatever was going to happen, it wouldn't happen without her consent. Consent, hell, she admitted ruefully. If that kiss last week was anything to go by, whatever happened was likely to have her enthusiastic cooperation.

As it turned out, neither consent nor cooperation was required. At the end of the evening, Reece took her home, walked her up to her door in proper date fashion and waited while she unlocked it. She turned to look at him, her heart beating just a little too fast. She waited, half-afraid that, whatever he wanted, whatever he suggested, she was going to give him a breathy little "yes" and melt like candle wax on a hot day. He studied her face for a moment, eyes dark and unreadable, and then his mouth quirked in a half smile. He brushed his fingertips across her cheekbone, murmured goodnight and turned and walked away.

Shannon stood in the half-open door, watching those long strides carry him over the damp, cracked concrete. For just a moment, a small unworthy moment, she hoped he'd trip over a crack, but he moved down the buckled walkway as easily as if it were broad daylight instead of misty darkness. She slipped into the house before he turned onto the sidewalk, shutting the door carefully, quietly and sliding the dead bolt into place before bouncing her forehead gently against the wood.

The next day, Thursday, Reece and Frank McKinnon arrived at the shop midafternoon, bringing sandwiches and coleslaw from Serenity Falls's one and only New York style deli, which happened to be run by a former Texan who'd never been farther east than Nebraska. But, whatever his antecedents, Willard Long knew his way around a pastrami sandwich. With rain pattering down on the street and dripping from the bright-striped awning out front and no customers in sight, they spread the food out on the classroom tables in the back of the shop and ate pastrami on rye and tangy coleslaw. Shannon tried not to notice how comfortable Reece was with her friends, how easily he fit into her life.

Friday evening, after the shop closed, Shannon rented a movie at the video store across the street. The owner was a middle-aged woman with a permanently harried expression and a teenage daughter whose sole purpose in life, according to her mother, was to turn her hair gray as quickly as possible. After dealing with the girl, who was currently handling the cash register, Shannon wouldn't have been surprised to see the woman's hair turn gray overnight.

Stitch—*Lacey is such a dork's name*—had pierced every conceivable body part so that silver rings and metal studs caught the light every time she moved. Not that she moved any more than she had to, preferring to point vaguely toward the possible location of any tape a customer might be seeking. Her only voluntary movement was the rhythmic up-and-down motion of her jaw as she chewed a never-ending wad of gum.

When Shannon brought up her selection of tapes, Stitch offered a running critique as she ran them across the scanner. The three tapes were, in no particular order, dismissed as dork-o-rific, total retro trash and a failed attempt to save the fading reputation of an over-rated director. A more sensitive person might have been offended. Shannon found herself biting her lip to keep from laughing out loud and thinking how much she was going to enjoy telling Reece about this encounter.

Somewhere in the back of her mind, she wondered if she should be worried that he was the first person she thought of or maybe worried that she was renting movies with him in mind, thinking of whether he preferred drama or comedy, wondering if he liked the old Preston Sturges classics. Still, where was the harm in it? It wasn't as if they were involved. Or at least not "Involved" with a capital letter and all the complications that implied. He was her neighbor—her *temporary* neighbor—and she enjoyed his company. There was nothing complicated about it.

So, Friday night turned out to be movies and pop-corn and the discovery that they shared a taste for screwball comedy and diverged sharply on the importance of Mel Gibson's blue eyes for the success of a film.

Reece didn't kiss her good-night, didn't even look as if he were *thinking* about kissing her good-night, and that was perfectly all right because they weren't involved. Right?

Saturday Frank and Kelly invited both of them over for barbecued ribs, and Shannon felt a little uneasy at the thought that the McKinnons were seeing her and Reece as a couple, which they definitely weren't. They were just neighbors and—maybe—friends but Kelly's casual comment that, since Reece lived next door, they could drive over together made it clear that no one was seeing them as a couple, least of all Reece because, if he thought they were a couple, he'd want to kiss her again, right?

Barbecue plans had to be canceled when the rain made an abrupt reappearance late in the afternoon. The small party moved indoors, including three cats and one large and not terribly intelligent golden retriever named Mortimer. They ate take-out fried chicken—the humans did, anyway—and played Trivial Pursuit, with much squabbling over alleged cheating and Frank's accusations that only alien brain implants could explain his wife's uncanny knowledge in the science and nature category.

The game was declared a draw when Mortimer came over to see what all the fuss was about and swept a plumed tail across the coffee table, scattering playing pieces every which way. Kelly hinted darkly that Frank had signaled the dog to destroy the game in a craven attempt to avoid going down to humiliating defeat. Since Mortimer's sweet disposition was matched only by his obvious lack of intelligence, no one put much credence in that theory, and the evening ended with the four of them eating butter pecan ice cream and discussing the relative merits of the Marx Brothers versus the Three Stooges.

Reece drove Shannon home through a steady rain, the hiss of the tires on wet pavement and the rhythmic slap of the windshield wipers providing a backdrop for their conversation. The late-night streets were almost empty, the streetlights providing intermittent light, approaching through the darkness and then passing. It felt as if they were the only two people in the world, as if everyone else had just faded away.

And somewhere along the way, she realized she was talking about her marriage, telling him about Johnny, about how she'd been working as a waitress in Stockton and he'd been there visiting an elderly aunt, about how he'd come into the restaurant for breakfast and then come back for lunch and talked her into letting him take her out for dinner.

"He had a wonderful smile," she said, staring out into the darkness, and suddenly, for the first time in years, she could *see* that smile, could see his face clearly, see the laughter that always seemed to lurk in the back of his eyes.

Reece didn't say anything. He didn't have to. It was enough that he was there, large and warm and solid. Maybe it was the darkness and the rain and the laughter they'd shared earlier but the words were suddenly spilling from her, and as she talked, she realized that she hadn't forgotten, after all. She just hadn't let herself remember.

She hadn't let herself remember the whirlwind court-ship, two weeks of dinners and movies and laughter and the crazy exhilaration of driving to Vegas to marry a man she barely knew, the nervous pleasure of real-izing that she was really married, that she was the cen-ter of someone's life now, just as he was the center of hers.

Sitting here in the dark, with the rain pattering against the roof of the truck and the rest of the world a distant, not quite real thing, the memories were sud-denly sharp and real and the words were easy to find. It felt good to talk about him, good to remember. And when she thought about it, she realized that she couldn't imagine talking to anyone else about this and she knew that should probably worry her, but for now it was enough to have the memories back, like a gift Reece had given her without knowing it.

Sunday morning Reece appeared on Shannon's door-step, empty coffee cup in hand, a pleading look on his face. Laughing, she invited him in and poured him a cup of coffee. They drank it in her kitchen, with rain sliding down the windows and an occasional distant mutter of thunder for accompaniment. When Shannon mentioned breakfast, Reece's eyes widened in mock fear and he quickly suggested brunch at a nearby bed-and-breakfast, known for their blueberry muffins and country-cured bacon.

Somehow, brunch drifted into a matinee of a new film, which they both agreed had been highly overrated and an early dinner at a café where they ate pot roast so tender it fell apart at the touch of a fork and mashed potatoes drowned in brown gravy.

And this time when Reece took her home, they stood

on her front porch, with a gentle rain hissing down around them, and he pulled her into his arms and melted her bones with a kiss. He pressed her up against the unlocked door, his big body hard and warm against hers, and she had a sudden image of him pushing the door open, taking her into the darkened house, into the softness of her bed. Her heart thudded with a mixture of fear and anticipation, but Reece was already easing back, his mouth softening on hers, his hands stroking gently up her arms until his palms cradled her face as he ended the kiss.

He stared down at her for a long moment, thumbs moving gently over her cheekbones. Shannon waited, hardly breathing. She wanted…she wasn't sure what she wanted. For him to kiss her again, for him to leave. She wanted to retreat into the safe little cocoon she'd spent the past three years building. She wanted to rip her way free of that cocoon and feel alive again. She was dizzy with the possibilities, scared and elated and terrified and eager.

Maybe Reece read something of that confusion in her eyes. Even in the dim glow from the porch light, she saw his expression change, soften. He lowered his mouth to hers, in a kiss as soft as a butterfly's wing, sweet as a baby's smile. And then he was stepping back, reaching past her to push the door open and nudging her gently inside, murmuring a good-night as he pulled the door shut behind her.

Shannon stood in the dark entryway, listening to the sound of his footsteps until they disappeared in the quiet hiss of the rain. Maybe, just maybe, she was in big trouble here.

The shrill ringing of the phone startled Reece out of a deep sleep. Heart pounding, he rolled out of bed, reaching automatically for the gun he no longer kept in the nightstand. By the second ring he was awake enough to realize he didn't need the gun, unless it was to shoot whoever was calling him at—he squinted at the clock—six o'clock in the damned morning.

Sitting on the side of the bed, feeling mildly light-headed from the adrenaline rush, he grabbed the receiver before the third ring. If this was some crazed telemarketer, he wasn't going to be responsible for his actions.

"Morgan," he snarled.

"Reece, it's Caroline."

The sound of his ex-wife's voice sent a fresh surge of adrenaline through him. *"Kyle."*

"He's fine," she said immediately. "Well, unless you count having no common sense and no consideration for anyone else as a *problem,*" she added with bitter emphasis.

Recognizing the tone of voice, Reece scrubbed one hand over his face and tried to shake the remnants of sleep and adrenaline overload from his brain. One of Caroline's less endearing traits was a tendency to choose dramatic statements over clear communication, but if Kyle was hurt, she'd have said so.

"What did he do?" he asked. Since it was obvious that sleep was no longer an option, he stood up and reached for the jeans he'd worn the day before, tucking the phone against his shoulder as he pulled them up over his long legs. Offering up a fervent thanks to whoever had invented portable phones, he headed for the kitchen and the coffeemaker.

"What did he do?" she asked in a tone that suggested he should already know. "What do you think he did?"

"Shaved his head, got a nose ring, joined a rock band?" Reece reeled off possibilities as he groped for coffee in the semidark kitchen. He could have turned on a light, but that would have been an admission that he was really awake at this ungodly hour, awake and listening to his ex-wife's increasingly strident voice.

"Ha, ha. I suppose you think this is funny. You're the one who told him to do this. Don't think I don't know that you encouraged this whole thing."

"What whole thing?" He measured coffee into the filter.

"Don't play stupid with me, Reece Morgan," she snapped. "This is our son's future at stake here. Maybe you don't care what happens to him but I do and I'm not going to just sit here and let him throw his whole life away. I should have known better than to think you'd—"

He set the phone down and leaned against the counter as he filled the carafe with water. Picking the phone up again, he propped it on his shoulder while he poured water into the coffeemaker, listening with half an ear as Caroline expounded on his many faults, most of which seemed to circle back to an appalling lack of sensitivity. It was an old story, one he'd heard more times than he could count when they were married.

"—know my feelings don't matter but I'd think you'd give some thought to what's best for your son. He's—"

Squeezing his eyes shut, Reece reached for his patience, reminding himself that she wasn't really trying to drive him insane.

"—only nineteen and he's *ruining* his life, just ruining it and—"

"Caro, it's six o'clock in the morning on this side of the country," he said, cutting her off midrant. "Way too early to spend time going over a list of my faults, which I'm sure are epic. Just tell me what Kyle has or hasn't done."

There was a pause and he knew she was debating about hanging up on him. He didn't have to see her to know she was weighing the satisfaction of slamming the phone down against the likelihood that he wouldn't call back, which would mean she'd have to face the humiliation of calling him again if she wanted to continue haranguing him. There was a practical streak under the histrionics and he wasn't surprised when she chose explanations over a dramatic exit.

"He's quit school."

"He can't quit. He's already graduated."

"Not high school," she snapped. "College. He quit college. He came home for Thanksgiving break and said he wasn't going back."

Reece stared at the coffeemaker, willing it to drip faster. This conversation would be much easier to take with caffeine.

"Did he say why?"

"He said college wasn't what he wanted to do right now. Apparently, what he wants to do is become a Hell's Angel," she added with heavy sarcasm.

Reece had a dizzying flash of his son dressed in black leather, chains and tattoos and bit back a groan as he reached for the coffeepot. To hell with letting the cycle finish.

"What are you talking about?" He poured half a mug of fragrant liquid, ignoring the sizzle as the coffee continued to drip onto the warmer. Shoving the pot back into place he stuck the mug under the faucet and added a splash of cold water.

''I told you, Kyle's quit school and become a...a—'' Three gulps of not-quite-scalding coffee and he could feel his brain coming online.

''Kyle bought a bike?'' he guessed.

''Yes, and don't try to tell me that you didn't encourage him to do it. I know you told him about that motorcycle you used to have.''

''Yes, but I didn't tell him to go out and buy one. What did he get?''

''What did he get?'' Caroline's voice rose to a level that probably had every dog within a two-mile radius of her elegant home barking hysterically. ''I tell you that he's gone off to kill himself on that...that *thing* and you want to know what it is?''

Reece leaned one hip against the counter and pinched the bridge of his nose. It was moments like this that reassured him of the wisdom of getting a divorce.

''Sorry,'' he muttered.

''You should be sorry you encouraged him to buy that thing in the first place.''

''Caroline, could we just skip the blame game? Whatever it is, it's all my fault. I accept that. Now can we move on to what's going on with Kyle? Why did he quit school? What did he say? Why did he buy the bike and where the hell is he right now?''

In the silence that followed, he heard her breath hitch and felt his irritation fade. Caroline was always at her bitchiest when she was worried. The more worried she was, the nastier she got. Obviously, whatever Kyle was doing, he'd scared his mother to death. He sighed and reached for the coffeepot.

"Tell me what's going on, Caro," he said quietly.

It was pretty straightforward, really. He already knew that Kyle had only agreed to start college because it was what his mother wanted. Kyle had told him as much when Reece had taken him out to dinner a few days after he graduated from high school. Looking at his son had been like looking at himself at the same age. The restless need to be on the move, to be going and doing.

I've been in school since I was six years old, Kyle had said. *That's two-thirds of my life. Now, I'm supposed to sign up for another four or five years of classes and papers. When do I actually get to have a life?*

Reece understood what Kyle was feeling, but he also knew how his ex-wife felt about the importance of getting an education, and it wasn't as if he disagreed with her. So, he'd encouraged Kyle to give college a try.

You can always quit, he'd said. *It's not like you're sentenced to life with no hope of parole.*

Thinking of it now, he winced, wondering if maybe Caro was right, if maybe he *had* encouraged Kyle in making this decision.

Apparently, after two months of classes, Kyle had decided that making his mother happy wasn't reason enough to even finish out the semester. He'd quit school, bought a motorcycle—and Reece still wanted to know what kind but knew better than to ask—and said he was going to do some traveling, see the country a bit before deciding whether or not to go back to school. Caro had tried to talk him out of it. Had, from the sounds of it, talked nonstop since the day after

Thanksgiving, which was when Kyle had told her what he planned. But Kyle had stood firm and had left this morning.

"He's going to end up in a dead-end job working in a factory or parking cars at a restaurant somewhere." Caroline's voice was choked with tears. "And that's if he doesn't end up dead on the road somewhere."

Reece couldn't really see Kyle settling into life on an assembly line or parking cars, but he wasn't particularly crazy about the idea of his son being on the road alone.

"Kyle's sensible," he said, trying to reassure himself, as well as his ex. "He'll stick to decent roads, take precautions."

"What about at night? I keep thinking of him sleeping in some awful park or campground."

"Kyle?" Reece exaggerated his disbelief. "Are we talking about the same kid here? You remember the last time I tried to take him camping? He wanted me to lug a damned mattress to the lake so he wouldn't have to sleep on the ground. Trust me, Kyle's idea of camping out is doing without room service."

Caroline's chuckle was watery, but at least it wasn't more tears.

"It's not like he's broke. He'll be fine, Caro."

"Maybe." She sniffed. "You know, he's using the money you set aside for his education."

"I put the money in a trust for *Kyle*. *You're* the one who decided it was for his education, and you agreed with me when I suggested giving him control of it after he graduated."

"That was before I knew he was going to do something stupid with it."

"You mean before you knew he wasn't going to do

what you wanted him to?'' Reece asked dryly. He dumped the last couple of swallows of lukewarm coffee in the sink and poured a fresh cup.

''Education is important, Reece. What is he going to do with his life if he doesn't get an education?'' She didn't wait for an answer but continued, her voice edging perilously close to a whine. ''All his friends are going to college. I don't see why Kyle had to be different.''

''First of all, I never said education wasn't important. Or have you forgotten the years I spent going to school at night? Second, he's nineteen. Who says he has to decide what he wants to do with the rest of his life right now? Half the kids in college don't know what the hell they're doing there, anyway. They're just waiting to grow up. Maybe he wants to do his growing up somewhere else.''

Caroline started to interrupt but he talked over her. ''And thirdly, when has Kyle ever been anything *but* different? This is the kid who wanted to learn to tap-dance when he was six and bloodied the nose of that obnoxious kid who lived next door for calling him a sissy.''

''Jimmy Karkowski,'' Caroline said immediately. ''He was a terrible bully and he was two years older than Kyle.'' Thirteen years after the incident, she still sounded indignant.

''And when Kyle was twelve and all his friends were riding skateboards or horses, he decided archery was the thing to do.''

''And you bought him that bow that was taller than he was,'' Caroline said reminiscently.

''He was sixteen when he decided not to play football and took up fencing instead and then added ballet

lessons because it improved his speed and control."
Reece paused to let the facts sink in. "Caro, the fact
that all his friends are going to college isn't going to
matter a whole hell of a lot to Kyle."

"No, I suppose not." Pride crept around the edges
of her lingering annoyance. "He gets that nonconform-
ist streak from you, you know."

"Yeah, right. I'm not the one who chained myself
to the gate of that ratty old house to keep the county
from tearing it down."

"That ratty old house was one of the few remaining
examples of Wilhelmina Matthewson's work. She just
happened to be one of the only nationally recognized
female architects at the turn of the century." She fired
up immediately, just as he'd known she would. "And
they were going to put up a concrete-block apartment
building."

Smiling into his coffee cup, Reece relaxed back
against the counter. Listening to her impassioned defense, he had a sudden image of her from the first year
of their marriage, curled up in a corner of the cheap
blue-and-gray-plaid sofa that had been one of their first
purchases as a couple, her light-brown hair caught up
in an untidy bun on top of her head, hands and mouth
moving a mile a minute as she explained how important her latest cause was and why he should take some
of his pathetically limited time away from work and
school to march in a picket line or put up posters or
attend a meeting in defense of whatever it was. He'd
viewed it as a challenge to see if he could distract her
from her current pet project, and he'd prided himself
on the fact that at least fifty percent of the time they'd
ended up in bed, which was the one place they'd been
completely compatible.

"You haven't heard a word I've said, have you?" The sharp question snapped him out of the past and into the present.

"Sure I have," he lied and grinned at the irritated little huff of breath that came over the line.

"I suppose you approve of Kyle throwing away his life like this." The words were sharp, but most of the edge was gone from her voice.

"Who says he's throwing away his life? Maybe he'll take a few months off, see the country a little and go back to school next fall."

"What if he doesn't?"

"Then that's his choice." He heard her draw a breath and continued before she could argue. "You raised him to make his own decisions, Caro. We agreed that that's what we wanted for him."

"But I didn't expect him to make a *stupid* decision like this," she complained, but the crisis was past. Nothing was going to make her approve of Kyle quitting school, but she was starting to become resigned to the reality of it.

"Stupid decisions are part of growing up. Kyle's a smart kid. He'll be okay." Privately he was wondering what kind of favors he could call in to have someone keep an eye out for the boy. Nineteen years old and hitting the road on a damned motorcycle. If he'd had Kyle in front of him, he'd be tempted to kick his butt up between his shoulder blades.

"He's just so young," Caroline sighed.

"Not that much younger than we were when we got married," he pointed out.

"And look how that turned out."

"I don't have any regrets. We had some good years and we ended up with Kyle."

"True." The silence that fell between them was easy, the kind that grew out of knowing each other for two decades, sharing a marriage, a child, going through a divorce and still managing to remember, most of the time, that they'd once loved each other.

"I suppose it's too late to ground him," Caroline said wistfully, and Reece laughed.

"You could give it a try."

"I'd have to track him down first." She sighed again. "I guess it's really early where you are, isn't it?" she said abruptly, as if it had just occurred to her.

That was so typically Caroline that Reece had to swallow a laugh. When she was focused on something, her concentration was so complete that everything else became background noise. He should count himself lucky that she hadn't called even earlier.

"Depends on what you consider early," he said amiably. "It's almost six-thirty. Some people might not consider that early at all."

"I guess I could have waited another hour or two to call," she said, sounding a little sheepish.

"That's okay. I had to wake up to answer the phone anyway."

She laughed and asked him how things were going with his grandfather's house, and he spent a few minutes filling her in on his cleanup efforts. Not that they'd been all that great, he admitted. He could have had the job done a couple of weeks ago if he'd put his mind to it.

"Are you thinking of staying there?" She sounded surprised. Not that he could blame her. His ex-wife knew how he felt about his grandfather. He'd lived in this town, in this house, longer than he'd lived anywhere else, but this had never been home. Coming back here had just been a stopover, a place to be while he decided what to do with the rest of his life. He certainly didn't want to stay here. Did he?

"I...don't know," he said at last. "Maybe."

He hadn't realized the idea was in the back of his mind until she mentioned it, but now that he thought about it, he realized that the idea held more appeal than he'd have believed possible a few weeks ago. He actually liked Serenity Falls, liked the combination of small-town nosiness and California indifference, the fake tile roofs and palm trees and architecturally barren strip malls cozying up with the occasional survivor from the Art Deco era. He liked picking up sushi, standing next to a farmer in dusty jeans and a gimme cap who was ordering California rolls and sashimi as comfortably as if it were burgers and fries. The mixture of down home and sophistication appealed to him.

And a certain long-legged redhead with pretty blue eyes appealed to him, too, he thought, letting his gaze slide out the kitchen window to the house next door. Shannon Devereux was high on Serenity Falls's list of positive attributes.

But that wasn't something he wanted to discuss with his ex-wife. He settled for telling her that the town wasn't the hellhole he'd remembered and admitting that the idea of settling down here had a certain appeal. When they hung up a few minutes later, they were back on comfortable terms with each other. He'd always thought it was ironic that it was only after the divorce that they'd learned to talk to each other. They were better friends now than they'd ever been when they were married.

He poured a fresh cup of coffee and contemplated Shannon's house. There was a light on in the kitchen.

He could see the golden glow through the curtains. She was probably making a pot of coffee, maybe popping a waffle in the toaster. The thought made him smile as he lifted his cup and took a slow sip.

They'd been dating for two weeks now, though he suspected Shannon would reject that description. But he didn't know what else you called it when a man and a woman saw each other every day, went out to lunch or dinner or sometimes both, went to the movies and generally spent most of their free time together. He wasn't sure where it was heading, but he knew where he wanted it to end up. He wanted it to end up with the two of them naked and horizontal on a nice soft surface. That would do for starters, but he was beginning to think that he wanted a lot more than just sex from his attractive neighbor.

"There's nothing wrong with having a relationship based on sex, as long as you both know that's what's going on." Kelly slid a stack of books into place and clipped a New sign to the rack in front of them. "There's no reason you can't have a blistering affair with Reece."

"Who said I wanted a blistering affair with him?" Shannon asked, trying—and failing—to concentrate on the invoices in front of her. Where were all the customers when you needed them?

"Oh, please," Kelly said, giving her a disgusted look. "What red-blooded woman between the ages of sixteen and ninety-six *wouldn't* want to have a blistering affair with that man? He's not only tall, dark and handsome, he's actually a nice guy. And I'd bet good money that he knows his way around a woman's body."

''Does Frank know you think things like this about other men?'' Giving up on the invoices—she'd just have to hope her suppliers were both honest and accurate this week—Shannon lifted half a dozen bolts of fabric from the cutting table and carried them toward the back of the store.

''We have a don't-ask, don't-tell policy.'' Kelly picked up the remaining bolts and followed Shannon. ''Look, you can tell me to mind my own business....''

''Mind your own business,'' Shannon said promptly.

''But the two of you practically sizzle when you're together.'' Kelly shoved a purple-and-green paisley onto the shelf. ''You can't tell me you haven't given any thought to sleeping with the man.''

''Thinking about it and doing it are two different things.'' Shannon found a spot for a sky-blue marble and slid it into place. She did think about it. She thought about it every time he kissed her at the end of one of their—they weren't *dates* exactly, though she knew it probably looked like that to other people. Whatever they were, they ended with a kiss. Or three. Long, slow kisses that left her heart pounding and her knees weak and then Reece would see her safely into her house and walk away. And she'd stand there, alone in the dimly lit entry and wonder what it would be like if he *didn't* walk away, if she invited him in for a nightcap. For a night of sizzling sex. ''Reece is only here temporarily. He'll be leaving soon.''

''So what?'' The remaining bolts of fabric thudded onto one of the classroom tables. Kelly set her hands on her hips and fixed Shannon with a look of mixed affection and exasperation. ''I'm not talking about a lifetime commitment here. So much the better if he's leaving. That will bring everything to a natural conclusion. No hurt feelings. No awkwardness.''

Shannon shoved the last three bolts onto the shelf at random. She felt pressured, not just by Kelly but by her own needs, desires.

''Why are you so determined to push me into bed with him?'' she asked, exasperated.

''I'm not. I'm determined to push you out of that...that safety net of yours.'' Kelly lifted one small hand, cutting off Shannon's automatic protest. ''Don't tell me you don't know what I'm talking about, Shannon Devereux. You haven't let yourself get really involved with anyone or anything except this shop, since Johnny died. I've introduced you to half a dozen perfectly nice men, and you haven't gone out on a single date with any of them. Now Reece Morgan comes along and the two of you are practically living in each other's pockets. He's gorgeous, he's nice, you enjoy his company and he'll be leaving, so you don't have to worry about anyone have expectations. Who better to have an affair with?''

The jangle of the bell over the front door saved Shannon from having to come up with a response. Ignoring her friend's irritated huff of breath at the interruption, she went to greet the elderly woman who'd entered. As she helped her pick out fabric to finish a quilt, she admitted to herself that Kelly's theory made a lot of sense. She had been wary of getting involved again, leery of where it might lead. But with Reece it wasn't going to lead anywhere, because he was only here for a short time. Maybe Kelly was right. Maybe a sizzling love affair would be a good thing.

Chapter 8

In typical southern California fashion, the weather had taken an abrupt turn from cool and damp to warm and dry. Reece's front door was open and Shannon heard the music coming through the screen door as she stepped onto the porch. The melody being picked out on the guitar was familiar but she couldn't quite place it. She cocked her head, listening, but the tune trailed off in a tangle of chords and a muttered curse and she realized it wasn't a CD she was hearing. Reece played guitar? The man was full of surprises.

She hovered on the edge of the porch, wondering if she should interrupt him and then wondered if she was hesitating out of consideration or out of cowardice. She'd never made plans to seduce someone before, and she was just a little nervous about the whole idea. But a plan was a plan and it had taken her a solid week to work herself up to this and she wasn't going to back out now. If her hand was not quite steady when she knocked on the door, no one else had to know.

She could see Reece through the screen. He was wearing a pair of jeans, old enough that the knees had faded to a soft, cloudy blue, and a gray sweatshirt with raveled cuffs. Sitting on the edge of the sofa, with the guitar resting on his knee and a lock of dark hair falling onto his forehead, he looked rumpled and sexy. And the way he smiled when he saw her... Shannon smiled helplessly in return.

"I didn't know you played guitar," she said as she pushed open the door.

"I haven't played in years. I gave my old guitar to my son five or six years ago when he wanted to learn to play. This was under my grandfather's bed. And as dead as these strings are, I'm not sure you can call what I'm doing playing." He plucked two strings. "They sound like old rubber bands."

"They sound okay to me." Shannon sat down on a worn leather hassock, elbows on her knees, hands clasped loosely together. "It's hard to picture your grandfather playing guitar," she said, thinking of the stern old man who'd offered her a brisk nod in greeting when their paths happened to cross and frowned disapprovingly at her haphazard landscaping efforts. "He wasn't exactly...folksy."

Reece grinned and shook his head. "Joe Morgan was about as unfolksy as it was possible to get. As far as he was concerned, 'The Star Spangled Banner' was the height of musical accomplishment. It was all downhill from there."

"Then, why the..." Shannon raised her eyebrows and nodded to the guitar.

"It was my dad's. His old Martin." He ran his fingers gently up and down the neck, his smile soft with affection. "This guitar has traveled more than most long-distance truckers. He lost it once in Buffalo, left it in some seedy little club and we didn't miss it until we were almost to Cleveland. He borrowed a guitar for that gig and then we drove all the way back to New York.

"I'm amazed the old man saved it, considering how he felt about Dad's music. I would have expected him to chop it up for kindling." Reece's hands cradled the guitar as if it were an infant. "The case was under his bed. Maybe he just forgot it was there."

"I take it your father was a musician?"

Reece looked suddenly self-conscious. "He and my mom cut some records in the sixties. Did pretty well with them. You might have heard their stuff on some of the oldies stations. Jonathan and Jennifer?"

"Your parents were Jonathan and Jennifer?" Shannon gaped at him in shock. "They were your parents? I love their stuff. I have their *Flowers in the Snow* album on CD."

"Do you?" Reece smiled, and picked out the first few chords of the title song. "Well, the little kid you hear singing very off-key at the end of 'All of You, All of Me' is yours truly."

"You're kidding."

"No. I was three years old. They had a baby-sitter all lined up, but she canceled at the last minute so they brought me into the studio while they were recording and told me I had to be very quiet. One of the engineers took a liking to me and gave me a mike to play with. I apparently sang along with Mom and Dad and he spliced it in on the end of the song." He saw her wide-eyed look and shrugged self-consciously. "Hey, it was the sixties. Peace and love and warmth and fuzziness breaking out all over.''

''So, you're practically a famous singer.''

''Yeah, well, my recording career pretty much began and ended with that ten-second bit.'' His fingers moved over the strings, drawing out a delicate melody.

Watching him, she tried to imagine him as a child, but she just couldn't transform six feet four inches of tall, dark and handsome into a chubby, dark-haired toddler.

''You were close to your parents?'' she asked, and then winced a little at the wistful sound of her own voice but Reece just nodded.

''Very close. We were on the road most of the time, playing clubs and festivals. We were never in one place very long so it was pretty much just the three of us.'' He picked out the opening to ''Scotch and Soda'' with absent-minded ease, the fingers of his left hand sliding up and down the neck of the guitar as he changed chords, while his right hand picked out the melody. ''We had a lot of friends on the road, though. I played cards with the Kingston Trio when we were all stuck in a snowstorm in Denver one time. Nick Reynolds was a demon at Old Maid. I sat in when my dad jammed with Pete Seeger and got to hear my mom sing harmony with Joan Baez.'' He looked up suddenly, his eyes bright in anticipation of her reaction. ''We went to Woodstock.''

Shannon's eyes widened. ''You're kidding. You were at Woodstock?''

''Me and half a million other people.'' His tone was dry, but his smile made it clear that he appreciated her reaction.

''Wow.'' Shannon drew her legs up under her, propping her chin on her knees as she watched him. "So, what was it really like? I mean, did you know it was a major cultural event?"

He shook his head, grinning. "Are you kidding? I was seven years old. I wouldn't have known a cultural event if it bit me on the nose."

"What do you remember about it?"

"Mud," he said promptly. "It rained, and there was mud everywhere. Way too many people and not enough bathrooms."

She shook her head, mouth pursed in disapproval. "Plebeian. You were witness to one of the great cultural events of the twentieth century and your only concern was whether or not there were enough bathrooms?"

Reece laughed and played a quick flourish of notes on the guitar. "By definition, all seven-year-old boys are plebeians. But, in my defense, no one who was there knew it was going to be a defining event for the Baby Boomer generation. It was just a concert, one that lasted for three days and had a lot of different artists. In the parlance of the time, it was a happening, man, but there was no way to know it was 'the' happening."

"I don't suppose you even remember any of the music," she said, looking disapproving.

"Not much," he admitted. "I remember Hendrix doing 'The Star Spangled Banner,' though. It was just about the last thing, and most of the crowd was gone by then." He plucked out a few chords, bending the strings a little to get a credible Hendrix-style whine.

"Was it amazing?"

"Well," he shrugged and looked self-conscious. "It was pretty noisy. Frankly, I thought something was wrong with the sound system."

Shannon flinched and moaned. "Oh, the waste, the waste. One of the great moments in American music and you thought it was a technical error."

"What can I say. I was a kid."

She laughed. It was easier to picture him as a tough seven-year-old, oblivious to the fact that history was being made all around him, than it had been to picture a sweet-faced toddler.

"It sounds like a fun way to grow up."

"It was." His smile took on a bittersweet edge and she knew he was thinking about his parents.

"How old were you when they died?" she asked softly.

"Ten." Reece didn't seem surprised that she'd followed his train of thought. "We were in Texas. They'd had a lot of rain. A *lot* of rain." His hands rested on the guitar but his eyes were distant, seeing thirty-year-old memories. "There was flooding, and some idiot had tried to cross a bridge that was closed. Moved the damned barriers out of the way and drove right out onto it. The car stalled halfway and the water was rising and, instead of getting out, trying to get back to shore, he kept trying to get the car started. Dad went out after him, slipped, lost his footing and went into the river. Mom went in after him. They pulled the bodies out a couple miles down river."

He ran his hand gently over the side of the guitar, rubbing it back and forth as if drawing warmth from the wood, his eyes on the idle movement.

Shannon let the silence stretch, not wanting to intrude on his memories, on his grief. She'd spent her childhood dreaming of having the kind of family he'd had. Now she had to wonder which was harder—dreaming and never having or having and then losing.

She thought of the Walkers, of their willingness to welcome her, to take her into their hearts, into their lives. What did it say about her that she could have everything she'd ever wanted, everything Reece had lost, and she was too scared to reach for it?

"What happened to the guy on the bridge?" she asked, seeking a distraction from her own thoughts.

Reece lifted his head and looked at her blankly, blinking like a man waking from a deep sleep. It seemed to take a moment for her question to sink in. "A cop got him out of the car. Turned out he was drunk and the bridge was the shortest route home. He couldn't figure out why anyone would have blocked it off." He stopped and shook his head, his mouth twisting with bitter humor. "He didn't even know Dad had tried to get to him, let alone that he'd been killed."

Shannon tried to think of something to say, some bit of wisdom, no matter how clichéd, to offer him but nothing came to mind.

"It must have been very hard on you, to go from living on the road like that, with your parents, to living here with your grandfather."

His sharp bark of laughter held little humor. "You could say that." He rested his forearm on top of the guitar, left hand wrapped around the neck. "My grandfather was career army. It was quite a jump from 'Give Peace a Chance' to calisthenics before breakfast."

"He did seem a little, ah, regimented," Shannon said, trying to think of something positive to say about the rigid, unfriendly old man she'd barely known.

"That's one way to put it," Reece said dryly. "He scheduled every minute of the day. Chores, homework, when I could see my friends, when I could watch television—educational programs only, of course."

"I gather you didn't get along."

"Not hardly." He shifted his grip on the guitar, fingers moving lightly over the strings, drawing out a bare whisper of sound. His eyes looked distant. "We fought like cats and dogs. I guess all that stuff about peace and love and living in harmony didn't sink in very deep with me," he said ruefully. "We butted heads over damned near everything. The older I got, the more he tried to control me and the harder I fought him. He wanted me to join the Boy Scouts and go to church. I wore my hair long, got my ear pierced and started smoking."

"You wore earrings?" she asked, laughing.

"Earring. Singular." Reece grinned self-consciously and reached up to tug his earlobe. "I was sixteen, and Rick McKinnon's girlfriend did it for me. Most of the time I wore a silver skull with red eyes but I had a gold hoop, too."

"I bet your grandfather loved that,' Shannon said, trying to picture him as a sixteen-year-old rebel with long hair and an earring.

"Oh, yeah." He laughed and shook his head. "He had a fit about the earrings, threw out some pretty ugly comments about men who wore earrings and cast serious aspersions on my masculinity. Said that between the long hair and the earrings, people were likely to mistake me for a girl."

Shannon stopped trying to tell herself that his grandfather had probably done the best he could. If the old man had been alive and standing in front of her, she wasn't sure she'd have been able to resist the urge to smack him. Hard.

"What did you do?"

"I bleached my hair blond and cut it short and spiky

so no one could miss the earring, and I started wearing eyeliner.''

"Eyeliner?" Shannon gaped at him for a moment and then started to laugh. "That must have really made his day."

"Not so's you'd notice." Reece smiled but there was something dark in his eyes, an old and bitter anger. "By that time I doubt if there was anything I could have done that would have pleased him. Not that I was trying. I was just marking time until I could get out."

"It's hard, being on your own at that age," Shannon murmured, remembering how lost she'd felt after her father died. They hadn't been close, but he was all she'd had.

"It was easier than living with him. I had quite a bit of money from my parents. Apparently, there was a practical streak under the flowers and peace symbols. I got control of the money they left when I turned eighteen, a couple months before graduation. I only stayed until graduation because I knew he didn't expect me to stick it out, and I was damned if I'd give him the satisfaction of quitting. I already had my stuff in the car when I went to get my diploma, and I walked out of the auditorium, got in the car and left. I never talked to the old man again." He stroked his fingers across the strings, a discordant jangle of notes that made her flinch.

"But he left everything to you," she said, gesturing with one hand to indicate the house. "He must have felt *something* or he would have left it to someone else or to a charity or something."

"Yeah, go figure. Maybe he got sentimental in his old age." He lifted the guitar, turning it faceup and studying it for a moment before leaning over to set it in its case. He snapped the latches closed and set the case up against the wall next to the sofa. "Maybe he just forgot to change his will. Who knows?"

Shannon thought about that. She couldn't claim to have known Joe Morgan. A few nods and an occasional "nice weather today" didn't even really qualify as even an acquaintanceship, but she'd seen enough to know that he managed his life with military precision, a place for everything and everything in its place, everything done to a schedule. He didn't strike her as someone who would have forgotten to change his will. If he'd left all his worldly possessions to his grandson, it was because that was exactly what he'd meant to do. It seemed sad to think that Reece would never know why.

"The new Costner film is playing at the Rialto," he said, changing the subject. "I was going to give you a call and see if you wanted to go tonight."

Distracted by the unexpected look into his past, Shannon had temporarily forgotten her reason for coming over, but now it rushed back to her and she felt the color come up in her face. She rose, sliding her hands in the pockets of her loose khaki slacks.

"Actually, I came over to invite you over for dinner. At my house."

"Dinner?" Reece's brows rose in surprise.

"Yes. I, ah, thought it would be nice to eat at home. More or less. For a change."

"I thought you didn't cook."

"I don't, but I've got this recipe for stuffed flank steak that's pretty well foolproof."

"Dinner at your house, huh?" His tone was...odd, and Shannon reluctantly lifted her eyes to his face.

He knew.

Her breath caught in her throat. He knew exactly what the invitation meant, knew where she hoped the evening would end, and the hunger in his eyes had nothing to do with flank steak. No one had ever looked at her like that before, like they were starving and she was a banquet. It was exciting and a little terrifying.

"Dinner," he said, smiling slowly. "Sounds good. What time?"

"Time?"

"What time is dinner?"

She flushed and dragged her eyes away from his. "Seven," she said. "Seven o'clock would be good."

That gave her three hours to either prepare for a seduction or run like hell.

By the time Reece knocked on the door, Shannon had changed her clothes five times and put her hair up and taken it down—twice. She'd bobbled the mascara wand, giving herself a new and highly improbable third eyebrow. Pantyhose had been donned and then discarded when it occurred to her that the only thing more awkward than trying to put a pair of pantyhose on was trying to get them off with any sort of grace.

The realization that she was getting dressed with an eye to getting *un*dressed in front of Reece momentarily paralyzed her, and she sank down on the side of the bed, staring at the wreckage of her bedroom, and wondered if it was too late to run. At an average speed of sixty miles an hour, she could be at least forty miles away before Reece got here.

The fact that she was actually considering running away from her own home was absurd enough to restore her sanity. Just because she'd planned to sleep with Reece tonight, that didn't mean she *had* to. He wasn't going to push her into something she didn't want. The problem was, she was pretty sure that what scared her most was that she *did* want it. Wanted him.

By the time the doorbell rang, she'd settled on a silver-gray skirt that swirled softly around midcalf and a coral-colored blouse that managed to do nice things for her skin without clashing with her hair. She left her hair down, letting it tumble in soft waves down her back. One last look in the mirror, a deep breath for calm—or maybe for courage—and she went to answer the door.

Shannon had expected dinner to be awkward, conversation weighed down by awareness of where the evening was heading, but that wasn't the case. She'd set the table in the small, seldom-used dining room, using the pretty floral china that had belonged to the mother-in-law she'd never known and had turned the lights low. The meal turned out well and she offered up silent thank-yous to the patron saint of bad cooks and the inventor of the crockpot.

The conversation flowed easily, just as it always did between them. Reece told her he'd received a phone call from his son. She already knew about Kyle's cross-country trek and, though Reece hadn't said as much, she knew he worried about the boy, even as he admired his independence. Kyle was on his way to Albuquerque to visit his mother's sister and showed no signs of regretting his decision to try life on the open road. Shannon told him about her plans for the inventory-reduction sale after the first of the year, making him laugh with descriptions of quilters in a buying frenzy.

After dinner she made a fresh pot of coffee while Reece built a fire in the fireplace. The day had been warm but the temperature had dropped enough to make the added warmth of a fire pleasant. Not to mention how it added to the atmosphere, she thought, as she carried the tray into the living room. The fire had caught and flames were crackling through the smaller kindling, licking hungrily at the larger pieces of wood on top.

"Is there some sort of secret society that teaches men how to build fires?" She set the tray down on the coffee table and gave the fire a disgruntled look.

"It's part of our genetic code," he said solemnly. "Hardwired in right next to our inability to ask directions and refill ice cube trays."

"I thought that was just being pigheaded and lazy," Shannon said, handing him his coffee.

"A common misconception. Really, we're just victims of genetic programming."

"Aren't we all," she said dryly.

Reece had settled on the rug in front of the fireplace, and she joined him there, leaning back against the sofa, legs curled beneath her. For a little while, the only sound was the soft pop and hiss of the fire.

When his hand settled on her ankle, sliding beneath the soft fabric of her skirt to rest on her bare leg, Shannon released her breath in a soft little sigh and tilted her face up to his. *Yes.* She wasn't sure if she said it out loud or only thought it. This was what they'd been building up to over the past couple of weeks, maybe since that first moment when he'd opened the door, shirtless and barefoot and she'd felt her stomach clench with an instant of pure lust.

Yes.

Maybe she did say it out loud, because she could taste Reece's smile when he kissed her, taste his hunger in the heat of his mouth, in the wet warmth of his tongue as it slicked over hers. As they kissed, she felt the last traces of nervous tension fading away and a new feeling taking its place, something soft and languid and hungry, so hungry.

Long, slow, wet kisses, his hands warm and hard against her skin, his mouth tasting the pulse that beat frantically at the base of her throat. Shannon let her head drop back into the cradle of his palm. His other hand slid around her waist, faint roughness of calluses against her skin, and she realized that he'd pulled her blouse out of her skirt so his fingers were splayed against her lower back. She could feel the imprint of each finger separately, as if he were branding her with his touch. Her own fingers were curled around his upper arms, feeling the solid strength of muscles through the fabric of his shirt.

She whimpered a protest when he lifted his head. No, no, no. She didn't want him to stop, didn't ever want him to stop. Her eyelids felt weighted down, too heavy to lift. It took a conscious effort to open her eyes and look at him. His hair was rumpled into heavy waves, and she had a sudden tactile memory of running her fingers through it, feeling it curl like warm silk against her skin. And his eyes... Oh, God, his eyes. The heat in them warmed a still, cold place inside her she hadn't even known was there.

"I know making love in front of a fire is supposed to be romantic," Reece said, his voice low and raspy. "But I've got two words for you. Rug. Burn."

It took her lust-addled brain a moment to process that and then she startled herself by giggling. His quick grin did nothing to cool the heat in his eyes. He rose to his feet, pulling her with him, wrapping his hand in her hair and tilting her head back, his mouth coming down on hers in a long, drugging kiss that left her weak and clinging to him.

"Bedroom," he muttered against her mouth.

"Bedroom," she agreed.

The trip took a lot longer than it usually did. He wrapped his arms around her and kissed her in the living-room doorway, pressed her against the wall in the hallway—twice—held her against the doorjamb in the bedroom and tasted the taut line of her throat. And then they were finally in her bedroom, the door shut behind them, the soft golden glow of the bedside lamp painting shadowy patterns on the double-wedding-ring quilt that covered the bed.

Reece drew back, his eyes holding hers as his fingers reached for the buttons on her blouse, and Shannon thought again, *Yes.* This was what she'd been waiting for, what she'd wanted. It felt like forever since she'd let someone touch her, hold her. Her gaze steady on his, she brought her hands up to his chest, fingers not quite steady as she began to unbutton his shirt.

When she'd thought about this—and she could admit now that she'd thought about little else for the last couple of weeks—she'd pictured it one of two ways. Either every move had been as graceful as if choreographed, the whole scene washed in a romantic golden glow, or there'd been urgency and hunger and clothes pushed aside, the two of them almost struggling with each other.

Reality fell somewhere between the two. The hunger was there, but the urgency was banked, leaving time for touching and holding and learning the planes and angles of each other's bodies. There was a certain grace in the slow dance toward the bed, the soundless drift of clothes slipping to the floor, pauses for long, hungry kisses, the heated slide of hands against skin.

What she hadn't imagined was how right it would feel. Now that the moment had arrived, there was no hesitation, no last minute doubts.

Reece's palms cupped her breasts as if made to hold her, and Shannon let her head drop back, shuddering with the intensity of the sensation as his thumbs dragged across her nipples, teasing them into hard peaks. He bent over her, and she gasped at the feel of his lips on her, tongue laving her gently, then the sweet, drawing pleasure as his mouth closed over her. By the time he moved his attention to the other breast, her knees were barely keeping her upright and her breath was coming in shallow little pants.

"Please," she whispered, not at all sure what she was asking for. Reece lifted his head, and she caught just a glimpse of the blazing heat in his eyes before his mouth came down on hers, hard and demanding. His palm flattened against the small of her back, pressing her close, his mouth devouring hers. And suddenly they were out of time. The almost languid progression toward the bed was at an end and need was thrumming in the pit of her stomach.

She wasn't aware of moving until she felt the bed against the back of her legs. His mouth still on hers, Reece reached past her, throwing back the quilt and blanket and then he was pressing her down against the cool linens, his big body following her down, covering her. He was so much bigger than she was and, for just an instant, she felt overwhelmed by the sheer size of him, but the little flutter of feminine panic burned away in the sheer heat of their connection.

Contrast. It was all contrast. The flat, hard planes of

his chest and stomach pressed against the softer curves of her breast and belly. The fever-hot thickness of his erection pressed against her, lean hips settling into the soft, damp cradle of her thighs. *So close,* she thought. *So close.* Fingers digging into the heavy muscles of shoulders, she arched, wanting him closer, needing...something. Everything. She arched again, knees sliding up along the outside of his hips, and felt the blunt press of his arousal against her. He groaned, hips jerking in involuntary response. *Almost. Almost.* And then she felt him tense and he was pulling away.

"Damn," Reece muttered against her ear. "Wait. I've got to get..." He shifted toward the side of the bed.

"It's okay. I've got... I, ah..." Words failed her and she settled for pulling open the nightstand drawer. "In there."

Reece's brows climbed, and his grin took on a wicked edge as he pulled out a condom packet. "I like a woman who's prepared."

She wondered if she should confess that she'd driven thirty miles to the next town to buy the box of condoms, rather than risk having someone she knew see her make such an intimate purchase, and then decided that didn't exactly fit with the image of a grown woman making a mature decision to embark on an affair. Of course, neither did the fact that she blushed as she watched him tear open the packet and roll the condom on.

But then he was back against her, fingers slipping through her hair to cradle her head, his mouth coming down on hers as his hips eased forward, finding, entering that first tiny bit and then pausing until she whimpered, arching toward him. As if that were the permission he'd been seeking, Reece sheathed himself in her welcoming heat. Shannon cried out with shocked pleasure, the sound muffled against his mouth.

It was all heat and movement and tension that kept building inside, pulling her deeper and deeper until she was drowning in sensation and the only reality was the man above her, within her. The solid weight of his body, the rough hunger of his mouth, the rasp of his breathing, the slide of his hands over her skin. It was almost too much, pleasure so acute that it rode the knife edge of pain. Shannon's breath left her in sobbing gasps as she struggled to contain it, and then Reece shifted, one hand cupping her bottom, tilting her up to meet his thrusts. The pleasure peaked, driving the breath from her lungs on a thin cry.

"I've got you," he whispered roughly. "Let go. I've got you."

Trusting him to keep her safe, she did. She let the sensation take her, let it spin through her in thick waves until her entire body burned with the heat of it and a red haze blurred her vision. Dimly, through the pounding in her ears, she heard his guttural groan, felt the hot pulse of his release, his big body shuddering with the force of it.

She had no idea how much time passed before the world started to creep back around the edges of her consciousness. For long, endless moments, it was all she could do to remember to breathe. Slowly awareness filtered back. Reece was still over her, within her, though he'd shifted his weight to the side to avoid crushing her. There was a distant satisfaction in the knowledge that his breathing was as ragged as hers. She felt as if she'd just tumbled through the eye of a hurricane, but she hadn't taken the trip alone.

It took a major effort to lift her hand and rest it on

his damp shoulder. It was nearly as difficult to turn her face into the hollow of his throat. He smelled of sweat and sex. She'd never realized what a heady combination that was. Without thinking, her tongue came out to taste his skin. He shuddered, and his hands tightened almost painfully on her for an instant. His head came up slowly.

"Are you trying to kill me?" he asked.

"No. Just…tasting." She let her hands slide up his back, liking the feel of sweat damp muscles under her fingers.

"You know, I've read warnings about girls like you."

"Have you?" She shifted her hips slightly, smiling a little when she heard him groan. "What did they suggest?"

"Give them anything they want," he whispered against her mouth.

Chapter 9

If she'd thought about it, Shannon would have said that it was poor planning to start an affair on a work-night. No time for wallowing in the morning, no time to sit and ponder the night just past and either bask in the glow or worry that you'd made a terrible mistake. Definitely, starting an affair should be left for Saturday night or, in her case, Sunday night since the shop was closed on Monday. But she hadn't thought of that ahead of time and, as it turned out, seduction on a Friday night worked out just fine.

She woke alone to the smell of freshly brewed coffee. There was a half-opened rose on the pillow next to hers, and she smiled as she brought it to her nose and inhaled the light sweet scent. She knew for a fact that the slightly tattered blossom had come from the overgrown rosebush that sat at one corner of her front porch but the gesture was what counted, especially when she saw that he'd taken time to carefully trim the thorns away. The image of Reece robbing her rosebush in the early-morning hours made her smile widen.

There was a note by the coffeepot. If he'd stayed, he'd have made her very—underlined twice—late for work. He hoped she didn't mind that he'd made himself at home in her kitchen. He'd see her tonight. Dinner?

Not exactly a love note, but Shannon folded it and tucked it in the pocket of her robe, anyway. She wasn't looking for love notes, she reminded herself as she poured a cup of coffee. This was an affair between two consenting adults, not the romance of the century. Still, it had been sweet of him to make coffee. She brushed the rose against her cheek and allowed herself a dreamy smile.

She went through the routine of getting dressed, driving to work and opening up the shop on autopilot. As she stocked the cash register and sorted through the stack of messages Kelly had left for her the day before, she spared a moment's gratitude for the fact that the other woman wouldn't be coming in until tomorrow. Hopefully, by then she'd be able to get this dopey smile off her face. Otherwise, Kelly was going to take one look at her and know exactly how she'd spent the night, probably down to the number of times they'd made love.

There was a woman out front, clutching a quilt and looking hopeful. Shannon glanced at the clock and decided that opening ten minutes early wouldn't set a dangerous precedent. The look of gratitude on the woman's face as she unlocked the door made up for the fact that she then pulled out twenty bolts of fabric, looking for just the right binding. Or maybe a night of wild sex just put her in a particularly mellow frame of mind, Shannon thought as she reshelved the rejected prints.

Saturdays were usually busy but, unlike most retailers, December was generally a slow month for quilt shops. Most people were too busy to start new projects at this time of year and what time they had for quilting tended to go into finishing gift projects they'd already begun. Customers trickled in throughout the day, but they were mostly dazed refugees from the rigors of holiday shopping, looking to spend a few quiet moments petting fabric and looking through patterns. She chatted with the people who wanted to chat and left the others alone to recover their shattered nerves in peace.

It was one of those days where everything went right except the things that didn't go right and Shannon found she really didn't care about those. She beamed at cranky children, smiled when a customer knocked over a display of patterns, soothed a tearful new quilter who'd managed to sew several pieces together both upside down and backward.

Not even Edith Hacklemeyer's pinched expression could impinge on her good mood. She agreed with Edith that the holiday season got more commercial every year, nodded through her complaints about the excess of lights on a house down the block from the two of them and complimented her on the latest totally boring, utterly unoriginal log cabin quilt she'd made. By the time the older woman left, she was so disarmed by Shannon's amiable mood that she almost smiled. She caught herself in time, though, remembering that she really didn't approve of Shannon for several reasons, not least of which was her friendliness with that Morgan boy. A muttered warning about him was greeted with a smile so dazzling that Edith pocketed her change and left the store without saying another world.

Humming under her breath, Shannon waved through the door before flipping over the Closed sign. Tomorrow was Sunday, and the shop didn't open until noon, which meant that she could sleep in if she wanted. If she had a reason to sleep in.

And maybe someone to sleep in with.

Reece's truck was not in the driveway, and his house was dark. Shannon was surprised at how disappointed she was. It wasn't like she'd planned to run next door immediately. Had she? She felt a niggling little twinge of uneasiness as she pulled into her own driveway and slid out of the car. She didn't want to lose sight of what this was. Reece would be leaving soon. Just because he hadn't mentioned it, that didn't mean his plans had changed. He'd come to clean out his grandfather's house and to take stock of his own life. Sooner or later he'd be moving on. And that was a good thing, right? That was one of the reasons she'd decided to take this step, because an affair with him came with a built-in ending. No expectations, no hurt feelings.

Just the way she wanted it, she told herself as she unlocked her front door, and if the thought sounded a little hollow, it was just because she was still caught up in that whole middle-class myth that love and sex went hand in hand, at least for a woman. But there was nothing wrong with sex going hand in hand with more sex, especially when it was really amazing sex. The kind of sex that made her tingle all over just to remember it. The kind of sex she sincerely hoped was going to be repeated as often as possible between now and whenever Reece left.

Shannon changed into a pair of softly faded jeans and a soft gray sweater that clung in all the right places. If Reece had dinner plans that involved anything more elegant than a coffee shop, she could always change, she thought as she pulled on warm socks.

A peek out the kitchen window showed the house next door was still dark. Not that she was waiting for him, exactly. It was just that she wasn't sure what to do about dinner. Right. That was it. Shannon grimaced as she ran water into the teakettle and put it on the stove. Really, it would be nice if she could lie to herself at least occasionally.

She'd just poured water over a teabag when the phone rang. This time of night, it was likely to be a telemarketer trying to sell her the vacation package of a lifetime or offering her a chance to buy a condo she didn't want or magazines she wouldn't read. She thought about letting the answering machine get it, but there was something compelling about a ringing phone.

"Hello?"

"Shannon?" It was a woman's voice, pleasant but unfamiliar.

"Yes."

"This is your, ah… This is Rachel. Rachel Walker."

Shannon's stomach knotted instantly. She knew what the other woman had stumbled over. *This is your mother.* Which of course she was. Why couldn't it have been a telemarketer? At least she'd know what to say to someone who was trying to sell her something.

"How are you?" When all else failed, fall back on the basics.

"I'm fine. And you?" Shannon could hear the strain

in the other woman's voice. She felt guilty for putting it there, guilty that she couldn't open her heart to her newly discovered family as easily as they'd opened theirs to her.

Thank God for social niceties, she thought as they limped through the polite inquiries. Shannon asked about Rachel's family—*her* family. Rachel asked how the shop was doing. Had the rain caused any problems? The weather was good for another minute or two, speculation about whether or not this was likely to be a wet winter, agreement that it would be nice to get enough water to avoid drought conditions next summer but not enough to cause mud slides. Rachel was telling her that Gage had been injured in a mud slide in South America a couple of years back, when Shannon saw lights flash across the ceiling. Her heart gave a little thud.

Reece was home.

It took a conscious effort to keep her focus on the conversation.

"Everything worked out all right, thank heavens," Rachel was saying. "And he doesn't spend nearly as much time out of the country since he and Kelsey got married and had Lily."

"It must have been difficult for you, having him gone so much," Shannon said, her ears tuned for the sound of Reece's truck door slamming. Would he call or would he just come over?

"Yes, it was," Rachel said, and something in her tone made Shannon wonder if the other woman was thinking of all the years she'd waited and worried about another child, one who couldn't even have the decency to focus on their conversation right now.

A newly familiar guilt twisted in her stomach. What was wrong with her? Keefe was right. She was the one who'd gone looking for them. What had she thought was going to happen? A quick handshake and a nice-to-meet-you and that was the end of it?

"Actually, I had a reason for calling," Rachel said, breaking the awkward little pause before it stretched too far. "I was hoping you'd be able to spend Christmas with us. Of course, I understand if you have other plans," she added quickly. "I don't want you to feel pressured or obligated at all. It's just that…well, it's been a long time since we had all the family together for the holiday."

More than twenty years, Shannon thought. She leaned her forehead against the wall and closed her eyes. For the last two decades, she'd been a part of a family she hadn't even known existed. They'd kept her in their hearts, held her memory close. Not even her fantasies had come close to the reality of what they wanted to give her. Why was it so damned hard to accept?

"I'd like that," she said, trying to put real warmth in her acceptance.

"You'll come?" The open delight in Rachel's voice made her flinch. She wanted to feel a connection to this woman. Shouldn't there be some sort of instinctive recognition of the bond between them? "That's wonderful. Everyone will be so pleased."

Everyone. As in four brothers and their wives and children. Shannon suppressed a shudder of dread at the thought of finding herself alone in the midst of a Walker family gathering. Except maybe…

"Would it be all right if I brought someone?" she asked impulsively. Reece might have other plans, but if he didn't, maybe he wouldn't mind spending the holiday acting as a sort of shield between her and her family. "It's a friend of mine. My next-door neighbor, actually."

"The tall, dark and studly one?" Rachel asked, and Shannon's eyes popped open as her jaw dropped.

"What?" she wheezed.

Rachel laughed, a warm, inviting sound that made Shannon smile despite her shock. "Keefe said he'd stopped by to see you on Thanksgiving and he mentioned that your neighbor was there."

"*Keefe* said Reece was tall, dark and, uh…"

"Studly," Rachel said, when she had trouble finishing the description. "Actually, I think that was Tessa's contribution. Keefe didn't really offer much by way of description, though he did say that David liked your Reece and since Keefe thinks the sun rises and sets in that baby, I think that went a long way toward making up for the fact that Reece had some claim on his little sister."

There were so many things to protest about this speech that Shannon didn't know where to start. Did she protest that he wasn't "her" Reece, deny that he had any claim on her, or object to the idea that Keefe had any right to an opinion about it if he did? Before she could decide what, if anything, to say, Rachel was continuing.

"I was surprised when Keefe said he'd dropped by, actually. Serenity Falls isn't exactly on the way to the ranch," she said, confirming what Shannon had already suspected. "I hope he didn't put any pressure on you."

"Pressure?" Shannon said, stalling for time.

"I know Keefe can be rather ferocious when it comes to family. All the boys are like that. I hope he didn't suggest that you were *obligated* in any way. I mean, to spend time with us. We very much want a chance to get to know you, but family shouldn't be about obligation.''

No, it shouldn't, Shannon thought, closing her eyes against the sharp sting of tears. That was what she'd been to her father—an obligation. To his credit, he'd never shirked that obligation. No matter how much he'd regretted taking her away from her mother, he hadn't taken the easy way out and dumped her on Social Services in one of the many cities they'd lived in. She chose to take that as a sign that he'd loved her, even if he hadn't been able to show it, but all her growing-up years had been colored by the feeling that she was a duty to him.

''So, if Keefe said anything to you,'' Rachel was continuing hesitantly, ''about Christmas or anything else, I don't want you to feel like you have to spend the holidays with us.''

''He didn't say a word about Christmas,'' Shannon lied. ''He and Tessa just stopped by to say hello.''

''Good.'' There was no mistaking the relief in Rachel's voice. ''Wonderful as it is to have you back in our lives, I know it's not as…easy for you as it is for us. I mean, we always knew you were out there, somewhere, but we came as a bit of a shock to you. I don't want you to feel pressured.''

''No pressure,'' Shannon said, swallowing the lump in her throat. Why was it so hard to accept what the other woman was offering?

She was no closer to an answer when she hung up the phone a few minutes later. She'd spent her whole life wanting a family, and now she had one, a family so full of warmth and welcome that they made The Brady Bunch look like the Manson family and now all she wanted was... Well, she didn't know what she wanted. That was part of the problem.

When the phone rang again, she eyed it warily for a moment before picking it up. Her hello was more cautious than welcoming.

"Hey."

Just that one word, but she felt her knees weaken and her mouth curve in the goofy smile that had been sneaking up on her all day.

"Hey, yourself." She leaned back against the wall next to the phone and smiled at the refrigerator on the opposite wall.

"You have plans for dinner?" Reece asked.

"Well, someone had left me a note suggesting dinner, but they haven't followed up on it yet."

"I am now." His tone made the words seem intimate, and Shannon felt her skin heating.

"What did you have in mind?" Lord, was that her voice? She sounded like the bottom of a whiskey bottle, all husky and smooth.

"Nothing fancy. You. Me. Food." Reece's voice dropped dramatically on the last word, and Shannon grinned even as she felt a shiver run down her spine.

"Sounds...interesting. Did you have a particular time in mind?"

"How about right now?" The doorbell provided punctuation to the sentence, and Shannon's heart was suddenly beating much too fast.

"I don't know," she said, hearing the breathless tone of her own voice. "Someone's at the door. Maybe they'll have a better offer."

"I doubt it," he said in a voice that practically breathed sex. "Open the door, Shannon."

Heart thumping against her breastbone, she pulled

open the door. He was standing on the porch and his smile…his smile finished the melting job his voice had begun. Shannon wrapped her fingers around the edge of the door and held on, trying to will some stiffness back into her knees.

"Hey."

"Hey," she managed, wondering if it would be bad day-after protocol to jump on him and drag him into the house.

"The wonders of technology," he said, snapping the cell phone shut and dropping it in his shirt pocket. Shannon realized that she was still holding the phone to her ear. She shut it off and let her hand fall to her side.

Reece stepped inside, sliding one arm around her waist and nudging her back from the door so he could shut it. "You hungry?"

She shook her head, her mouth too dry to speak. Reece's smile took on a feral edge that made her pulse jump. Her hands came up to cling to his shoulders, and she realized she was still clutching the phone when it smacked against him. Reece reached up to take it from her, setting it on the little half-round table that sat against the wall at the same time he lowered his head to let his mouth take hers. You had to love a guy who could multitask.

It was the last coherent thought she had for several minutes. Reece didn't lift his head until he'd managed to melt every bone in her body and she was clinging to him like a shipwreck passenger holding onto a floating plank.

"I was going to take you out to dinner," he said, feathering soft kisses across her eyebrows, which she instantly decided were an erogenous zone.

''I've got frozen dinners in the freezer.'' She threaded her fingers through the dark-brown silk of his hair.

''No toaster waffles?'' He'd worked his way down to her ear, catching the lobe between his teeth and worrying it gently.

''Breakfast,'' she gasped, arching into his hold. ''We can have those for breakfast.''

''Sounds like a plan to me,'' he murmured against her mouth.

And that was the last thought either of them gave to food for quite some time.

If she'd known that having an affair would be this much fun, maybe she'd have embarked on one sooner, Shannon thought, watching Reece and Frank out on the patio. It was fifty degrees out and the sky was overcast, the air already smelling of rain, but Frank's Christmas present from his parents, an assortment of aged beef, had arrived the day before, and he was determined that the steaks had to be grilled over a mesquite fire, which was why he and Reece were huddled over the built-in barbecue, watching the steaks cook and slowly turning blue.

''Just like watching primitive man broil up a haunch of mastodon,'' Kelly said, pulling out the chair next to Shannon's at the kitchen table and sitting down.

''If primitive man had a gas barbecue and Gortex jackets.'' Shannon said dryly.

''Yeah, that does sort of take the man-against-nature element out of it, doesn't it?'' Kelly spooned sugar into the cup of tea she'd just made.

The kitchen smelled of the roasted garlic that had gone into the mashed potatoes and the earthy scent of steamed broccoli. Two of the cats were curled up on the cushioned window seat, and Mortimer slept in the corner, feet twitching as he dreamed of chasing rabbits.

"So, Reece is going to spend Christmas with your family." Kelly's tone was elaborately casual, and Shannon resisted the urge to sigh. It had been foolish to think that Kelly would be able to resist the urge to comment.

"That's the plan." She glanced out at the patio and saw that the first scattered drops of rain had begun to fall, grinned at the sight of Reece holding a red-and-black-plaid umbrella over the barbecue while Frank tended the steaks. "His son is spending the holiday in Albuquerque with his aunt, so Reece didn't have anything planned."

She thought she'd hit just the right casual note but she didn't really expect Kelly to let it go at that. For all her delicate appearance, she had the tenacity of a pit bull.

"I know I suggested that you have a wild affair with the man—and I haven't said a single word about the fact that you've obviously taken my advice," she added with a look of angelic pride that made Shannon snort and roll her eyes. "But don't you think that taking him home to meet the family is a little…I don't know. Commitment-y?"

"It's not a big deal." Shannon shrugged. "I'm not really taking him home to meet my family. I mean, they're my family but they're not…" She frowned and decided that trying to define what the Walkers were or weren't was just too confusing. "He didn't have any plans and I just thought spending the holiday at…well, with the Walkers would be better than spending it alone. No big deal."

Kelly look doubtful. "I just don't want to see you get hurt."

"That makes two of us," Shannon said lightly and tried not to look too desperately grateful when the door opened and Frank rushed in, cradling a platter of sizzling steaks as if it was a pot of gold dust.

She looked past him at Reece, who was shaking the rain off the umbrella before setting it outside the door. Kelly didn't need to worry about her. She wasn't going to get hurt. She knew exactly what she was doing. Didn't she?

Chapter 10

When Reece married Carolyn, he'd discovered he was also, to some degree, marrying her family, which consisted of two sisters and a mother. Caro's mother had thought her daughter was too young to get married—in retrospect, she'd had a point—and her sisters, both older than Caro, agreed. So, he was no stranger to suspicious, even downright hostile family gatherings. But three women with a niggling romantic streak didn't hold a candle to four large, protective older brothers.

Whatever hesitation Shannon might have about being part of the Walker family, it was obvious to Reece that they didn't share her doubts. She might have been taken from them and missing from their lives for twenty years but, in their minds, she'd remained a part of their family circle, and they were as protective of her as if they'd watched her grow up. The last time he'd been looked at so suspiciously had been by a band of terrorists, and he'd been trying to convince them that he really was a harmless American tourist. Well, at least he didn't have to worry about Shannon's brothers shooting him. Probably.

The other thing about the Walkers was that there were so *many* of them. When he and Shannon first arrived at her mother's house in Los Olivos, the phrase that came to mind was "a cast of thousands," but after introductions and a cold beer, he was able to sort it out to a little over a dozen people. Four brothers and their wives, three children, an infant, at least two cats and a dog the size of a Shetland pony, Rachel Walker, who was, he supposed, the matriarch but was too small and pretty for the word to fit, and a tall, older gentleman named Jason whose connection was easy enough to figure out once Reece saw the way he looked at Rachel.

The thing that struck him immediately—well, right after the deeply suspicious looks aimed in his direction—was that they all seemed to like each other. Not just love each other in that we're-family-so-we-have-to-care way but actually *like* each other. There was an easy camaraderie among the four brothers, and even the assorted wives and children all seemed to like each other.

His ex-wife's family had been much smaller, but the only thing they seemed to agree on was that they didn't trust him. The Walkers argued about everything from the proper way to build a bridge—one of them was a structural engineer but that didn't seem to stop his brothers from arguing with him—to whether or not cranberry sauce should be smooth or chunky—they seemed to split pretty evenly on that one. But under the squabbling, there was a sense that they were a unit, all of them against the world, if necessary.

It was clear that they considered Shannon a part of that tight-knit circle. It was equally clear that she saw herself as an outsider. Watching her uneasy interactions with the rest of her family, Reece was torn between the urge to shake her for being too scared to take what they were offering and the desire to pull her into his arms and hold her until the lost look was gone. Not that he was going to get much chance to do that. He wasn't sure which was most intimidating—the suspicious looks from her brothers or the open curiosity of their wives. Both had a definite dampening effect on the libido.

When Shannon had asked him if he'd like to spend Christmas with her family, it hadn't been hard to figure out that what she really wanted was a shield. He'd never thought of himself as a knight errant type but he was willing to give it a shot. Besides, two days and a night away sounded appealing.

In the two weeks since they'd become lovers, they spent at least part of every night together, but he couldn't quite shake the niggling feeling that they were doing something illicit. Maybe it was the knowledge that Edith Hacklemeyer was probably peering through her curtains, counting how much time he spent at Shannon's, making note of the exact hour of arrival and departure, though if she was noting his departure, she was keeping some pretty late hours. No matter how many times he told himself that Cacklemeyer was welcome to draw any conclusions she cared to, he still had to fight the urge to creep through the hedge like the straying husband in a bad farce. Two days away with Shannon would make a nice change. On the drive to Los Olivos, he indulged in visions of sleeping in and then waking up to make long, slow love in the morning.

Unfortunately, as it happened, any sleeping in he did was going to be at the whim of his roommate and, as he recalled, six-year-old boys were not big on sleeping late, especially on Christmas morning. He looked at the six-year-old boy in question and stifled a sigh. It should have occurred to him that, unless they stayed in a motel, there was no way he was going to be sharing a room with Shannon. So, here he was, at her brother's house, while she was ensconced in a spare bedroom at her mother's house, miles away.

"Sorry we don't have a real guest room," Gage Walker said, pushing open the door to his son's room and flipping on the light. "We talked about doing an addition last summer but Kelsey got a second greenhouse instead."

Contemplating the action-figure-strewn floor, the sports equipment propped in the corner and, more ominous than the rest, the bunk beds, Reece wondered if he could convince anyone that it was his lifelong ambition to sleep in a greenhouse.

"You can have the bottom bunk," Danny Walker offered, continuing before Reece could offer his heartfelt thanks. "It's harder for grown-ups to climb 'cuz they're old and stuff."

Catching Gage's wince out of the corner of his eye, Reece swallowed a grin. Yeah, these were the moments when parents reconsidered the joy of having children.

"Thanks, Danny. That's very considerate of you."

"Yeah, Mom said I should be 'specially nice 'cuz Dad and Uncle Sam and Uncle Cole and Uncle Keefe were pro'ly gonna give you grief." Oblivious to his father's strangled moan of protest, Danny eyed Reece speculatively. "Are you Aunt Shannon's boyfriend?"

"I...yeah, I guess I am." It had been a long time since he'd thought of himself as anyone's "boyfriend." The word conjured up images of high school proms and groping in the back seat.

"Do you kiss her and everything?"

Painfully aware of Gage's interested look, Reece coughed to clear his throat. "I, ah, kiss her," he admitted, leaving the question of "everything" out of it.

"Yuck." Danny screwed his face up in distaste. "Kissing's gross."

Reece and Gage exchanged an amused look. "You'll change your mind when you grow up," Gage told his son. He reached out to ruffle the boy's hair. "It's getting late, and I know you're going to be up early, tearing into your stocking. Go brush your teeth and get into your pajamas and tell your mom good-night."

"Aww, Dad." Danny caught his father's eye and swallowed the rest of his protest. Heaving a sigh, he pulled a pair of Spider-Man pajamas out from under his pillow and dragged his way out of the room.

"He's really good at the pathos thing," Reece commented after they heard the bathroom door shut.

"Yeah, if we could put that act on Broadway, we'd make a mint." Gage ran his fingers through his dark hair. "He'll keep you up all night if you let him. When he gets rolling, he can talk nonstop for hours, and he's wired because of the holiday. I don't know where he gets the energy. Kelsey says it's just because he's a kid, but I think he's battery powered." He looked at the bunk beds and sighed. "You can sleep on the couch if you'd rather, but I can tell you from personal experience, that's it's not really built for sleeping."

"I'll be fine." Reece sidestepped several small plastic bodies in varying states of undress, an exotic-looking space-age gun and a battered stuffed tiger, and tossed his overnight case on the lower bunk. "It's been a while since my son was this age, but I think I remember it well enough to hold my own."

"You've got kids?" Gage looked surprised, as if it was the first time he'd considered Reece apart from his relationship with Shannon.

"Just one. Kyle's nineteen and just quit college to take a cross-country trip on a motorcycle."

Gage moaned. "Oh, man, it's never going to end, is it? I mean, when I'm ninety, I'm still going to be worrying about him, aren't I?"

"Probably." Reece grinned. "I think it pretty much goes with the territory."

A thin wail came from the baby's room and Gage turned instantly toward it. "The master's voice," he muttered. He glanced back over his shoulder at Reece. "Kelsey made some incredible cinnamon rolls. They're supposed to be for tomorrow morning but I think you might get a special dispensation, being a guest and all. Let me see what Her Highness needs and I'll meet you in the kitchen."

"Am I supposed to steal the cinnamon rolls or talk her out of them?" Reece asked.

Gage stopped in the doorway to his daughter's room and looked back, blue eyes gleaming. "Whatever works."

Reece shook his head. He wondered if stealing cinnamon rolls qualified as some sort of male-bonding ritual. If so, it seemed a small enough price to pay to have at least one of Shannon's brothers looking at him with something other than acute suspicion. Besides, it had been years since he'd last tasted a homemade cinnamon roll.

When Shannon was growing up, Christmas had been a modest celebration. There were gifts. Her father had leaned toward the predictable: dolls in pretty dresses giving way to bicycles and then, when she reached her teens, gift certificates to the local mall so she could buy herself something nice. He also expressed his appreciation of whatever she got him, whether it was glue-smudged construction paper artwork or the lopsided ashtray for the cigarettes he didn't smoke. Like Thanksgiving, Christmas dinner had generally been eaten at a restaurant with the sound of piped-in carols to fill any silences.

There was music at the Walkers', too. She caught snatches of it now and again. Kermit the Frog alternated with Garth Brooks and Tchaikovsky, reflecting the taste of whoever happened to be closest to the CD player when it came time to change the CD. She was fairly sure the Tchaikovsky was courtesy of her oldest brother's wife, Nikki, and Garth Brooks was Cole's choice, but Kermit's serenade appeared suspiciously soon after she saw Keefe near the stereo. The scary thing was she wasn't sure he'd put it on for the children, and the idea that her large, tough brother was a secret Muppets fan was mind-boggling, to put it mildly.

Then again, everything about this day was mind-boggling. There was noise and laughter and food—large quantities of all three. Children and animals darted through the rooms of Rachel's modest home, weaving in and out among the adults and furniture with total disregard for life and limb. There was always an adult hand nearby to slow a careening six-year-old or steady a wobbly toddler's steps.

There was no question of everyone being able to sit at the table so the meal was set up on the kitchen counters and served buffet style. It wasn't a meal with a recognizable beginning, middle and end. People served themselves, found a place to sit or stand and ate, then went back for seconds or thirds or, in the case of Cole and Gage's little boy, Danny, possibly fourths.

It was a classic American family Christmas, in all its chaotic glory, and Shannon felt like a little kid with her nose pressed up against the candy-store window, looking in on all that brightness and warmth. The fact that it was her choice that put her on the outside looking in didn't ease the feeling. They included her in their family so easily. Hell, they included *Reece* as comfortably as if they'd known him for years, and he seemed to fit right in. Why was it so hard for *her* to reciprocate?

"God, where did you find that?" Shannon had been staring down at her eggnog, as if trying to find the meaning of life in the pattern of nutmeg sprinkles, but Sam's question, warm with amusement, made her look up.

Mary, Cole's daughter, had come into the room, clutching a guitar in her arms. The instrument was nearly as big as she was, and she had her arms wrapped around the body, the neck sticking up in front of her face, blocking her view so that she had to twist her head to one side to see where she was walking.

"It was in the closet in the little bedroom," she told her uncle. "I found it yesterday and Grandma said I could get it out. She said you used to play it, Uncle Sam."

"Yeah, about a thousand years ago." He took it from her when she handed it to him. He edged forward on the sofa and strummed his fingers across the strings. The sound that resulted was musical only by the very loosest of definitions. A chorus of moans was punctuated by a sharp, pained bark from the dog, and the fat black-and-white cat who'd been snoozing on Tessa's lap leaped to her feet with a startled hiss and shot from the room.

When the laughter died down, Mary patted the top of the guitar and gave her uncle a hopeful look. "Play something, Uncle Sam."

"Honey, I haven't played guitar in twenty years." Sam shook his head apologetically. "I wasn't very good even when I did play."

"Reece plays guitar." Shannon was a little startled to hear herself speak, and she bit her lip, giving Reece a quick, uncertain glance, not sure he was going to appreciate being volunteered like that. But he didn't seem to mind. He'd been leaning against the mantel—it was easier to digest standing up, he'd said—but on finding himself the recipient of hopeful looks from both Sam and Mary, he pushed away from the support and reached to take the guitar from Sam, who was more than eager to hand it over.

"Why don't you go get that stool I saw in the kitchen," he told Mary, "and I'll see if I can tune this thing."

Shannon saw Mary's father start to get up but his wife's hand closed over his arm. He looked at her and she shook her head warningly. He hesitated and then settled back into his seat, watching as Mary ran from the room with Danny close behind her. The silent exchange had taken only an instant but it reminded

Shannon that Mary had had heart surgery a few months ago. Rachel had called to tell her about it and she'd sent flowers and a box of candy, receiving a thank-you note back a few weeks later, written in a surprisingly neat childish print. At the time she'd told herself that she didn't want to intrude on the family but, in retrospect, it seemed incredibly thoughtless that she hadn't made more of an effort. They were trying so hard and she had given…nothing.

"Reece is practically a famous singer," she said, hoping he'd forgive her. "His parents were Jonathan and Jennifer, and he sang on one of their songs."

There were exclamations and Reece smiled and shrugged and explained how he'd come to be immortalized in song. By the time he was done, Mary and Danny were back with the stool. Reece thanked them and sat down, bracing the guitar on one knee, fingers twisting the tuning pegs as he brought the old strings into something approaching harmony with one another.

"I seem to be doomed to play guitars with rubber bands for strings." He looked up and smiled at Shannon and she smiled back, wondering if he was remembering the same thing she was, that the last time he'd complained about guitar strings, the first time she'd heard him play, had been just before they slept together for the first time.

Aware of the color creeping up her face, she looked down at her eggnog. Better not to think about that right now, not with her whole family looking on. She'd been surprised by how much she'd missed him last night. It hadn't even been two weeks, but she'd grown accustomed to the feel of him in the bed next to her, to falling asleep with her head on his shoulder. The narrow bed had felt large and empty, and that was maybe a little scary, considering the fact that this was supposed to be a temporary thing. It was the built-in temporaryness of it that had made it safe. But last night she'd been lonely without him, and that didn't seem to fit in with the whole "safe" thing.

Reece was playing a rather unique version of "Old MacDonald Had a Farm." At least Shannon didn't remember any emus in the version she'd learned. Not to mention aardvarks and antelope—contributions from Sam and Keefe. Mary and Danny were laughing, delighted with this unique vision of agrarian life. Little David, too young to know the difference between an aardvark and a Holstein, stood in the middle of the floor, rocking back and forth and clapping his hands to the rhythm of his own particular drummer.

Shannon was struck again by the realization that Reece was more at home with her family than she was. Then again, there was no pressure on him, no sense that, no matter how much they tried not to push, they were all watching her, hoping to see something of the child she'd been, the woman they'd hoped she'd become.

Suddenly restless, she set her glass down and stood up, slipping between her chair and Nikki's pretending not to see the other woman's questioning look, pretending not to notice the way Rachel's eyes shifted away from her grandchildren's happy faces. If she left the room, no one would come after her, but they'd wonder and they'd worry. Maybe she couldn't be whatever they'd hoped she'd be but she could at least avoid making herself even more of an outsider than she already was.

So, instead of fleeing out the door, out of the house and maybe just trotting her way back to Serenity Falls, she wandered along the outskirts of the room, as if that's what she'd intended all along, finally ending up near the piano. Old MacDonald was now raising sharks, which, according to Danny, make a growling noise that sounded a lot like the same noise his new Tonka truck had made earlier in the day.

Shannon risked a quick glance in that direction, half expecting to find everyone looking at her, but they were apparently absorbed in the impromptu concert. Relieved, she sank down on the piano bench. Obviously, her ego was running amuck. Or maybe it was paranoia spiraling out of control. Since when did she go around assuming that everyone was looking at her?

There were pictures on top of the piano, and she picked up a framed photo, studying the four solemn-faced boys and the little girl standing in front of them. She wished she could remember what it had been like to be a part of that obviously close-knit family. All she had were a few dim memories—a pink stuffed dog, the sound of her own giggles as someone swung her high in the air, hands picking her up and dusting her off when she fell down. Laughter and music, a lot like today, except...

"I remember someone playing piano," she said abruptly and then flushed when she realized she'd spoken out loud, interrupting the song. She started to apologize but Rachel spoke first.

"Gage used to play," she said quietly. "You liked to sit and draw pictures while he practiced. He was teaching you to play 'Chopsticks' when your...when you went away."

Shannon nodded, looking away from the almost painful look of hope on the other woman's face. Gage was watching her, something dark and...scared?...in his eyes. She smiled a little, wanting to take that look away.

"I still can't play 'Chopsticks,'" she admitted. Laughter greeted the comment, more than it deserved but it eased the sudden tension.

She wasn't sure how, because it hadn't been her suggestion and she knew it wasn't Gage's idea, she found herself the recipient of an impromptu piano lesson. It wasn't long before she had Danny on her lap and Mary crowded on the end of the bench next to her as both children tried their hand at pounding out the rhythmic little piece. It was mildly humiliating to find that they both picked it up faster than she did.

"Children learn easier," she said defensively when she hit the wrong keys yet again.

"Nah, you were always tone-deaf," Gage told her, grinning heartlessly at her outraged gasp.

"Maybe you're just a lousy teacher," she suggested with a dangerously sweet smile.

"Me and Mary learned okay," Danny pointed out, twisting his head to look up at her. "You've just got two left feet, Aunt Shannon."

"And both of them are on the keyboard," Gage murmured wickedly.

Shannon's offended glare was derailed when Mary patted her on the arm and said, "Don't feel bad, Aunt Shannon. I bet you're real good at lots of other stuff."

"Nonmusical stuff," Gage added helpfully, and Shannon lost the battle with her laughter.

A few minutes later, in answer to his niece's request for some "real music," Gage was making his way hesitantly through "Moonlight Sonata." Watching his long fingers skim over the keyboard and hearing his frustrated mutters as he stumbled over something that had obviously once been easy for him, it occurred to Shannon that, for a little while, she'd actually forgotten that Gage was her "brother" and had just enjoyed his company.

The idea was startling. She shifted her hold on Danny, whose head was starting to loll back against her shoulder as the day's excitement caught up with him. Maybe it wasn't the *Walkers'* expectations that were the problem. Maybe it was her own. Really, they hadn't asked for anything more than a chance to get to know her. She was the one who was hung up on the whole "family" label and what she *should* be feeling, which was stupid, really, because you couldn't force feelings.

It was amazing how much easier things were when she wasn't trying so hard, Shannon thought a few hours later as she stood on the front porch saying goodbye to her family. They even, almost, *felt* like family. Not that there had been some miraculous movie-musical-style moment of connection where bluebirds were singing and everyone was dancing with joy, but there was a tentative sense of *beginning,* a feeling that, given time, the connections would be there.

"Thank you so much for coming." Rachel Walker's smile was warm, her eyes just a little too bright. "It meant a lot to all of us."

"It meant a lot to me, too," Shannon said. "I...I really do want to get to know you." Her glance included her brothers. Their wives and children had already said their goodbyes and gone back inside. Reece was waiting in the truck.

"We want that, too." Rachel's voice was not quite steady. She hesitated a moment and then held out her arms. It wasn't the first time they'd hugged, but it was the first time Shannon had felt like she belonged. Her eyes were stinging when she pulled back, and she aimed a shaky smile at her brothers before turning away and hurrying down the dark pathway.

Reece had the truck running, and the interior of the cab was nice and warm. She felt him glance at her and was grateful of the darkness that hid her expression. Not that she was sure what it was since she wasn't sure what she was feeling but, whatever it was, she didn't want to talk about it. She'd had enough emotional dissection for one day. She didn't—

"As soon as we're out of sight of your four large and intimidating brothers, I'm going to pull the truck over in some secluded spot and ravish you."

Reece's tone was conversational, and it took her a moment to process what he'd said. When she did, her breath caught and her mind went perfectly blank for an instant before coming back online with a rush of need that left her flushed and breathless.

"I've never been ravished in a truck." Was that her voice? She sounded like she'd been smoking cigarettes and drinking whiskey for the last month. She sounded downright wanton.

"No?" In the light from a street lamp, she saw Reece's fingers flex on the wheel. "New experiences are supposed to expand the mind."

"I've heard that." She slid her hand across the seat and set it on his thigh, nothing overt, just her fingers resting lightly on him, feeling the flex of muscle and the heat of his skin through denim. "I'm always eager to learn."

He slanted her a look that had an almost palpable heat. "I'm counting on that."

Chapter 11

The week between Christmas and New Year's was gray and rainy, but New Year's Day dawned with bright sunshine and clear skies. The talking heads in Pasadena tried not to look too smug about the fact that, yet again, the sun was shining on the Rose Parade.

"I think someone's made a bargain with the dark side," Shannon said. "Only demon interference could explain why it never rains on the parade. Is that a bear?"

Reece squinted at the screen, trying to see through the fuzzy snow. "I think it's a dog. It rains on the Rose Parade."

She snorted. "Yeah, like twice in the past two hundred years. You can't tell me that's not a product of some hell world."

He eyed her speculatively as he reached for his coffee. "You've been watching too much *Buffy the Vampire Slayer.* Maybe it's just really good luck. Maybe

Pasadena-ites are just really deserving people and this is their reward. Besides, they weren't having the parade two hundred years ago.''

''Sure they were.'' She leaned forward to select a miniquiche from the platter on the coffee table and then pointed it at him. ''It's a little-known fact that the Californios held a parade right down Colorado Boulevard every year on New Year's Day. They decorated their, um, donkeys with native flowers and gave prizes for who had the most attractive...ass.''

Reece groaned and threw a crumpled-up napkin at her but she just grinned and popped the quiche in her mouth.

He still wasn't sure why they were sitting on his grandfather's ancient sofa, watching the Rose Parade in all its fuzzy glory and eating leftover hors d'oeuvres from last night's New Year's Eve party at the McKinnons'. Last night was the first time they'd ended up in his bed instead of hers, but that didn't mean they couldn't walk across the driveway to her more comfortable sofa and, if she wanted to watch a bunch of flower-bedecked floats, wouldn't it be nice if she could actually *see* them?

But watching the floats through a blizzard of bad reception apparently didn't bother her and neither did faded upholstery and springs that were prone to...spring in unexpected places.

When he'd awakened alone in bed, he'd assumed she'd gone back to her house. He crawled out of the tangled sheets and nearly tripped over a pillow, which he had a vague memory of having thrown out of the way sometime the night before. The memory was enough to put a smile on his face as he headed for the shower. They'd definitely started the new year off on a high note. With luck, they could continue on that same high note later this afternoon.

Now, two hours later, he was wondering if Shannon would be amenable to nudging that timetable up. She was curled up on one end of the sofa, her hair caught up in a messy knot on top of her head. She was wearing faded jeans and one of his blue workshirts, half-unbuttoned and knotted at the waist. He didn't need X-ray vision to know she wasn't wearing a bra. The soft, gentle sway of her breasts when she moved made his mouth water and made other body parts perk up with an eagerness that seemed downright greedy considering the previous night's activities.

She frowned and tilted her head as if hoping a different angle might clear up the picture on the screen.

"You know, if you want to actually *see* the parade, we could move this next door," Reece said, running his thumb over the top of her bare foot.

"We could," she agreed, but made no move to get up.

Reece shrugged mentally. It was her choice. His interest in the parade pretty much began and ended with... Well, actually, it never really began. He couldn't even remember the last time he'd seen it. Maybe when Kyle was little.

"Now, that's definitely a bear."

Reece turned his head obediently to look at the screen. "In a grass skirt?"

"It's a Hawaiian bear. They're very rare. They live in caves in the lava and only eat poi and moon pies."

"Did anyone ever tell you that you're a terrible liar?"

"I am not." She gave him an offended look. "I'm a very good liar."

"You know, liars never prosper." Reece's fingers closed around one slim ankle.

"I thought it was cheaters who never prospered." Shannon let him tug first one leg and then the other flat on the sofa, her eyes going wide and dark as he crawled up the length of her body. Her voice took on a breathless edge. "Liars are supposed to have flaming pants."

"Well, it was a relatively little lie. I don't think it's necessary to extract the full penalty." He hovered over her, weight braced on his elbows, hips nudging gently against hers, letting her feel his arousal. She smiled, a slow, feline curl of her lips that went straight to his groin.

"Maybe I could get some sort of dispensation for good behavior?"

Reece lowered himself slowly until his body pressed hers into the faded upholstery. "Depends on how good you are," he murmured, swallowing a groan when she shifted, sliding those sinfully long legs up alongside his hips so that he lay in the cradle of her thighs.

"Oh, I can be very…very…*very*…good." She brought her head up and caught his lower lip between her teeth, worrying it gently.

"You're missing the parade." He slid his hand upward, palming her breast and rubbing his thumb over the nipple, feeling it harden beneath the thin cotton of his shirt.

"What parade?" she whispered against his lips.

It was a slow, languid kiss, the heat between them banked with the knowledge that they had all the time in the world. Shannon opened her mouth to him, her tongue fencing teasingly with his, hands moving restlessly up and down his back, sliding over the thin cotton of his T-shirt.

Reece rocked his hips, teasing both of them with the feel of his trapped erection rubbing against her through two layers of denim. She moaned, a soft, hungry sound that cranked up the heat between them a notch. Urgency began to replace languor, lazy pleasure giving way to need. His hand slid between them, tugging at the knot she'd tied with the tails of his shirt. He needed to feel her skin against him, bare and warm and flushed with hunger.

It took a moment for Reece to figure out that the bell he was hearing wasn't part of the background mutter from the television.

"There's someone at the door," Shannon said, tilting her head to give his mouth better access to the sensitive skin under her ear.

"Probably someone selling something," he muttered, catching her earlobe between his teeth.

"At eight-thirty on New Year's morning?" Shannon's hands shifted, settled on his shoulders and pushed.

"They'll go away," he told her. He gave up on the knot and slid his hand under the shirt. She shuddered, body going boneless beneath him as his fingers closed over her bare breast.

The bell rang again, and her eyes popped open. Reece groaned and lowered his forehead to hers, admitting defeat.

"It might be something important," she whispered with a touch of apology.

"Yeah? Well, this is pretty damned important, too," he muttered. Reluctantly he slid his hand out from under her shirt and pushed himself up off the sofa. He

took a few deep breaths, willing his arousal to subside
to a point where he wasn't likely to be arrested for
public indecency, and stalked to the door. Behind him,
he heard Shannon shifting around, sitting up and probably putting herself back together. Dammit. Of course,
that wasn't all bad. Getting her untidy again wasn't
exactly a hardship. That thought might just be enough
to save the life of whoever was ringing his doorbell.
For the third time.

His expression less than welcoming, Reece yanked
the door open. The young man on the other side of the
screen grinned at him.

"Hi, Dad."

Chapter 12

There was nothing like being caught practically *in flagrante* very *delicto* by your lover's son to really kill the mood, Shannon thought. She glanced down to make sure everything was properly buttoned and tied. It was at least the tenth time she'd checked in the past fifteen minutes, but you couldn't be too careful. Not that she thought it likely that Reece's son didn't have a pretty good idea of what she and his father had been doing when he arrived, but there was no sense in making it obvious. Any *more* obvious.

When Reece introduced them, his eyes had skimmed over her, taking in the tousled mess of her hair, the man's shirt knotted at her waist and her bare feet before cutting to his father, also barefoot, rumpled and looking more than a little panic-stricken. Kyle's eyes flashed with speculative amusement but he didn't say anything, for which she was pathetically grateful.

Looking at him, Shannon thought she would have

known who he was, even if she'd met him in the middle of Times Square. The resemblance between him and his father was striking. Kyle matched Reece for height, but his body was leaner, still holding some of the lankiness of youth. He had the same thick dark hair and strong jaw, the same smile. It was like looking at a picture of Reece taken twenty years ago, except for the eyes. Where his father's eyes were dark brown, Kyle's were an unexpected clear, pale emerald. Shannon was willing to bet that he had girls trailing after him in hordes.

"Are you sure you want to cook?" Reece asked, eyeing her uneasily as she pulled a carton of eggs out of the refrigerator.

Breakfast had been her suggestion when it began to look like the three of them were going to stand in the living room forever. Reece had seized on the suggestion gratefully. It was obvious that his son's unexpected appearance at such a delicate moment had thrown him off balance. They'd moved into the kitchen, leaving the television muttering to itself, fuzzy images of pretty floats drifting past unseen. She'd poured a cup of coffee for Kyle and freshened her own cup and Reece's before poking through the refrigerator to see what the options were. Her suggestion of omelets had been met with enthusiasm on Kyle's part and cautious approval on Reece's.

She knew what he was thinking and couldn't resist teasing him. She gave him a sweet smile. "I'll make one of my special omelets."

"Special?" Reece asked warily. "What's in them?"

Kyle gave his father a surprised look. "Haven't you ever heard the saying about not looking a gift cook in the mouth?"

"Experience has taught me that it's better to be safe than sorry," Reece told him. He leaned back, bracing his hands against the edge of the counter and looked at his son. "The first morning I met her, she tried to feed me Froot Loops."

"That's not so bad," Kyle said. "I like—"

"And Pepsi," Reece added heavily.

"*On* the Froot Loops?" Kyle asked, his expression so exactly echoing his father's that Shannon nearly choked on a giggle.

"Not *on* them," she explained. "*With* them."

Kyle looked like he didn't think this was much of an improvement but was too polite to say so.

"And then, when I politely declined," Reece continued grimly, "she tried to feed me toaster waffles and grape jelly."

"It's a perfectly nutritious breakfast," Shannon protested. "The waffles provide a serving of grains and the jelly counts as a fruit."

Kyle eyed her with something approaching awe. "Did he eat them?"

"No." Shannon pursed her mouth into a prim line and slanted a laughing glance at Reece. "He made up some ridiculous story about being allergic to grape jelly."

Kyle cleared his throat and looked self-conscious. "Actually, it's a hereditary thing. I, ah…"

"Turn purple," Reece suggested, and Kyle seized on it gratefully.

"Yeah, I turn purple when I eat grape jelly. It's a very rare condition." He tried to look regretful. "So, if your special omelets have grape jelly in them, I'll have to pass."

"Grape jelly in an omelet?" Shannon's brows rose

in shock. "Don't be silly." She waited a beat and then gave them both a big, bright smile. "Everyone knows you always use orange marmalade in omelets."

Reece made breakfast. When Shannon offered to at least help, he instructed Kyle to keep her away from the stove, even if he had to use physical force. Laughing, Shannon began setting the table.

Conversation was easier than she might have expected. Kyle had his father's gift for telling a story, and his cross-country trip had given him plenty of those. He hadn't said anything about why he was here or how long he planned to stay, but, reading between the lines, Shannon had the distinct feeling that he was less than enchanted with life on the open road. She wondered if he'd come to Serenity Falls planning to spend time with his father and how that would fit in with Reece's plans. He hadn't said anything about leaving, but he hadn't said anything about staying, either.

She looked down at the remains of her omelet and wondered if the hollow feeling in the pit of her stomach was because she'd eaten too fast.

Shannon excused herself as soon as they were done eating, saying that she had some shop samples she wanted to finish up. She hadn't really planned on doing anything but spending the day with Reece, but she thought he and Kyle could probably use some time together and maybe it would be a good thing for her to spend some time alone, remind herself of how much she enjoyed being on her own.

When Reece got up to walk her to the door, Kyle made a point of the fact that he was going to clear the table. Shannon caught his eyes, saw the amused knowledge in them, and felt herself blush.

"I'll see you later today?" Reece asked, his hand settling on her lower back as they stood in the open doorway.

"Don't you think Kyle might want to have you to himself for a bit?"

"No." His hand slid up, nudging her gently closer. "He said he's planning on staying for a while. We'll get plenty of time together." He lowered his mouth to hers in a soft, quick kiss. "You know, it's great to see him, but his timing stinks."

Shannon felt the color come up in her cheeks, a mixture of desire and embarrassment. She lifted her hand to his face, tracing the solid line of his jaw. "It could have been worse," she murmured. "He could have shown up a few minutes later."

"God, yes." Reece laughed and dropped another, harder kiss on her mouth before she slipped out the door.

When Reece returned to the kitchen, Kyle had just finished rinsing the plates and stacking them in the drainer. He turned to look at his father, drying his hands on a red-and-white-checked towel.

"Nice neighbor." There was nothing suggestive in Kyle's tone but Reece felt himself flush.

"Yes. She's very...nice."

"Pretty, too," Kyle said mildly.

"Very." Reece fought the urge to shove his hands in his pockets like an erring child. Dammit, *he* was supposed to be the grown-up here.

"She the reason you've hung around here so long?" There was nothing but curiosity in Kyle's question.

"Part of it." It felt good to say it out loud and Reece

leaned back against the counter opposite Kyle and waited to see how his son would react to that.

Kyle nodded. "Yeah, I can see why. She's a hottie."

Reece laughed. "I hadn't thought of her that way, but I guess she is."

"Yeah." Kyle folded the towel and set it down before bracing both hands on the counter and leaning back against it in unconscious imitation of Reece's pose. "So, you *pissed* at me for quitting school? You didn't say much when we talked on the phone."

Reece shook his head. "I told you before that it was your decision and I'd support you whatever you decided to do."

"Yeah? Mom said pretty much the same thing but she just about had a cow when I told her I was quitting."

"She wants what's best for you," Reece said, choosing his words carefully. "And she's more...definite in her ideas of what's best."

"You mean she likes to run everyone's life," Kyle said dryly.

Reece started to defend his ex-wife, met his son's eyes and shrugged instead. "Your mother's a very strong-willed woman."

"Yeah." Kyle grinned and relaxed back against the counter. "Charles says she's pigheaded as a mule." Charles was his stepfather.

"Does he?" Reece let his mouth curve upward. "Well, I always did like Charles."

"Me, too. He's good for Mom because he only lets her manage him as long as she's pushing him to do what he wants to do."

"What did Charles say about you quitting school?"

"Said he thought I was an idiot, but everyone had a right to be an idiot when they were nineteen."

"Sounds reasonable." Reece cocked his head in question. "Are you sorry you quit?"

"No." Kyle's answer was prompt. "I may go back, but I just couldn't face another four or five years of school right now. It would be different if I had something I wanted to do, some career in mind, but I don't."

"Well, I guess you're entitled to take some time to decide what you want to be when you grow up," Reece said, and Kyle smiled, relieved.

"I thought I might hang around here awhile, maybe get a job. I mean, I've got plenty of money, thanks to what you've put away for me, but I don't want to use that just to live on. Besides, I figure working for a while might help me figure out what I want to do. If you don't mind me hanging around, that is."

"Well, it'll be a real hardship but I think I can bear up under the strain." The dry comment seemed to be the reassurance Kyle needed.

"I don't suppose Shannon has any younger sisters?" he asked, grinning.

"No, she's got four very large older brothers," Reece said, grimacing and Kyle laughed out loud.

"Man, you do like to live dangerously, don't you?"

Reece laughed, but he thought Shannon was likely to prove far more dangerous than her brothers.

Shannon hadn't planned on spending New Year's Day sewing samples for the shop but, since she found herself with the day unexpectedly free, she decided it wasn't a bad idea. Since getting involved with Reece, she hadn't spent much time sewing, and it was a pleasure to immerse herself in pattern and fabric. She'd always enjoyed sewing but, since buying the shop, there was the added challenge of trying to guess what was most likely to inspire her customers to part with a significant portion of their discretionary income.

Humming along to Chris Isaak's version of "Yellow Bird," she cut out brightly colored squares. She'd piece them together and then appliqué a pair of funky looking cats on the background, finishing up with a multicolored-stripe border that would pull in all the colors from the center of the quilt. She'd already ordered three bolts of the stripe, taking a chance that her customers would like the playful look of it as much as she did. It never hurt to show them how the fabric looked in an actual quilt.

Halfway through the afternoon, she stopped and went into the kitchen to make herself a cup of hot tea. She sat at the kitchen table and nibbled on a chocolate chip cookie while she waited for the water to boil. The wall hanging was coming along nicely. She just might get it done this evening. The stripe wasn't due in to the shop for another week or two, but it couldn't hurt to whet people's appetite ahead of time by hanging the sample up early. She'd done that last summer with a pretty little print featuring fairies riding bunnies and had sold two bolts of the fabric the afternoon it came into the shop.

The teakettle began to hiss and she got up to catch it before it started whistling. She'd just poured water over a tea bag when she heard someone tapping at the back door. Startled, she turned, her expression relaxing in a grin when she saw Reece looking through the window.

"What are you doing at the back door?" she asked as she unlocked it and let him in.

"I snuck through the hedge," he said, holding out his arm to display a thin scratch. "Damned thing bit me."

"It's a hedge. It's supposed to keep people out." She led him over to the sink, pulling a paper towel off the roll and dampening it before dabbing it against the scratch. "Should I even ask why you were going through the hedge?"

"Because I'm an idiot," he said, taking the paper towel from her and tossing it in the sink and then sliding his arms around her waist. "Because my nineteen-year-old son is staying with me and I'm suddenly feeling terribly wicked and dirty old manish."

"Did Kyle say something?" Shannon asked, frowning. She reached up to pluck a leaf from his hair. Kyle hadn't seemed upset by the idea that they were involved, but maybe he'd just been hiding his feelings.

"Kyle said he was going to go take a shower, then take a nap and if I had anything I wanted to do or anyplace I wanted to go, I didn't have to worry about him." Reece's smile was equal parts amusement and irritation. "He might as well have given me permission to go off and do illicit things. It was embarrassing as hell and he knew it, the brat."

"You could have thrown him off the scent by staying home," Shannon said. She hooked her fingers through his belt loops and tugged him closer, her pulse jumping at the feel of his arousal pressed against her belly.

"No, I couldn't. I don't have that much self-control." He bent to taste the sensitive skin under her ear and Shannon tilted her head to give him better access, her eyes fluttering shut.

"So why the back hedge?" she managed, sighing as his teeth closed over her earlobe.

"I don't know, it just seemed to fit in with the whole illicit affair thing. Sneaking through hedges in the dark of night."

"It's the middle of the afternoon." She turned her head to catch his mouth with hers.

"You've got to use your imagination." He slid one hand between them and began slipping open the buttons on her shirt—*his* shirt. "But next time, I'm bringing a chain saw."

Grinning, Shannon leaned back against his hold. He took advantage of the space between them and tugged the shirt open. She'd put on a bra since this morning and he frowned in mild disapproval before flicking the front catch open, baring her breasts.

"Now where were we?" he murmured, watching her with dark, hungry eyes. He cupped one soft mound, stroking his thumb across the peak.

"Right…right about there." It was difficult to talk when her brain felt like it was melting right along with her bones.

"Or maybe right…here?" The last word was a whisper against her breast. She shuddered as his tongue laved her nipple, painting it with quick little strokes that brought it to aching hardness. Her fingers curled into the solid muscles of his upper arm, and her head fell back as she arched, offering herself to him.

There was something deliciously wicked about standing here in the middle of her kitchen, bare to the waist, sunlight pouring through the back window—Sunlight. Window. Shannon's eyes popped open.

"Reece! The curtains are open."

"No one can see into your backyard," he murmured, licking a patch along her collarbone.

She shivered. He was right but...

"Someone could sneak into the yard," she said.

"Trust me, anyone who tries to sneak into your backyard is too busy trying to stop the bleeding from wounds inflicted by that hedge to have time to peer through the window." But he straightened and looked down at her, lust and exasperation mixed in his expression. "I'm trying to ravish you."

"I know." She slid her fingers through his hair, made her smile coaxing. "Have I ever mentioned that I have this fantasy about being ravished in my bed?"

He frowned. "That's sort of a boring fantasy, isn't it? What about the deck of a pirate ship or a treehouse in the jungle?"

"Splinters and mildew," she said, edging him toward the door.

"Splinters and mildew?" he repeated blankly.

"Pirate ship. Deck. Splinters," she clarified. "Jungle. Humidity. Mildew. And bugs." She shuddered. "Big bugs. Not my idea of a fun time."

"I think we need to work on your fantasy life," Reece said. Without waiting for a response, he bent to slide one hand under her knees and scooped her up into his arms.

Gasping, Shannon threw her arms around his neck, her pulse skittering with excitement.

"Is this where you carry me off to your jungle lair?" she asked breathlessly.

"I was thinking more along the lines of your bedroom." Reece angled her legs out the door and carried her down the hall. "Do you know how far it is to the nearest jungle? Not to mention the cost of renting a lair this time of year.''

He dropped her on the bed and followed her down, his mouth catching hers, swallowing her laughter. His hands caught hers, pinning them to the pillow beside her head. The soft cotton of his sweatshirt pressed against her bare breasts, abrading her nipples, and suddenly the playfulness vanished, burned away in the heat that flared between them.

She pulled her hands free, tugging at his shirt, needing to feel him against her, skin to skin. Reece released her mouth long enough to pull his sweatshirt off over his head, tossing it aside. He reached for her jeans at the same moment that she reached for his, and they rolled on the bed, her choked laughter mixing with his muttered imprecations as they struggled with the heavy denim. A seam ripped with a sibilant hiss, and then he was stripping her jeans down her legs, taking her peach-colored panties along with them. She arched into him, hands slipping on sweat-damp skin as he shoved his jeans down, urgency too great to take time to get them off. She could feel his hands shaking as he gripped her hips, fingers digging into her skin hard enough to leave bruises but she didn't care.

She cried out as he slid into her in one long, heavy thrust, filling her, completing her, making her whole. And then it was all heat and movement and sound. Her breath coming in panting gasps, his guttural groans, the soft, wet slap of flesh on flesh. It was too much, she thought, too much. Her body bucked as if to throw him off even as her legs tightened around his hips to pull him closer.

''Now,'' he whispered against her throat, against her ear. ''Now. Give it to me now.''

As if the words were all she'd needed, she felt herself spin out of control, her entire being concentrated on the spot where they were joined. The pleasure spiraled out, tighter, harder, hovering on the knife-edge of pain until it burst apart in a shower of lights and sparks, dancing red and gold under her eyelids. Her arms tightened around Reece and he shuddered and groaned against her.

Minutes or hours later she felt him stir. He'd shifted to one side and lay sprawled on his stomach, his knee bent, leg resting across her hips, one arm across her waist, face buried in the curve of shoulder and neck. His hand moved slowly, tracing a warm line up her side, finally curving around her breast in a casually possessive gesture that made her heart stumble with a mixture of pleasure and uneasiness. Maybe it wasn't a good thing for him to feel possessive. Maybe it was dangerous that she liked it so much.

But it was hard to worry about it when he lifted his head, giving her a smile that said he was unabashedly pleased with himself, with her and possibly with the world at large.

"Now, that's how to get the new year off to a good start."

There was really nothing to do but kiss him.

Shannon had never been a big believer in New Year's resolutions. She didn't believe there was anything mystical about January first. It was just an arbitrary number on a calendar invented by mankind to make it easier to keep track of things. It was also a busy time if you happened to own a quilt shop. With the holidays just past, every quilter on the planet seemed to be seized with a determination that *this* year, they were really going to make quilts for everyone they knew and they were going to start them all in January. It was also time for that annual rite of torture known as taking inventory and the big inventory reduction sale that preceded it.

As a general rule, the first part of January passed in a haze of long hours and hard work, and this year was no exception. But she had distractions this year that she hadn't had before. Well, one distraction. One large distraction. One large, very distracting distraction. It was a little frightening to realize how easily he'd fit into her life and what a large hole he was going to leave if he left. *When* he left, she reminded herself regularly. It wasn't a question of *if* he left. It was just a question of when.

And that probably seemed so depressing because she had some sort of low-level flu that she couldn't seem to shake. She must have gotten it from Kelly, who spent three days out sick right after the first of the year, but she hadn't gotten as bad a dose. She was never sick enough to stay home but she was tired all the time and vaguely queasy. It was the illness that was making her feel so vulnerable and…needy, because she'd known from the beginning that Reece was leaving, and she couldn't possibly have been stupid enough to fall in love with him.

Falling in love at forty wasn't all that much different from falling in love at twenty, Reece decided. There was still that nervous little jiggle in the pit of his stomach when he saw the object of his affections, still all those niggling uncertainties about whether or not she loved him in return and whether or not they could build a future together. He was planning on it. Definitely planning on it. He hadn't mentioned it to Shannon yet. She was…well, he wasn't sure what she was. Skittish? Wary? Either one fit. It was understandable, really. When you looked at her past history, there was nothing in it to encourage her to throw herself into emotional commitments.

Her father had taken her from her family and, though she hadn't exactly said as much, it was pretty clear that he'd been emotionally distant. Fear of being found out had kept him from settling anywhere for very long, and the frequent moves had meant that Shannon didn't get a chance to build long-lasting ties with anyone. And then, when she got married, her husband died just a few months later, leaving her alone again. It was no wonder she was having a hard time opening herself up to the Walkers, no wonder she always kept a little part of herself distant from him.

But things were changing. He knew she'd talked to her mother a couple of times in the month since Christmas. Maybe they were not yet to the point of having heart-to-heart, mother-daughter talks but Shannon seemed more at ease with the idea of having family, of having those ties. And, whether she admitted it or not, she'd let him in, too.

She loved him. He thought. Probably, she did. He hoped. God, he hoped so. Because he'd finally figured out what he wanted to be when he grew up and, much to his astonishment, he wanted to stay in Serenity Falls and build a life with Shannon Devereux. He wanted that a lot.

He wasn't going to push it, though. He didn't want to push her. They had plenty of time. He knew what he wanted. It was just a matter of getting her to admit that she wanted the same thing.

* * *

The way to a man's heart was supposed to be through his stomach. Reece had decided that, in these days of genderless thinking, the same could apply to a woman. In this case, he was hoping that the way to a coffee lover's heart was through a cup of Jamaican Blue Mountain coffee, freshly brewed and hand delivered. Considering what the beans cost, he was willing to bet they'd been hand delivered straight from Jamaica, one bean at a time.

Shannon was dressed for work when she opened the door. A loose ivory-colored sweater worn over a pair of rust-colored slacks, her hair tumbled around her shoulders in a spill of warm red-gold curls. A pair of scruffy blue slippers completed the outfit, and Reece grinned when he saw them.

"Nice shoes."

"Thanks," she said, offering him a vague smile, apparently accepting the compliment as if it had been sincere.

"I'd change them before you go to work," he suggested, poking one slipper with the toe of his running shoe. "Unless you're trying for the bag lady look."

"What?"

"The slippers?" he said gently. "Not exactly high fashion attire."

"Oh." Shannon looked down at her feet and nodded. "I guess you're right. I'll…change them."

"You okay?" he asked as he followed her into the house.

"Fine. I'm fine." She rubbed her fingers across her forehead. "I'm just a little distracted, I guess. Thinking about…stuff. Things. Thinking about things."

"You sleep okay?" He set the thermal pot down on the counter and slid one hand behind her neck, drawing her forward into his kiss. She pulled back a little and then seemed to almost collapse against him, sliding her arms around his waist.

"Pretty good," she mumbled into his shirt.

"Still got that flu bug?" he asked, brushing a kiss over the top of her head. "Maybe you should see a doctor."

She stiffened as if jabbed with a cattle prod, pulling out of his arms and taking a step back. "I'm fine." Her tone verged on snappish. "I've just got a lot on my mind. With the shop and everything."

"Okay." Reece lifted his hand, palm out, placating. "Just don't let yourself get too run down."

"I won't." Shannon looked away from him, pushing one hand through her hair. "I didn't mean to snap."

"That's okay." He pushed down his concern and smiled. "I come in peace and I come bearing gifts."

Shannon's smile didn't quite reach her eyes. "Isn't there some warning about 'Beware of Greeks bearing gifts'?"

Reece took two mugs off the hooks under the cupboard. "Yeah, but lucky for you, I'm not Greek and this isn't just any gift." He unscrewed the top on the thermal mug and the rich scent of coffee immediately wafted out. He inhaled deeply as he poured it into cups. "This is Jamaican Blue Mountain coffee, freshly ground, freshly brewed and freshly delivered."

Smiling, he turned and held a cup out to Shannon. She looked at it, looked at him, swallowed once, swallowed again. The color drained out of her face and she gave him a helpless look and clapped one hand over her mouth before turning and bolting for the bathroom.

Reece stood there, staring after her, coffee cup still extended. Through the door, he could hear the unmistakable sounds of her throwing up. Slowly he pulled his hand back, stared down at the cup for a moment and then turned to pour it back into the carafe, along with the cup he'd poured for himself. He tightened the lid on the carafe and rinsed both cups thoroughly and then opened the back door for good measure, letting in cold, clean air.

After several minutes he heard the water come on in the bathroom. Judging the smell thoroughly dissipated, he shut the back door and then leaned back against the counter, waiting. It was a long wait and he had plenty of time to think. He thought about how pale Shannon had been lately, how distracted she'd been the past few days. He thought about the fact that they'd been lovers for more than six weeks, had spent almost every night together and she hadn't once said anything about it being a bad time of the month for her. He thought about how careful they'd been. Most of the time. Almost all of the time. Almost.

He waited, hearing nothing but silence and wondering if she was on the other side of the door, hoping he'd go away. But he wasn't going to go anywhere until they'd talked, until he'd asked a few questions. He'd lead up to it gently. No sense jumping to conclusions. Maybe she just had the flu. That's probably all it was, and he didn't want to sound accusing.

The bathroom door finally opened, and Shannon came out, looking pale and hollow-eyed. Looking anywhere but at him. Flu, he told himself. The flu could really wipe a person out, make them throw up when they smelled coffee. That's all it was.

''Shannon?'' He waited until she looked at him, saw the answer in her eyes even before he asked the question.

''Are you pregnant?''

Chapter 13

Shannon looked at him, not saying anything, not denying it.

Not. Denying. It.

Reece swallowed hard and fumbled for the back of a chair, pulling it out and sinking into it. The silence was so complete that he could hear the clock on the wall ticking the seconds away.

"Shannon?" It came out on a croak and he stopped, cleared his throat and tried again. "Are you…pregnant?"

Her eyes slid away from his, slid back for an instant and then away again. "Maybe," she said at last. "Probably. A little."

He stared at her blankly, his mind spinning back to Christmas night, driving back from her mother's house, pulling off the highway into a deserted rest stop, parking away from the lights. The two of them in his truck, risking hypothermia and breaking several public indecency laws. No condom. Not even a highly inadequate gesture of premature withdrawal. They hadn't talked about it, hadn't discussed it and made a logical, adult decision. There had been one frozen moment when they'd both realized what they were doing, the risk they were about to take.

She'd been sprawled on the seat beneath him, blouse pulled open, skirt pushed up around her waist, eyes glittering in the darkness, the wet heat of her pressed against him. So close, so close. And he'd waited, frozen, wishing he hadn't packed the condoms in his overnight case, which was in the back of the truck, knowing he should pull back. It was the right thing to do, the responsible thing to do. And then she'd arched against him, taking him inside that first tiny bit, and his breath had hissed between his teeth and he'd stopped thinking.

They hadn't talked about it afterward, either. Not really. Helping her pull her clothes back together, he'd said something about letting him know and she'd cut him off with a quick gesture of one hand and a blush that he could sense more than see. And that was the last thing either of them had said about it.

"A little?" he said finally. "I don't think you can be a little pregnant. It's sort of an either-or kind of thing." He tried to smile but couldn't quite manage it. "Have you been to a doctor. Are you all right?"

"No and yes." Seeing his blank look and apparently realizing that his brain was not exactly working at full speed, Shannon clarified. "No, I haven't seen a doctor yet. Yes, I'm all right."

"And you're sure you're…" He gestured vaguely toward her stomach.

"I did one of those home pregnancy tests. It…they're supposed to be pretty accurate."

"Yeah, I guess they are."

Silence descended again. Reece stared at the clock, watching the second hand make one full sweep around, trying to wrap his mind around this new information. He was going to be a father again. He and Shannon were having a baby. Shannon was having his baby. No matter how he phrased it, he couldn't make it seem real.

"You're feeling okay?" he asked. "Besides the coffee thing, I mean."

"It's not just coffee." Shannon was tracing aimless patterns on the table with the tip of one finger, her eyes on the movement. "But other than the fact that food is pretty disgusting, especially first thing in the morning, I seem to be fine. I've...got a doctor's appointment tomorrow actually."

"Good. That's good." A doctor's appointment. She'd made a doctor's appointment. She'd taken a home pregnancy test and made a doctor's appointment and she hadn't said a word to him.

"When did you plan on telling me?" he asked, and saw Shannon flinch away from the edge in his voice.

Her eyes shot up to his and then darted away. "Soon. I thought I might be...but I just... I did the test thingy this morning. I'm still sort of getting used to the idea myself."

Yeah, he could relate to that, Reece thought. He pushed down the annoyance, told himself it was stupid to feel like he was the last one to know. He wished she'd told him when she first suspected, but maybe that was unreasonable. If she'd needed a little time to deal with this on her own, that was her privilege. But if she thought she was going to *continue* dealing with it on her own, that was her mistake.

"We need to talk," he said.

"I know but I can't right now." She looked at the clock with poorly concealed relief. "I need to go open the shop." She stood up and pushed her chair under the table.

As if she was ending a damned board meeting, he thought irritably. The legs of his chair scraped across the floor as he rose. Her eyes widened, and she stepped back from the table as if afraid he was going to lunge across it and grab her. It was tempting.

"Shannon." Reece stopped, drew a breath and reminded himself to stay calm. "Can't Kelly do that for you this morning?" he said finally. "I really think this is important."

"It is." Shannon edged toward the door. "It's very important and I want to talk to you about…about this but it wouldn't be fair to call Kelly at the last minute like this. Saturdays are our busiest day and she's already scheduled to come in this afternoon. Besides, it's not like I'm sick." She flushed when Reece shot a pointed glance at the bathroom door behind her. "Not *sick* sick," she amended. "Just because I'm… Women in my condition work all the time, and if I'm going to be doing this for the next eight months, I'd better get used to it."

"The next eight months? So you're going to have the baby?"

Shannon was halfway out the door but his question made her stop and look at him, her eyes wide and startled. "What?"

"It's a simple question, Shannon. Are you planning on having the baby?"

"Yes. I'm sorry. I should have told you that right away. And I'm sorry if that's not what you wanted to hear but I want this child.'' Her voice wobbled and then steadied. ''I want it and I'm going to have it. You don't have to feel obligated to—''

''To hell with that,'' he snapped, cutting her off. He was around the table and reaching to catch her hands in his before she could move. ''Don't start telling me I'm not obligated, like it's a dinner check we agreed to split.'' She tugged on her hands but he tightened his grip, refusing to release her. ''Shannon, we need to talk about this. Call Kelly. Please.''

''No.'' She shook her head, looking down at their clasped hands. ''Please. I need... I can't do this right now.'' When she looked up at him, her eyes were full of tears and all his frustration slipped away, leaving only the need to comfort but, when he tried to draw her closer, she pulled back, shaking her head frantically. ''Please, Reece. I had this— I was going to tell you tonight. I had it all planned out. Dinner and...and everything. I didn't expect you to—'' She stopped and drew a deep breath, visibly grabbing hold of her composure. ''I can't do this now, Reece. I know it's not fair and I'm sorry but I just...can't.''

He couldn't ignore the plea in her eyes. His hands tightened over hers for an instant and then he released her. ''Okay. Tonight.'' That sounded almost like a threat, and he drew a deep breath, forcing back the urge to insist that they had to talk now. This minute. ''We'll talk tonight. We'll have dinner and we'll talk.''

''Thank you.'' Her obvious relief stung, but he told himself not to take it personally, which was pretty damned stupid, really, since it didn't get much more personal than this.

''No toaster waffles,'' he said, and she gave a wavery little laugh that made him want to grab her and hold her and never let her go. He settled for brushing his fingers over the curve of her cheek. "I'll bring dinner."

"Okay." She managed something approaching a real smile. "I've really got to get going."

He nodded and stepped back. "I'll see you tonight. And, Shannon?" She'd started to walk away but turned back to look at him. "Everything's going to be all right."

She hesitated and then gave him a jerky little nod. Reece turned and stared at the sunny kitchen. Twenty minutes ago he'd walked in here with nothing more on his mind than sharing a cup of coffee with the woman he loved, the woman he thought just might love him in return. Instead of a cozy cup of coffee and a few stolen kisses, he'd found out that he was going to be a father again, and all his plans for wooing and winning Shannon had just taken a sharp left turn into the unknown.

Reece had no idea how long he'd been standing in the middle of his grandfather's kitchen, staring blankly at the faded-print curtains while he tried to absorb the idea that he was about to become a father for the second time. He heard Kyle's bedroom door open and then the bathroom door close. A few minutes later his son shuffled into the kitchen, wearing holey gray sweatpants and an equally tattered black T-shirt, his dark hair sticking out in every direction.

"Hey." Kyle muttered, his attention focused on the coffeemaker. He frowned when he saw it was empty. "I thought I smelled coffee."

"Yeah."

Kyle turned to look at him, eyebrows raised. "So, you drank the whole pot already?"

"No." Reece shook his head, forced himself to focus. "It's in the thermos. I...took some over to Shannon's."

"Yeah?" Kyle got out a cup and reached for the thermal carafe. "I thought I heard you go out earlier."

He twisted off the lid, and Reece felt his stomach lurch as the rich, dark scent filled the room. God, was morning sickness catching? Kyle glanced at him, lifting the carafe and arching his brows in question. Reece swallowed and shook his head.

"No, thanks."

"More for me," Kyle said, grinning as he twisted the lid back on and picked up his cup. He closed his eyes in bliss as he took the first sip. "Oh, man, this is the good stuff, isn't it? That Moroccan Brown Trenches stuff."

"Jamaican Blue Mountain."

"Same difference."

"If you don't know the difference between Jamaica and Morocco and a trench and a mountain, maybe you really should go back to school," Reece said dryly.

Kyle's grin was unrepentant. "Geography never was my best subject."

"No kidding." Reece hesitated, debating about whether or not to tell Kyle about Shannon's morning bombshell but he was going to have to know sooner or later. "Look, I...I need to tell you something."

Kyle lowered his coffee mug, his expression concerned. "Are you okay? You're not sick or anything, are you?"

"I'm fine," Reece said quickly.

"Good." The sudden tension eased from Kyle's

shoulders. "Usually, when someone says they need to tell you something, it's bad news."

"It's not. Not bad news, I mean." He was half sorry he'd started this, but now that he had, he might as well finish it. It wasn't the sort of thing that could be kept a secret, even if he wanted to. "It's...I..." He saw the concern creeping back into his son's eyes and sighed. "Shannon's pregnant."

Kyle stared at him, looking almost as stunned as he'd felt when he first found out. Reece let the silence stretch, letting his son absorb the full impact of the news.

"Wow," Kyle said finally. He looked down at his coffee cup, lifted it partway to his mouth, then set it down on the counter with a sharp little click. "Wow, that's just... I take it you guys didn't plan this?"

"Hell, no, we didn't plan it." Reece shoved his fingers through his hair. "It just...happened."

"It just happened?" Kyle raised his eyebrows, his disapproval obvious. "What, like an act of God?"

"No. We...I didn't..." Reece felt himself flush under his son's disapproving look. "It was just one time, dammit."

"One time?" Kyle's mouth tightened in a way that was uncomfortably reminiscent of his mother. He jabbed his finger in Reece's direction. "*You're* the one who told me there was no excuse for carelessness. Right after you showed me what a condom was and how to use one."

He sounded angry, and Reece couldn't blame him. He'd been criminally careless and now...now...Jesus, he didn't know what happened now. He sank down on a kitchen chair, all but fell into it and scrubbed his hands over his face.

"It was stupid," he said tiredly. "Just...really stupid."

"Yeah, it was." Kyle was apparently not in the mood to cut him some slack. "What are you—What is Shannon going to do?"

"She wants to keep the baby." That much he was clear on. He had the feeling some of the details of their conversation were gone forever, lost in the buzz of panic and denial that had filled his head but he was sure of that. "She said I didn't have to feel obligated—"

Kyle's disgusted snort cut him off. "She doesn't know you very well, does she?"

"No." He sighed, relieved that his son *did* know him, knew him well enough to know he'd never walk away from his own child. Never *want* to walk away from his child.

He heard Kyle stirring around but didn't lift his head until a coffee cup appeared on the table next to his arm. "I'd add a shot of whiskey if I knew where it was."

"Don't have any." Reece picked up the cup, wrapping both hands around it.

"Maybe you should get some," Kyle said dryly, and Reece surprised himself by laughing. It only lasted a moment but it made him feel better. He sat up, straightening his shoulders as he lifted the cup and took a swallow of coffee.

Kyle pulled out the chair across from him and sat down, his expression serious as he looked at Reece. "Dad—"

Reece held up a hand to stop him. "Please, no lectures on safe sex. This whole conversation has way too much role reversal going on already."

Kyle grinned. "Oh, man, and I was just about to get all public service announcement on you."

"Yeah, well, don't." Reece looked across the table at his son and shook his head, his smile rueful. "No offense but I always figured that, if we ever had to have this conversation, I'd be on the other side of the fence."

"Hey, my dad really drummed the importance of safe sex into my head."

"Smart ass," Reece muttered.

"So, what are you going to do?" Kyle asked after a moment.

"Talk to Shannon." Reece set his cup on the table and cupped his fingers around it, drawing warmth from the thick porcelain. "She had to go open the shop, so we didn't get much chance to talk."

"She couldn't get somebody to cover for her?" Kyle asked, looking surprised.

"I don't think she wanted to," Reece admitted with a sigh. He leaned back in his chair, suddenly aware that he was as tired as if he'd been up for forty-eight hours straight instead of—he glanced at the clock—God, was it only ten o'clock in the morning? He caught his son's concerned look and forced a half smile. "She just found out for sure this morning. I think she needed a little time to get used to the idea."

"Yeah, I guess I can understand that." Kyle turned his coffee cup between his hands, keeping his eyes on the aimless movement. "What do you want to do? About the baby and Shannon, I mean?"

The answer came more easily than he'd expected. "I want to marry her."

"Because of the baby?" Kyle looked up at him, green eyes sharp and focused. "I've got to tell you, I don't think that's such a hot reason to get married. I mean, I know you're going to want to be involved with the kid and everything but there's more to marriage than just raising kids."

"Yeah, I kind of figured that out about the time your mother and I split up," Reece said dryly. He stood and picked up his coffee cup to carry it to the sink, ruffling Kyle's hair on the way past. "I appreciate the sage advice, though."

Kyle grinned and ducked away from his hand. "Yeah, not everyone is lucky enough to get the benefit of advice from someone who might have majored in psych if they'd stayed in college."

"Psych? I thought you were planning on archeology. Get a fedora and go off in search of adventure."

"I was thinking about it but then I found out that there's a severe shortage of four-star hotels on dig sites and you know how I feel about camping out. Nature Boy, I'm not." He'd turned in his chair to watch Reece rinse out his cup. "And don't think you're going to distract me from the subject at hand by bringing up my abandoned education."

Reece shook his head as he set the cup in the drainer. "You get that pigheaded streak from your mother."

"Yeah? She says I get it from you." Kyle pushed back his chair and stood up, jabbing his empty cup in his father's direction. "I'm not a kid anymore, Dad. I may not have your vast experience with relationships." He grinned and dodged the cuff Reece aimed at the side of his head. "But that doesn't mean I don't know a bad idea when I hear one. And marrying Shannon just because she's pregnant is a bad idea."

"How about if I marry her because I love her?" Reece rested his palms on the edge of the counter and leaned back, waiting for Kyle's reaction. It was the first time he'd said it out loud and it sounded surprisingly not-startling. It sounded...good. Right.

"Yeah?" Kyle tilted his head and gave his father a considering look.

"Are you okay with that idea?" Reece asked, suddenly worried that maybe he should have led up to it more gradually.

Kyle looked surprised. "Why wouldn't I be?"

"Well, you know, me getting involved with someone else, maybe getting remarried." He shrugged uncomfortably.

"You mean because I might have some lingering fantasies about you and Mom getting back together?" Kyle's tone was dry as dust and Reece grimaced.

"Okay, so forget it. It was just a thought."

"That's okay." Kyle gave him a patronizing pat on the shoulder as he rinsed out his cup and set it to drain. "Leave the psychological stuff to those of us who thought about taking classes."

"Smart ass."

"You're starting to repeat yourself." Kyle leaned one hip on the counter, arms crossed over his chest. "I think Shannon is great. She's nice and she's fun and what red-blooded American boy doesn't dream of having a gorgeous stepmother?"

His grin held an edge of mischief and, for just an instant, Reece saw the boy he'd once been. He felt a pang of nostalgia for the years gone by and then a sharp little jolt at the realization that he was going to get to watch another child grow up.

Kyle straightened away from the counter and looked at his father, his expression suddenly serious. "I think you guys are really good together. I think it would be great if you got married.''

Well, that made two of them, Reece thought. Now, all he had to do was convince Shannon that it was a great idea.

She was *not* running away from home, Shannon told herself. That would be childish and immature. She was simply taking a long drive to give herself a chance to think. A really long drive that had, so far, involved no thinking more complex than whether to leave the radio on or off. And there was nothing at all strange about the fact that she had started that drive in the middle of a busy Saturday, leaving the shop in the semicapable hands of two part-time employees.

Kelly had been coming in, she reminded herself, trying to soothe her guilt pangs. Actually, the fact that Kelly was due to arrive had been a driving factor in her decision to flee like the craven coward she apparently was.

Her fingers tightened on the steering wheel, and she released her breath on a long sigh. There. She'd admitted it. She was running away from home. She was running away because she knew Kelly would take one look at her and know something was wrong. Shannon wasn't up to deflecting her questions, she didn't want to lie and she wasn't ready to tell the truth.

Apparently, when it came to fight or flight, she ran like a jackrabbit.

But she couldn't run forever, and two hours of aimless driving was about her limit. Or maybe not so aimless, she thought as an exit sign loomed up in front of her. She felt a jolt as she realized where she was and, almost as if in a dream, she flipped on her turn signal and took the exit for Los Olivos.

Ten minutes later she was standing on Rachel Walker's front porch, watching the surprise in the older woman's eyes change to warm welcome.

Chapter 14

Shannon had heard it said that home was the place you could go where they had to take you in. She wasn't sure about the "had to" part of it, but there was certainly something wonderful about showing up on someone's doorstep and having them just...take you in. Rachel didn't ask any questions, didn't comment on her unexpected arrival. She just smiled and held the door open.

Shannon's eyes stung and she blinked hard. "I hope you don't mind me just dropping in like this." She laughed and hoped it didn't sound as thin to the other woman as it did to her. "I was in the neighborhood."

Rachel looked surprised. "I thought you'd decided to come after all."

"After all?" Shannon repeated blankly and saw a sudden flicker of concern in Rachel's eyes.

As soon as she stepped inside, she became aware of the dull roar of sound she'd come to associate with large numbers of Walkers gathered in one place. She heard someone laugh and a child's giggle. Obviously, most if not all of the family was here.

"I didn't—" With half-formed thoughts of retreat, she stepped back, but Rachel caught her arm and tugged her the rest of the way inside, shutting the door firmly behind her.

"Don't be silly. If you're not up for seeing everyone, we can sneak you through the kitchen. Sam and Nikki are staying in the big guest room but there's no one in the small spare room. I can stash you there." She was moving forward as she spoke. "The children wanted pizza so no one's cooking tonight. You should have heard the argument over what to order. Keefe can't stand pepperoni and Cole made gagging noises when Nikki said she liked anchovies. I suppose it's setting a terrible example for the children but, honestly, *anchovies?* So, then Danny wanted ham and pineapple but Kelsey says he doesn't actually like the pineapple, he just likes the *idea* of it."

Shannon let the words flow over her. No response seemed to be required, which was just as well. Somewhere in between the pepperoni and the pineapple, she'd remembered that this weekend was a joint birthday celebration for some combination of family members. Exactly who escaped her at the moment. Now that it was too late, it occurred to her that there had been a lot of cars parked out front. Rachel had invited her to join them and she'd said she'd try but weekends were a busy time at the shop. But not so busy, apparently, that she couldn't run like a rabbit at the first little problem, if you could call an unplanned pregnancy and a totally confused life a "little" problem.

Rachel led Shannon into the kitchen, bypassing the

crowded living room, but the kitchen wasn't entirely empty. Hippo, Rachel's enormous dog, lay sprawled in the middle of the room, taking up a large portion of the available floor space, and Sam stood in front of the open refrigerator door.

"So, was that Mrs. Klausman complaining about the— Hey, Shannon." His smile held the same easy welcome his—*their*—mother's had, and she wondered again why she'd found it so difficult to open her heart to these people. "How are you?"

"I'm fine." Her voice wobbled, surprising her. She saw Sam's eyes sharpen with sudden concern and felt her heart stutter. If he started asking questions, she was going to dissolve in a sobbing heap. Hormones, she thought. It had to be hormones.

Sam started to say something, caught his mother's eye and stopped. "Shannon's tired. I'm going to get her settled in the little bedroom," Rachel said.

"Sure." If he thought it was odd that a perfectly healthy young woman would be so exhausted by a two-hour drive that she had to lie down, he didn't say anything. "Pizza should be here in a half hour or so," he said. "If you feel up to joining us, I promise to fend the ravening hordes off long enough to make sure you get a piece."

"Thanks." She smiled, grateful enough for the questions he didn't ask to forgive him for making her stomach roll with the mention of pizza.

Rachel led the way down the back hall to the bedrooms. "I'll need to get some linens for the bed. Keefe, Tessa and the baby are staying at Gage and Kelsey's. With Lily there and Danny, they're already set up for children. Besides, Tessa's apparently been bitten by the green-thumb bug and I think she's hoping to convince

Keefe that what the ranch really needs is a greenhouse like Kelsey's.''

Shannon let the words flow over her in a pleasant wash of sound. She knew, though she didn't know how she knew, that Rachel didn't expect a response or even for her to really listen. It wasn't until she was standing in the small bedroom she'd occupied at Christmas, watching Rachel pull the duvet off the bed that something occurred to her.

''I didn't say anything about spending the night,'' she said, coming forward to take the duvet and drape it over the small armchair in the corner.

''Didn't you?'' Rachel picked up a sheet from the stack she'd brought in from the linen closet. She spread it across the mattress with a quick snap of her wrists. Shannon moved automatically to tug it into place. ''I guess I just figured that, since it was so late in the day, you weren't likely to be heading home tonight.''

At the mention of home, Shannon flinched. Reece. She'd told him they'd have dinner together so they could discuss the situation. She glanced at the small alarm clock on the nightstand. ''Could I use your phone?''

''Of course.'' Rachel finished smoothing the bottom sheet out before straightening up and fixing Shannon with a look that held concern but no demand. ''You can use the one in my bedroom, if you like.''

''Thanks.'' Shannon started toward the door, remembered the half-made bed and pivoted back. ''Let me—''

''I'll get this.'' Rachel waved her hand at the door. ''You go make your call.'' When Shannon hesitated, she arched both brows. ''Go on.''

Shannon went. For all her small size and gentle appearance, there was a certain air of authority about Rachel Walker that made it easy to imagine her raising four boys by herself.

Rachel's bedroom was painted a soft white and furnished with a light oak bed and dressers. The overall effect was both airy and restful. The phone was on the nightstand, and Shannon sank down on the edge of the bed, staring at it for several long moments before reaching for it. She had it all worked out, knew exactly what to say when Reece answered the phone. It all flew out the window when she heard Kyle's voice.

"Kyle? It's, ah, Shannon. Is your dad there?"

"Hi, Shannon. No, Dad went out to pick up some stuff for dinner. He should be back any minute now. Are you at home? 'Cause I think he was planning on cooking dinner here and then taking it over to your place."

"Actually, I'm not home." Shannon tried for casual and managed strained. She cleared her throat. "I...I was calling to tell him that I couldn't do dinner tonight after all. I decided to...visit my...family and I'm going to spend the night here."

"Are you okay?" The concern in Kyle's voice made Shannon's eyes sting.

"I'm fine. I just— It's my brother's birthday." She was almost positive it was Cole's birthday but she was probably going to go to hell for using it as an excuse like this. "I thought I should—"

"Dad told me about the baby."

"Oh." So much for polite lies. Shannon made a conscious effort to ease the tightness of her grip on the phone. "I, ah..."

"It's none of my business," Kyle said, interrupting her, which was just as well, since she had no idea what she was going to say. "I just wanted you to know that I'm okay with this." He laughed a little. "I mean, I'm not going to be overcome by a sudden attack of sibling rivalry or anything."

"That's good to know." *Sibling?* She closed her eyes while she absorbed that idea. She'd barely begun to deal with the idea that she was going to have a baby and now her child had a sibling. A brother. God. She drew a shaky breath. "I've got to go, Kyle. Tell your dad…tell him I'm sorry about dinner and I'll…I'll call him."

She barely waited for Kyle's goodbye before hanging up the phone. Sitting on the edge of Rachel's bed, she clasped her hands between her knees, shoulders hunched as she contemplated the pale-green carpet at her feet. She really needed to get a handle on this whole thing. The baby. Reece. Her life.

Sighing, she pushed herself to her feet and left the room. A muted clamor drifted from the living room, male voices, a childish giggle, a woman's laughter. She felt a brief, wistful urge to join them, let herself be absorbed in the noise and the warmth that seemed to be an integral part of any Walker family gathering. Sighing, she turned away.

"I'll find you something to sleep in later," Rachel said as Shannon entered the small bedroom. She smoothed one hand over the floral-print duvet and twitched a corner of a pillowcase into place. "I don't think you'll need it but there's an extra blanket in the closet, just in case."

"Thank you. It's very nice of you to take me in like this." Shannon managed a lopsided smile. "I don't usually show up on people's doorsteps like an orphan of the storm."

"You're always welcome here, Shannon. You know that." Rachel studied her a moment and then seemed to come to some decision. "I know it doesn't feel like it to you but we're your family and we're here for you. I'm here for you. I promised myself I wouldn't pry, but it's obvious that you're upset about something, and I just want you to know that if you want to talk, I'm a pretty good listener."

Shannon started to tell her that she appreciated the offer but really didn't want to talk but what came out was: "I'm pregnant."

The flat statement seemed to echo in the small room, as if she'd shouted it loud enough to ruffle the neat blue-and-white-striped curtains. Rachel drew in a quick, startled breath, her dark eyes widening in shock.

"I take you don't want to be pregnant?"

"No. I mean, I didn't plan on this but, now that I am, I...I want the baby." She was surprised by how much she wanted it. It seemed odd that a few weeks ago, motherhood had been nothing but a distant, maybe-someday possibility, but now that it was a reality, she couldn't remember a time when she *hadn't* wanted this.

"Reece doesn't want the baby?" Rachel probed gently.

"No. I...actually, I don't know." She hadn't really given him a chance to express any feelings one way or the other.

"You haven't told him?" Rachel looked surprised, and Shannon immediately felt defensive.

"I told him. I told him this morning."

"And what did he say?"

"Not much. I... Well, I sort of..."

"Come sit down," Rachel said, sitting on the edge

of the bed and patting the spot beside her. "Tell me what happened."

It was surprisingly easy. Shannon told her about Reece moving in next door, about how the fact that he was only there temporarily had been a *good* thing and then they'd...well, it was just one time but they'd been careless. She felt her face heat as she said it and was glad that she was sitting next to the other woman so she didn't have to meet her eyes. God, she couldn't believe she was telling her mother about her sex life. And then about the "flu" she couldn't seem to shake and how stupid she felt that the truth hadn't occurred to her sooner.

Rachel patted her hand. "Well, you know, every now and again, you hear a news story about some woman who didn't know she was pregnant until she gave birth, so it could have been worse."

That surprised Shannon into a choked laugh. "I suppose that's some consolation. At least I figured it out before I went into labor."

"So, tell me what Reece said when you told him," Rachel said, folding her fingers around Shannon's and squeezing a little. "I liked him when he was here at Christmas. I'm going to be very disappointed if he was a jerk."

"He wasn't." Shannon kept her eyes lowered, staring at their linked hands. There was comfort in that simple touch, a connection she hadn't realized she needed. "He told me not to worry, that everything would be okay."

"That's it? That's all he said?"

"I...didn't really give him a chance to say anything else," she admitted in a low voice. "I'd just found out that I was...about the..." She stopped, huffed out an exasperated breath. How was it possible that she could *be* pregnant and not be able to *say* the word? "I'd just found out about the baby." She got it out in a rush. "I wasn't ready to talk to him about it so I told him we'd have dinner and talk."

"Dinner tonight?"

Shannon nodded, her cheeks warming with a guilty flush.

"I don't understand," Rachel said slowly. "I would think you'd want to talk to Reece, want to find out what he's thinking. Are you afraid he won't take responsibility? Because, I have to say, he didn't strike me as the kind of man who would do that."

"No. No, I know he'll want to live up to his obligations." Shannon's hand tightened around her mother's, the fingers of her other hand plucking restlessly at the duvet. "He'll probably offer to marry me."

"And you don't want that?" Rachel asked gently. "Do you love him?"

Shannon opened her mouth, closed it without speaking and drew a shuddering breath. Straight to the heart of it. The question she'd been avoiding asking herself. But now that it was asked, the answer was obvious and devastating. That night in the truck, the night their child had been conceived, there had been one frozen moment when she could have stopped what was about to happen. A word, a hesitation, and Reece would have pulled back, would have ended it. She'd looked up at him, the hard planes of his face limned in moonlight and she'd had a sudden image of herself, belly rounded with the weight of his child and she'd wanted that with a fierce hunger she'd never felt before. It had been a deep visceral *need* inside to have his child, a part of him that would be hers to keep even when he was gone.

She'd never felt that way about anyone. She'd loved Johnny, and she'd mourned him deeply, but what she felt for Reece was so much more, so overwhelming.

Did she love him? So much it terrified her.

"That's not the point," she said carefully, and wondered if that sounded as much like an admission to Rachel as it did to her.

"I think it's very much the point, but I won't argue with you about it." Rachel squeezed her hand gently. "Why don't you tell me what you think the problem is?"

"I don't want him to feel obligated. Not to me or the baby."

"But why shouldn't he feel obligated? It's his child, too. His responsibility."

"No." The single word was sharp and hard. Shannon drew a shallow breath and repeated it more quietly. "No. I want more than that for my baby and for myself. I don't want Reece to feel *obligated*." Her tone made the word an epithet. "My father was *obligated* to take care of me. All my life, I knew that's what I was to him. A responsibility. An obligation. I didn't know why until I found out what he'd done, that he'd taken me away from you. He took care of me. I always had plenty to eat and a decent place to live but there was…" She shook her head, at a loss for the words to explain what had been missing. She'd never done without, and yet she hadn't had the most important things— love and warmth, a sense of belonging.

"I don't know why he didn't just leave me on somebody's doorstep somewhere, but maybe, after he took me away, he felt obligated to take care of me. I won't be an obligation to anyone ever again and neither will my child.''

There was a moment's silence before Rachel spoke, her voice thick with tears. ''Oh, Shannon. I'm so sorry.''

For the first time since they'd sat down, Shannon looked at her mother, saw the pain in her eyes. And the love. ''It wasn't your fault,'' she whispered.

''Maybe not.'' Rachel shook her head a little. ''I can't tell you how many times I asked myself if there wasn't something I could have done or said, if I shouldn't have realized somehow what he was going to do, that he was going to take you away from us.'' She lowered her eyes to their joined hands. ''It took me a long time to accept what had happened—at least as much as anyone could accept losing a child. I don't think I would have survived if it hadn't been for the boys. They needed me, but I needed them even more. Life went on, more or less, but there wasn't a single day went by that I didn't think about you, wonder where you were and if you were happy.''

Her voice broke on the last word, and Shannon felt tears start to her own eyes. After a moment Rachel cleared her throat and went on more briskly.

''I won't pretend to know what was in your father's mind, why he did what he did. It was not a good divorce.'' She lifted her head and met Shannon's eyes. ''It wasn't a good marriage and that was as much my fault as his. It was too soon after losing my first husband. I was scared and alone and scared of being alone. Your father and I were a poor match from the beginning and we should have ended things sooner. By the time I did end it, I was carrying you. I know every parent thinks their baby is perfect but you were so…wonderful. And all the harsh words and misery between your father and me just didn't matter anymore. It seemed so amazing that something so…perfect had come out of something so…flawed.''

Her expression tender, she reached up to brush Shannon's hair back from her face. "You were such a happy little girl. Your brothers adored you. It was like you were our reward for all the bad things that had happened. You…completed the family somehow, as if we'd just been waiting for you."

Shannon felt something dissolve inside at the love she saw in the other woman's eyes, some long-held barrier disappearing, taking a lifetime of loneliness with it.

"I don't know why he took you away. Maybe it was because he was afraid that, as long as you had us, you wouldn't need him. Maybe taking you was just an impulse and then, once it was done, he didn't know how to turn back. I'm not sure it matters anymore but I won't pretend to forgive him for it. Maybe if I were a better person I could, but I can't. What he did, what he took from us…from you…" Rachel's eyes grew suddenly fierce, and her fingers tightened around her daughter's. "You were *never* an obligation, Shannon. Not to me, not to your brothers. And I don't believe for a minute that either you or this baby are nothing but an obligation to Reece. Don't make decisions before you at least hear what he has to say."

"I'm scared," Shannon whispered.

"Of what?" Rachel stroked her hand over her daughter's bright hair.

"What if it doesn't work? What if he does want to marry me and we give it a try and it doesn't work or what if something happens to him? It hurt so much when I lost Johnny but what I feel for Reece is so much— It's more than I thought I could ever feel for anyone. It would kill me to lose him.''

"If you don't take the chance, you've already lost him," Rachel pointed out gently. "How are you going to feel if you turn him away now, shut him out of your life, out of the baby's life without ever seeing what you could have together?" She cupped her hands around Shannon's face, her eyes dark with love and compassion. "If you don't take the chance, honey, you'll spend the rest of your life wondering what you could have had. Maybe it won't work out. And maybe something will happen to him, maybe you'll lose him, but wouldn't you rather have a few months or years with him than no time at all?"

Shannon blinked against the sudden sting of tears. She was tired and confused and scared. Her whole life had been turned upside down and she didn't know what to do to put it right side up again. Her vision blurred and she blinked again, feeling the hot slide of a tear as it spilled over.

"I'm sorry," she whispered, bringing her hand up to press her fingers to her trembling lips. "I'm sorry."

"Hush." Rachel's arms were strong and warm around her, pulling her close, holding her tight. "Everything's going to be okay. Just let it out." She pressed her cheek against the top of Shannon's head. "Let it out, honey. I've got you."

And Shannon turned into the offered comfort, crying out all her fear and confusion on her mother's shoulder.

He'd given her twenty-four hours, Reece thought as he flipped on the turn signal and made the turn onto the street where Rachel Walker lived. If Shannon needed more time, she could tell him as much and he'd leave. Maybe he'd even be able to resist the urge to throw her over his shoulder and take her with him.

He considered himself a patient man. Contrary to the nonstop-action sequences so beloved of Hollywood, covert ops was largely a waiting game. Patience was a necessity if you wanted to grow old and die in bed. And he was a reasonable man. When Shannon had dropped the bombshell that he was about to become a father and then said she couldn't talk about it right then, he'd demonstrated both patience and reason. He hadn't insisted that they had to talk *now*. He'd accepted her need for a little time to come to terms with the changes this made in her life—in both their lives.

And last night when Kyle had given him Shannon's message that she wasn't safely next door, resting quietly the way any newly pregnant woman with an ounce of sense would be, but had instead, apparently, driven over a hundred miles by herself, he had again demonstrated his capacity for calm reason by not leaping into his truck and tracking her down. Okay, so Kyle had been instrumental in that decision, pointing out that showing up on her mother's doorstep and demanding to know what the hell she thought she was doing smacked of an overly possessive attitude at best and teetered on the edge of stalkerdom.

So, he'd done the reasonable thing and stayed home, charring the two filet mignons he'd bought to have with Shannon and overcooking the asparagus so badly that, when Kyle asked him what it was, it didn't even sound like sarcasm.

After a mostly sleepless night, he'd demonstrated yet more patience—not to mention good manners—by not calling Rachel's house at 5:00 a.m. when he finally gave up trying to sleep and got up. He'd only checked five times to make sure the phone was still working between then and eleven o'clock, which showed restraint. At noon, when she still hadn't called, he'd decided that patience and restraint could only take a man so far. Kyle had gone for a run, which made it the perfect time to leave since his son would probably have advised yet more patience and had, in fact, threatened to body tackle him when Reece hinted at driving to Los Olivos at six in the morning. Leaving while Kyle was gone prevented more arguments and possible physical violence.

Now here he was, and from the looks of it so was Shannon's entire family. Muttering a curse under his breath, Reece parked behind a truck he recognized as Keefe's and got out. Slamming the truck door did *not* suggest that his patience was running thin. It just slipped out of his hand. Really hard.

Somebody must have seen him coming, because the front door opened as he pushed open the front gate, and by the time he reached the porch, four large, male bodies stood between him and the house. Reece stopped at the bottom of the steps and looked at them. Patience and restraint, he reminded himself.

"I came to see Shannon." Well, it was stating the obvious but he had to start somewhere.

"Oh, yeah?" That was Cole, looking less than patient and restrained. "She didn't say anything about expecting you."

"I wanted to surprise her."

"Seems like you're just full of surprises," Keefe said, his tone so neutral it hovered on the edge of hostile.

Apparently, she'd told her family about the baby and

her brothers were laying the blame squarely at his feet. Not that he blamed them. Reece felt himself flush but he didn't say anything. He'd already endured a lecture on safe sex from his son. He was damned if he was going to start offering excuses to Shannon's brothers.

"Why don't you tell Shannon I'm here and she can decide whether or not she wants to see me?"

"If she wanted to see you, she would have called," Cole said.

The logic was irrefutable, but Reece was not in the mood for logic, and his store of patience and reason was fast running out, too. He put his foot on the first step and looked at the four of them steadily.

"If I have to go through all of you, I will."

Gage arched one brow and his mouth twitched with something that looked like amusement. Cole looked as if he was thinking about launching the first punch. Keefe's eyes were steady, cool, his expression impossible to read. Sam tilted his head a little, blue eyes bright and interested.

"I think he means it," he commented.

"Good." Cole took a half step forward, and Reece braced himself. Damn, this wasn't exactly the best way to start off a relationship with what he hoped were his future in-laws, and Shannon was not going to be happy if he broke her brother's nose. He wasn't sure how she'd feel if it was *his* nose that sustained the damage. Either way, he had a feeling that a plea of "he started it" was not going to cut it.

Sam's hand came down on Cole's shoulder. "Let's not be hasty here." He looked at Reece. "At the risk of sounding like a character out of a bad novel, you mind telling us what your intentions are?"

Reece thought of telling him it was none of his

damned business, but that wouldn't get them anywhere. Besides, maybe they had the right to ask.

"I plan on marrying Shannon."

"Because of the baby?" Keefe asked.

"No. Because I'm in love with her." Reece could feel his patience thinning, fraying along the edges.

"Cut the guy some slack." That was Gage. He stepped back, using a shoulder to edge Keefe back with him. "Shannon's a big girl. If she doesn't want to see him, she'll say so and *then* we can throw him out."

It was said with a look of cheerful malice that startled Reece into a smile. "Bring help," was all he said as he came up the steps and shouldered his way past the four men.

"She's in the kitchen," Sam said as he pushed open the door, and Reece supposed that was as close to being given their blessing as he was going to get at the moment.

She was indeed in the kitchen. He stopped in the doorway, feeling a tightness he hadn't even realized was there suddenly ease in his chest. She was sitting at the kitchen table, wearing black leggings and a gray flannel shirt that was so much too big for her, it had to belong to one of her brothers. A ray of sunlight spilled through the window over the sink and caught in her hair, catching red-and-gold highlights in the thick waves.

She looked...perfect, and for a moment it was enough to just stand in the doorway and look at her. He would have stood there admiring the view for even longer, but Shannon wasn't alone. The entire distaff side of the Walker clan and their offspring were also crowded into the big kitchen, and he barely had time to draw a relieved breath before Addie saw him standing there.

"Oh, dear." Her voice was hardly more than a murmur, but with some sort of female sixth sense the other women immediately turned toward him. Finding himself suddenly the focus of so many pairs of eyes—even the children were looking at him—Reece fought the urge to check and make sure his fly was zipped. Ironically Shannon was the last one to register that something had changed. She was bent over the coloring book she was sharing with Cole's little girl, and it wasn't until Mary nudged her that she looked up and saw him.

"Reece." Her eyes widened into startled blue pools. He couldn't read either welcome or rejection in her expression, just surprise.

"Hi." As opening lines went, it wasn't exactly original. "I thought we should, ah, talk," he added, painfully aware of their audience, who made no attempt at a polite pretense of not listening.

All eyes swiveled to Shannon, waiting for her response, and Reece had no illusions about being able to either intimidate or persuade *this* batch of Walkers. If Shannon said she didn't want to talk to him, he might as well just turn around and go home. She hesitated, and he was surprised to see her eyes seek out Rachel's. The other woman gave her an encouraging smile, and Shannon flushed a little before looking at him and nodding.

"Okay."

As if on some prearranged signal, everyone was suddenly in motion. Reece stepped through the doorway and out of the way of the sudden exodus. He'd worked with military commanders who would have envied the efficiency with which the kitchen emptied, leaving him alone with Shannon and a silence so thick it was a tangible presence.

He moved closer to the table, his eyes devouring her. It was less than thirty-six hours since he'd seen her, but it seemed much longer. Yesterday morning he'd been reeling with the sudden knowledge that he was going to be a father. Now that he'd had a chance to get used to the idea, he found himself looking for some outward sign of the changes taking place inside her body.

"I was going to call you," she said. She was twisting a purple crayon back and forth between her thumb and forefinger, her eyes on the nervous movement. "I'm sorry about dinner last night."

"That's okay. Kyle enjoyed the steak. He would have enjoyed it more if I hadn't burned it, but then he wouldn't have had the pleasure of complaining about my cooking."

She smiled a little but didn't look up. Reece shrugged out of his denim jacket and draped it over the back of a chair. He pulled out another chair and sat down, facing her.

"So, why'd you run?" he asked conversationally.

"I didn't run," she said, her head jerking up and her eyes meeting his for the first time since that brief contact when she first saw him. "I...wanted to see... It was Cole's birthday."

"Uh-huh. And did you remember this before or after you got here and saw the whole family was already here?"

She held his gaze a moment longer, and then her eyes slid away. One shoulder lifted in a sheepish half shrug. "After," she muttered. "But I wasn't running away."

"You stick with that story," he said kindly, and was rewarded by a muffled snort of laughter. Still cautious, he reached out and closed his hand over hers, tugging until she turned to sit sideways on the chair, facing him but still not looking at him. She was apparently fascinated by the pattern on the floor. Still, she didn't pull her hand from his, and Reece figured he'd take his encouragement where he could find it.

"I had this all planned out. I was going to cook you a romantic dinner to impress you with my culinary skills and I was going to ply you with a reasonably adequate wine, because neither of us can taste the difference between that and a really good wine, and then, when I had you well fed and maybe just a teeny bit drunk, I was going to ask you to marry me." Her hand jerked convulsively in his, but he held on, refusing to let her pull away.

"When I found out about the baby, I had to rethink things a bit. The wine was out. I was going to go for the maximum cliché and propose on Valentine's Day but I had to move my timetable up a bit. I—"

"Wait." Shannon's hand was suddenly gripping his painfully tight. Her eyes were riveted to his face. "You were going to ask me to marry you *before* you found out about the baby?"

"That was the plan." He raised his eyebrows. "Is that why you ran away? Because you thought I was going to do the noble thing and offer to marry you just because you were pregnant?"

"I thought you might," she admitted. "And I didn't run away."

"You ran like a jackrabbit and why does everyone

think I only want to marry you because you're pregnant?''

''Who else thinks that?'' she asked, her eyes widening.

''Your brothers, who all look like they'd like to see my head part company with my body, by the way. And my son, who told me that getting married just because of the baby would be a mistake. That was right after he lectured me on safe sex.''

''Did he really?'' One corner of Shannon's mouth quirked up in a half smile.

''Smirk if you like but he was pretty upset. I expected to find myself grounded at any moment.''

''That must have been…interesting.''

''Let's just say I'm not anxious to repeat the experience,'' Reece said dryly. Shannon's eyes were bright with laughter, and Reece felt something unknot in his stomach. It was going to be okay. There were still things to say, questions to be asked, decisions to be made, but it was going to be okay. He reached for her other hand, and she didn't try to pull away this time.

''So, what do you think?''

''About what?''

''About marrying me but not because of the baby.'' His rubbed his thumbs over the back of her hands, watching her face.

''I think it's an…interesting idea,'' she admitted shyly. ''Did you, um, have a *reason* for wanting to marry me before you found out about the baby?''

''Just the same reason I have now.'' He shifted closer so that their knees were touching. ''I love you. I'm in love with you. I want to spend the rest of my life with you. Are those reasons good enough? Will you marry me?''

Shannon lifted her eyes to his face, her expression searching, worried. "I thought you were only going to stay until your grandfather's house was cleaned out."

"I could have had that done weeks ago."

"You hated Serenity Falls."

"When I was a kid." Reece nodded. "But it wasn't really the place. It was the circumstances. I was sort of thinking of starting a business. A bookstore, maybe, or a toaster-waffle franchise."

When she laughed, Reece decided he'd been cautious long enough and leaned forward to scoop her out of her chair and onto his lap. She gasped and clutched at his shoulders.

"Idiot." Since she was already curling into his hold, her head on his shoulder, Reece decided to take it as an endearment. He wrapped his arms around her and pressed his cheek against her bright hair.

"So, do you think I could get an answer here?"

"Yes." Shannon's voice was dreamy. Her fingers were toying with the buttons on his shirt, opening the top two so that she could slide her hand inside, pressing her palm over his heart.

"Yes? Yes what?" Reece prompted. He didn't really need an answer. She was giving him that now, lying in his arms like this, letting him hold her. Still, it would be nice to hear the words. "Do you love me? Are you going to marry me?"

"Yes to everything." She turned her head to press a kiss against his throat. "Yes, I'll marry you. Yes, I love you. Yes, I think you'd make a terrific bookstore owner or toaster-waffle king or anything else you want to do. Yes, I'm happy about the baby. Yes, I do believe in happily ever after."

"That's a lot of yeses." Reece swallowed to clear the sudden huskiness from his voice.

"Yes." He felt her mouth curve against his throat. "I'm feeling very agreeable. Enjoy it while you can. I'm told I may get very cranky in a few months."

"Oh, yeah?" Reece settled his hand over her flat stomach, imagining it was possible to feel the quick beat of the new life she carried. "Are you going to get cravings for pickles and ice cream?"

"Absolutely not." Shannon raised her head and looked at him with eyes so full of love that he felt it all the way to his soul. "I'm strictly a Froot Loops and Pepsi girl."

*   *   *   *   *

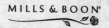

0407/51

MILLS & BOON®

Desire ™ 2-in-1

STRICTLY LONERGAN'S BUSINESS by Maureen Child

Kara Sloan was his ever-dependable, quiet assistant…until in a month of sharing close quarters Cooper Lonergan surprised her with a night of seduction.

PREGNANT WITH THE FIRST HEIR by Sara Orwig

Matt Ransome will stop at nothing to claim his family's one heir, even if it means a name-only marriage to a pregnant stranger. But perhaps it wouldn't be in name only for long.

DYNASTIES: THE ELLIOTTS

MR AND MISTRESS by Heidi Betts

Scandal threatens to rock the Elliott family when business mogul Cullen Elliott wants to make his pregnant mistress his wife! Misty's past was scandalous…

HEIRESS BEWARE by Charlene Sands

Wealthy Bridget Elliott lost her memory and fell for a sexy stranger. All Mac Riggs knew about Bridget was that she came from money, but he wanted to uncover her secrets…

FORCED TO THE ALTAR by Susan Crosby

Her handsome millionaire protector, Zach Keller, was insisting that for her safety they must marry. She had to find a way to deny him or have an unforgettable wedding night!

SEDUCTION BY THE BOOK by Linda Conrad

For two years he had isolated himself on his Caribbean island – could stormy passion with Annie Riley help him to overcome the past?

On sale from 20th April 2007

Available at WHSmith, Tesco, ASDA, and all good bookshops

www.millsandboon.co.uk

MILLS & BOON®

INTRIGUE™

RILEY'S RETRIBUTION
by Rebecca York
Big Sky Bounty Hunters

A master of disguise, Riley Watson infiltrated Courtney
Rogers' Golden Saddle ranch to capture a sinister fugitive.
Riley was caught off guard by the pregnant ranch owner and he
vowed to protect Courtney from a deadly showdown…

MORE THAN A MISSION
by Caridad Piñeiro
Capturing the Crown

She'd murdered the heir to the throne, and now the assassin
was firmly in undercover agent Aidan Spaulding's sights. But
Elizabeth Moore looked more like a princess than a prince-
killer…and she faced the greatest threat of all: one to her heart.

BEAUTIFUL BEAST
by Dani Sinclair

When an explosion ended Gabriel Lowe's military career and
left him scarred, his life became a shadow of what it once was.
But the beautiful Cassy Richards was determined to warm his
heart before an old enemy cut short both of their futures.

CAVANAUGH WATCH
by Marie Ferrarella
Cavanaugh Justice

When Janelle Cavanaugh's assignment took a deadly turn, she
was given a ruggedly handsome, but infuriating, bodyguard.
Risking his life was part of Sawyer Boone's job. Risking his
heart was quite another matter.

On sale from 20th April 2007

Available at WHSmith, Tesco, ASDA, and all good bookshops
www.millsandboon.co.uk

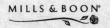

MILLS & BOON®

INTRIGUE™

MY SISTER, MYSELF
by Alice Sharpe

When Tess Mays discovers she has an identical twin, she thinks her life is finally coming together. But with her sister in a coma, Tess stumbles into an arson investigation, assuming her sister's identity to exonerate the father she never knew.

THE MEDUSA GAME
by Cindy Dees
Bombshell – The Medusa Project

Isabella Torres is part of the Medusa Special Forces team. She must protect an Olympic figure skater receiving death threats – then the Medusas discover something far more sinister. With Gunnar Holt as her partner, can Isabella keep her cool?

STRANDED WITH A STRANGER
by Frances Housden

Wealthy, pampered Chelsea Tedman never expected to be climbing Mount Everest with a mysterious, alluring stranger. But only Kurt Jellic could get her up the perilous mountain to solve the mystery of her sister's fatal fall.

STRONG MEDICINE
by Olivia Gates
Bombshell

The Global Crisis Alliance had been Calista St James' life – until she'd been blamed for a botched mission and dismissed. Now, the GCA want her back for a dangerous rescue operation and Calista must work with the gorgeous man who'd fired her.

On sale from 20th April 2007

Available at WHSmith, Tesco, ASDA, and all good bookshops

www.millsandboon.co.uk

0407/46b

In 1875, a row of tiny cottages stands by the tracks of the newly built York – Doncaster railway…

Railwayman Tom Swales, with his wife and five daughters, takes the end cottage. But with no room to spare in the loving Swales household, eldest daughter Mary accepts a position as housemaid to the nearby stationmaster. There she battles the daily grime from the passing trains – and the stationmaster's brutal, lustful nature. In the end, it's a fight she cannot win.

In shame and despair, Mary flees to York. But the pious couple who take her in know nothing of true Christian charity. They work Mary like a slave – despite her heavy pregnancy. Can she find the strength to return home to her family? Will they accept her? And what of her first love, farmer's son Nathaniel? Mary hopes with all her heart that he will still be waiting…

Available 16th March 2007

www.millsandboon.co.uk   M&B

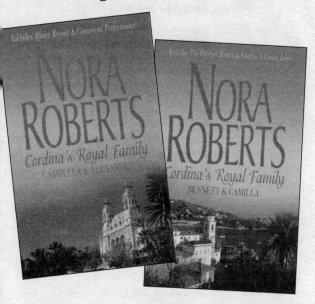

"The mountain always looked dark, but the older I got that year, the darker it got."

It is 1967 and eleven-year-old Charlie York lives in Angel's Rest, deep in the mountains of the American South. His town is a poor boy's paradise – until a shotgun blast kills Charlie's father and puts his mother on trial for murder.

When reclusive veteran Hollis Thrasher is also linked to the death, Charlie must embark on a dangerous midnight journey so that the truth about what he witnessed that fateful day can finally be revealed.

Available 16th March 2007